JUST LIKE PROPER GROWN-UPS

Christina Hopkinson

WINDSOR
PARAGON

First published 2012
by Hodder & Stoughton
This Large Print edition published 2013
by AudioGO Ltd
by arrangement with
Hodder & Stoughton

Hardcover   ISBN: 978 1 4713 3093 3
Softcover   ISBN: 978 1 4713 3094 0

British Library Cataloguing in Publication Data available

Printed and bound in Great Britain by
TJ International Limited

To Anthony and Sylvia Hopkinson,
who tolerated and even encouraged my stroppiness.

CHAPTER ONE

STARTING TO SHOW

It was always a surprise to those who knew Lucy to discover that she had an enduring attachment to the diktats of women's magazines. They provided a running commentary on her life so that however successful and efficient she became, there was always something that could be improved. As she waited on the doorstep of Tess's flat she did a quick inventory of her appearance. Women of a certain age, she knew from her reading, should forego cleavage but displayed legs were fine, so long as they were encased in opaques. Check. Her face was only dimly reflected in the glass, but she could see how cross she always looked these days. Her hair was too flat, but she'd had no time to do the necessary candy-flossing to big it up before coming out.

As she was buzzed in and confronted with Tess, she felt any confidence she had brought alongside the bottle of mid-market Italian wine evaporate. Her friend looked radiant, almost younger than when they had first met twenty years before.

'My darling,' said Tess. 'You look tired.'

'Thanks,' said Lucy. 'Nothing like people saying that to make you feel a hundred and three.'

'Speaking of which, happy belated birthday.'

'Is it? Happy, I mean? It feels like one more plank of wood towards the coffin.'

'Don't be silly. We're still young.'

'Well, *you* look it,' said Lucy. 'You look amazing.

1

I read somewhere that these days Botox and teeth-whitening are considered "basic maintenance". Can you believe it? Not in my world. It's as much as I can do to brush my teeth of an evening.' She squinted some more at Tess's unlined face. 'Are you, have you?'

'Had work done, you mean? Funny how they call it work, when it's really about being quite lazy, isn't it? Letting someone else sort out your face for you.'

'Not a face-lift, obviously, but Botox, injectable fillers, collagen, hyaluronic acid—anything like that?'

'You seem to know a lot about it.'

'Well, have you?' Tess's face looked as though it had been plumped out. Yes, it was plump, but in a good way. It was too irritating that after all these years of being told that thin was everything to have to readjust your vision to embrace a sort of localised chubbiness, restricted to the apples of your cheeks and your lips.

Tess laughed. 'No, I'd tell you if I had. But you should see Mummy these days. She's like one of the people who put their car into reverse to try to get the mileage down before flogging it. She's had so much Botox that her forehead's got that shiny oversized skating-rink look that you see on actresses, and she has these weird little lines'—Tess pointed to the sides of her nose—'right here. It's like all her wrinkles have sought sanctuary there, so she looks like she's making a rabbity face all the time.' Tess crinkled up her own face and bucked her teeth in illustration. It only served to emphasise the dewiness of her skin.

Lucy looked at herself in one of Tess's silver spoons, which was speckled with age. Everything

2

in Tess's home was vintage and mismatched in the artless way that is such hard work to achieve. The only new thing seemed to be Tess's glow. 'Oh god, even in this, I look terrible. Now that I'm doing a bit of TV, do you think I should get some work done? My forehead looked like corduroy when I saw myself on-screen. Ned asked the other day, "Mummy, why's your face all stripy?"'

'You're on the news talking about pension reform; I hardly think people want to see a baby-faced expert. I can't believe I'm hearing this from you, of all people—you were my ally in not being boring about looks and weight.'

'I don't have a problem with my weight. That's an easy calculation: calories in minus calories expended. That makes sense. But I can't control this. I find myself actually paying attention to adverts that promise luminescence and a reduction in the appearance of fine lines. What are the seven signs of ageing that they talk of anyway?'

'Talking nonsense in your case. I rely on you to be sensible.'

'How bloody grown-up.'

They were interrupted by the doorbell. Lucy looked with surprise at the man—or, some would say, boy—in low-slung jeans and a logo-ed top, staggering under the weight of several large brown paper bags. She'd seen him many times before, but to see him out of context was like seeing a priest out clubbing. What on earth was he doing here at Tess's flat?

'My darling,' said Tess as she kissed his cheeks, 'you're dwarfed by these bags.'

'Not that it takes much to dwarf me,' he said.

'Shush, you're not that much smaller than I am.'

3

'Bless you, but despite my boyhood hopes, I'm always going to be eight years younger and three inches shorter than you. Your side got all the tall genes.' He smiled at Lucy. 'Hi, I'm Michael.'

'I know. Well, I know you as Mr Wasiak.'

'Yes, he's a Wasiak, my cousin on Mummy's side,' said Tess. 'How do you say cousin in Polish?'

'*Kuzyn*,' said Michael. 'It's very tricky. You're about as Polish as fish and chips.' He turned to Lucy again. 'How do you know my name?'

'Because you're Mr Wasiak from Moreton Primary. I'm Lucy, mother of Rosa and Ned, Year 2 and Reception. You've never taught either of them. Though I've heard great things about you.'

He reconfigured his look of blankness into one of enthusiastic recognition. 'Of course, Lucy.'

'How weird that all this time I never knew you were Tess's cousin. And strange to see you outside school. I don't like to believe that teachers have lives outside school.' Lucy was always rather priggish when she heard other parents talk about friending the teachers on Facebook. Teachers weren't allowed to have drinks or sex; they should dissolve on walking out of the building.

'Lucy and I were besties at university,' said Tess.

'But I've heard so much about that Lucy,' he said. 'All the stories about what you girls did in your youth.'

'Sweetheart,' said Tess, 'some of us like to believe we are still in our youth.'

'Of course.' He looked at Lucy in reassurance. 'Well, do call me Michael and I promise not to tell on you in the staff room if you get drunk. So, Tess, who else is coming? They told me at the deli that it's dinner for five. It's all very mysterious, you

4

never give dinner parties.'

'Sierra, the latest and longest-lasting assistant at the gallery. Just your type—big and gorgeous. You'll want to eat her up, if she doesn't gobble you up first. And Owen, another friend from the old days.'

Lucy groaned.

'You know you love him really,' said Tess.

'Really not.' The announcement of Owen's attendance chipped away still further at Lucy's confidence. 'Does he still have such an, ahem, engaging way with women?'

'You are mean,' said Tess. 'Although I saw Fred the other day, who told me a good joke: what's the difference between Owen Williams and a public lavatory? The loo can't be engaged and vacant at the same time.'

'Boom, boom,' said Lucy.

'What are you talking about?' asked Michael.

'Owen has quite a history with the ladies,' said Tess, exchanging glances with Lucy. 'Quite a history.'

*   *   *

Michael found himself falling quickly into his traditional role as Tess's helpmeet, unpacking, unwrapping and uncorking, in part to hide the fact that he had no memory of ever having seen Lucy at the school. There were so few teachers and so many parents that it wasn't fair to expect him to recognise her, especially since she had that generic layered and highlighted mum-bob.

He leaped to the intercom when the doorbell buzzed.

'Tess, you gorgeous creature, open up and let me ravish you,' a deep voice boomed, sonorous through the speaker. Michael wished he could have left its owner out in the cold night, feeling his ears ache even with the man held at a remove. He pressed the door release button and was almost flattened by the force of the man's entrance.

'And here he is,' said Lucy. 'The lovely Owen.'

He gave Michael a bone-crushing handshake with a self-consciousness that suggested he knew his own strength, then turned to Tess. 'You look fabulous, absolutely gorgeous. Tits look particularly great.'

They do, thought Michael, they really do look marvellous, though he'd never have been so uncouth as to comment on them. And in his head they were always reverently referred to as breasts. Women like Tess didn't have tits.

'Oh please,' said Lucy.

'Oh please what? You want me to compliment your tits, too, Lucy.' He turned back to Tess. 'And where's the lovely Vondra?'

'Owen is Mummy's favourite man in the world,' said Tess to Michael, who liked to think he occupied that position.

'Something to do with the fact that he says things to her like, "and you must be Tess's gorgeous sister",' said Lucy.

'And it's great to see you too. What are you up to?'

'Work, kids, house, you know.'

'Not really, no. I've just got a new car actually.'

'What is it?' asked Michael, who had no interest in the subject whatsoever.

'Alfa Romeo.' There was a pause, which Owen

decided to fill with: 'Looks as good topless as you do, Tess.' He winked, not in a lascivious way but in a knowing, 'this sexist drivel is actually me being postmodern' way. At least that's what Michael hoped, since he didn't want to admit that his cousin could have a friend who was idiotic rather than ironic.

'And that's what I love about him,' Tess said to Michael. 'He really embraces this silly playboy image of his.'

'To the extent,' added Lucy, 'that it must be hard to know where the image ends and the person begins.'

Owen began talking about the size of his bonus, which he did with full innuendo. His tone was low and slow, like a record being played at the wrong speed, yet everything about him spoke of a life lived at full pelt. Michael found himself sucked into the beta half of the room, discussing the state of local secondary schools with Lucy. He was relieved when the bell went again.

Sierra, he assumed. Tess was right, she was his type: tall and slightly over-ripe.

'Tess, you look fierce, I love those shoes.' Her voice veered from squeak to husk, from snob to scrub, all in the space of one sentence.

'But yours are amazing, too. Vintage?' asked Tess.

'Yeah, of course. I don't like having new stuff in my wardrobe—it's just like so boring and so unsound to buy new stuff in shops.'

'Apart from Topshop,' said Tess.

'Of course, Toppers is different,' said Sierra. 'And you're totally working a statement earring. Those are edible. Like little chandeliers that you might find in a doll's house. Teeny tiny chandeliers.'

*   *   *

The food was lavish, all chargrilled artichokes and aubergines coupled with obscure smoked cheeses, alongside grilled salmon and beef in different but complimentary shades of pink.

There was a brief lull in the conversation. 'Lucy was asking me earlier what the seven signs of ageing were,' said Tess.

'Senility, incontinence . . .' replied Owen.

'Casual racism and elasticated waistbands,' added Michael. 'While middle age is all about investment dressing. You know, an investment coat, usually in camel.'

Lucy cringed at his words. She had now moved way beyond the investment coat towards the investment saucepan, one of the expensive ones with copper bottoms.

'And owning a spice rack,' continued Michael. 'Surely that's the definition of adulthood. Actually, surely the definition of a grown-up is anyone who's ten years older than you.' He looked at Tess.

'Rounding it up are we now? I think she was thinking more about skin elasticity and so on,' Tess retorted.

'Not really,' said Lucy. 'Can we drop it?'

'It depends, I suppose,' continued Michael, 'if you're talking about ageing physically or mentally. Ageing might mean growing up. Which would mean the acquiring of wisdom.'

'Or acquiring a house,' said Sierra. 'I think you're a grown-up when you own property. My mum doesn't.'

'I knew I'd grown up when I'd made my first million,' Owen announced.

'That's nice,' said Lucy.

'Oh, what, you think it's when you've got a watertight pension plan in place?'

'If the definition of growing up was making a million, then almost all of us would still be considered adolescents.'

'You're just jealous you didn't use your degree to make as much money as I have.'

'Do stop arguing, children,' Tess interrupted.

'You're right,' said Lucy. 'I know that ageing isn't just about crow's feet. I remember my midwife saying you don't really grow up until you either have a kid or one of your parents dies.'

'Says you, the woman with children, ergo Little Miss Mature,' Owen snorted.

'I'm not saying I agree with that theory. Just that it's an interesting thought, you know, about the conveyer belt of life.'

'I've a dead parent,' said Tess. 'That makes Lucy and I even, by that reckoning of grown-upness.' She paused. 'For the moment.'

*   *   *

Sierra was very drunk and very happy, basking in the glow of male attention.

'Sierra, unusual name,' Owen purred, leaning in closer. 'After the Ford Sierra? A classic eighties car.'

'Nah, after the Sierra Nevada. I was conceived there.'

'In Andalucia?' said Lucy. 'How lovely. We went to Granada—so beautiful, the Alhambra's

9

just exquisite, though you do have to get there very early to avoid the crowds. We booked these special tickets in advance.'

Sierra laughed. 'Nah, it was a club in Vauxhall. My mum and dad used to go there and legend has it that I was the result of a session in the toilets in the late eighties. Class.'

'More champagne?' Tess asked.

'Got anything stronger, sweetheart?' enquired Sierra. 'Why don't I make us all up some cocktails. You got the voddy in?' She stood up and felt the heel of her shoe wobble. Or was it her leg? Either way, she hoped it would give an alluring wiggle to her walk. She found a tray and filled it with assorted spirits. Tess had a spice rack, she noticed, and pillaged a bottle of Tabasco from it.

'Just look at that arrangement,' said Tess. 'It's like that game we used to play at children's parties, you know the one with the tray filled with objects and you looked at them then they got covered up and you had to remember as many of them as you could?'

'Kim's game,' said Lucy. 'Except they don't play it at children's parties any more because it's not expensive enough. It's all "let your children play football with a Premiership team", or have a real live zoo in the back garden.'

'Shall we play it now, then?' suggested Sierra. 'Can you remember these? We've got vodka, some sort of lemon drink from Italy, some freshly squeezed OJ, something purple. Fuck that, let's just get mixing. Yeah, much better to drink than to remember. I want to drink to forget. I warn you, guys, my cockies are absolute killers. A couple of these and I'm anybody's.' She locked eyes with

10

Owen for as long as she dared when she said it.

*   *   *

'This is all marvellous. I love you all,' proclaimed Michael after two of Sierra's concoctions. Job done, she thought. 'I love you, Tess, for getting all these marvellous people together. But you are naughty not to have got us together sooner.'

'Naughty, naughty, naughty,' echoed Sierra.

'But nice,' said Owen.

'Not nice,' Michael countered. 'Nobody could ever accuse you of being nice. You're merely marvellous. A toast to the hostess.'

'A toastess,' said Owen.

'A toast to Tess, a testes,' Sierra giggled.

'She's our host-tess. A toast to toasts,' said Michael. 'Or just toast. Toast, just a little piece of toast. My sisters used to sing that song. Do you remember it?'

Tess and Lucy murmured assent. 'I don't,' said Sierra. 'Is it, like, really old or something? More toast, please.'

'Beer, beer, I want more beer,' sang Owen in a beautiful baritone. 'All the lads are cheering, get the bloody beers in. Or champagne, if you insist. No thanks, Sierra, your cocktails taste like washing-up liquid.'

'Cheeky,' she said, giving him the punch that schoolgirls give boys they think are way buff.

'You're all right,' said Michael to Owen.

'Why, thank you.'

'No, really, I thought you were a bit of a knob when you came in, but you're all right. Turns out you're not a total arse.'

11

'A nice arse,' said Sierra. 'A pert one,' she added, in case her first comment had been too subtle. 'You two must come and have lunch at the gallery one day with me and Tess.'

'Or even if Tess isn't there,' said Michael. 'We don't care about her any more.'

'And this is why I never introduced you,' Tess said, but she was smiling. She was still holding a full glass of champagne, undrained despite the repeated toasting that surrounded her. Sierra was vaguely aware that the other two women had not been knocking back the drinks with quite the same speed as she had.

'Actually,' declared Tess, 'I've got you together for a reason. I've got an announcement to make. Well, it's more of a favour.'

'You look like the cat that got the cream,' Michael said to his cousin. She was smiling, but her hands shook and she spilled some of her champagne. 'Spit it out. The announcement, I mean, not the cream.'

'Spit it out,' said Owen. 'You never used to.'

'Oh please,' Michael protested. 'That's my cousin you're talking about.'

'Did you two . . .' asked Sierra.

'Hardly,' said Lucy. 'For about three minutes.'

'I can assure you, Lucy, it lasts a lot longer than three minutes. With me, anyway.'

'He's not exactly one for commitment, Sierra.' Lucy shook her head. 'Tess, please tell us what we can do.'

Tess cleared her throat theatrically. 'I'd like to ask you . . . I'd be honoured if . . . I'd like to ask the four of you to be godparents to my child.'

The four of them stared at her, their glasses

12

lifted in preparation but as yet unchinked. Michael decided to drink his anyway.

'Well?' asked Tess.

'Yeah, whatever, of course I will, babe,' said Sierra.

'As and when you decide to have a baby, I'd be delighted and proud to be his or her godmother,' Lucy said.

'I wouldn't,' said Owen. 'I'm bloody sick of being a godfather. I've got ten or eleven or something already.'

'You must be so popular.' Sierra leant towards him.

'Rich,' said Owen.

'And unlikely to have children of his own,' Lucy added. 'You know that thing I was saying about commitment earlier, Sierra.'

'Would you really not want to be godfather to my child?' asked Tess.

'Of course I'd be godfather. I'll make an exception for you. Just don't do it too soon.'

'Too late.'

'What?' said Lucy. 'I knew something was up! You haven't had more than a glass of champagne. I noticed you weren't drinking. I knew it. You look so different, too.'

'I look fat.'

'No, not fat. You've put on weight, but only on your face.'

'And chest,' added Owen.

'You look incredible,' said Lucy. 'Really well. God, if you could bottle it up and sell it in Harley Street, you'd make a fortune. It's like the elixir of youth. You're glowing. I only ever glowed with the gleam of vomit on my chin. But you look amazing.'

13

'I feel amazing. They say now that morning sickness is psychosomatic. I don't feel sick at all.'

'How many weeks are you?'

'Twelve, nearly thirteen. I've had the first scan. I'm due in August.'

'God,' said Michael.

'No, god*parent*—I want you to be a godfather.'

'God,' he repeated. 'You know I don't do god.'

'What the hell are you doing?' said Sierra. 'What about the gallery? And your friends? You can't be pregnant. Why didn't you tell me? Who the fuck's the father?'

'It's nobody you know,' said Tess.

'Well who?'

'We didn't, did we?' joked Owen.

'Stop messing around,' said Sierra, feeling simultaneously more drunk and more sober. 'Who's the father?'

'He's a doctor, blond hair, blue eyes, six foot something.'

'Sounds like a sperm donor,' said Michael. 'They're always six foot and then some. Always scientists, too, though who wants to go out with them in real life? Often blond. Women seem to have an Aryan thing going when it comes to their sperm donors.'

'He is a sperm donor, actually,' said Tess.

'Not literally, though,' said Lucy. 'Figuratively, surely.'

'No, I do mean literally. He is a sperm donor.'

'No,' exclaimed Michael, giving the word at least four syllables. 'What, one of those ones off the Internet? I've read about them. These sites where you order some sperm and a motorcycle courier comes round.'

14

'You're pregnant by a sperm donor off the Internet? Deliberately?' asked Lucy.

'It's quite hard to get pregnant by accident, really. At my age.'

'But why?'

Tess shrugged. 'Just because I don't have a man in my life, I'm not allowed a baby?'

'No, of course not. I absolutely applaud you for pursuing your right to have a child. It's just that I thought you were different, above fretting about biological clocks. That's what you always said, anyway—that you didn't want children. I admired you for it, for being different. And you don't even like babies. Not mine, anyway.'

'Don't be silly, I adore your little ones and their little faces and so on.'

'But why now, when you've always said you didn't want them?'

'Please, so many questions. Pregnancy's so tiring.'

'It's really, really fantastic,' said Lucy, hugging Tess. 'I honestly couldn't be more pleased for you, but at the risk of sounding like the bad fairy . . .'

'Bad fairy godmother,' said Sierra, who was responding to the news by drinking another of her detergent cocktails.

'At the risk of being negative, do you know how much work is involved in bringing up a child?'

'Lordy, how hard can it be? I'm sure I'll manage.'

'But really, it's such hard work . . .'

'That you get Jamie to do it for you. That's enough, Lucy. I get the picture.'

'I still don't understand,' said Michael. 'If you wanted sperm, why didn't you ask someone you knew? You could have asked me.'

'Don't be silly, you're my cousin.'

'Second cousin. It's because I'm short, isn't it?'

'Daft boy. It's because I didn't want to share the responsibility with anyone. It's something I want to do and I want to do it on my own.'

'Well, you can't,' said Michael. 'I read that they're changing the law. Donors aren't anonymous any more. And there was that boy who found his dad's DNA on the Internet. You know, it was in America. The Child Support Agency will be on to Mr Tall Doctor man, or make that Mr Tall Medical Student, given that he's flogged his load for a tenner . . .'

'I think it's more than that, actually.'

'Well, he'd better put it in a high-interest account,' said Michael, 'as one of these days he might find himself having to support a child with expensive tastes.'

'We'll worry about that when we need to, won't we? Owen, you're being quiet. You will be a godfather, won't you?'

He nodded.

'Sierra? Michael?'

They, too, mumbled assent.

'With such enthusiasm,' said Tess, then laughed.

'Obviously you know you can count on me,' said Lucy. 'We really need to pull together to make sure that you never feel the lack of . . . support.'

'I know, that's why I've chosen the four of you to be godparents. You're all so special in your own ways. You don't have to tell me how much it, he or she, is going to change my life. I know that. But I'd like to hope that in a little way it will change yours, too.'

CHAPTER TWO

LACKLUSTRE SKIN

Lucy pretended to be asleep as she watched Jamie get out of bed at dawn. That way she could admire how he had just enough stomach definition to be attractive, but not so much that he looked like he spent too much time exercising his abs and drinking protein shakes.

He lifted up his T-shirt to scratch said abdominals and Lucy felt herself lust like a builder at a blonde. Then she found herself wondering whether he was going bald on the top of his head, in just the sort of spot that a television presenter would be tempted to spray on that fake hair which looks like strange-hued candy floss. Was it wrong to hope that dramatic hair loss was imminent?

Jamie was giving her a lie-in, as she'd been the one to go out the night before. He was thoughtful like that. He'd give the kids breakfast and clean up afterwards. He was perfect.

She pulled herself up after a dozily unsatisfying snooze and stared at herself in the mirror. She started with one of her favoured manoeuvres, which was to pull up her eyebrows to see what she'd look like with a brow lift. She wasn't particularly sure what the point of lifting one's brows was, but it was one of the most popular surgical procedures around, so clearly having unlifted brows was a bad thing. Maybe her eyelids were getting a bit saggy after all, one step closer to drooping over her eyes. She stopped tugging since she figured that this

17

would only make it worse. She imagined a surgeon with a marker pen drawing circles and dotted lines around them. She moved on to her forehead, which she pulled back. She wanted it to look cushiony like Tess's did now that she was pregnant.

She then stood up and pulled at her stomach. This was the most satisfying of her manhandlings, seeing what she'd look like after liposuction. Although she was slim, back to the weight she had been before children, she had a flap of residual fat that no number of sit-ups would eliminate. When she did a downward dog in yoga she'd see it dangling, which made her feel anxious and unyogic. She clasped the flesh around her middle. The surgeon would draw a dotted line around it, maybe with a scissors symbol at one end. Then perhaps they could take the white shiny fat from inside the flap and inject it into her cheekbones for a pillowy modern look. 'The new new face', she had seen it called.

She went down to the kitchen, where Rosa and Ned were filming themselves on her phone.

'You look rubbish anyway,' Ned said to Rosa as they played back the footage.

'No, I don't, I look like a pop star,' Rosa retorted. This latest phase was even worse than the princess one, and Lucy was surprised to find herself mourning the Snow White and Rapunzel dresses that had been consigned to the bonfire (metaphorical, given their highly flammable man-made fibres).

'Look at my costume,' Rosa went on, pointing to her midriff, exposed below her knotted up T-shirt. 'I'm fierce.'

'It's my film and you'll do what I say,' said Ned, a

four-year-old Alfred Hitchcock with an iPhone.

Lucy didn't need to drink to feel hungover. 'Please, darlings, stop fighting. Guess who I saw last night? Mr Wasiak, you know, from school.'

'Oh my god!' shrieked Rosa, and Lucy lacked the energy to admonish her. Teachers at this age were accorded celebrity status when spotted in the supermarket, as if they were too glamorous for such mundane realities. 'Evie says he's the nicest teacher in the school. I hope I get him next year.'

'He seems lovely,' said Lucy. 'He's my friend Tess's cousin, but I never knew that. Isn't that funny?' Which it was, to her—that Tess should not know the names of all the schools of all her friends' offspring, nor ever make the connection between Michael and Lucy, but she supposed it was like the way you never noticed how many different sorts of buggies there were on the pavements of the city until you had one of your own.

Jamie was on the phone, saying, 'Yeah, man,' a lot and bandying around some technical terms like 'edit' and 'Avid'. He barely looked at her, absorbed, just as he had been for the last few months, by the renaissance in what he called his 'film-making career'. She hated herself for always mentally wrapping it in inverted commas.

'So,' she said to him when he finally tore himself away from a conversation about 'viral shorts' that had nothing to do with infectious disease. 'Guess who's pregnant?' A look of sheer terror flashed across his face. 'No, not me!' Yeah, right, she thought.

'Who?'

'Tess.'

'That's good news.'

'Yes, it is. It's lovely. Really lovely.'

'Is there a Mr Tess?'

She shook her head and mouthed, 'D. O. N. O. R,' at him, glancing towards Ned and Rosa as she did so, who ignored her in favour of bickering over who got to rip open a herbal tea bag and scatter its contents across the floor.

'Really?' he said. 'How very modern.'

'Yes. Strange, though. It doesn't make sense.'

'Why not? She's your age, isn't she, so she's not getting any younger . . .'

'Thanks for that.'

'Reproductively speaking, forty's pretty old.'

'Thirty-nine. Tess and I are thirty-nine. We're all thirtysomethings—you too.' It was a fairly brief window, two and a bit years, in which she could say this of her and Jamie. 'It's odd, she never wanted children—or that's what I always thought. And with a donor . . .'

Jamie looked at her intently. 'Women do that, they use men. Anonymous or otherwise. They do it all the time. The only surprise, I guess, is that she should go down the anonymous route. It's not like she couldn't have anyone she wanted.'

'True. Though there's no correlation, is there, between levels of attractiveness and finding somebody to settle down with?' she said. 'In fact maybe there is, but it's an inverse correlation. The more beautiful you were or are, the less likely you are to settle down.' This is the point, she thought, when you're supposed to say, 'But you're beautiful'. She had been, if only she had known it, and if only Jamie had known her then.

When she was younger, her friends used to call her the Love Actuary, on account of her cool, statistical evaluations of relationships. She'd warn them off men whose parents were divorced, citing a 70 per cent higher divorce rate for their offspring. She'd tell them that no, it was highly unlikely they'd get back together with the man who'd asked for a trial separation. She'd tell Tess that only three per cent of alpha married males leave their wives for the mistress, at which Tess would laugh and say, 'Well, darling, yes—that's the whole point.' This ability to predict the future based on empirical evidence and hard maths had been equally useful as a party piece as it had in her career as a pensions expert.

She wondered whether there was a correlation between attractiveness and relationship longevity, an infidelity calculation? Lack of marital satisfaction plus opportunity minus chances of getting caught equals likelihood of an affair. The better looking you are, presumably the more opportunity you have, especially if you work in an environment where women outnumber men. That would be Jamie, then.

Falling in love, she had read, was only an evolutionary device to bind men and women together for the few years necessary to produce and wean children. Since this job was pretty much done, people like Lucy—normal people—would soon have affairs. How glamorous that sounded, for up until now, only Tess had indulged in affairs. The very word sounded starry to Lucy, although she supposed the reality was probably all about static electricity shocks on the nylon carpets of budget hotels, tedious lies about interdepartmental awaydays and snatched shags in the two-hour window of a children's party.

That's it, she thought, you'd have to have standing-up sex in toilets or rammed up in the toy cupboards at church halls. It would be frantic, even rough, dry yet surprisingly satisfying, dirty thoughts whispered into ears and stifled screams of pleasure. She felt herself blush as she looked towards Jamie, who was now wiping the wooden kitchen table, his muscles flexing as he leaned over it, and she thought of herself coming between his torso and the pine top with its stubborn crayon marks and sticker remnants. Yes, she wanted sex like that, dirty illicit sex. She wanted sex like that with Jamie.

*   *   *

Michael had believed that dropping the bombshell of Tess's pregnancy on his mother and three sisters over Sunday lunch would make him rejoice in the news. True, they had been gratifyingly shocked, dumbstruck for all of ten seconds—something of a record—before bombarding him with judgements wrapped up in questions: the how could she, the what was she thinking, the who will bring up the poor mite.

It seemed to him that they talked about nothing but the Franklins in his parents' house. It was as natural as commenting on the weather. Tess's mother's life had always seemed to him to be like one of those blockbuster novels that he'd borrowed from his older sisters when they were growing up. Vondra had bounced from Warsaw to New York to London, annulling husbands and unpleasant incidents on the way, until she'd found, by fortunate coincidence, lasting happiness, wealth, status and the birth of one manageable child as the second

22

Lady Franklin.

All the while, her cousin, Michael's mother, had remained in the London suburb where she'd been born after the war and had swelled the Polish population with her four children. The division of glamour had repeated itself in the next generation, with Michael enjoying a privileged position as Wasiak envoy into the exotic land of the Franklins.

And now, something was wrong. He was still Tess's chosen one—being made godparent was proof of that—but in getting pregnant she'd lost some of her sheen. His sisters, once their shock had subsided, began to crow. After all, they'd managed to produce seven children between them. And with husbands, too. Poor Tess, they all said, and a part of him agreed.

He tried to analyse why he felt so low as he walked from the Underground to school on Monday morning. It was what was known as a 'mixed' neighbourhood, which pretty much described any area of London, but this one in particular, as was reflected in a primary school where 25 languages were spoken and a handful of families probably spent more on their holidays than the entire annual income of the others.

He saw a woman in a pair of shiny running tights coming towards him. When the parents dropped off their kids at school, he could tell the difference between the mothers who wore tracksuit bottoms because they were cheap and comfy and those who wore them because they were on their way to personal trainers.

'Hello, Michael,' she said.

'Oh, hello, Lucy. I didn't recognise you.'

'No, well, I don't tend to wear this outfit for

dinner.'

He looked at her get-up. As well as the tights, she had on some sort of silky blouson hoody with a zip and reflective strip across the back. This would have been designed to reflect light when zipping up mountains or down darkened streets. Since she was running on the pavement, it most reflected the fact that she took her hobbies seriously enough to dress them in expensive specialist gear. 'You run,' he said, although it was as obvious from the hardness of her thighs as her clothes.

'I'm heading to work, but this way I avoid public transport and get my exercise.' As she spoke, she started fiddling with the phone strapped to her arm. 'Sorry, just stopping the clock. Don't want to bring down my average time. Five k in twenty-six minutes.'

'Great. How funny that we'd never met before Saturday and now here we are again.'

She looked disappointed. 'But we had met before then. At the school tour, don't you remember? About four years ago, when I was looking for a school for Rosa?'

He did now. He'd won a bet with the headmistress over which of the parents would ask about the school's gifted and talented programme. Women like her always asked about how the school coped with the very clever children, despite having no evidence that their three-year-old was in any way special. Then when they were outflanked by the child for whom English was an additional language (whom he preferred to call bilingual), they'd blame the school for this lapse.

'Of course. And running also means you avoid the school run.'

'Though I'd love to take them to school. It just makes more sense for Jamie, their dad, to do it.'

Of course, Ned and Rosa's dad was Jamie—aka 'fit dad', as he was known by the mostly female staff and, judging by the gaggle of women around him in the playground, the other mothers. Michael would never have put the two together as a couple, but he could see the resemblance to both parents in the children. The girl was tall for her age and big, not fat exactly, but probably already excelling at swimming and fretting about her stomach. The little boy had an alpha swagger and a team of minions that rather belied his angelic looks.

'So, Tess's news?'

'Yes,' she said. 'Tess's news.'

'An immaculate conception.' As he said it, he realised that it was. No messy sex or shared fluids for Tess. He imagined beautiful doctors in white coats, like the sort that people the Laboratoires Garnier, their horn-rimmed spectacles only enhancing their good looks. And Tess in the midst of them, having a baby conjured within her.

'Indeed. It is immaculate. Or something.' She looked as though she wanted to say more, but put the earphones back on, started the stopwatch and ran away from him.

*   *   *

The title of the message was 'Godparents'. Owen was in no particular hurry to open it.

Just trying to organise a good time to get the three of you round or to meet up to discuss Friday's big news!

25

Owen shuddered at Lucy's exclamation mark, which sat awkwardly like a paper hat on the boss's head at the Christmas party. He never used exclamation marks in email. He tried to avoid punctuation full stop.

Being the godparents to Tess's baby is going to mean a lot of responsibility for the four of us and I think it would be great to work out what roles we're fulfilling and in what ways we can best help out. As a working mother, I know the juggling, stress and financial implications involved in bringing up children even if Tess doesn't (not yet!) and it makes sense to divide some of this up between us. I'd also look forward to getting to know you all better, especially Sierra and Michael.

There followed a complex algorithm of potential dates. He fired off a reply before looking at his diary.

I'm responsible for irresponsibility therefore probably not needed at meetings.

It was bad enough that he should find himself inveigled into having another godchild, but now he was being expected to do more than go to the toys section on Amazon twice a year. Owen was neither callous enough to forget his godchildren's birthdays without conscience nor caring enough to remember them with reliability. He usually compensated by taking their parents out for belated but lavish meals where they would order the most expensive champagne while complaining about the cost of babysitters.

His phone went.

'I presume your email is a joke.'

'Lucy, always a pleasure.'

'If you don't want to help at all I think you ought to tell Tess now so that she can find a godfather who is prepared to pull his weight.'

'Don't you think you're taking this all a bit seriously?'

'Tess wouldn't have asked us all to be godparents at this stage if she hadn't wanted us to take active roles in its upbringing.'

'Says who?'

'Says her. She said we're all very special, which you'd remember if you hadn't been quite so drunk.'

'Was not.' Lucy could bring out the inner child in Owen. Sadly, it was the inner screaming-tantrum, spaghetti-throwing toddler rather than a cute frolicking moppet.

'Are you honestly telling me that you can't spare an evening to discuss things with Michael, Sierra and me.'

'Now you mention it, I'd be happy to see Sierra. To discuss godparental duties.'

'She's young enough to be your god-daughter.'

He did his roué laugh for her benefit.

'You are revolting. What is it with you and twenty-somethings? You went out with them when you were eighteen and you're still going out with them now. Twenty-two is to you what fourteen is to Humbert Humbert.'

'You can talk.'

'What's that supposed to mean?'

'Your choirboy husband.'

'He's seven years younger than me and he's not my husband. It hardly makes me Mrs Robinson. That is so sexist of you, Owen, there's such a double standard about men being younger than women. I bet you never go out with women who are only seven years younger than you. You probably think any woman in her thirties is positively geriatric.'

'I just find that women turn at about thirty. Maybe even earlier. Twenty-seven, perhaps.'

'Just send me a list of the dates that you can make. See you.'

'Wouldn't wanna be you.'

'For god's sake, Owen, grow up. You may sleep with teenagers but it doesn't mean you have to speak like one.'

'Why don't you stop being so old? Anyway, my girlfriend's twenty-three, actually.'

'Whoopee-do. Bye, Owen. Read my email and get back to me, will you?'

Ruby was 23. It was her birthday some time this month. Owen checked the calendar on his screen. Shit, Ruby was 24, 24 today. Why hadn't she reminded him? He knew there had to be some disadvantage to having a girlfriend as sweet and undemanding as Ruby, and now he'd discovered what it was. They don't bang on about their birthdays enough.

And she was so sweet. He'd leave work, exhausted, and there she'd be, a delightful fluffy puppy of a girl, an aromatherapy-oil-filled bath of a woman he could wallow in. Imagine coming home to Lucy. He'd work even longer hours to avoid the combat. Even Tess, in his experience, was prone to low moods and high expectations. And Ruby was so beautiful both inside and out.

Ruby deserved to be looked after on her birthday. He pulled strings to get a table at his favourite restaurant for that evening and nipped off to the nearest jewellers. There he allowed himself to be steered in the direction of a purply-blue stone that was neither amethyst nor sapphire.

'Tanzanite,' said the shop's owner, whose gnarled hands made his wares look even more precious by comparison. 'It's a rare form of Zoisite.'

'Zoisite?' asked Owen. 'Isn't that a fake diamond?'

He smiled. 'No, sir, that's Zirconia. Tanzanite is a precious stone, rare and beautiful. Like your lady friend?'

Owen surprised himself by falling for it. It was almost the colour of Ruby's eyes, which were compared to Elizabeth Taylor's by those of a certain age, his parents' generation—or that of her grandparents, as she'd remind him.

'And which finger would sir be wanting it for? The wedding finger?'

He laughed.

'If your lady has slim fingers, it will currently fit on the index or middle finger. But I could make it narrower for a wedding finger.'

'That won't be necessary. Phew.' He made a gesture of clichéd male relief in wiping his forehead. In truth he'd never noticed the width of Ruby's fingers, but he'd never gone out with a girl with fat anything, ankles, thighs, fingers or otherwise. 'I think she's got thin fingers. She'll wear it on her index finger, I'm sure.'

Later, he found himself looking at Ruby's tanzanite-coloured eyes over dinner. 'You look lovely,' he told her.

'You look tired, Owen.'

'I am a bit.'

'You work so hard.'

'I do.' He hadn't quite recovered from Sierra's cocktails. Little minx that she was, with those enormous tits of hers. 'I work damn hard.' Ruby stroked his leg under the table and then pushed her toes into his groin. He began to feel cross-eyed with lust.

'How was your dinner on Saturday? With whatshername?'

'Tess. Good, great. She's pregnant.' Ruby's tanzanite eyes brightened. 'There's no father. She got some sperm. Bought sperm, I mean—off the Internet, I think.'

'She is really old, isn't she? I want to have babies before I'm thirty.'

'You do?' The wine had been described by the sommelier as fruity and engaging. He felt the same as he drunk another glass and enjoyed Ruby's ministrations under the table.

'Of course. I feel really sorry for these kids with old mums, getting asked why their granny picks them up from school. My mum's only forty-five.'

Not far off my age, and nice looking in those photos Ruby had on her phone. The generations were getting all confused; Lucy had jumped over him to become so much older, using her economics degree to specialise in pensions while he'd opted for the boy-fuelled world of investment banking. Tess was technically old to be a mother but he was shocked that she should have been allowed to get pregnant in the first place, as though she were some schoolgirl. She should have always remained ageless: too sophisticated to be a teenager, too self-centred to become a parent. Ruby and he would have beautiful children, perhaps with her eyes and his dark skin. He'd carry them in one of those sling things and there would probably be just enough room for a car seat in the back of the Alfa. If Tess could do it, so could he.

'Your mother is more or less the same age now as my father was when he had me.' Adopted me, he corrected himself inwardly. Or, as his mother was continually correcting him, 'chose' him. 'We love you more because we chose you,' she would repeat. 'We picked you out because you're special,' which always seemed a rather tactless remark given the presence of his younger sister, Caron, who had not been chosen but begotten the old-fashioned way.

'I feel really old,' said Ruby. 'No, I do. I may not look it, but I'm really mature. I sometimes feel like I'm the older one in this relationship and you're the mad kid, don't I? I know what I want.'

At that moment, Owen did too. 'Happy birthday, darling.' He gave her the gold and green box. She took it in her hands, her—as he noticed for the first time—incongruously chubby-fingered hands. How could somebody so slim have such fat fingers?

'Owen, it's lovely.'

'It matches your eyes. I thought to get a ruby would be a bit obvious.'

She held out her hands and he hovered the ring over her middle finger, then inelegantly wedged it down. It was stranded above the knuckle. He pulled it away and tried the index finger, which was even more of a mismatch. His mind was telling him to put it on her little finger and quick, but there was some terrible force that pulled it down towards the fourth finger of her left hand. Her ring finger, it's called a ring finger for a reason. Don't do it, his head said. Do it, said her sweet face and his hands that now seemed divorced from his conscious mind, like some rogue limb in an old-fashioned horror film. He put it on a finger quickly. He wanted it to glide down and it did, sort of; there was a small tussle halfway, but it got there. It fitted that finger as if he'd had it measured. It was her wedding ring finger.

She looked at him, fearfully. He felt her telescope away from him and then he heard the words, 'Ruby, will you marry me?' not said by him, surely not, but it sounded like his voice, it *was* his voice, and then a yes, a yes, please, of course, Owen. She clutched his face with those bunch of banana hands and he heard other words form in his head, articulating sharply in a way that they didn't normally. No. Not. Again. Not again. God, Owen, not again. The words formed noiselessly inside and above him, like the clearest thought bubble on the simplest cartoon. He later remembered the words, but at the time he allowed them to be drowned out by a champagne cork popping and a girl gushing and a restaurant applauding.

CHAPTER THREE

APPEARANCE OF PORES

Sierra noticed that Tess was already doing that thing of resting her hands on her back and arching it, which looked as though she was trying out the part of a pregnant woman rather than genuinely needing to do it.

'I just couldn't get up yesterday morning,' said Tess, arriving by taxi 27 hours after she had been due to appear. 'Sorry.'

'Don't apologise, you're the boss.'

'True. I'm going to be a totes understanding one, too—one who is very generous with maternity rights and time off for antenatal appointments.'

'I'll remember that for when I get pregnant.'

'You're not planning to, are you?'

'Hell, no. Not until I'm much older. Or never. What are your plans, anyway, for the gallery? We need to go over the schedules.'

'It'll be fine, don't worry about it. Nothing will change. I don't see why everyone makes such a big deal about having a baby. Your mother didn't change her life when she had you, did she?'

'Wish she had. She took me everywhere with her, clubbing and everything. Says she used to leave me with her coat and get given a cloakroom stub for me.'

'There you go.'

'It made me miserable. I'd have loved a boring mother.'

'Don't say that. You wouldn't be you if your mother hadn't had all those musicians and fun people around. You wouldn't be interesting, funny, unusual you.'

'I might be all those things with an education,' said Sierra.

'You're getting an education, here, where it matters and with a salary.'

With any luck, thought Sierra, who'd been looking through the accounts before Tess's arrival.

33

'Do I get a pay rise when you go off on maternity leave, then?'

Tess laughed. 'We'll see. How is your mother, anyway?'

'We're getting on very well at the moment. That'll be because for the last few months she's been in some mountain range I've never heard of in southern Spain with a load of skanks with dreadlocks and dogs on pieces of string. Honestly, Tess, when she gets back I've so got to get out of there.'

'Silly thing, I lived at Mummy's until I was much older than you.'

But Mummy's is a large house with acres of swagged curtains in a posh bit of London, while Mum's is a one-and-a-half-bedroomed shithole on an estate that would be demolished if it weren't so popular with film crews looking for somewhere gritty.

*   *   *

It had been a strange and wonderful surprise to Lucy that she should have been gifted with a whole new set of friends at what felt like such a great age. These women were not her contemporaries, but parents of her children's contemporaries. Was there a term for this? Probably something hideous like 'momtemporaries'.

There was no doubt, she thought, as she looked around at the Year 2 mothers she was having a drink with, that they were considerably less glamorous than the friends she'd sought out in her previous incarnations. At school, she'd been in the top set both academically and socially, though the best in the former and definitely scraping by in the latter. Then at university, where she'd met Tess, she'd always found herself drawn to those that exuded the social and sartorial confidence that she herself had always lacked.

She loved these women, she genuinely did, but today she yearned for a conversation with a woman like Tess, an 'other', who could tell her what life was like out there, beyond home and office, who'd take her to a world where there were choices and forks in the road. Tess would no longer be an other, she'd just be another version of all that Lucy was already familiar with, only seven years behind. She'd want to discuss routines and solids and Lucy was not sure she could face it, because she never wanted to go back there and because sometimes she so desperately did. Children did this to you—they made you yearn for the next phase, sleeping, walking, talking, reading, but once these were reached you were sad at the passing of that previous age.

'So, apparently,' said Liz, 'there's such a thing as "youngest kid goes to school syndrome".'

'Which is?' asked Clare.

'It's when your youngest goes to full-time school and you have a terrible crisis over your life, like a mid-life one, and you think "is this it?". Then you get a divorce or have an affair. Apparently it's always happening.'

'That would account for the slightly febrile atmosphere at the PTA quiz night,' said Clare. 'Honestly, the pheromones were flying.'

'Is this true?' asked Lucy. 'Is this recognised as a crisis point in a woman's life?'

'Not yours,' said Liz. 'You've got a proper life

away from your children. No, it's prevalent among women who've put their own life on hold to look after the kids.' Or men, thought Lucy, with a shiver of panic. 'And they start putting their energies into hitting on their builder or having crushes on inappropriate people,' Liz continued.

'I am so crushing on that cute Mr Wasiak,' admitted Clare.

'Ah, bless,' said the others in unison, for Mr Ah Bless was how they usually referred to him as they barely resisted the temptation to ruffle his hair.

Clare turned to Lucy. 'I am so jealous that he's your new best friend.'

'Hardly,' Lucy replied, 'and I'm not sure we're his type, anyway.'

'Mind you,' said Liz, 'I can think of many things I'd rather be doing with my newfound freedom than shagging some teacher or random dad from school. It's not as if I've the energy to do it with the dad I've got at home.' She began to regale them with stories of her recent night away with her husband and without her children.

'Was it wonderful being away from the kids?' asked Jenny.

'Yeah, I suppose. Though I had to have sex, obviously, which was a bit of a chore. Obviously.'

The other six snorted in recognition. 'When all you wanted to do was sleep and try all the free toiletries,' said Clare.

'Exactly,' Liz agreed. 'Lie back and think of the body crème. That sounds all wrong—let me make it clear that does not mean lie back and think about putting the body crème anywhere filthy.'

'Why not reinvigorate your lovemaking with some gentle role-play or smearing your lover's body in exotic foodstuffs?' Clare aped the directives of a women's magazine. 'My arse, as if you'd mess up the sheets like that. They never talk about clearing all the gunk up afterwards; I mean, where's the eroticism in that?'

'Bless him, he's so easily sated and I can't even give him that pleasure more than once every full moon. Luckily, a bit like my old PE teacher, he seems to find the fact that I have my period for at least three weeks a month entirely credible.'

The louder the laughter, the more discomforted Lucy felt. She had gone out for drinks with some dear women with whom she could discuss secondary school options and whether anybody was already getting their child tutored, and instead found herself trapped in some sort of cackling middle-aged hen night.

'God, I know,' said Jenny. 'What's even more tragic is that he asks me whether I'm satisfied by these nano-romps we have—as if—and I find myself nodding to avoid a prolonged prodding which stops me from getting back to my book.'

'Tell me about it.'

'You're very quiet, Lucy,' said Clare. They all turned to look at her. 'Do you not share our problems?'

'No, well, I . . . I don't know,' she replied.

'I do,' said Liz. 'You so don't share our problems, do you, with your young, ridiculously hot husband?'

'He's not my husband. And he's not that young. He's 32.' Well, he will be quite soon, anyway. She liked the few months of the year that he was seven years younger than her, rather than the other half, when it was eight. His next birthday would be celebrated, as always, as the children's were. Theirs were good things, you see. Lucy's were not, so they were left unmarked and unremembered.

'He looks way younger—like he should be in one of those vampire films or breaking into song in a high school canteen. The phrase "wouldn't kick him out of bed" could have been invented for him.' Liz looked at her. 'I bet you're doing it all the time. Not that I blame you.' Lucy bristled at the inappropriate turn of the conversation, not excused by the 250ml wine glasses littering the table.

'You are, aren't you?' Clare insisted. 'Mind you, I'm not surprised with Little Mr Should Have Been in a Boy Band. I should be so lucky.' Clare's husband was very twinkly and to Lucy rather lovely, but he was always the man asked to be Santa Claus at the school's Christmas fair.

'I promise you, I'm not swinging from the chandelier.'

'That new one you've got in your hall?' asked Liz.

'Apart from anything else, it's far too delicate,' Lucy added.

'Now we're talking,' said Clare. 'Have you seen what Lucy's done to her living room? Bloody lovely, it is. That wallpaper is just gorgeous.' And the conversation moved on to the safer confines of interior design.

* * *

Owen and Tess lasted five minutes in the nursery department on the fifth floor of the department store before escaping to the safety of the overpriced bar tucked away in the square behind.

'That was the seventh circle of hell,' said Owen.

'The eighth,' said Tess.

'I see your eighth and raise it to a ninth. That was the ninth circle of hell.'

'How many circles of hell were there, anyway?'

'As many as there are makes of pram. Jesus, that saleswoman seemed to be convinced I gave a fuck about complex travel systems.'

'It had wheels, didn't it?'

'But no motor. You know my liking of vehicles corresponds entirely to how much they fuck up the planet. I didn't even get to flash my plastic. What an abortive trip.'

Tess flinched. 'Unfortunate choice of words. Oh dear, I'm not sure I'm ready for this.'

'And I never shall be. Why on earth did you drag me into your nightmare?'

'Because I wanted you to pay for all that stuff,' said Tess. 'You are so much richer than anyone else I know and I feel that your godparental contribution should be more financial than emotional.'

'Hear, hear,' he said, chinking a martini glass to her Virgin Mary. 'Here's the deal. You can have my credit card details and spend as much as you like, just so long as I don't ever have to go to that brightly coloured cesspit again. Why didn't you take Lucy?'

'Too much advice. My head is spinning from the last detailed conversation about whether to buy an electric or hand-held breast pump.'

'Urgh. I wish I'd never asked.'

'Exactly what I thought.'

'Are you sure you know what you're doing, Tess?'

'Yes, definitely. I've decided to go for the electric

39

one.'

'Don't be evasive.'

'No, that's your prerogative, isn't it, Owen?'

'I'm going to be honest.'

'How unusual.'

'Shut it. I'm trying to be all emotional here. Have you really thought this through?'

'I didn't know you cared,' she said and held her stomach protectively.

'Of course I do. You know I do. You're like a . . .' He paused. He wasn't sure what Tess was to him if he was forced to express it other than in the language of banter. Not a sister, definitely not a sister—someone less like the lumpen Caron he couldn't imagine. Not a lover, either, though they had been. Not an ex, because that suggested the past, when it was the present, too—and, he hoped, the future, his engagement notwithstanding. Tess was unique and so was their relationship. What word was there to describe the woman you idolised continually, slept with occasionally and wanted to wallop intermittently? Was there one word to describe the strange hybrid of mistress and mystery that Tess was to him? 'I don't know, sort of best friend.'

'Sweet,' she said.

'Seriously, Tess. It's hard, not knowing who your father is. I should know.'

'Rubbish, darling, you've got a father and a mother. You're always saying that the fact that they adopted you didn't make any difference. Gary is more father than you'll ever wish for.'

'Gareth. His name is Gareth.'

'Of course. The Welsh thing.'

'I suppose I've got two fathers. Dad, who is

40

fantastic and I wouldn't wish for anyone else. And the other one, the biological father, who's pretty irrelevant.'

'And it hasn't done you any harm at all, has it? Besides, this little one . . .' She pointed at her stomach again. It was almost as if she needed reminding of it herself. She'd keep glancing at it in the same way she might a new phone with lots of mysterious applications. 'This little one is going to have me around so I think that more than makes up for any lack of father, don't you.' A statement rather than a question. 'You didn't know who your mother was. That's probably more the cause of your problems, wouldn't you think?'

'What problems? I don't have any problems.'

'I can't win. One minute you're saying you're so terribly deprived by not knowing who your real father is and now you're saying you're absolutely fine. What's it to be, Owen?'

'I'd just like to know what you think my problems are.'

'OK. You have a problem with commitment.'

'Look who's talking.'

'Which you try to mask with all these unsuitable engagements. Have you ever wondered why you keep getting engaged but never married?'

That was a question he avoided asking. He knew that he'd got into the habit of saying 'I love you' too quickly, of giving it away too generously. It wasn't that he didn't mean it, it was just that he always had more love to give away. It was a currency that had gone through hyper-inflation and now he had a wheelbarrow full of I love yous. He needed to devalue, to find a way of recalibrating it or he'd find himself telling the new girl on reception that he loved her. He knew that his I love you was worth a baht while Ruby's was worth a pound. They needed at least to be trading in euros.

He paused, poised to tell Tess that she was wrong, that yes, he had got engaged again, but this time it was going to happen. He looked at her knowing, cat-like face and stopped himself. 'I don't know, Tess. Maybe it's got something to do with not knowing who my father is . . .'

'Mother,' she corrected him.

'All right, not knowing who my mother is.'

She leaned back, sipping her drink triumphantly. 'I told you so.'

*   *   *

Michael arrived at Lucy's before the others. He'd stayed at school to prepare some of what was no longer called homework, but 'home learning', and then had a drink with his fellow teacher Rachel, who'd kissed him passionately outside the pub, much to the amusement of some enormous teenagers sitting on the wall, who he belatedly recognised as having been angelic primary school pupils only a few years before.

'Nice house,' he said to Lucy and it was, with its pale grey walls and upcycled armchairs. 'Very grown up.'

'Is that a good thing?' she said. 'I'm beginning to worry whether I could do with becoming a little less so. Here, have some tapas.'

Michael looked at the carefully displayed slices of Manchego and anchovies and was about to say something about the grown-up-ness of the snacks, no crisps for her, but looked at Lucy's frowning face and thought better of it.

He examined the photographs that had been stuck with magnets onto the wall. 'He's very good looking, isn't he?'

'Ned?'

'Yes, him too. But Jamie.'

'Yes, he is.'

He was touched to see that on her wall calendar, amid the reminders about swimming sessions and book-changing days, she'd added 'Tess, seventeen weeks'. Lucy can do all that stuff, he thought, so I don't have to.

Sierra and Owen fell into the house, with the slightly self-conscious air of people who were trying to create the impression of intimacy, or perhaps something more complicated—people who were trying to create the impression of hiding their intimacy but not doing so very well.

'Owen saw me walking from the tube,' explained Sierra. 'He kerb-crawled me in that fabulous car. I felt so glamorous, like that Julia Roberts in *Pretty Woman.*'

'Ah, that fantastically realistic exposé of the life of a prostitute. Isn't selling your body just so glamorous, so empowering?' said Michael, who prided himself on his feminism. 'Apart from the drugs, the pimps and the clients who rape you.'

Sierra looked at him blankly.

'Do you want some wine?' asked Lucy brightly and Michael vowed to be nice.

'Gorgeous kitchen table,' said Sierra, caressing the antique pine. 'I love kitchen tables, they make me feel sort of nostalgic, though I'm not quite sure what for as I never had one growing up. It's like a proper grown-up house this, isn't it?'

'I suppose so. That's what I keep being told, anyway.'

'And you're such a grown-up. You've got children and everything. Mind you, it didn't make my mum grow up, having me. There was a point when our ages actually crossed over, she regressed as I progressed and at about thirteen I overtook her. She's still not really a grown-up, she's on like a gap year in Spain, except her gap year's been going on for decades. Still, at least I get the flat to myself. Not that it has a proper kitchen table in it.' The carapace of Sierra's robustness cracked for a moment as she stroked the wood as though it were the most calendar-cute kitten. 'I don't know what's more exciting, this house or Owen's car. I feel, like, all mature today, what with being picked up by an older man and now sitting in a proper eat-in kitchen.'

'So,' Lucy said, once her fellow godparents each had a glass of wine and an authentically Iberian nibble in their hands. 'It's been a month since Tess's announcement.'

Michael clasped his hands together. 'Gossip. Tell me honestly, what did you think about Tess's bombshell?'

'It's great that she's doing what she wants to do,' Lucy replied.

'Don't be so prim,' said Owen. 'You were more judgemental than any of us.'

'I was more sober than any of you. And I know the realities of having children, that's all. It's very hard to do alone.'

'You're so conventional.'

'What do you mean? I've always supported non-nuclear families and a woman's right to choose in whatever sphere that might be.'

'You think a child should have two parents, a mother and a father, all happily married.'

'Hardly, I'm not even married myself. But maybe a little bit. I always thought I'd do it on my own if necessary, that women didn't need men, but since having children I think it's wrong—no, that's not the right word—that it's a shame to deny them knowledge of where they come from.'

'My mum's on her own,' said Sierra.

'I'm sorry, I didn't mean to say she's not a good mother.'

Sierra shrugged. 'She's not, really.'

'Do you know your father and his family?' asked Lucy.

'Yeah, I grew up with them some of the time. Sort of. Holidays and stuff.'

'Exactly,' said Lucy. 'You know where you've come from, where you get your green eyes from, how your parents met, how your grandparents met even. And presumably your parents didn't set out to bring you up separately. Tess has chosen that from the outset, she has very clinically decided that her child will not only have no father, it will have no knowledge of a father.'

'Let's get this straight,' Owen said to Lucy. 'You don't mind parents being separated, but it's vital for a child to know who their father is.'

'There's lots of research into it. The lack of a role model can affect your relationships in later life.'

'What about adopted children?'

'I think a lot of—well, some—adopted children do have problems with identity. That's why they try to find their birth parents.'

'Adopted children are weird if they don't try to

find them?'

'I didn't say that. Damaged, maybe.'

Owen stretched his arms out and then put them behind his head. 'You do know I'm adopted, don't you?'

'Ouch,' said Michael. He and Sierra had been watching this exchange with a mixture of fascination and fear, like children being forced to listen to Mummy and Daddy arguing in the front seat of the car.

'I did know that, now I think about it. Sorry . . .'

'You're sorry? You've nothing to be sorry about, I love my parents. They're my parents, you see, adopted or not.'

'Good, I'm really pleased for you, Owen, that's fantastic. Can we get back to Tess and our role as godparents? Here, let me top up your glasses. More boquerones, Sierra, queso Manchego?' She rolled her 'r's and shortened her 'o's with the sound of a woman who'd done at least one course of Spanish language evening classes. 'I've made a list of the things we ought to discuss, the different roles that we can fulfil as godparents. Tess said it herself, she wants us to be involved in our own special ways.'

'And your role is?' said Owen.

'I'm a working parent with a professional understanding of the financial and legal implications of all that it entails—life insurance, pensions provisions, et cetera.'

'I'm the party one,' said Sierra. 'I asked Tess and she's cool with that. What with me being so much younger and everything.'

'I'm the one with the wallet,' said Owen. 'Tess has made that very clear.'

'What am I? What godparent am I?' asked

46

Michael.

'I think you're the gay one,' said Lucy, with her understanding, some-of-my-best-friends-are face on. 'You've always got to have a gay godparent. Mother, single girl, rich bachelor and confirmed bachelor—bingo, full house.'

'Rich man, poor man, bugger man, thief . . .' intoned Owen.

'But I'm not. I'm not gay,' Michael said.

'Aren't you?' the other three asked, united for the first time that evening.

'No, I'm not. Whatever gave you that idea? What has Tess told you?'

'Nothing. I don't think she ever said you were. I just assumed. I'm sorry,' said Lucy. 'Not sorry, of course, there's nothing wrong in being gay.'

'But why do you all think that?'

'You are quite . . .' said Sierra.

'What? What am I?'

'A bit camp,' Sierra replied hesitantly. The others nodded their assent.

'And a primary school teacher. Aren't they, usually? And you were saying how handsome Jamie is,' said Lucy.

'Well he is. Doesn't mean I fancy him. Or that I'm gay.'

'Of course not,' said Lucy. 'And if you were . . .'

'But I'm not. I don't mind you thinking I'm gay, though I'm a bit surprised at Tess giving you that impression, but it's just that I'm not. Don't look at me like that, as if I'm in denial, trying to hide it. If I were and trying to hide it, don't you think I'd choose a better disguise than being a slightly effete boy? If I were gay, I'd be more like Owen, all macho and thrusting car and rugger buggery.'

47

'I don't play rugby. Any more.'

'So if I'm not the gay one, which godparent am I? The related one?'

'No,' said Lucy. 'You're the Catholic one—you're on the Polish side, aren't you? Tess probably wants to get the baby christened a Catholic, so she needs a Catholic godparent. So useful for schools, though she's probably going private.'

'I wouldn't bank on it,' said Sierra. 'Have you seen the gallery's accounts recently?'

'But I'm not religious,' said Michael.

'I don't think that really matters,' said Lucy. 'You've just got to have a nominal Catholic, from what Tess has told me.'

'Who renounces the devil,' he said.

'Coo-el,' said Sierra, 'that is like so Gothic. Do I get to do that too?'

'But I can't, I'm not a Catholic. Well, I am a Catholic, but I don't believe in god,' said Michael.

'An atheist Catholic, then,' said Lucy.

'Sort of.' How could they understand that to Michael, being a Catholic was like being an alcoholic? He need never touch another drop, but he would always define himself as such: my name is Michael Wasiak and I'm a Catholic. *Ex*-Catholic. An ex-Catholic who doesn't believe in god. It was all bound up in his foreignness, in the old-school Polish community, which now said things like, 'Bloody Poles are everywhere,' about the new immigrants, who they felt were giving all the old-timers a bad name. He defined himself by his religion without feeling the need actually to believe in god.

'Well, that's all right then,' said Lucy. 'I think you just have to be baptised a Catholic to be the

Catholic godparent. I don't know that they check what actually goes on in your brain.'

Michael shook his head. The first time he properly thought about god was the last time that he believed in his existence. He was seven and had just learned that Father Christmas didn't exist and that sex did. On hearing the latter, he said to his sisters, 'The Virgin Mary never did *that*,' at which they had laughed and told him, no, she didn't— that's the whole point, der, she's the *Virgin* Mary. Michael then made the association between sex and god, or in reality, the disassociation. If there was sex, there was no god.

God and Tess, they too were bound up, his devotion to one completely replacing his duty to the other. His feelings of childish admiration for Tess mutated into full-on lust and she became the goddess in his new religion, the talisman, the icon that he prayed to.

'I can't do it,' he said. 'I just can't do it. It sounds stupid, but I hadn't really thought about the god bit of being a godparent.'

'Nobody ever does,' Owen told him. 'Least of all the kid's parents.'

'I don't mind sharing the fun duties with you,' said Sierra.

'I don't think the fun really kicks in yet,' said Lucy. 'Here's my list, which takes us up to the birth. I suggest we meet every couple of months, with or without Tess, just to keep ourselves up to speed with tasks. Here goes: antenatal appointments, birthing partner, nursery equipment buying, driver for getting to the hospital, decorating the nursery . . .'

'I could do a mural for that,' said Sierra.

'Thank you. Perhaps you could also help with the hospital bag—she needs aromatherapy oils, lip balm, things like that. And Michael?'

'I'll say ten Hail Marys and an Our Father.'

'Please don't sulk,' said Lucy.

'What's left for me to do, anyway? I don't want to be at the birth.'

'I'm going to be a birthing partner as I've been through it myself. Ned was a natural birth, I didn't have any drugs, just gas and air.'

'Like my mum, she loved that gas, wanted to take a canister home with her,' said Sierra. 'Mind you, it's funny her boasting for once about not taking the drugs.'

'So what does that leave me?' Michael repeated.

'I told her to sign up for hypnobirthing classes, to meet other mothers and to get some breathing tips. She was worried that people would think she was a lesbian if I went with her.'

'See,' said Michael. 'It's not just me.'

'Maybe you could go with her to those. And if there's a problem with me going to the birth, you can be the substitute.'

'I am not going to the birth.'

'Only in an emergency. At least if you do the class, you'll know about the breathing. You can go for the twenty-week scan, too—that's coming up. Maybe she could schedule it for half term or after school or something. Anybody got any questions? Good, now we can relax and talk about something else.' There was a pause. 'Owen, how's your girlfriend? Ruby, isn't it?'

'You've got a girlfriend?' Sierra touched her throat.

'She's not my girlfriend any more.'

50

'Oh?' said Lucy.

'She's my fiancée. See what I did there?'

'What's that, your fourth fiancée?' said Lucy.

'Third.' He wasn't counting Bianca.

'I can think of at least three others. When's the big day? I'll buy myself a hat.'

'We haven't set a date yet. Perhaps we could have a double wedding, Lucy.'

'Ha ha. What's she like, anyway?'

'She's lovely,' said Owen. 'She's a lovely person.'

'So's my girlfriend,' announced Michael, with emphasis. 'She's called Rachel and she's a teacher.'

'My boyfriend's lovely, too,' said Sierra. 'His name's Josh. I've always got a boyfriend. I haven't been single for longer than a fortnight since I was fourteen. In fact, I haven't been single at all if you count the overlaps as time in lieu. I think I've been single like minus a few months.'

'Do you think that's healthy?' asked Lucy. 'I've done my time on my own, when I was thirty or so, and I think it really helped me work out what I wanted in life. You have to know that you can be alone, that you don't need a man.'

'Well, I do. I need to be with someone. I get really crabby if I don't get enough sex.' Sierra looked at Owen. 'Really, I do. In fact, I'm going round to his house tonight.'

*   *   *

Even the lift home in Owen's car couldn't cheer up Sierra. She felt soiled, more like a proper prostitute than Julia Roberts this time round. What had she been thinking? All that stuff about loving sex, ooh, needing sex, I love boys, I do. She had sounded

51

like some see-through-panty-wearing starlet on the pages of a lads' mag. She might as well have stuck her finger in her mouth and her bum up in the air for all the dignity she had exuded.

She hadn't wanted a lift in Owen's car, but he'd made a big point of his chivalry. All her insistence that she make her own way seemed to goad him further into converting his Alfa into a trusty steed. Then there was something about the way he referred to her newly announced boyfriend as 'this Josh person' that made her want to prove something.

She looked across at him. He had the profile of an Italian footballer, long-nosed and long-haired—well, long for a straight City type, anyway. He was whistling. Not in a cheerful, window-cleaning fashion, but as an impediment to conversation. Sierra was undeterred.

'She's nice, that Lucy, when you get to know her. Not as uptight as I'd thought. A really good cook, too—wasn't that food lovely?' Owen grunted a vague assent.

Sierra wished she was in a minicab with Michael. She wanted to gossip about the evening, to discuss Lucy's lists and all the photographs of children stuck to the fridge door alongside the forms you get from school with tear-off slips at the bottom, the ones her mum never got round to filling in. She'd wanted to ask him what he really thought about Tess's pregnancy. Most of all she wanted to expunge the horrible sense of shame of having boasted about her libido. She had really liked Owen. She hadn't known how much until she'd found out about the girlfriend. Sorry, fiancée.

'Is it her real name?'

'Whose real name?' Owen sounded distracted, like a father being asked a persistent question at the Science Museum by a pesky seven-year-old. The way her dad had sounded on those Saturdays they'd spent together.

'Your girlfriend's. Sorry, fiancée's.'

'Well, Sierra, as it happens, no, it's not. She changed it when she was fifteen.'

'Why? What from?'

'You'll have to ask her. So where does your young man live exactly?'

Your young man? Patronising arse. 'My boyfriend lives just over there on the left. You can drop me here, that's fine.' He insisted on driving to right outside the terraced house.

She glanced back at the car. Owen was waiting to see that she'd got safely to the door, of course. Patronising arse times two.

Aware that Owen was watching her, she knocked firmly on the door. It opened. Sierra looked at Josh to try to see what Owen would see from his vantage point. All right looking, she supposed, a bit of fat creeping onto a skinny frame, his face with the startled pallor of someone who spends all day and all night looking into screens of varying sizes.

'Sienna,' he said.

'Sierra.'

'Oh, yeah, Sierra.' He paused. 'What the fuck are you doing here?'

CHAPTER FOUR

DRY IN PLACES

Lucy felt emboldened by a bottle of wine, the sex scenes in the film they had watched that night (*Brokeback Mountain*—what was it about two absurdly good-looking men indulging in forbidden love that was quite so intoxicating?) and a random, yet very lurid fantasy that she had entertained about being straddled across the ancient rocking horse that Jamie had inherited from his grandmother (which in reality was very rickety and creaked in a way that would alarm both the children and the neighbours). She was so encouraged by these things that she began to make the epic journey across the unfrozen tundra of their king-sized marital bed.

Jamie had his back to her and was wearing not only underwear, but pyjamas on top of that. 'Jammies', they called them, when trying to wrestle Rosa and Ned into them each night and out of them in the mornings. This was the reverse alchemy of language brought on by parenthood, rendering sexless all that was previously erotic—tits become boobs, cocks are now willies, vaginas are lulus or some other silly made-up word that sounds like either a girl's name or a species of wildflower.

She leaned across and stroked the back of his head. She felt him stiffen, and not in a good way. She persevered and lifted up his pyjama top to stroke his back.

'That's nice,' he said.

She ignored the tightness in his voice and used

this as encouragement to shimmy across the bed and press her chest into his back. No resistance. She pressed harder and then moved her crotch in and round. Even with the wine and the thoughts of inappropriate sex, she still felt far too nervous to begin to think about enjoying herself. And if it got that far, and she hoped it would, she feared she might be too dry with stage fright for him to be able to enter her with ease. Say he managed to do that—and it wasn't a given, not at all—then things could still go wrong, the delicate journey could be so easily derailed. Even if it all actually happened— and the chances, she knew, were so slim as to begin to feel negligible—she wouldn't actually enjoy it, though she'd give every indication of doing so, because she'd be so concerned about getting there, completing the act, being able to say to herself that it had only been five minutes or one day or only a week since they last had.

But it had been almost five months since they'd had sex. There were already three calendars that swirled in Lucy's head: the school year, the financial year and the actual year. To those she now added the forty weeks of Tess's pregnancy and, unmarked, the time that had elapsed since she and Jamie had last done it.

It was easy to remember the date, as there'd been an argument over Rosa's Halloween costume.

'I don't want to be a witch,' she'd screamed.

'Fine, be a ghost then.'

'No, I want to be a dancer.'

'But dancers aren't very scary.' Lucy knew that Halloween was a US import but she was keen that this American habit of girls dressing in random 'sexy' costumes should not make it through customs. 'I suppose you could be a zombie dancer if we put some talcum powder in your hair.'

'But then I'll look ugly.'

'That's sort of the point.'

'Let her dress how she wants,' Jamie had said, and Rosa had hugged him while he cut up Lucy's favourite cashmere bed socks to turn into legwarmers.

She hadn't been able to switch off her irritation at him throughout the trick or treating, or four hours later when they'd had sex. If only she'd known then that it was to be the last time for so long, she'd have made the effort to enjoy it.

She now dared to put her hand around his waist and began stroking his still flat stomach. Her attention briefly flitted to thoughts of the husbands of the women in the pub, how your hand could get lost in the folds of their bellies. That might be quite nice, she thought treacherously, to feel all thin and superior in comparison. She concentrated again on the line of hair that went down from there to inside his pants like the cursor on a computer, this way please, following it with her finger. She caught her breath with the anxiety of what she'd find inside those pants, surely worn as some sort of cotton-mix contraception. Her hands felt for it, what she was looking for, and right until the last minute she felt optimistic.

Nothing. Well, something, obviously, but shrunken and flaccid with not even the merest glimmer of stiffening hope to offer her. She tried for a while but it was she that felt impotent as she rubbed ineffectually and it eluded her grasp like jelly.

'I'm tired,' he said, shrugging her off.

'So am I,' she said brightly, in her 'this museum is fun, isn't it, kids?' voice, the one she used for getting Rosa and Ned to walk up hills. 'Yes, I'm tired too.' I'm fucking tired of this, I can't bear the humiliation and the loneliness any longer.

'Night then,' he said, pulling away from her.

'Yes, good night. Sleep well.' I shan't. She lay awake, sobbing silently until the tears that pooled in her ears began to overflow and dampen her pillow. She was sleeping in the wet patch again, just not the one she had hoped for.

* * *

Josh is my boyfriend. My boyfriend, Josh. This would be true to say now, he is my boyfriend, thought Sierra, trying it out once again. My boyfriend, Josh, yeah he's in computers, going to be totally minted one day, he already earns like a thousand a day as a consultant, or something like that, when he works—he's freelance, lots of fingers in lots of pies, yeah portfolio career, that's what he calls it.

It still didn't quite ring true, though it was, it really was. Before the night of Lucy's dinner, it had all been lies—well, apart from the bit about him being in computers. He really wasn't her boyfriend then, not even close. Their how-we-met story needed a bit of work, it definitely wasn't one to tell the grandchildren.

Sierra had been to a pub gig of some band who mutilated themselves on stage, or pretended to, she didn't know which was more pathetic. Afterwards, everyone had gone back to a flat that some bloke pretended was a squat but later it had emerged his dad had bought the disused factory as a development project and was paying him handsomely to keep the bona fide squatters out. There were some schoolgirls, not even sixth-formers by the looks of them, a couple of much older men, the band and then some randoms, including Sierra.

Her friend Chloe was letting the lead singer of the band eat the scabs off the grazed knee she'd got while playing hockey. Chloe was doing her best not to look revolted as Mad Dave, as he called himself, made a great thing of crunching the congealed blood between his crooked teeth. We've all done it, thought Sierra, eaten a childhood scab or picked our own nose or even luxuriated in the rank smell of our own farts, but really, it just didn't work with anybody else's. It wasn't transgressive and cool, it was just disgusting and pointless.

She wandered through the rooms, which were decorated with detritus that its makers would probably call art. Pieces of crap—not literally, though that wouldn't surprise her. Working in a gallery meant that she was qualified to make such pronouncements. Qualified—she liked the word and repeated it in her head; she'd never felt herself to be qualified in anything but negotiating between her parents and navigating between their worlds. In a room not much bigger than a cupboard, she came across a boy playing with his phone and she introduced herself. She gave him a blow job, for want of anything better to do, which he made the right noises about, though he did continue to surf as she did so. She could have sworn he was still concentrating on it while he came, in fact. He offered her some indeterminate pills and tweaked her nipples and that was that. She didn't think she'd ever see him again. They'd made each other friends online, though that was overstating it, and she'd gathered that he lived near where the party had been—he'd offered a vague invitation to 'come round some time', but she hadn't ever thought she ever would.

Then there was the night she went round after Lucy's dinner.

When he'd asked, 'What the fuck are you doing here?' she'd repeated, 'What the fuck,' emphasising the 'fuck' in as erotic a manner as she could muster in the hope that he would let her in quickly and for as long as it took for Owen to just fuck on off so she could give up on this charade. It had worked and she'd gone in.

'How did you know where I lived?'

'You told me, remember. Hardly a state secret, anyway—it's all over your page.'

'Do you want to come in, then?'

She nodded. Surrounded by the family photographs at Lucy's, learning about Owen's engagement and Michael's girlfriend, she couldn't face going back to her mum's flat alone. But here with Josh, she still felt pretty lonely.

'You was lucky I was in.' Sierra flinched at the bad grammar, especially since she guessed it was an affectation. 'You could have woken my flatmates.' They couldn't feel any more like strangers to her than Josh did. She'd probably spent longer with her head inside his underwear than looking at his face.

'Yes, I'm sorry. Really rude of me. I can go.'

He shrugged, so she stayed. They had sex, she felt she owed him that. There were three computers in his bedroom as well as the phone welded to his

59

hand. She worked really hard at it and he finally came and she did the yes-yes-ooh-yes-yes and then she pretended to sleep, putting the pillow over her head to cut out the glare from the screens and the clickety-clack of the keyboards as he continued doing whatever it was he did.

*   *   *

'Hello, Sierra,' Michael said as he entered the gallery after school one Thursday.

'All right?' she replied. God, she was sexy, he thought. So his type, but he got the distinct impression that he wasn't hers. Things with Rachel were already stagnating. He wondered whether he wasn't the marrying type, but not for the reasons that some people always suspected.

'Did you get home OK the other night? After Lucy's?'

'No. I went to my boyfriend Josh's.'

'Ah, yes, your boyfriend. Josh. Is Tess here? I'm accompanying her to the hospital for something called a sex scan, which is odd because of course the sex came twenty weeks earlier. Although not, I suppose, in Tess's case.'

'Actually,' said Tess as she came in, 'I think you'll find they call it an anomaly scan these days, but well done you for doing your homework with the *What to Expect When You're Expecting* book.' She kissed Michael and he was surprised at how different her body already felt against his. 'But hopefully they'll be able to tell us what it is.'

'A baby?'

'Very funny. A boy or a girl, obviously. Let's go.'

The waiting room at the hospital was painted

in Elastoplast pink, with posters exclaiming 'Breastfeeding is best feeding' and 'If you would like a photograph of your scan, please tell us beforehand. Photographs are available for a cost of £3.' The posters were a clumsy mixture of prescription and aspiration, one with a close-up of a baby sucking a breast, while the woman's other hand was curled around a (presumably non-alcoholic) cocktail, complete with parasol.

Tess was jiggling her leg, either with anxiety or desperation to go to the loo. Apparently she needed a full bladder for the scan. She'd been on edge from the moment they'd entered the hospital. 'Come on, come on. Why's it taking so long? Excuse me, but my appointment was for 4.30 p.m. How much longer am I going to have to wait?' Her voice became even more imperious than usual. There were mothers like this at school. Believing that even if they weren't paying for it, some people deserved better service than others.

'Why's it called an anomaly scan?'

'Because they're looking for anomalies.'

'Like what? Two heads?'

She shook her head. 'For god's sake, Michael. Perhaps you weren't the right person to bring along here, after all. Let's just call it a twenty-week scan, shall we?'

'Halfway through your forty weeks, then? It's half baked like those baguettes you can buy in the supermarket that you finish off in the oven. Or it would be an incubator in this case.' She shot him a look of pure venom. 'I think I'll shut up now.'

He was trying, he really was, but nothing was enough for Tess. He'd now learned the difference between a radiographer and a sonographer, that pregnancy is not nine months but 40 weeks, that they date it from before the woman's even conceived. But he was never going to say the right thing or be the right person, some sort of tall handsome doctor type who was the real father and could supply genes, kindness and money to the proceedings.

And he learned, ten minutes later, looking at her gel-covered belly, that a pregnant stomach isn't the hard, glorious thing that he'd imagined it might be. It just looks a bit fat.

She clutched his hand with a force that he'd have thought she'd reserve for the birth.

'There's the heartbeat,' said the sonographer, 'and the hands and the feet.'

Just like on the television, thought Michael, and he would play the role of doting dad.

'Amazing,' he said. This was the bit where he was supposed to cry. He didn't feel emotional. He didn't even feel particularly interested in the baby, only in Tess's reaction to what was happening. So far he just knew that it was not so much gaining a godchild as losing his cousin.

Godchild. Oh god. He must have a conversation with her, some time—not now, obviously—about this whole god business.

He watched as the sonographer took a series of black and white snaps of unidentifiable cross sections that reminded him of bone marrow at the butcher's.

'How's it looking?' asked Tess.

The sonographer smiled. 'Fine, normal.'

'Normal's good.'

Michael had never heard Tess express that view before. Normality was always perfectly ghastly or an abomination or so dreadfully dull. He looked at her eyes filling with tears. He'd never seen her cry, either. She looked back at him and smiled, as if for that second she too believed in him as the father. He squeezed her hand and they looked at the pictures on the fuzzy black and white screen and he pretended, just for one moment, that they were the normal parents to this wonderfully normal baby.

'Would you like to know the sex?'

Tess nodded.

The sonographer kept on moving her mouse across the stomach. 'It's hard for me to get a good picture. Shake your belly a bit.' Michael stopped feeling sentimental. 'That's better . . . wait a second . . . yes, I think that's it. You do know whatever we say isn't definitive, don't you?'

'Go on.'

'Especially not if it's looking like a girl.'

'A girl?'

'I'd say that it's almost certainly a girl.'

'A girl.' Michael and Tess looked at each other. He felt he was warming up to this role. 'Or a boy with a very small winkle,' he added.

Tess groaned. 'Please.'

'Unlikely in our family,' he said, trying out being Owen for size. 'Know what I mean?'

'Really,' said Tess. 'It doesn't suit you. And anyway, please.'

He hugged her, getting gel on his jumper.

*   *   *

Ruby had told him that Welsh pottery was very sought after these days, but to Owen there was nothing glamorous about the country of his birth.

63

Unless you owned it, of course, or at the very least great tracts of it, as had seemed to be the case with those friends of Tess who were always described to him as Welsh despite the lack of accent or ability to speak the language.

'But I don't understand why you don't want me to come with you,' Ruby had said. 'I'm your fiancée.' She liked the word, Owen had soon found out; she liked all French words, in fact: she dabbed her face with a serviette, drank rosé and spent her salary on Crème de la Mer that she got using her employee's discount card at the glossy department store. He wondered whether he hadn't taken himself into a cul-de-sac.

He couldn't explain why she wasn't allowed on his trips home, to her or even to himself. He felt ashamed both of his family's lack of glamour and his fiancée's surfeit of it, or at least of a certain sort of painted-on and easily removed with cleansing wipes glamour.

'Your parents must be dying to meet me,' she had said.

This was an unfortunate use of the word dying. Amid all the other thoughts Owen was trying to suppress was the worst one of all: his father would die soon of the disease that was turning the pink coral of his lungs to desiccated and blackened lumps. Visions of mortality were unavoidable at his parents' house as his father left notes on every surface reminding his mother of the things she had to do, with printouts of bills stamped 'paid' to try to explain to her something of the modern world. What would she do, his father said, she barely knew how to write a cheque, let alone use a cashpoint machine. He'd been the first person Owen knew to

64

get telephone banking, soon followed by an online bank account, while his mother had never even used a photocopier. She copied recipes out from library books by hand and had a ring binder that came ready divided into sections for hors d'oeuvres, soups and starters, mains, desserts and special occasions.

Life for Owen's mum seemed to have calcified in the seventies. Not the fun, free-loving, pot-smoking, revolutionary or punk version of that decade, but the impoverished, dull, tinned-spaghetti-eating, hidden-in-the-attic suburban sibling of that glittering era. The insides of the cupboards in their kitchen still had the wallpaper with the brown and orange curvy-sided cubes tangoing across it, a pattern matched by the drawer-liners that had once been scented. His mother left all that was newfangled to his father.

'Owen, you look so handsome.' His mother hugged him on arrival, trampolining him against her chest. Mari hadn't read the pieces about how bigger crepey-breasted women shouldn't wear high-necked or cleavage-displaying tops and she alternated between the two. Today she'd gone for the former option with a polo neck and her waist cinched by a wide suede belt with a covered buckle that matched her boots. Between those and the above-the-knee skirt a wodge of flesh was on display. All women seemed to maintain a look reminiscent of the one they wore at the peak of their physical allure, which, according to science, was at age 24. That figured with Mari. That was the year she'd married Owen's dad, the same year they had adopted him, the year after he was born.

He wriggled away from her embrace like a small

65

child from a hairy-faced aunt. 'Where's Dad?'

'On the computer. You know what he's like. Do you think I should be worried?'

'About what?'

She giggled. 'Sexy stuff.'

Owen escaped to the room that had been his teenage refuge and now fulfilled the same function for his father.

'All right, Dad?'

His father's handshake was stiff, it always had been—hovering, not knowing whether it should mutate into something more intimate—but now the rest of him was just as awkward. He pressed on the sides of a second-hand office chair to lift himself up, slipping slightly while its wheels ricocheted away. Owen could picture him doing the same thing in a wheelchair.

'Mustn't grumble.'

'Oh, but you must.'

'I will then. I'm rubbish and I'm getting worse.' He coughed by way of illustration and then swallowed back the tide of phlegm.

'Mum's worried about you looking at porn on the web, but I can see it's much, much worse than that.' The screen was filled with the tentacles of messages on an emphysema support group site with titles such as 'Broncoscope, what's it like?' and 'Lung nodule question'.

'It's good for me. Makes me feel better. Turns out I didn't smoke for long enough to have caused it. Twenty per cent of cases aren't caused by smoking.'

'Good. I think.'

'Which means it's genetic. Another thing I should have thanked my parents for. They always

66

did call me ungrateful.'

'The things your parents give you,' said Owen.

'You can have my encyclopaedias when I die.'

'Thanks, Dad. Don't, though. Don't die just yet.'

'We've got dinner to get through for starters,' he said and coughed at the prospect.

*   *   *

Owen struggled with his consommé. His father, he noticed, had foregone the croutons that floated in his own. Bad for his throat, he said. Mari ate hers with relish, claiming there were negative calories in vegetable soup. She knew the calorific cost of every foodstuff and the taste of none of them.

'How's life in the big smoke?' she asked.

Owen caught his father's eye, who then coughed theatrically. 'Same as ever.'

'Lots of money?'

'Enough.'

'Good for you, son,' his father said. 'You'll have enough to retire with soon.'

'I don't see the point of that,' retorted Mari. 'You'll need some to support a family. When you have a family. Have you got a bird at the moment?'

'A bird? A dolly bird? A chick?'

'I don't know what you call it these days. Something horrible like "partner", I don't doubt. What about that nice Tess? Is she single?'

'She is.'

'She'd make a lovely mother.'

'Indeed. She's pregnant.'

'But you just said . . .'

'She bought the sperm. From the Internet. It's full of that sort of thing.' Owen would never tire of

67

goading his mother. In the car on the way he'd tell himself that he wouldn't, but on walking through the frosted-glass door, he'd transform himself. 'Tonight, ladies and gentlemen,' he seemed to be announcing, 'I'm going to be a peevish adolescent with a hotline to my parents' points of irritation.'

'I knew nothing good could come from the computer,' said Mari. 'The poor mite, it won't know who its father is.' There followed an awkward pause.

'But at least it will know its mother, that's what Tess says,' said Owen. 'At least it will know who one of its parents is.'

His mother's face fell and she began to splutter. 'But still. She'll be a single mother. That must be hard, I think.'

'I think she'll be all right.'

'Why didn't she just have a baby with you?'

'Because she didn't want to. Nor I with her. We're not a couple.'

'Your mother's right,' said Gareth. This wasn't, though—he and his father were the team against her, the positions weren't supposed to shift. 'It's high time you settled down.'

'You were way older.'

'And look at me now. I'm not going to live to see my grandchildren.'

'I can't squeeze in some kids just because you're obsessed with your own mortality. Hassle Caron, she should be reproducing for you, not me—give you some proper grandchildren.'

'Owen!' his mother cried, but didn't need to continue. She ran out of the room. He knew he should feel sorry, but he just felt irritated. He'd never had a fantasy about who his real mother was.

68

It wasn't that he felt Mari was as perfect a mother as he could wish for, just that he wasn't really that interested. Who his father was, on the other hand, that was a different matter. He used to fill the empty spaces of car journeys to the coast with thoughts of how Dad, Gareth, was his real father. How he'd lived some colourful life before being sucked into marriage and a job as a lab technician, where he'd dallied with an exotic dancer who had died in childbirth but had begged Gareth to look after their dark-eyed boy. Whereupon he'd come back to the boring town of his birth and found an idiot like Mari to marry, merely to create a family for the baby.

He had told neither his parents nor Tess about his engagement. He didn't stop to think why.

CHAPTER FIVE

DECREASING NIGHT VISION

And here I am again, thought Sierra. Apart from that first time when she'd met Josh, they hadn't seen each other outside of this house, which she tried to persuade herself made them like doomed lovers in a film with subtitles, compelled to live out their love within four walls. He was playing a shoot-'em-up game on the Playstation with three other blokes in the living room, which she'd only just discovered was also one of the housemate's bedrooms. What she had thought of as a throw for the sofa was in fact a duvet, and none too clean at that.

She sat there watching the four boy-men playing

their game and making a lot of kah-pow-die-fucker noises as they did so. There was another girl there—Sierra thought her name was Biff, or that might have just been another video game accompaniment sound. She didn't speak and so Sierra didn't either, instead they sat there like silent cheerleaders, spectators at their menfolk's chosen sport. She thought about going as he was so not worth this embarrassment, but felt paralysed by the thought of the further embarrassment of leaving. Would standing up in a huff show that she cared? She didn't, really, she hadn't even much liked him, but she wanted him to like her and the more he seemed indifferent, the more she found herself wanting to prove him wrong.

'Let's go,' Josh at last said to her and she wondered whether they'd get out to the street of a thousand bars that was only ten minutes' walk away, but no, he meant to his bedroom. Her stomach rumbled with hunger and she could hear the sounds of the game being played below through the uncovered floorboards.

He sat at one of the laptops and she put her hand inside the zip of his trousers.

'That's good, baby.' Since this was more syllables than he'd uttered to her all evening she felt encouraged. 'Real good.' His accent had become somewhat Americanised. 'Right there, yeah baby. Now fuck my arse with your finger.'

'Really?'

'Yeah, fuck it hard.'

'OK.'

'Talk to me, tell me all about it.'

'About what?'

'How good it feels.'

70

'Right. It feels so good. Baby, feel my finger, do you feel it?' Oh god, she herself could feel something and she didn't like it. She wanted to wash her hands immediately. Could she wipe her hand on the duvet or something or might there be some Kleenex knocking around?

'You like that, baby, you like it a lot,' he said.

No, not really, I don't like it all. Why would I? 'Do you like it?'

'Love it, babes, love it.'

'Yeah, me too.'

Sex hadn't been like this that first night. It had been pretty straightforward. Nothing to write home about (though who exactly writes home about their latest sexual adventure, even with parents as permissive as hers), but quick and efficient at least.

'And you love it, you love my big fat cock, don't you?'

It's not that big. Or fat, for that matter. 'I love it. It's so big, fuck me with your big fat cock.' Yes, do. Let's just get this out of the way so I can wash my flipping finger.

He turned her over onto her hands and knees and she hoped that this meant he was going to at least attempt to pleasure her with his fingers, not because she could really be bothered to come, but because at least it would show some effort on his part. He lifted up her skirt and pulled down her tights and then stood up. She was beached with her bum exposed to the cold air. He fiddled with one of the laptops and then came back to her.

They engaged in a tussle while he tried to stick it in the wrong hole. Jeez, what was it with guys these days? Chloe said that there's some agreement they've all signed that says anal's the new oral. She wanted to guide him but was trying to keep her finger, the one she'd used on him, as far away as possible. Once he'd finally got inside her, she gave an encouraging, 'Oh yeah, that's good,' and realised that she was not the only one saying these words.

She lifted her head to find that the laptop was showing some porn. It was vanilla, a couple of women and a man, some sex toys, but she did wonder why he wasn't happy with the live entertainment that was already provided. It felt a bit like those people who go to concerts and watch the whole thing through their mobile screens, filming the event instead of just enjoying it.

'Oh god, yes, yes,' she said when she felt he was on the verge of coming. Yes, finish it now, why don't you.

'I'm fucking you, I'm fucking you,' he said, which didn't need saying, 'and I'm going to come.' Good, get on with it. 'I'm going to come, I'm going to come, bitch, I'm going to come.' He pulled himself out, ripped off the condom and came over her back just as the money shot appeared on the screen in front of her, giving new meaning, she supposed, to the term 'simultaneous orgasm'.

He lay down and she waited for him to turn off the screen, but it rolled straight into the next feature. She felt like getting up and leaving.

'You are so beautiful, Sierra,' he said. 'You're the fucking best.'

So she stayed.

*　　　*　　　*

'Do you miss alcohol?' asked Lucy, who was enjoying her own glass of red.

'Like life itself,' said Tess. 'Hell, I'm getting myself a glass. I was saving up my "one to two units once or twice a week" for this weekend, but I need it now. And then, probably.'

'In America, you're not allowed any at all. Barmen refuse to serve it to you and you can get arrested for child abuse, apparently.'

'Did you drink when you were pregnant?'

'No, I didn't have a drop,' said Lucy, 'but actually I think that was a misinterpretation of the statistical evidence about the effects of alcohol and the prevalence of foetal alcohol syndrome, and I believe there is very little in the way of empirical hard facts due to the impossibility of deliberately plying a sample cohort of pregnant women with booze.'

'Which, in English . . .'

'Means sit down, I'll get you a glass of something.'

'Champagne, please.'

'I envy you,' said Lucy on her return.

'Why?'

'It's such an exciting time, the birth of your first child. I think it must be like your first hit of heroin—you spend the rest of your life trying to replicate it. It's all ahead of you.'

'The broken nights, the loss of independence, the penury . . . That's what everyone keeps telling me about.'

'But that bit when you first see this stranger who at the same time you know so well,' Lucy sighed. 'It's the best. Like falling in love without any chance that they'll stop phoning you or sleep with someone else.'

'Have another, then.'

'God, no. I think Jamie would divorce me. Well, he'd divorce me if we were married.'

'Well, yes, lucky me not to have to worry about my husband leaving me.'

'Sorry, I didn't mean that. I'd love to, in a way, but I think I'd just be trying to stave off my own feelings of mortality.' Lucy caught sight of her tired face in the mirror behind Tess's head. 'There's just something about having children that makes you hyper-aware of the passing of time. It's like having one of those big countdown clocks like they have in Times Square on New Year's Eve constantly running on the film of your life. One million, two thousand, three hundred and four seconds until death. So many birthdays to celebrate. We're having a party at the beginning of May for Jamie's birthday, by the way. I was going to invite you and the other godparents. As you know, we never celebrate my birthday.'

'Not even your next one?'

'Especially not my next one.'

'You're making parenthood sound very melancholic,' said Tess.

'I don't mean to. Of course, the kids getting older is a good thing, you read these awful stories of disabled adults who are like giant babies, but it goes so fast. Well, that's wrong, the minutes go slowly, but the years speed by. You can spend your life wishing away the hours and then before you know it, the youngest has gone to school full time.'

'Golly,' said Tess. 'And there was I thinking everything in your life was perfect. But now that I've joined your club, I'm allowed to hear about the downsides. Great.'

'Sorry,' said Lucy. 'Actually, I never thought

74

you'd have children.'

'Thanks.'

'No, I mean it in a good way. As a compliment. I should have told you, I guess, but it never seemed necessary. I really admired the way that you didn't seem to be locked into the same timeline as the rest of us—the late twenties, hit thirty, hit thirty-five thing that seems so rigid, so biological despite our brains and our education. You seemed to be a rather glorious throwback to an age where people did or didn't have children, but it didn't seem to define them. Perhaps because if it didn't happen then there was nothing you could do about it, you couldn't freeze your eggs or borrow someone else's. You just lived your life.' She needed Tess to be living that life so that she could believe it existed, a parallel world without a family, which was OK— brilliant, sometimes, in fact. It comforted Lucy to know that if she hadn't met Jamie, nabbed him, grabbed him, things would have been all right. She'd probably exercise a lot more, she'd spend her considerable salary on herself and on a fine selection of scented candles and expensive cushions.

'That's nice of you to say,' said Tess. 'And you're right, in a way—it's not something I ever really thought about, the having children thing. I used to be rather befuddled by those articles about sad, eggless women. And now it's not so much that I feel I have to have a baby, I just . . . I don't know, I don't want to regret not having one. Let's not forget, because nobody ever lets us, that we're staring into the barrel of forty. One can feel pretty odd being the only woman our age without children.'

'Rubbish,' said Lucy. 'There are loads of you.'

75

'Where are all these women? Where were my role models? Where are the single childless middle-aged women? Stuck in flaming Anita Brookner novels, that's where, mooning around in their cardies.'

'Not true. There are plenty of wonderful childless women. Like Katharine Hepburn.'

'I give you Ms Hepburn for her stylish way with a wide-legged trouser, but she's hardly contemporary.'

'Oh, you know, all those actresses. And I'm always reading about career women not having children.'

'Career women, such a damning phrase. You're the one with the career, not me.'

'You've got the gallery.'

Tess snorted. 'You think that's a career?'

'Of course.'

'It's nonsense. It might as well have been a deli or a florist or a bookshop. Something funded by a wealthy man, in this case my father. I get more money from renting out the flat upstairs than from the gallery.'

'I never knew. You always seemed so shiny.'

'Well, yes,' she said. 'I was always destined for great things, wasn't I? Problem is that you have to work hard at them like you do. I inherited so much from Daddy, but not his famous work ethic.'

Lucy would always have guessed that she'd have felt reassured by Tess showing vulnerability, but it shocked and even repulsed her. 'Have you thought of any names?' was all she could think of in reply.

*   *   *

Lucy knew about the timeline because she herself had been so neurotically aware of it. At 28 she had started to have her visions of mortality, or at the very least visions of being 30, and charging up from behind that, 35 and 40. No one could accuse her of not knowing about a woman's fertility and the five times table. She had always had a phobia of being comfortably coupled up throughout her twenties, only to find herself single at 30, with no man and no experience of finding one since freshers' week at university.

Despite this fear, or perhaps because of it, that was exactly what happened. She'd met Mark at university, they'd lived together on graduating, then bought a flat, which was so sensible, it really was, got them onto the housing ladder so much earlier than everyone else. And then they decided that they needed an eat-in kitchen, so they'd traded up to a place with its own front door and the pine table that she still used, looking dated amid the galvanised steel worktops. There, they'd had grown-up Sunday lunches so that their friends could regale them with stories of their chaotic lives and jokingly call them Mum and Dad.

One day, she suggested that she and Mark put together a timetable for the next stage, one which would involve turning the box room into a nursery. She feared that he would turn male on her, say he wasn't ready, but he greeted the idea with enthusiasm. She should have been happy, but a muscle in her mind went ping, like the way it does when you turn your head too quickly. She looked at Mark—lovely, lovely Mark—and she knew she couldn't stay with him for the rest of her life. In reality, she shouldn't have stayed with him for longer than a term at college, but as a teenager she'd read an interview with a successful entrepreneur who'd said it's so important to couple up and settle down young so that you don't have to waste your energy in your twenties and thirties on trying to find somebody. That appealed to her sense of efficiency, in the same way that roasting a pair of chickens at the same time to have three days' worth of leftovers did, or running to work and then stretching in the shower.

So there she had been, 30 and single with little previous experience of being in such a position. When she'd last been on her own, answerphones had been the latest technology, but now she was faced with a whole battery of ways to be courted and contacted—or, as she urged herself, to court and contact. She made up her mind to date no one who wasn't father material.

Then she met Jamie, and for once in her life, she did something ill thought out.

*   *   *

Sierra had cramp in her hand, but still nothing from Josh. She was worried she might be giving him a Chinese burn, she'd been working on it so long and hard. He shrugged her off and went to his computer. Her pride wouldn't let the piece of hardware beat her in a race to get his software hard. Or something like that. This was the sort of language he liked her to use, an awkward combination of bad language and bad puns, both equally blush-making.

She put her hands down her pants and felt glad that at least she could fake it.

'It's good, oh yes, I'm wet,' she drawled, having

78

caught the American accent off the films that Josh liked.

'Fucking computer,' he said and she thought, yes, you probably would like to, wouldn't you? 'Got to get this virus off.'

'Babe, give up and come here. Let me take your mind off it.' They didn't talk much, but Sierra felt confident that they could have sex at least. Well, she had been confident, but that was before his most high-res laptop went on the blink.

'I'm looking at you, babe, I'm thinking of you,' she said. Still nothing. It didn't matter how much porn he streamed into her head, she still found this speaky bit tricky. 'And your cock.' For god's sake, what more do I have to say?

'What's it like?'

Here we go. 'It's so big. It's so hard. It's big and it's hard.' No it's not, she thought, checking it out behind the cotton of his underwear. It's small and floppy. She took her dress off so that she was wearing nothing but a rather fetching set of vintage knickers and a bra. Was it a bit skanky to wear second-hand undies? Not if they were fifties and satin and in exquisite condition. He smiled. Well, it was a start. He grabbed his phone off the desk and held it up between them. 'Keep talking,' he ordered. He was looking at her through the prism of his phone and pressing the record button.

'I'm wet thinking about you.'

'Show me,' he said, pointing the phone at her crotch.

At last he was hard.

*   *   *

79

The lift was broken again, but Sierra still felt relieved to be home. She liked her look to be eclectic but after a night at Josh's, the eccentric mix of styles she wore was frequently made actually artless instead of merely trying to appear so. Her Celia Birtwell print dress was not warm enough for the day's weather and so was worn over a pair of Josh's flatmate's tracksuit bottoms and a pair of heels.

She felt dirty, and not just because she hadn't taken spare underwear to Josh's. Though she called Josh her boyfriend, she couldn't say they were 'going out' since they had never actually left his place. Like their relationship, they weren't going anywhere. She couldn't see the point of not seeing him, since there was no one else on the horizon. But then again, it was quite boring when she was there. The constant chat like a demented radio you couldn't switch off. Well, if there was a radio station that played a never-ending stream of 'ooh, baby' and 'fuck me', which there probably was and if so, Josh would know exactly what its frequency was. Last night's episode had been particularly hard work, since she had continually been told to manoeuvre herself into a position where he could film them with his phone. It wasn't enough for him just to stick the camera somewhere in the vicinity, he had to be able to look through to see what he was filming, too, which involved limbs criss-crossing like a game of Twister. Straight afterwards he'd watched back what he'd filmed, and Sierra could have sworn he was more excited by watching them having sex than by actually having sex.

No, she'd knock it on the head soon. It's not like anybody would get hurt, unlike some of those women in his films. The bottles weren't made of real glass, were they? And even if they were actresses experienced in this field, it had to hurt, didn't it, being penetrated so multiply?

Sierra's stilettoed feet negotiated the omnipresent pools of water along the walkway until she reached her door, painted purple, her mother's signature colour. Funny that, whenever women have an obsessively favourite colour, it's always purple. Pink for girls, purple for women.

Her key didn't turn in the upper lock. She tried again. She tried a third time, now with a shaking hand. It was already open; it had already been opened. Please, no, not another break-in. The door swung easily, unencumbered by the pile of exhortations to get a credit card and pizza delivery leaflets that usually blocked her entry after a night away. Please, no, let them not still be here, was her second silent plea.

She sniffed perfume in the air and felt sick. Parure by Guerlain.

CHAPTER SIX

VELOCITY OF BLOOD FLOW

Lucy was in bed alone, not that it made much difference. It was past midnight before Jamie came in.

'Where have you been?'

'Doing the film, obviously.'

They were like a couple in a weather house. They got up to do the breakfast shift, but he'd go back to bed after dropping off the kids, having stayed up all night poring over those endless snippets of footage he and his three mates—sorry, 'guerilla film-making collective'—were creating.

'I wish you'd tell me.'

'You're not my mother.'

Well, she thought, I might as well be. Oh god, that's what he thinks when he looks at me; no wonder he doesn't want to have sex. 'It's just that if I know when you're coming back then I can make a decision about whether to get to sleep before you come in or wait until you come back, if you see what I mean.'

'You want me to ring you to tell you exactly where I am.'

'No, just to let me know when you're coming home. I don't see why it's so big a deal.'

'Neither do I.'

'How's it going? The film.' She knew she was on safe ground here.

'Fan flipping tastic,' he said, smiling for the first time. 'I totally reckon that we can use the short as a trailer, get it onto YouTube and then watch it go viral while we sort out a feature-length script.'

'Do you really think people are going to get it from a three-minute clip?' The concept of the film had been explained to Lucy—it was about aliens slash reality TV stars slash celebrities who control earthlings via their phone signals—many times, but she still didn't really understand the point of it.

'Course they will. It's going to be massive, you'll see.'

He went to get undressed in the bathroom like a coy maiden. She knew that he would not return until she had gone to sleep so she turned off the lights and made ladylike snoring noises. He always went to bed half an hour after her, under the pretext of suddenly being engrossed in something on his computer or on TV that he couldn't leave.

She lay in bed, using her thespian skills to do fake sleeping when they could have been so much better employed. In lieu of physical contact, she replayed the day over eight years ago that was still the sexual highlight of her life.

Lucy had been very good about donating blood before she'd had Rosie and Ned, doing it at least three times a year thanks to reminders that she put in the calendar on her computer. She liked the sense of righteousness it gave her, but more the physical high that was how she imagined medieval saints felt on fasting.

She left the office at noon and signed herself in at the blood donor centre, enjoying the congratulations she got on coming so soon after her last visit. As she read through some documents from work, she didn't notice the young man who had sat down beside her. Even if she had, she probably wouldn't have thought anything other than possibly an objective appraisal of his good looks. Now when she looked back on that day she could picture him sitting on the plastic stacking chair with photographic precision, but she was like a child constructing a false first memory for she knew that she had not really examined him until later. It would not, she thought on reflection, have occurred to her to feel attracted to him or anything so crass, given his obvious youth and beauty.

She was called in, had her test and then lay on the raised bed so that the bloodletting could begin. The young man from the reception area was lying beside her on a trolley bed less than a metre away. She glanced over to him and surprised herself by noticing how muscular his arms were now that he'd removed his jacket. Despite this muscularity, his veins looked pretty below his smooth skin and a more luminous turquoise than she'd ever noticed on anyone else. He was clenching and unclenching a foam ball that he'd been given to get his blood pumping into the collection bag quicker. She'd been given one too. She saw that his muscles were flexing as he did so with a hypnotic effect. She concentrated on her own bag of blood and squeezed her foam ball with all her strength. She glanced over and caught his eye and realised that they had synchronised their exertions and were going harder and faster on the balls. Almost muffled by the sound of a song playing on the radio, she could hear her breathing and then above that, in time, his. She became terrified that he'd look away, so she did first and saw with surprise— and some disappointment—that her bag of blood was filling fast. How could that be, when she felt that all her blood was rushing towards her crotch. She looked at him again and their eyes locked. They carried on squeezing their foam balls together and apart until she felt herself flood the way that sometimes happens in dreams, her face flushed and she knew beneath her clothes her chest would be speckled with the stigmata of sexual satisfaction.

'You're done,' the nurse said, unhooking the bag.

'Sorry, yes. Of course. Thank you.'

'And you are too,' she said, turning to the man lying on the bed beside Lucy. 'At exactly the same time.' They looked at one another and Lucy allowed herself a coquettish smile. It seemed as though her inhibition had been drained along with that 470ml of blood.

'Now then, biscuits? Squash or tea?' said the nurse.

'Tea,' they replied with one voice.

'Milk no sugar.'

'Same here.'

'And I'll have a Bourbon biscuit, please,' she said.

'Make that two Bourbons,' added the man.

Lucy lay back and tried to process what had just happened, desperate to quell the quivering that she still felt, but too embarrassed to put her hand there and too scared to go and lock herself in the loo. She could hardly admit to herself that she had just had a moment more erotic than in all of those ten years with Mark. She looked around at the posters on the wall telling her what a good thing she was doing and it all seemed so very inappropriate, like being in church or something.

She sat up and her head began to spin.

'Be careful,' said the nurse. 'You might feel faint.'

Lucy had given blood dozens of times and had never once felt this before.

'Stay on the bed with your feet hanging down,' said the nurse. 'And wait for your tea.' She swivelled round and the man did the same so that they were now facing each other.

'Do you know what?' he said.

'What?'

'I don't much like tea. I'd rather get a coffee.'

'Me too,' she replied. 'I'm Lucy, by the way.'

'Jamie.' He leaned over and shook her hand. She felt faint again.

The rolling mat, gutted Camel Light and torn Rizla packet had been left to mingle with Sierra's bowl of muesli. She stared at them without censure. Better joints than tabs or needles, she always used to say to no one other than herself.

Once Sierra had got over the shock of the prodigal mother's return, she began to, if not enjoy having Susie there, at least tolerate it. Better her mother than a flatmate, someone who'd leave their underwear hanging off the radiator and bring back strange men. Though, come to think of it, that description pretty much fitted Susie too.

'What the fuck?' she had said on recognising her mother's signature scent and realising that no one had broken into the flat, but that the reality was potentially more destructive. And on seeing Susie, despite everything, she ran into her arms and wanted to be spun around by her, which was equally illogical since she weighed at least a stone more.

In the end, they'd had a good evening, Susie telling her about the night she was born and how much she had loved her instantly. Sierra had heard the story before, but never tired of it. Her mother had gone clubbing that night and a Polaroid was taken by the decade's favourite chronicler, a now-reclusive photographer called Dez. The picture was still one of Sierra's favourite possessions in the world. Her mother was skinny, despite being eight and a half months pregnant, a series of ins and out, like a twisted strand of DNA. Her beautiful blonde hair, so beloved of advertisers but eventually butchered into a buzz cut to please a fashion editor at *The Face*, and decorated with a faux-tribal turban. She wore a cropped gold bolero jacket that hung neatly above her bump, while below it was a stretchy Lycra tube dress that she still owned and wore off the shoulder. Beneath the jacket, Sierra could just make out a conical bra that she wore over the dress and that showcased her pregnancy-swollen breasts. 'I couldn't afford maternity clothes,' Susie said, 'and anyway, in those days nobody made such a big deal about it, no special shops or anything.' Sierra thought about the way that Tess was already fetishising her stomach with swagged jersey bought from boutiques that sold nothing else. Susie's tights were decorated with Aztec patterns, a tricky look to pull off for anyone above a size tiny.

Nobody thought Susie shouldn't have been dancing that night. She was so heavily pregnant that she was a freak, but at the club freakery was venerated. She had bumped bellies with Leigh Bowery and mimed giving birth on the podium. She had jumped the queue in the ladies' to appease her put-upon bladder and laughingly mimed taking a tab of acid. Her favourite joke was to pretend to go into labour and her fellow clubbers would shout 'hot towels'. She'd been given free drinks all night and had a dozen dancers kiss her stomach as though it were a talisman. It was not that she had gone out that evening because she feared she wouldn't be going out once the baby was born, she'd gone out to show that nothing was going to change.

It was only when a man wearing a plaid skirt and jelly shoes skidded in Susie's broken waters did she think of going to the hospital. She was waved off by clubbers who forgot her a minute later and walked the half-mile to the hospital with Sierra's father. Everyone told her how first labours were really long, 'but you just popped out Sie, no drugs, no nothing, just the high of life and a couple of vodka Ts. One minute you were dancing inside me as I danced inside the club, an hour later and you were out.'

Sometimes it seemed to Sierra that her mother still hadn't stopped dancing. Nor had she stopped revelling in being a freak. Certainly she had been very different from the mothers they had met at playgrounds and school gates.

Susie was still asleep and would be when Sierra left for the gallery. It reminded her of a thousand school mornings when she'd made her own packed lunch, often out of the canapés that Susie had blagged from launches the evening before. She had looked with envy upon the cream cheese sandwiches and prawn cocktail crisps her friends ate.

She let herself into the gallery, again. Tess had not arrived before her since the evening of the announcement. The walls looked to be sagging under the weight of gloomy pictures, unscarred by the yearned-for acne of the red 'sold' spot. Tess hadn't made any plans for a new exhibition. Sierra would just have to do it for her.

*   *   *

It was unfortunate for asthmatics and those with chronic obstructive pulmonary disease that the use of inhalers had become so sinister. Owen remembered amusing his friends with his best

88

Dennis Hopper in *Blue Velvet* impression that he'd do after stealing his dad's inhaler. His father had been wheezing all the way back then. It wasn't so funny now.

Doctor Gunawardena didn't wear a white coat, but grey flannel trousers and a polo neck that looked as though it had been bought from a prep-school outfitters. When she spoke, she seemed like a prodigy child that should be on a daytime chat show, spouting unintelligible phrases for the delectation of the masses.

His wife, his doctor and his son sat listening to Gareth's polyphonic coughs, phlegm layered with a bass note of throatiness and finished with a high-pitched splutter and a wheeze.

'So, Doctor,' Owen began. 'Doctor, er . . . Doctor. What are the options?'

'My options, what are my options?' said Gareth.

'We're hoping that some non-invasive ventilation will save your father . . .'

'Me, save *me*. Talk to me, I'm still alive. Just,' Gareth insisted.

'Yes, of course. Initially we'd like to continue with the non-invasive techniques in order to prevent the need for mechanical ventilation.'

'And if that doesn't work?'

'Gareth,' protested Mari.

'Obviously we'd continue with the inhalers and the antibiotics.'

'They don't work. End-stage COPDers need to have LVRS, don't they?'

'There is some evidence that lung volume reduction surgery can improve QOL,' said Dr Gunawardena.

'Quality of life,' explained Owen to Mari, his

years in banking having given him a tourist's smattering in the language of acronym. 'Some evidence, you say?'

'Pretty shaky evidence,' said Gareth.

The doctor smiled at him, the first sign of warmth that Owen had seen flicker across her preternaturally young features since their meeting had begun. 'Been at the Internet again, Mr Williams?'

'Isn't that the first thing anybody does when they're given bad news by you lot these days?'

'It's a disorder in itself.'

He began coughing again and they all sat in silence, examining the tardy health warnings about smoking that papered the walls of the doctor's office. He stopped, they exhaled, he began again.

'Basically,' he said between barks and growls, 'they'll try lung reduction and then they'll put me on the waiting list for a transplant. If I'm lucky— ha, lucky.' His father had mastered the art of the mutant cough-laugh. 'I'll get a lung transplant and that might relieve some of the symptoms of end-stage lung disease. Am I right, Doctor?'

'We wouldn't recommend a transplant operation for a man beyond a certain age.'

'Which means I'm not worth giving a new lung. Basically, I'm screwed.'

Mari giggled nervously at the use of a swearword with sexual connotations.

'Listen,' said Owen, his voice deepening. 'I don't want to hear what the NHS can and cannot afford. We can pay. I can pay anything, whatever it takes. Money no object, what's the best route?'

Gareth hushed him. 'It's the same, son. It's the same. Your money's no good here.'

Gareth was buoyant in the car home. He sat beside Owen in the front of the Alfa, while Mari occasionally leaned forward to stick her head between them and make driving more difficult. Owen batted her away, not for the first time believing her to be an irritating child who was only moments away from whining about how long the journey was taking or wanting to stop to go to the loo.

'I found one site that claims that I should start with the laughing cure,' said Gareth.

'The Laffin Cure?' asked Owen.

'No, laughing, l-a-u-g . . . Apparently, it provides us with a natural inner massage and can account for a thirty per cent improvement. Now that makes me laugh. Then I need to get some wormwood and give myself a yoghurt enema and apparently I'm sorted.'

'The Internet's not all good, is it?' said Owen. 'But modern medicine's amazing, isn't it, Dad? What that doctor was saying about lung reduction surgery. Someone at work's mother had it and said it was incredible. And transplant surgery, what a thing that is. I remember the first successful heart transplant, don't you? And now we don't think anything of it. I can pay for it, if they won't do it; I'll pay for it.'

'I'm not doing it, none of it.'

'Please, Dad.'

'I'm not doing it.'

'But it's technology. It's the brave new world. It's the white heat of technology, it's computers and keyhole surgery and—'

'I'm not doing it.' Firmer this time, followed by a pause.

'How's your friend Tess getting along?' said Mari, who could never see a gap in conversation without wanting to plug it with a Polyfilla of guff. 'Having a baby on her own and all that. Can't be easy for her.'

'Fine, I think. She's got a nice line in maternity wear.'

'There's more to it than that, though. She must feel lonely, not having anyone to share her worries with.'

'I suppose.'

'I hope you're going to be around for her, be supportive.'

'Don't you start. I get enough of this from Scary Godmother Lucy. She's always on at me about taking my responsibilities as a godparent seriously. It's not like I'm the baby's father or anything.'

'Aren't you?'

'No, I'm not. For God's sake.'

'That's a shame.'

Owen rolled his eyes.

'Please, Owen.' His father this time.

'What? Look after Tess?'

'No, have a family. If only I'd done it sooner, had you.' Owen didn't correct him. 'Then I could have seen my grandchildren grow up. But instead, here I am, an octogenarian who can't breathe who's going to be dead in a few months with nothing to show me that life is going to continue beyond the next generation.'

'Caron's trying,' said Owen. 'I'm sure they'll sort it out soon.'

'Nothing to show me.'

Owen pulled into the drive and leaped out to open the garage door. He stared at the neat plastic boxes within, the way that they slotted together to form a perfect surface of large boulders like an Inca city, a dry stone wall of possessions marked 'OWEN: school', 'CARON: skating'. There was one marked 'DAD'. Not Gareth, just Dad.

He went to help his father out of the car, but waited before rolling the car forward into its womb. 'I'm getting married.'

There was a pause. Then his mother squeaked while his father just looked at him, expressionless, as though hope and scepticism had cancelled each other out. 'No, really, this time I'll go through with it. She's lovely.' She is lovely, he thought to himself; really, she is. 'Ruby, we've been together for a year, maybe less, I might have mentioned her. She's beautiful and kind and caring and she'll look after me.' He glanced at his mother, of whom his father always used to say the same, though as far as Owen could see it was the other way around. 'And I'll look after her.'

'Owen,' breathed his mother. 'We can't wait to meet her.'

'She can,' his father contradicted, gesturing towards Mari. 'It's me that can't wait.'

*   *   *

'I'm a bit confused,' said Sierra to Michael. 'Is it a child's party or an adult's? I mean, what are those zig-zaggy thingies called?'

'Bunting,' said Michael, surveying the proper cloth decorations in tastefully faded colours. 'It's called a family party, darling, I think it's supposed

93

to be nice to include the children, and it's certainly nice for them to watch their parents get steadily drunker as the afternoon progresses. It's Jamie's birthday. He's an adult. Just. I mean, have you seen him? A child-man—that Lucy's a cradle-snatcher.'

'You can talk,' said Sierra.

Michael looked at her in confusion—she was indeed that much younger than him, but how did she know about the lustful feelings he was harbouring?

'Haven't you been crushing on Tess for years?'

'I suppose so, but it's not like we've done anything, let alone had children. And really, look at him. He's always strutting round the school in his fashion jeans, while the rest of the men are wearing dad shorts—you know, the ones that come down to the knees with all the pockets for fishing tackle and the like.' It never stops, thought Michael—among the parents as much as the children, there are the cool blokes and the rest.

'How old is he, anyway?'

'Thirtysomething—one or two, I think.'

'That's the same age as my Josh. How funny.'

'Is he coming?'

'No,' said Sierra, sharply. 'He's, like, so busy with work at the moment. What about your girlfriend?'

'Nah, didn't work out.' Michael felt a moment of mourning for Rachel. She'd played a bit part in his life, but on ending it with her he'd been forced to recognise that he'd had a starring role in hers. She'd wept and wondered why, when everything was going so well, and he'd thought, *everything*? There was almost nothing. They'd barely had a conversation and not one proper date. He didn't miss her, but he did miss having a default person to

94

think about in bed—though this had only worked until he actually slept with her and discovered that she cried after sex. As for Tess, her pregnancy meant she was no longer reliable in this regard. He looked at Sierra, inelegant in six-inch heels, like a child who's playing dress-up, and he thought, yes, she'll do.

'Let's go and talk to the Madonna over there. She's looking so beatific these days, isn't she?'

'If you say so,' said Sierra.

'I know, I know,' Tess laughed, looking down and then back at Michael. 'You may stare.'

'At what?' asked Michael. 'All right, I admit it. They are magnificent.' Maybe Tess could stage a re-entry into his fantasy top three.

'I feel gorgeous. Not that I've got anyone to lavish my gorgeousness on. Isn't there some hormone that increases a pregnant woman's libido? I feel incredibly . . .' She paused. Please don't use the word 'horny', thought Michael. Don't destroy all the ideals I hold of you. 'Erotically charged.'

Michael had always suspected that Tess was fundamentally uninterested in sex, hence all those older men with their flagging libidos. Maybe he'd been wrong all along.

'Nice of Lucy to invite us.'

'I think she wants to get us used to having lots of children around. It's stopped raining, hasn't it? Have you been outside?'

Michael shuddered. 'Noise, sludge, tears, violence—it's like the Somme out there. I'm tempted to desert.'

'Hello, Michael,' said a woman bearing handmade paper chains, musical instruments and a bag full of hats. She herself wore a Viking helmet.

95

She said his name self-consciously, he thought, as we did as teenagers when we were told we could call friends' parents by their first names. Nowadays, they just do that from the start. He recognised her, vaguely, from school.

'This is Sierra and Tess,' he said, leaving her to fill in the rest, since he knew her only as Jake's mum—or, to give her her full title, Jake that little thug from Year two's mum.

'I'm Liz.'

'Are you a mate of Jamie's?' asked Sierra.

'Yes,' said the woman, the pigtails of her Viking helmet swinging. 'I'm a friend from school.'

'You look a bit old to be at school,' said Sierra, and the woman laughed, though Michael knew that she'd meant it genuinely. Liz was one of those mothers who almost did believe themselves to be at school, and whose social life was now lived through their kids' friends. He only had to look at her to know that just like the four godparents, she hadn't been invited by Jamie but by Lucy, in the same way that the mums chose who to invite to the kids' parties.

Liz turned away from Sierra towards Tess. 'Are you the famous Tess?'

'I suppose so,' she said. Yes, thought Michael, she's always been *the* Tess.

'With the sperm donor pregnancy?'

Michael squirmed, but Tess remained gracious. 'Yes.' She stroked her stomach. She was doing pregnancy very well, but then she did most things well except, as his mother would observe, settling down with a nice young man.

'Lots of my friends have done the donor thing.'

'How interesting.'

96

'Yes, some of my best friends are gay,' she said. Michael stared at her, but the comment was apparently made without irony. 'Which service did you use?'

'The one of my choosing,' replied Tess, continuing to stroke her belly.

'But which donor agency? Would you recommend them? My friends are always asking me. I don't know, they think I know everything about parenting—which actually I sort of do. I'm always on the look-out for recommendations.' She said this as if she were asking about a new restaurant or a holiday destination with a kids' club.

'Without wishing to be rude, is this any of your business?'

Liz gamely pushed on. 'But can you keep the father anonymous and all that? Can you do that any more—they've changed the law, haven't they? Does that worry you?'

'And how did you conceive your child?'

'I've got two, actually,' Liz said.

'Them. Were you on top? Did you keep your legs up in the air afterwards? Had you and your partner been trying for long?'

'Wow,' said Liz. 'I really don't think this is appropriate.'

'Exactly.' With that Tess glided away, taking Sierra with her.

Michael could not help but admire the way she'd handled the interrogation, while at the same time rather wishing that she'd answered some of those questions, which he had many times wished he had the courage to ask. He smiled at Liz apologetically and then he too made his excuses.

Owen was stuck by the wall with a beer,

discussing football with renegade fathers, while Ruby was having an involved conversation with a seven-year-old about boy bands—'Well, I'm not much more than a kid myself, am I?' She mouthed something at Owen, either 'I love you' or 'I love kids'.

Michael joined him. 'I get enough of the little blighters in my day job.'

'I work in the City,' said Owen. 'It's not a dissimilar environment. You seen Tess?'

'She's off somewhere with Sierra. Looking amazing.'

'She's got the look of such a dirty girl, that Sierra.'

'I was referring to Tess.'

'Do you think?' said Owen. 'Pregnant women don't really do it for me.'

'There are porn sites specialising in pregnant women.'

'Yeah,' said Owen. 'But then there are sites specialising in dwarves and shaved grannies. Doesn't make it sexy.'

'You and Tess . . .' Michael stopped. Owen raised an eyebrow. Michael felt obliged to carry on and had drunk enough beers to be able to. 'Was it serious?'

'No. One of those college things. Then one of those twenty-something things. Maybe even thirty. Didn't know I'd ever slept with someone that old. Fuck buddies.' Owen noticed Michael wincing. 'It was her. She never wanted anything more serious, to be honest.'

'It's her father.'

'That obvious?'

'Yes, it's so Freudian, I know. Darling Tess,

tries so hard to be different, but she's just another daddy's girl.'

* * *

'Are you sure you want to go through with the pregnancy?' said Sierra, opting to use her posh voice that day to rise above the din. 'What a world you're joining.' A toddler removed the chocolate biscuit from her hand and slipped it into his own. 'Don't you come near me with that,' she warned him. 'This is Pucci.' She waggled her finger in mock anger, causing the little boy to peal with the rat-a-tat laughter that sounds perilously close to tears. She grabbed a wet wipe from one of the many packets dotted around the kitchen like ashtrays at a real party and started playing a dodging rugby tackle game with the child until she got both his hands and rubbed his face. 'I win, I win,' she shouted, arms aloft, and her opponent ran away.

'It's fun,' said Tess.

'So fun that you've not moved from the only comfortable chair in the kitchen.'

Tess fanned her face. 'Not so fun today. Feel a bit hot. I never thought I'd say it, but I miss winter—there's no bloody air in here, is there? But the children bit, that will be fun, it will. Look at their little shoes and their little faces, so easily pleased. Which buggy do you think I should get? Do you think Bugaboos are passé?'

Sierra shrugged. 'What do you think of that Scarlett? Owen's girlfriend.'

'It's Ruby, and she's his fiancée. You're so transparent. She seems very sweet.'

'Look at her little shoes and her little face,' said

99

Sierra.

'Now, now. It's not like you're the older woman yourself.'

'Least I don't squeak. And tell all the boys how much I love football while putting my head to one side and twiddling my hair.'

'Take it from me, you don't want to get involved with Owen. He'll leave you with nothing but an engagement ring and a broken heart. And that's if you're lucky.'

'Didn't happen to you.'

'No, it didn't.' For a second Tess looked sad. Sierra supposed it must be hard for Tess, thinking about other people getting married and stuff. They were approached by the party's other childless attendees.

'Hello, Owen.' How to play it? thought Sierra. Cool, obviously, but cool could so easily be sulky and it wasn't as if she had any right to be sulky. Though he had flirted with her that first time and it hadn't been her imagination. He should be punished for making her think that he fancied her, thus causing her to fancy him, and then bringing along that vile—she was vile, with her fake bake and what looked like hair extensions—girlfriend and humiliating her. She'd never have fancied him in the first place if he hadn't come on so strong—well, maybe just a little bit with those dark eyes and the car and the confidence. In the end she settled on: 'Having fun?'

She was now flanked by both Owen and Michael. There might even have been a bit of jostling. This cheered her considerably.

'It's all right, I suppose. I don't know what I was expecting with a party starting at three in the afternoon. There is one hell of a lot of children,' said Owen.

'I'm kind of used to kids from my dad's family—he's got three,' she told them.

'Your brothers and sisters,' said Michael.

'Half.'

'Half brothers and sisters.'

'Two boys and a girl.' Technically they were her siblings, she supposed, but they seemed more like cousins or even acquaintances, their lives were so different from hers. Her father had got married ten years ago to a woman who was younger than Tess was now. Sierra could never quite understand why. Not her father's motives, but her stepmother's. She was a property developer, rich, dynamic, good looking. Maybe she had got used to taking on old wrecks and restoring them to their former glory, increasing the value of the property in the process. Although come to think of it, her father would have been more or less Owen's age at the time of his wedding. Oh please, the thought of it.

'I've got five nieces and two nephews,' said Michael. 'I love them. It's like being a grandparent—all the benefits of children with none of the boring bits like potty training and discipline. It's their mothers I have problems with.'

'I suppose that's what I get with my lot,' said Sierra, but she didn't suppose Michael's love for the children in his life was seasoned with a grinding of envy. Not for the house with the Aga or the attic bedrooms filled with hand-crafted wooden toys, but for having a father who knew when their vaccinations were due, made them chicken and broccoli pasta and read them stories every night. He was one of those older fathers who acted as

101

though they were the first men in the world to have children, when in fact it wasn't even the first time that they themselves had had them.

*   *   *

Tess had spirited Owen away and they were leaning together so closely that it was hard to know whose dark hair belonged to whom.

'So, are you going to marry this one?' asked Tess. 'Ruby.'

'Of course,' said Owen. 'Why would I have got engaged to her otherwise?'

'You tell me. Although you didn't bother telling me about your latest engagement when we met up. Funny that you should have been so reticent. Almost as if you're ashamed.'

'I'm not. And I'm engaged because I love her and it's time I settled down.'

'Settled. Down. Not very nice words, are they?'

'Neither's "lone", as in "lone parent".'

'I'm not on my own, don't worry about that.'

Owen looked at her and realised that whenever he pictured Tess she always was alone: arriving at and leaving parties; drinking her daily espresso; clipping round the gallery. The last time he'd really thought about Tess as part of a unit was when he'd first met her at university and she and Lucy were so inseparable that one student thought that Tess's surname was Enlucy, as in Tess and Lucy.

'Why did you do it?' Owen asked. 'This donor thing, the baby.'

'Because I wanted to. Simple as that.'

'I never thought of you as maternal. There was that time your period was late and you were terrified.'

'I was twenty-five. Things change.'

'You never thought about coming to me?'

'It's not about you, Owen.' Tess smiled. 'Hello, Ruby, let me have a look at your gorgeous ring.' It was, in truth, hard to avoid, given that Ruby's left hand had been melded to her forehead throughout the afternoon.

*   *   *

Lucy entered the designated music room and immediately felt like a parent coming into a den where joints were being smoked.

'There you are, Jamie,' she said brightly. 'Do you mind just helping me wash up some glasses? It doesn't matter how many times you do the calculations, you never hire enough glasses, do you? You really ought to order what you think you need and then an extra ten per cent. Actually an extra twenty per cent, probably.' She was boring herself, let alone anyone else. Jamie was hanging out with the people he'd invited, rather than all the suitable neighbours and families and godparents that Lucy had got along on his behalf. No doubt she'd be nagging him to write thank-you letters to them for all the bottles of champagne and quality hardbacks they'd brought as presents, too. She felt intimidated by his filmie mates, buff in their trompe l'oeil T-shirts, the ones who claimed to have portfolio careers but were supported by wealthy parents, just as Jamie was funded by a high-earning wife.

Jamie dutifully came with her. He always did. Whatever was going on with him it didn't change his behaviour, which was on the whole perfect, as everyone would tell her. She wished he'd tell her to fuck off or fight with her, but he never did. He never did anything to her, that was the problem.

She could hear a noise in the kitchen.

'What's going on?' she asked Michael as she dashed into the room. He hyperventilated in response. 'Sierra?' She gestured towards Tess, who was still sitting on the only comfortable chair in the kitchen, but was doubled up and clutching her stomach and moaning. 'Stand back, everyone, give her some room. Jamie, call 999, get an ambulance.'

'Really?' said Sierra. 'Shit, what's happening? Does she really need the hospital?'

'She's pregnant and in pain, yes of course she needs an ambulance. Anyone who's not a doctor, get out.' Lucy wished that they hadn't got into that dispute over the party wall with their neighbour the obstetrician. 'Tess, sweetheart, can you talk?' Tess let out a terrifying groan. 'Does it feel like cramps?' Tess nodded. 'Everything's going to be all right. You and the baby are going to be all right.' How pregnant was she? Twenty-something weeks, 24, it's too early, way too early.

'Come with me,' Tess managed to exhale.

'Of course. I'll be with you all the time.'

'Is it going to be OK?'

'She'll be fine, I'm sure.'

'Not the baby. Me. Oh god.' She bent over and then vomited onto the floor, some of it spraying into Lucy's lap.

'You'll be fine, you'll both be fine.' Lucy grabbed a wet wipe to get the sick out of Tess's hair and to scrub at her dress.

'I'm sorry, so sorry.' Tess retched again, but Lucy grabbed a bowl that had been holding high-end salty snacks. 'I was never supposed to have a baby. I knew it.'

'Really, you'll be fine. I promise.'

CHAPTER SEVEN

Blotches and Age Spots

'Lucy will let us know, won't she?' Sierra was curled up on Michael's sofa. He noticed that she took her shoes off on entering the house and asked permission to put her feet up, which surprised him, since somehow he thought her manic way of dressing would be reflected in a reckless approach to other people's upholstery.

It hadn't seemed appropriate to stay at the party once Tess had left in the back of an ambulance, though Michael had noticed that some of Jamie's friends were staying on, with various small children ensconced in front of a DVD, while the adults (if that's what some of the men with their Crayola-coloured T-shirts and artfully dishevelled hair could be called) carried on drinking.

'I've texted her. I'm sure she will if she can.'

'It's funny,' said Sierra, worrying the skin around her fingernails. 'Well, not funny, obviously—wrong word. It's strange because I felt a bit snarky about Tess having a baby in the first place, and here am I so worried that she won't. Do you know what I mean?'

'Yes, I do, exactly. Why did you feel not entirely pleased about her being pregnant?'

'I don't know. Just shocked, I suppose. And

worried she'd change. And worried that she wouldn't, too. It was a bit mad. I wasn't expecting it and I didn't think it suited her, but maybe it does somehow. What about you?'

Michael looked at Sierra, who had stretched her long body across the sofa he'd so carefully chosen, modern but with a retro edge. He could easily imagine her naked, since she'd look like an eighteenth-century nude, all luscious with that slightly glazed half-victor, half-victim look of those models. 'You know, the same. Something just not quite right about it all.' He suddenly felt very scared for Tess and his as yet unborn godchild. 'If I believed in god, I'd be praying right now that they both be OK. That stupid Liz woman told me that if a baby dies in the womb at this point you still have to give birth to them properly—you know, go through labour and everything. I wish Lucy would call. I'm going to look it up. "Cramping in early pregnancy", is that it? When did she have her twenty-week scan? It was about a month ago, wasn't it? So she's like twenty-four, twenty-five weeks. When can you have a baby and it be all right and not look like one of those premature ones with all the tubes and the hairy skin?'

'Please don't,' said Sierra. 'Switch it off. I'm sick of computers, really I am.'

*   *   *

'I don't want to be here,' groaned Tess.

'I know it's not ideal, but they'll sort it out, I'm sure,' said Lucy, stroking her forehead.

'I hate hospitals.'

'I know, but it's the best place for you. You and

106

the baby.'

She groaned again. 'I don't fucking care about the baby. I should never have got pregnant.'

*   *   *

The hospital had been brilliant so far. One look at a pregnant woman doubled up in pain and there was no staff shortage or suggestion that they were wasting anyone's time. Questions were fired off, stomach examined, blood taken. Eventually, Tess was whisked off to obstetrics and Lucy was left alone with her phone. She checked her messages. A text signed from Michael and Sierra. Lucy noted the joint nomenclature. She didn't know either of them, not really, but she wished she were with them. She wished she were anywhere but here.

She'd been good at dealing with the doctors. Bad signs: cramp, stage of pregnancy, she'd answered all the questions they had fired at Tess while the patient had groaned ominously like a woman in labour. Good signs: no bleeding.

She had bled when pregnant with the embryo that turned into a foetus that had turned into the baby that she and Jamie had named Rosa. They call this bleeding spotting, but in reality, it was more streaky than spotty. The pregnancy hadn't been planned, not really, but they had both been surprised at how terrified they'd been at the prospect of losing it.

After Ned, she was sure that she wanted no more children. She had two, a number unlikely to offend population control advocates and probably the maximum you could really have in her career without losing some of your hard-won privileges.

One girl, one boy, all neat and tidy, symmetrical with the parents. So no more children, god willing, and there would be no more changes to her bloodletting until the menopause.

The blood would dry up but other things would replace it. She had read a rather terrifying article about postnatal urinary incontinence. She had started the article with the smug certainty that it wasn't her problem since she could sneeze and laugh without fear despite her two non-caesarean births, but then she read with horror that a woman can be fine after the births but once the menopause hits, then the bladder can weaken in a delayed response to childbirth. The average age of onset of the menopause was 51. Jamie would be in his early forties. What were the chances that he'd love a leaky flushing woman? It made her sound like a broken toilet. No wonder he was repulsed by her age, she was beginning to repulse herself.

*   *   *

Michael came back into the living room to find that Sierra had answered his phone. He felt disconcerted by this, as if he'd caught her trying on his underwear. She was grinning and giving him a thumbs up.

'What the fuck?' she said to whoever it was on the phone. 'Is this normal? I'd better go, Michael will be wanting to know the good news. Yeah, thanks so much for calling. Big kiss from me, and from Michael I'm sure.' She mimed a smooch, dropped the phone and jumped up and over to him. She was about his height—who was he kidding, she was an inch or two taller—and almost lifted him up

108

as she enveloped him in her arms. 'Fan-fucking-tastic news,' she said as he stared into her breasts and the dark pink bra that held them. 'Tess and the baby. They're fine. Just fine.'

'What happened?'

'It was food poisoning, that's all. Just really bad, horrid, come-on-really-suddenly, winter vomiting.'

'But it's not winter.'

'Whatever. It's all fine.' She laughed with the glee of it.

Michael wanted to capture this feeling of happiness, capture it and bottle it and then drink it. It would be sweet and sparkling and very potent. 'We should celebrate,' he said.

'Yeah. No, I'd better get back to my mum.' She groaned. 'Like, how old am I? She's moved back in to my place—well, I suppose it's her place—not for long, I hope, and I ought to make the most of her.'

'Of course,' he said. 'I'll walk you to the tube.'

*   *   *

'Mum, Dad, this is Ruby.' He watched as his mother and Ruby did what looked like a traditional Irish folk dance as they put their hands out to shake, removed them and embraced instead, then did another jig around one kiss or two.

'I'm so happy to meet you,' said Mari.

'No, I'm so happy to meet you,' said Ruby.

'You're lovely. Owen, you didn't tell us how pretty she was.'

'And you look so much younger than you are, Mrs Williams.'

'Mari to you. I'm so thrilled to have a daughter. A second daughter, of course—I've got Caron already.'

His father, observing the two blondes, didn't get up from his armchair. Owen didn't like to think of him as being in his eighties, but he was, and today he looked even older. Ruby bounced over to him, then paused for a second. She's revolted, thought Owen. She's looking at him and thinking he's someone's grandfather, not father. Ruby's parents were sporty types, her mother always on her way to Yolates or Bums, Legs & Tums at the gym, her father still playing Sunday league football. He wondered, for the first time, whether Ruby ever thought she was too young for Owen. He'd only ever questioned it himself. Did Ruby at that moment fast-forward to a time when she might be caring for an octogenarian Owen, while still as girlish as Mari? Owen thought not. Why, he himself had never even got as far as fast-forwarding past their wedding day. He felt so old today, so very tired, after all the drama of Tess's trip to the hospital, followed by getting up at dawn, on a Sunday, to make an ill-advised day trip to Wales just so Ruby could get to meet his parents.

Ruby gave Gareth a hug, which, since he was still sitting in his armchair, was physically awkward. She ended up kissing the top of his head—he had lots of hair still, thick and black like Owen's, everyone said so, commented on their likeness, those that didn't know and even those that did. This kiss meant that Ruby's chest was thrust into his father's face. There was something stomach-churning about the juxtaposition of her fertility and his decrepitude. It conjured up images of Anna Nicole Smith and J. Howard Marshall. He even thought he caught the glimmer of a lecherous smile on his father's face as

110

he emerged from the bosom.

'I'm so happy to be here,' Ruby said. 'Now I feel properly engaged.' This was a cue for cooing over the ring and discussions about placement. Ruby pulled a sheath of wedding magazines from her bag and she and Mari were off.

'You look well, Dad.'

'Don't lie.'

'Actually, you look terrible.'

'I'm going to die.'

'Not this again. You can't tell.'

'I am. There are so many things I need to talk to you about.'

Owen glanced over to the women. Ruby was in full flow. 'I thought about getting a wedding planner—you know, they wander about with a hands-free phone, shouting stuff—but I thought, I don't trust anyone with my vision.' A vision that was currently compromised by the fact that Ruby was still lacking a date, or even a season, for its realisation.

'What do you want to talk to me about?'

'About how we got you,' he whispered, drawing Owen down to his level. 'About where you come from.'

'Don't you think it's a bit late for the whole "where babies come from" talk?'

'I'm serious.'

Owen felt that he had stopped breathing; his father's rasps were breath enough for two. 'We don't need to talk about this now, do we?' Owen was torn between a yearning to hear the truth at last and a fear that he would be told.

'All right, we won't. But don't think you'll get it on my deathbed. They don't do good deaths any

111

more.'

'What do you mean?'

'Nobody's allowed to suffer. You're hooked up on a machine and out of it on drugs. There are no dying words, dying wishes, not any more. There isn't even a good old death rattle. People just go, with hardly any difference between them being alive and being dead.'

'That's your beloved technology for you,' said Owen.

'I don't want it. I've lived my life loving technology, but I don't want to die with it.'

'All right,' said Owen. He suddenly felt disappointed at the prospect of not being told what he had avoided hearing ever since finding out that he was adopted. 'Fine. Do you want to tell me what it is you wanted to tell me?' He tried to sound casual.

'Your mother, I mean your real mother . . . What do they call it these days? Your biological mother . . .'

Owen was dizzy, he was drunk on expectation. He waited to hear his father's husky revelation, but instead the air was cut through with a shrill, 'Owen's father always liked me in green, though I don't think you can beat a bride in white, don't you agree? Especially a lovely young blonde like you. Don't you think, Owen, can't you just picture Ruby in a beautiful ivory dress? Can't you? Picture it, go on.'

'Strapless, Vera Wang, full skirted,' detailed Ruby. 'Or a sheath-like shimmery thing, seeing as how I'm so slim.'

'That sounds lovely, dear.'

'I can get a discount from the store.'

'Yes, Owen said you worked in a shop. That must be fun, having a job and everything, a proper career girl.'

'I'm a model and actress really, I just work there for the designer discounts,' Ruby explained. 'I'm going to give it up when we get married.'

This was news to Owen, though he didn't react since he was too distracted by the news untold to him by his father. He looked at Gareth, but it was as if he was being carried away on a sea of wedding conversations, never to be allowed to talk to him again that weekend.

'Go on, Dad. What did you want to tell me?'

But Gareth just shook his head and said, 'Later.'

*   *   *

'It's very tidy round here,' Sierra said to her mother, when she got back from having a long lunch with Chloe and Chloe's uni friends, the ones she sometimes pretended were her own.

'Why, thank you.'

'Well done. Seriously, I'm impressed.' She looked at her mother, who'd turned to put the kettle on. The kettle that had actually been polished and was sitting on a kitchen surface as clean as it had been when it had just been Sierra living there.

Her mother looked embarrassed by this praise.

'What brought this on?'

'Oh, you know, spring clean.'

'I don't know, actually. Well, I do, but I didn't know that you knew. You know what I mean. Why have you tidied, Susie?'

'Some people are coming round tomorrow.'

113

'Friends?'

'Friends of friends, some people I know from Spain.'

'That's nice.'

'They need to rent a place in London.'

'Right.' She looked at Susie's apologetic face. 'I don't understand.'

'It's been very lovely to be here, but I don't belong. I'm too much of a free spirit for uptight grey old England, don't you think? I need to be somewhere more Latin.'

'As far as I can make out, you hang out with a bunch of British and German hippies.'

'That's not true. Well, it is sort of true, but we spend a lot of time selling our wares at the local market. The Spanish love us and all that we can offer.'

'Bet they hate you.' Smelly drug-dealing scuzz, thought Sierra. Not her mum, though; she believed that Susie was just selling her flower jewellery and her bad landscapes. 'You don't even speak Spanish.'

Susie looked sad. 'You've never understood what it's like to be a free spirit, my love.' She stroked her daughter's hair.

Sierra shook her off. 'What's this to do with the flat, anyway?'

'Although the local people really get my work, they can't necessarily pay for it, if you see what I mean. I need an income. I've looked up rents on Gumtree and I could be getting more than enough profit to live on if I rent out this place.'

'It's not yours to rent out. It doesn't belong to you.'

'It's my name on the council contract.'

'It's illegal to sublet.'

'To be honest, poppet, I'm not sure I'm even supposed to be letting you live here instead of me. Do you want the council to start investigating that?'

'You're throwing me out? It's my home. The nearest thing I've got to one, anyway. I've been the one to repair it, furnish it, fix that stupid tap you're using now. You're the most fucking useless mother ever, do you know that?'

'That hurts me, that really does. I've done nothing but love you.'

'You've done nothing. And now you're making me homeless.'

Susie threw herself at her. 'I feel horrible about it, really I do, but I'll die if I have to stay in this repressed country.'

'Well, go and earn a living in Spain, then. Don't expect me and the flipping taxpayer to subsidise your eternal gap year.'

'My art.'

'My arse. It's not art. It's being a lazy useless sponger who thinks that the world owes her a living. You'd rather see me homeless than make some compromises, wouldn't you? You think you're so lofty, so idealistic, but you're worse than the greediest banker, or some bloke mugging old ladies. What sort of a mother are you?'

'Being a mother doesn't mean sacrificing your sense of self.'

'Well, maybe it should.' Sierra walked out of the flat with a satisfying slam of the door. The feeling of triumph subsided as quickly as she feared the building would in the near future, judging by the large cracks in the walls. She had a £20 note in her pocket and her mobile, but not a lot else. She stared at her phone. The person she most wanted to call was Michael, but that would be weird, wouldn't it?

She paused, then scrolled through her contacts.

'Hello, it's me. Can I come round?'

*　　　*　　　*

A rainy Sunday with children and one parent with a hangover was not a recipe for familial happiness.

'Shall we put them in front of a video?'

Jamie snorted. 'A DVD, you mean?'

'Yes, of course. A DVD, obviously.' He always reacted with derision when she referred to taping a programme off the telly. In the early days, she'd regaled him with tales of growing up in a Britain with only three TV channels and no video recorders. He'd listened with wide-eyed disbelief, like a child being told about the Blitz.

'Which one do you want?' she asked Rosa and Ned. Idiot, she thought, why am I giving them a choice? There had been a brief period when they had coincided in a love of Disney Princesses, but Rosa now considered herself too old and Ned too male to enjoy them. 'This one?'

'That one doesn't have a proper ending,' said Rosa.

'What do you mean?'

'With a wedding and things, yeah.'

Lucy cringed. Their children had parents whose lives directly contradicted such claptrap, but the forces of global capitalism were too much for their puny powers. Fractious negotiation followed before they agreed on a film, which Lucy checked was 96 minutes long. An hour and a half of offspring

116

inanimate in front of animation.

'What do parents without TVs do?' she asked Jamie.

'Do they even exist?'

'Apparently. Though it often turns out that they just watch DVDs on the laptop instead.' Much as Jamie was doing now.

'Do you think,' he asked, 'that it's scarier to have an alien implant an explosive in your brain through your ear, or up your arse using devices hidden in public toilets?'

'Your head. Your bum. I don't know. Neither?'

'Or like a really powerful but microscopically small bomb that you breathe in through the spores in the air?'

'Maybe. Listen, Rosa and Ned will be occupied for the next 96 minutes. Why don't we take a nap?'

'You go ahead. I really want to get this done.'

It wasn't as if she wasn't tired, she thought, as she pulled the duvet over her head, but she'd been using nap as a euphemism. If it wasn't, it was an awfully granny-ish word to be using, though she consoled herself with the fact that '40 winks' would have been worse.

*   *   *

One of Josh's flatmates let Sierra in when she got there and waved her upstairs. She felt awkward, like she shouldn't be there, but why not? She'd had a row with her mum and he was her boyfriend, wasn't he? She suddenly wondered whether the flatmate hadn't been trying to tell her something. She was about to push the door open, when instead she knocked.

'Who is it?'

'It's me, Sierra.'

'Oh, right,' said Josh, who had by now opened the door. 'Why d'you knock?'

She glanced around the room. She didn't know what she had been fearing for it looked exactly as it always did, darkness illuminated by screens. 'You would not believe what's been happening to me.'

He had sat back down at the laptop and was typing away. 'Try me,' he said eventually.

'So I was at this party and my boss, you know the one who's pregnant, we thought she'd gone into labour or was losing the baby or something . . .'

'Look at this,' he said and turned his laptop around to her.

'That's disgusting,' she said once she'd managed to work out what was going on, which necessitated her putting her head to one side.

'Don't be so uptight.'

'I'm not,' she protested. 'You know that, babe.' She took her top off by way of illustration.

'Stroke your nipples and tell me a story,' he said, holding his phone up to her.

'She hadn't lost the baby, it was just food poisoning. And today I went out and when I got home, my mum said she's going to sublet the flat and I don't know what to do.'

'Not that sort of story. Tell me how it makes you feel.'

'Pissed off with my mum.'

'For fuck's sake, Sierra, stop dicking me around. You know what I mean.'

'Of course I do, I just don't want to talk about how I'm all wet, oh baby, you're making me wet. I'm upset and I want you to be interested in me.'

'I am interested in you.' He put down both his phone and his laptop; Sierra had thought they were surgically welded to his hands.

'Thanks.' Her need to talk about Tess and her mother had now evaporated, and she wanted to exploit this unique moment of lo-fi sexual contact between them. 'That's nice,' she said as he kissed her nipples and moved down to her stomach. It was, too. It must have been the first time she had felt genuinely excited by him. She was almost relaxed.

He moved downwards and lifted her skirt so that it came over her face. Her view of the room was now obscured by the brocade of her latest purchase, a flouncy fifties piece in gold and cream. She could begin to imagine that she was somewhere else, with someone else—a smart hotel in an obscure European city with Owen, who'd order something flashy from room service, money no object.

Josh tugged at her knickers. She was keen for him to do so, but desperate for him not to speak so that the pretence could endure.

'Fucking hell, Sierra, what's this?'

She sat up, shoving her skirt away from her face. 'What's what?'

'It's disgusting.'

'What?'

'It's so hairy. When did you last get a wax, babe? I swear to god it wasn't like this when we last hooked up.'

Three weeks ago, or was it four? Not that she could afford waxing on the salary Tess paid her; a quick going-over with a razor was as near to a Hollywood as she got, nicks and all. 'My pubic hair disgusts you?'

'Yeah, a bit. A lot. Fuck me, Sierra, I had no idea

119

you were such a bearded lady.'

'I'm not particularly. I'm quite normal, actually, it's just that I didn't know I was coming round to see you.'

'Whoah, babe—Phil Spector wants his wig back.'

Suddenly Sierra felt a rush of rage—at Josh, at her mother, at Owen for an unknowable reason. 'This,' she said, pointing downwards, 'this is what pubic hair looks like on women outside a porn film.' She remembered her mum having a T-shirt saying 'This is what a feminist looks like'. She wanted some underwear with the legend: 'This is what a twat looks like'.

'No, babe, that's an awful lot of hair. It's like fucking Dumbledore down there.'

'No, it's not. It's what women over the age of twelve have. It's what happens if you don't constantly wax and trim.'

'Well, maybe you ought to.'

'This is the pubic hair of a real woman,' she said with as much dignity as it's possible to have when you're struggling to get your knickers back on. 'It's just a shame you're not enough of a real man to enjoy it.'

He shrugged and turned back to his computer. She had never felt the desire to hit someone as violently as she did at the moment. Instead, she put on her shoes and walked out of the room, out of the house and out of his life.

'I was faking it, you know,' she shouted up at his window. 'You're shit in bed.'

Sierra found herself out on the street once again, with less money, one less option as to where to go and even further from a warm bed.

CHAPTER EIGHT

LINES AND WRINKLES

'I suppose this really means that you're going to have a baby in a couple of months' time. I'm excited, in a weird, almost pervy way.' Michael looked over at Tess at the wheel of her child-unfriendly Fiat, seat belt strapped over and under her bump, bondage for a belly.

'Don't be,' Tess said. 'I've already been to a pregnancy yoga session and the novelty of looking at twelve fat ladies soon wears off. Then there's only the stale custard creams and herbal tea to look forward to.'

'You do keep your clothes on, don't you?'

'Thank the lord.'

'And what am I, anyway? What's my role?'

'You're my birthing partner. The course is called hypnobirthing for couples.'

'And we're the couple?'

'In your dreams.'

Indeed, thought Michael, in many of them. 'What is this hypnosis, though? Do I get to swing a watch in your face and say, "You are feeling sleepy"? And then make you run around like a chicken to general hilarity?'

'You're so amusing. It's a breathing and self-hypnosis technique that's going to mean I'll be able to spit this baby out in an entirely painless fashion. Apparently.'

'According to my sister, birth is like pulling an orange out of your nose. I'd really like to see you breathe through that one.'

'Thanks for that, Michael.'

'Mind you, she also said that she loved children, especially when they cry, for then someone takes them away.'

'Do shut up.'

'I'm only joking. It's not like you're not going to want to be with your baby. I know how much you must have wanted it to have done what you did.'

'Absolutely.'

'How's Sierra?'

'Why do you ask?'

'Politeness.'

'Really?'

'Don't give me that smug look, or I'll tell you some of the graphic tales my sisters have told me about what childbirth has done to their nether regions.'

'I said enough. Sierra's all right, I suppose,' said Tess. 'About to be made homeless. I came into the gallery the other day to find that she'd slept the night there after rowing with both her mother and her boyfriend.'

'Have they broken up?'

'I don't think you can chuck your mother.'

'More's the pity. You know what I mean.'

'I think so. He sounded a bit of a cock, to be honest. And her mother's a nightmare. She's planning to sublet their place so she can swan around some Spanish commune, while Sierra finds somewhere else to live on her pittance of a wage.'

'Maybe you should pay her more, then?'

'I wish I could, really I do. I can barely pay her what I do.' She smoothed down the folds of yet another of her maternity contraptions, some sort of ruched garment designed to be worn in myriad ways.

*   *   *

The hypnobirthing class was being held in a nondescript hall in a nondescript area, yet everyone entering its portals believed that they, and they alone, were going through a uniquely interesting experience. Tess pressed the bell and they shuffled nervously, both hoping that no other couple would join them on the doorstep so that they'd be trapped as if in a lift, obliged to make conversation. Their wish was not granted.

'I see we've come to the right place,' said the man, a muscular, sporty-looking type, the sort who had bullied Michael when he was at school, and he saw every day in proto-form now that he was a teacher. With this remark he prodded Tess's bump. She flinched. 'I'm Charlie,' he continued, 'and she's up the duff,' pointing at the small, round woman beside him.

'Uptheduff,' said Michael. 'What an unusual name.'

Charlie guffawed. 'Nice one. The name's Debs.'

'Hello, Debs,' said Michael. He had only agreed to this charade on the assumption that it would be full of right-on types and nice lesbian couples. It was a sign of just how mainstream the alternative had become that someone like Charlie should find himself learning to meditate and drinking tea that tastes of wee.

They were buzzed in and made their way into a room scattered with brown and orange swirly patterned beanbags and cushions. Tess must hate this, thought Michael; there was no need for such a lack of style.

They were the last to arrive and in amid the beanbags there were already six couples. The animals came in two by two, hurrah, hurrah, he thought as he looked at the fathers sitting behind their partners, all of them to a man showing how supportive they were with some aggressive back massaging.

'What are we doing here?' he hissed at Tess.

'I don't know. Lucy said that now I'm entering the home straight I need to know how to give birth. Attending this will halve my chances of a caesarean birth, according to her beloved statistics.'

'And that's a good thing?'

Michael read the sheet they'd been handed. There were glowing testimonies to the power of hypnobirthing techniques, all signed off with vagueness: 'Thanks a million, Rebecca, Brighton'. It read exactly like a website for a dodgy diet pill.

The teacher, whose purple drawstring trousers and fleece top clashed somewhat with the scatter cushions, ushered Michael and Tess into a squashed corner. 'We'll be partnering up later. You four can go together,' she said, gesturing towards Charlie and Debs.

Michael avoided catching Tess's eye.

The first exercise was about learning everybody's names, nice names like Ben and Katie, Will and Megan. Michael noticed that all the women, and most of the men, were wearing wedding rings, despite the apparent hippy vibe.

'Now,' said the teacher or instructor or mentor, 'let's talk about how pregnancy's been for all of us so far. We'll start with the men: tell us how many weeks pregnant you are and how it's been so far for you. Ben.'

'Hi, we're thirty-two weeks pregnant.' Ben rubbed his wife's stomach vigorously. 'Pregnancy's been great for me.' Nervous laughter. 'And she's been great, there's been no sickness or anything and we're just so excited about our baby.'

'We're also thirty-two weeks—in fact, we're due on the same day, aren't we?' said the next man, and the two couples looked at each other excitedly, thrilled to have found a common bond within the institutionalised friend-making process. 'Let's hope there won't be a fight over the birthing pool.' More laughter. God, thought Michael, this lot will laugh at anything, it's like a pigeon landing on Centre Court at Wimbledon. 'Pregnancy's been a wonderful journey and I'm so proud of the way that Katie's coping with it all.'

So it continued. Michael intuited a pattern. Use of the first person plural when talking about pregnancy, some sort of flippant remark to deflect the seriousness of it all, followed by an achingly sincere comment on how beautiful it all was. He found himself distracted by trying to guess who was the most pregnant by the size of their bump.

He looked at Tess. She was, he remembered, about six months pregnant. What was that in weeks? Next they'd be boasting about how many days pregnant they were, how many minutes had passed since conception. He mouthed 'How many?' to her. She clutched and unclutched her fists twice and then stuck out all her fingers. 'Twenty-eight?' he whispered. She nodded. The others were all more pregnant than her, that crucial three or four weeks making them seem ahead in a vital race and gifted with some strange maturity. In what other world would mere weeks make any difference?

Michael's palms sweated as his turn came nearer. I'm a teacher, he thought, I'm used to standing up in classes and making myself heard.

'The wife's thirty-one,' said Charlie. 'No, she's not aged thirty-one, I mean that's how many weeks pregnant she is. She's a bit longer in the tooth than thirty-one, more's the pity.' Even in the laugh-happy environment of the room, Charlie's joke provoked no giggles. 'Anyway, yah, pregnancy. Best thing about it is that she does all the driving and her tits are huge.' Some shocked sniggering this time round. 'Worst thing, she's bloody hormonal in the mornings. But it's all worth it, I suppose. Nah, we're really excited about it. Want to have a whole football team of the little brats, actually.'

Michael was so thrown by this performance that his turn snuck up on him. He looked at Tess. Her bare feet were perfectly pedicured. If he'd known they were expected to go barefoot he might have put some Vaseline on his soles too. Her chin was raised and her back was straight, but Michael knew her well enough to know that she was rattled.

'We're twenty-eight weeks,' he said. Tess looked at him; she was encouraging him to go on, wasn't she? 'Looks like we're the babies of the group.' He got his obligatory laugh. 'We're so happy to be pregnant.' He put his arm round her and felt her flinch beneath it. He looked at her—she was definitely the most beautiful, the best dressed, had the neatest bump. He did feel proud, he really did. 'I'm so proud of Tess, I think she's doing so brilliantly. I never hear her complain. My life's hardly changed a bit so far. But obviously it will. I'll do everything I can to carry on making this as good as possible for her, before and after the birth.'

'Ah, bless,' he heard murmured around the room. He was good, really good. Not for nothing had he stepped in as Fagin when Archie Jameson refused to go on in the Moreton Primary's Year 6 leavers' production of *Oliver.*

*   *   *

Tess waited until after they'd got into the car and driven well away from the suburban street. She waited through the breathing exercises, the ones that had made Michael feel quite drunk. She waited through the herbal teas when they'd been allowed to chat to the others without the invigilation of the instructor, and so had asked normal questions, unrelated to pregnancy, like what do you do and where do you live (with Tess, obviously, had been Michael's reply, thus fulfilling a childhood fantasy to live in that rather smarter borough). She didn't say anything when they were asked how they met— we're cousins, second cousins though, you know our mothers are cousins not sisters, Michael had said; oh, that's all right then. She'd endured Michael massaging the bottom of her spine with gusto. She'd not broken when he'd given out the loudest primal scream.

But in the car, Tess did not hold back. 'What the hell do you think you're playing at, Michael Wasiak?' It was said quietly, almost casually, as Tess stared at the road ahead.

'What do you mean?'

'You were only supposed to be my birthing partner.'

'So?'

'You know what. What was all that "We're twenty-eight weeks, we're very happy, I'm so excited about becoming a father"?'

'I never said that.'

'Well, you implied it. I didn't ask you along to be a pretend father, I asked you along for support.'

'I thought I was quite convincing.'

'You were. You almost had me fooled for a while. I was wracking my brains trying to remember when I'd slept with you, moved in with you, decided to spend the rest of my life with you, and then I remembered: gosh, I never did, he's just a sad fantasist who's using my hypnobirthing classes to make good a thousand schoolboy daydreams.'

'Hang on, Tess. I did it for you. I couldn't bear all those smug couples and those men talking about how "we're pregnant". I didn't want them feeling sorry for you and you being the only single mother, independent parent, whatever. You could have gone to a single mothers' class if you'd wanted to, but you wanted to go to the fathers and mothers one.'

'Mothers and partners,' she corrected. 'Partners.'

'Hang on, you said it was hypnobirthing for couples.'

'Couples consisting of mothers and partners.'

'Partners in the life partners sense of the word, not bloody birthing partner, as well you know. Not that I'm your birthing partner anyway. I just couldn't bear for any of those people—for the awful Charlie, or the nice Ben and his even nicer wife—I just couldn't bear for any of them to be talking about you afterwards, speculating.'

'You're so conservative, when did you get to be

like this? Is that what you think, that I should be ashamed that I'm doing this on my own? Jeesh, why is everyone making such a fuss about it?'

'No, no, of course not. I just thought that you might prefer it if we . . . I don't know.'

'Instead they're just speculating on what an odd couple we make.'

'I thought we made quite a good couple. Better than that Lizzie and Tom for starters. Rare example of a pair where he's way better looking than she is.'

Tess giggled. 'By some way. Did her nose actually touch her chin? Like a Habsburg?'

'And that Abigail, don't tell me that she was just carrying a baby.'

They laughed. Then Tess sighed. 'I don't know, Mishe. I don't know what I wanted you to say when it came round to us. I was having to do breathing exercises just to stay calm as we creaked round the room listening to all those men talk about what brilliant fathers they're going to be. Part of me was relieved when you insinuated that we were as normal as the rest of them.'

'Hey, who wants to be normal?' Michael's tone was of forced jollity. This was as close to vulnerability as Tess had ever come to him.

'Not me.' She echoed his tone, but it was weaker; the next echo would have faded out completely.

'Tess, you're not going to be on your own, you've got me and Aunt Vondra and Lucy . . .'

'But I won't have "I'm just so damned proud to be a father and if men could lactate I'd breastfeed my child" though, will I?'

'You don't need them. You're Tess. You've never needed anyone; you've always been like a cat—people are lucky to love you, not the other way round.'

'Lucy keeps telling me how hard it is and how she doesn't know how I cope and every day she says to herself she doesn't know how she'd do it without the saintly Jamie.'

'But people do, don't they? Millions of them and few with your resources.'

She laughed at this comment.

'I promise I'll be there for you, Tess,' he said. 'I'll be there every day. Honestly, having a kid with two parents, judging by that lot, is just too bourgeois for you, too smug, too . . . I don't know, cloying, boring and normal. They're the supermarket basics range biscuits that were handed round, while you're a hand-rolled langue de chat dipped in seventy per cent cocoa solids chocolate.'

'You're right, of course. Why, I could be married to Charlie and have a baby and a hairy-backed husband to look after on top of that. I'd have had to have had sex with him, at least once, to have conceived.' They urghhed in unison.

*   *   *

Ruby massaged Owen's feet. She had become even more the geisha since they had been to his parents' house. She and Mari had not stopped talking after his mother unleashed the beast of Ruby's bridal fantasies. His own parents' wedding had been rushed and cheap, a registry office with just two witnesses. Later, his sister Caron—stolid, unlovely Caron—had denied Mari any mother-of-the-bride excesses, since she had not wanted any fuss or frill. Even though a traditional-wedding-dressed Caron

130

would have looked all too Michelin man, Mari had still wanted to give her the big day she had never had, and to bond over mother-and-daughter pampering days at the beauticians.

He'd rung his father a couple of times, but he had not been able to talk—that's what he had said. Each time, Owen had had to steel himself with a glass of whisky. He didn't even particularly like whisky, it was an old man's drink, but it just seemed like the stuff he should be knocking back to talk to his dad about where he'd come from. He had a sort of deep-breath, I'll do it at seven, nervousness each time that reminded him of calling girls before he'd realised that the girls were always hoping for his calls. He'd even lit a cigarette each time he called Gareth, then held his hand over the phone each time he had a drag so his father couldn't hear his insensitivity.

In the intervening days, Owen had found himself speculating about who his real parents were more than he had done since he'd been eleven. Once adolescence had hit, he'd been too concerned with where he was going to think about where he'd come from. Occasionally, odd things would have rekindled a brief interest, which would then be followed by a low mood. He wondered for a time if his father wasn't Fred West, the multiple murderer. It seemed plausible. He was the right age, didn't live too far away, slept with the sort of girls who would give up their baby for adoption. He'd watched every news bulletin, pored over the one photo that was reproduced over and over: Fred West as a bad-toothed troglodyte, leering out at him, with thick black hair and large features, looking like Owen's own picture of Dorian Gray, a hideous, grotesque version of himself.

That's the thing about being adopted. It's not just the pop stars and aristocrats that you fantasise about being your parents, it's the bad people too. Did Tess know this? Didn't she ever worry that one day the baby would grow up and walk down the street and stare into the face of every man of a certain age and colouring and wonder, is that him? That every time her child found themselves in bed with a new lover they'd have a quick flicker of fear that they might be related to their conquest. Especially when in bed with those that looked like you. It wasn't as if Owen was particularly narcissistic, if anything he went for blondes, but if you'd slept with as many women as he had, you were bound to come across some that could pass as your sister or half sister. Did Tess ever think about that?

Every day, the others, the non-adopted, casually reminded Owen of the difference between him and them. You're so dark, where do you get that from? My father's very musical, is anybody in your family? I'm from Yorkshire, my family's always lived there. I hate my eczema, I get it from my mother; she was plagued with it as a baby, but it's cleared up now. My elder brother tried to kill me when I was a newborn—he was so jealous that he climbed in the cot and my parents came in just in the nick of time.

It only got worse when his contemporaries began having their own babies. All that talk of types of birth and the wonderful moment when a father first sees his baby and being forced to look at identikit photos of a bleary-eyed mother holding a Gollum-like creature immediately after birth. It made all his friends, self-centred as they were, interested in their own births, asking their parents for the first time what it was like and what they had felt, and Owen knew he'd never have that privilege.

Ruby was the worst person for heightening his lack of knowledge about his provenance. She was proud of her genetic inheritance, seeing as it had resulted in long legs, thick hair and, apparently, a fast metabolism. 'I can eat and eat as much as I like—I'm always having burgers, aren't I, Owen?—but a size six still falls off me. Just lucky I guess, my mum's the same, and my nan—you should see her, people always think she must be my mother she's so young looking, the women in my family really keep their figures.'

Ruby's readings of new-age books called things like *Take the Thorny Road* only furthered Owen's isolation and irritation. 'You've got to find your birth mother,' she'd say to him, thinking that she was being supportive. 'If you don't know where you're from, how can you tell where you're going?' and 'Maybe your fear of commitment before you met me is due to your birth mother's fear of committing to you when you were born.'

'I just hadn't met the right girl yet,' he'd say. Hadn't, haven't. Almost the same thing.

*   *   *

Sierra had always been tidy. Her pencil case at school had been a source of pride—some photographer friend of her mum's used to bring her back Hello Kitty stuff from Japan. Every evening the case, its contents and her little plastic Hello Kitty rucksack would be laid in readiness for school the next day, everything matching even down to her two beloved hairgrips and her cartoon-covered knickers.

'Are you going to get dressed today?' she asked on her way out to the gallery. 'Or even get up at all?' Susie lay in Sierra's old bedroom, spilling out of a single bed, still with that natural, non-surgically enhanced skinny-body-big-tits combination so beloved of modelling agents. Rings of discarded pants interlocked across the floor, while coffee cups grew swirls of mould.

For Monday mornings, Sierra always reverted back to the routines of the first day at a new school, of which there had been fourteen, what with all the flicking between private and state that had gone on, as well as moving from borough to country and back again.

'Mum, are you getting up?'

'Don't feel well,' Susie mumbled. Sierra sighed, but her mother did have a gleam of sweat on her face that wasn't commensurate with the chilly May morning. She went and sat at the end of the bed.

'What's wrong?' Sierra felt her mother's forehead. This seemed the right thing to do, but she wasn't sure what she was judging.

'Don't know, don't think I can get up.'

Sierra glanced at her watch. 'Why don't you move into my bedroom?'

'*My* bedroom,' her mother corrected.

'You've been away for almost two years. What was I supposed to do?'

'I'm just saying.' Susie lay back with a moan.

'What time did you get in last night?'

'Don't know.'

'Were you taking anything?'

'What is this? The Spanish Inquisition?'

'Look, Mum, I don't want to hassle you, but I've no idea what's going on. It's been two weeks since you basically told me I had to get out and now I don't know. Are you definitely not subletting?'

'I told you, they thought it was a shithole.'

'Not my fault.'

'Never said it was.'

'So what, Mum? Are you going back to Spain or what?'

'I'm waiting,' she said and turned away with her eyes shut.

'Waiting for what, Mum?' Her mother simply stared at the wall. 'Why don't you get a job or something? You can't lie here forever. Go back to Spain if you have to, just sort yourself out and tell me what's going on so I can make some plans of my own about what's happening to my flat, your flat, our flat, my home, I don't know. What is going on?'

Susie just curled herself up further and told Sierra to 'Fuck off, I never asked . . .'

'Asked what? Asked to be born?' said Sierra. 'Whoo, get you—what are you, fourteen?'

'I never asked for you to interfere with my life.'

'And I've never asked for anything. And now I'm wishing that you'd just go.'

'I will, then.'

'Good.'

'Yes, good for me. I've got plans, you see. I'm all right, thanks.'

'Which are?'

'Not telling.'

'Fine.'

'Fine for me,' Susie said.

'Better for me.'

Sierra realised that this conversation could go on

infinitely and chose to believe that by being the one to walk out, which she needed to anyway if she was to get to the gallery on time, and she really hated being late, then she was the grown-up. As ever.

*   *   *

Lucy was in the bathroom, staring at herself in the mirror as she wiped her face with cleanser. She scrubbed at her frown lines, but they weren't so easily rubbed away. She knew that her face wasn't bad for someone her age—she thanked her parents for not having ever taken her skiing and for the rarity of foreign holidays—but it didn't matter. It wasn't enough to be not bad for her age, she wanted to be good for someone Jamie's age. She wiped harder, but she couldn't eliminate the tiny pockmarks that had recently begun to appear around her chin, or the way the skin above her eyelids had begun to hover over her eyes like those houses you see in photographs to illustrate coastal erosion. The odd wiry white hair had begun to appear amid her highlights. Two pregnancies had caused her gums to recede so that she had become literally long in the tooth. She, the natural sceptic, the eternal rationalist, had begun to spend obscene amounts of money on lotions, potions, serums and fluids. She had exfoliators to take off the old cells, replenishers to put the new ones on; creams for brightening and emulsions for tightening; serums that were intensive and creams that were non-invasive. Previously she'd had one cream for everything and it was available from the supermarket, now her body was divided up into tiny pieces with a specific lotion for each area— different ones for her neck, eyelids, chest, thighs and stomach; an unguent for her knees, another for her elbows. She even had gel that promised to restore the lustre of her eyelashes.

She who had never been vain, she who had prided herself on her natural good looks if she'd prided herself on her appearance at all.

'You're still in here,' said Jamie, walking in as she massaged cream into her neck.

'Sorry, I won't be long.'

She watched him in the mirror. She noticed his eyes flick from the cupboard to her and then back to the cupboard again. She tried to read his expression. She thought she saw panic with a top note of revulsion in there. He couldn't get out of the room fast enough.

They had eaten supper together, at least, and talked about Rosa and Ned, as usual, then retired to their separate televisions. They should never have got the second screen.

She looked back at her neck and then her face and tried to see herself through his eyes. He had definitely been panicked or horrified by something. She picked up one of her tubes of fluid. She wasn't stupid, she knew that scientifically it was unlikely that smearing something on the epidermis would bore its way through the dermis and into the subcutaneous tissues to revitalise them. And yet, and yet.

If she didn't believe that creams worked, then she was left with two options: a) Learn to love her wrinkles as a sign of the wisdom and experience that life had brought her, or some other cod psychological exhortation, or b) Leave behind the gateway drug of moisturiser and go onto the hard stuff.

She Googled fillers and brow lifts again that night. She was a feminist, of course, but wasn't there an argument that if you were doing these things for yourself, then it was empowering? And in a world where a woman's earning capacity is compromised by ageing, then it was a logical response to make yourself look younger by whatever means. If she were to do it—and she wasn't definitely going to, it was just a thought—but if she were to, then it would be for herself and nobody else.

Jamie was still downstairs doing whatever it was he did to arrive in bed half an hour later than her. She closed her eyes and pretended to sleep, all the while thinking of an after photo of herself.

CHAPTER NINE

CLINICALLY TESTED

The school holidays were never as long as people thought they were. The way others spoke of them, you'd think Michael barely made it to work, let alone put in all the long hours and the weekends, which made the fact that he had to go away at the same time as just the sort of people he'd most like to avoid even more galling.

Not this year, though, for he was staying put in advance of Tess's August due date. It was odd, he thought—not for the first time—that the baby would most likely be born in August. The pushy parents, the Lucy types, had their children in autumn so that they'd always be the oldest in their class. Surely Tess with her artificial conception would have thought this through beforehand?

He was spending a lot of time at Tess's gallery. He didn't like to examine his motives for this too closely. It was the baby—yes, it was the baby, due in only a month's time. He was being a dutiful godparent, without the god bit.

'How's things?' he asked Sierra, when he'd finally finished discussing the benefits of a birthing plan with Tess. She looked a little wan, very different from the vital girl drunk on cocktails he remembered from the first time they'd met.

'Fine.'

'Tess told me that you're having some problems. With your mum?'

'That, yes. I don't know what's happening now. Nobody wants to pay £1,500 rent for the flat. But she'll either get so desperate that she lowers the price, or she'll find someone desperate enough to pay it.'

'Well, if you need somewhere to kip, I've got a sofa bed.'

She shrugged. 'I'll manage. I always do. I'm a survivor.' She stuck her chin out and Michael expected the karaoke music to start and for her to do a belting dance routine off the desk. He went back to talking to Tess, leaving Sierra frowning at a spreadsheet on the computer.

'Have you read up about perineal massage?' he asked. 'Honestly my darling, you need to try and, ahem, prepare yourself down there to preserve yourself for your next lover.'

'My lover,' said Tess, giving it a Gallic spin. 'I don't really mind. It was never that big a deal to me anyway, this sex thing.'

'By this sex thing, do you mean sex?' She nodded. 'You're just saying that because you're so pregnant.'

'No, really, it wasn't. I liked to have it once in a while just to remind me what it was like—that's why Owen was so useful, just to scratch that itch, and then I'd think oh yes, I've ticked that box for this month or year or whatever, all the sharing of beds and toothbrushes. Too much intimacy. I know I'm not the tidiest of women, but I don't like other people's mess. No, when it comes to sex, I've always been of the "I'd rather have a nice cup of tea" brigade. Well, a nice chilled glass of champagne in a long, tall flute glass. Not one of the flat ones— they make it taste slightly metallic and remind me of ghastly weddings in the middle of nowhere.'

'Really?' asked Michael.

'Definitely. I can't be doing with those silly glasses.'

'Not the champagne. The sex. You really don't care about it?'

'No. It's like Poussin or Issey Miyake pleats or white truffles. So overrated, don't you think?'

'No, I don't think sex is overrated,' Michael said. He crossed his legs and then caught sight of Sierra looking at him. She still thinks I'm gay, he thought. She can look at me crossing my legs and assume that's because I'm so camp it's the way I naturally sit. He lowered his voice. 'It may be everywhere, it may be the thing we talk about more than anything else, it may be ascribed magical powers and change the world and we may be told that it's everything that anybody wants, but no, I don't think it's possible to exaggerate its wonder. I don't think there are poets who can do it justice, there aren't

140

drugs as good, there's no painting in the world that can even be the tenth part of that moment, just before . . . oh, you know, when your brain fills up and empties all at the same time. Every time I have sex I get this amazing revelation of wow, this is what it's like, it's this combination of the familiar and yet every time the utterly unexpected and I think, yes, I should do this all the time.'

'How nice for you,' said Tess. 'Though I must say I'm rather disappointed. I didn't think you were quite so blokeish about the whole thing, that you'd be a bit cooler, more insouciant about it. Take it or leave it, you know. But instead you're a clichéd man. You sound like Sierra.'

'Why like me?' Sierra asked and Michael wondered how much of the conversation she'd overheard.

'A sex addict,' said Tess.

'Hardly,' said Sierra, shrinking behind the computer.

'While for me,' Tess went on, 'beds are all about napping. It's time for my siesta. Sierra, sweetheart, can you help Michael carry this through to the back office?'

'But I was going to get going on the cataloguing.'

'Do it later, there's no hurry.'

'But there is, don't you see, we have to get rid of this lot and get started on the New Florals. It's got to happen before you drop. Please, Tess, you know what the dates are.'

'Why don't you just rest here in the sun?' suggested Michael. 'Let Sierra get on with all the work back there.'

'It's my office and I'll nap if I want to.'

Michael and Sierra lugged the chaise longue into

141

the windowless back office. They stood next to each other as they pushed it into the corner, away from the computer.

'Sorry, I didn't mean to bash,' said Sierra.

'You didn't,' said Michael.

They stood up and looked at what was to be Tess's bed for the afternoon. It felt like they were intruding on her solitary sleep and it felt like they were intruding on one another. It was not so much that they were alone that bothered them, rather that they were without Tess. It had only happened once before, that evening when they thought Tess was going to lose the baby.

They came back into the main part of the gallery. Sierra's face was flushed with exertion. Michael felt the need to cross his legs again.

'Not many sold,' he said, avoiding looking at her.

'Tell me about it. Tess hasn't done a stroke of work since announcing her pregnancy. The accountant's been lecturing me about how bad things are looking and I don't know what I'm going to do while she's away; there's this great big hole in the schedules in November and we're screwed if we can't put something in it.'

'Could you not take on some help?'

'I'm planning to, but I can't do Tess's job. I don't have the contacts, the confidence.'

'It doesn't look like you'll do much worse,' he said. 'Maybe you just need to try something completely different. These are large, expensive . . .'

'And unsold.'

'So you need small, inexpensive . . .' he cued her.

'And sold. You're right, I know you are. I'm thinking about it, but I just worry that everything worth doing has been done already. By someone

142

more powerful and influential than I am. And anything worth doing is going to need a lot more notice than I've got.'

'Could be your big break.'

'I doubt it.'

'Can I ask you something? Something personal?'

'Yes.'

'Do you buy Tess's donor story?'

'What do you mean?'

'My mother says that Vondra doesn't think it's a donor baby, since Tess has told her something completely different. And I was just thinking it's bad timing that it's due in August.'

'Too right, all the big art fairs are in the autumn.'

'Stranger and stranger.'

'But she is quite old and stuff, her biological clock and things.'

'For someone else, maybe, but I genuinely never felt the clock ticked for her. Did you ever hear Tess talk about wanting children?'

'No, but I don't think she would with me. We talked about work and when we were kids and going out, but not stuff like that. She'd be more likely to talk about it to Lucy, wouldn't she?'

'I suppose. It would be interesting to ask her.'

'Do you think she's not telling the truth about it, then?' asked Sierra.

'We know she's lied to someone, but who's to say it's not to us, rather than her mother?'

'But why?'

'I don't know. I really don't. But I'll find out, I promise you.'

*　　　*　　　*

Lucy had made a list to take with her. Always useful to have something written down—or in this case, typed—so that she could add to the list on the left: 'Things I don't like'. There was never any need to add to the list on the right of the page.

It was made very clear to her that she would be meeting with a practitioner. The word was repeated. Not a doctor, in other words. Lucy liked qualifications, she had quite a few herself, and practitioner was just the sort of lily-livered cop-out of a word she hated. Practised what exactly? The piano? It turned out that the whole issue of semantics was confusing—what exactly was the difference between clinical and cosmetic dermatology? Why had she found herself at a dentist's—sorry, dental clinic—when nobody was going to touch her teeth? It seemed appropriate, somehow, that this work should take place at the dentist's, since people who did this sort of thing, people like her, always compared it to cosmetic dental work. 'I don't see how it's any worse or unfeminist than having your teeth brightened,' they'd say. 'Or dyeing your hair.' Though it was, of course, which they all knew.

She was further disconcerted to find that the practitioner was female. She had bought into the whole Pygmalion aspect of such intervention and hated herself for feeling that she wanted a man to sculpt and perfect her. It is my right, she repeated to herself, to spend the money that I earn how I like. It is an investment in my career and in my relationship. Empowerment was her mantra. Reinvigoration, rejuvenation, reinvention. I will reinvent myself as someone who is adored—a goddess, a sexual being.

The waiting room was kitted out like a mid-end airport hotel, all beige walls, mahogany finishes and bland abstract art.

If the practitioner had not been a woman, then maybe Lucy would not have stared at her so, to examine her face for signs of too little or too much work.

'How can I help you?' Amanda asked. Yes, first name, it was all very cosy. Lucy gave up trying not to stare and quickly scanned her face. No ice-rink forehead to imply Botox, that was a good sign, and not a lot of wrinkles either. Lucy would have put her in her mid-thirties. Which, given where they were, could be anything from 25 to 55. Mid-thirties, that was where they all wanted to be, wasn't it? Not teens or twenties because we were all so badly dressed then and unworldly. Thirty-three or 34, that's the age. Or 32, Jamie's age. His friends' age. Lucy sadly hadn't enjoyed her few years at the perfect age, too busy at the time being conscious of the quality of her eggs rather than her exterior.

'That's the question I'd like to ask you,' said Lucy. 'What do you think I need?'

'You don't need anything, of course.' Oh, she's good.

'No, of course not, but what do you think would make me look a bit . . .' Not younger, that wasn't it exactly '. . . more cheerful. Well rested.'

Amanda nodded. 'You want to make sure that what you look like on the outside matches how you feel.'

'Yes.' No, thought Lucy. It's not as if I feel all young and gorgeous on the inside. I feel quite old. My legs are stiff in the morning, I fall asleep in front of the television, I don't understand social networking and I want a phone that just rings people. My pupils no longer seem to adjust to sunshine so I need to wear shades even on a dull spring day. I now look at sunglasses as not cool rock star-ish accessories, but as much a sign of age as a Zimmer frame and liver spots. I feel all cantankerous when people use idiotic portmanteau words like manny or cankle. 'How do I do that? Look younger, I mean? I don't want to have that shiny forehead thing going on.' Lucy had come armed with a scrapbook of celebrities whose photos were often marked with headlines like 'When surgery goes wrong' or 'When bad surgery happens to good people'.

Amanda laughed. 'You'd need at least £5,000 worth of Botox and fillers to achieve that look.' Achieve? 'Everyone comes to me telling me about the celebrities they don't want to look like. What they don't realise is that for every one that's overdone it, there are a thousand who look fabulous and tell the magazines that it's all due to their healthy diet, good genes and an expensive moisturiser. Or worse, a cheap moisturiser from their local supermarket. Do you mind?' She leaned over to take a closer look at Lucy's face. 'Your frown lines are probably your biggest issue, then these grooves by the sides of your nose. I'm guessing you're none too happy about your lower eyelids, too?'

My lower eyelids? 'I suppose so.'

'Your face makes you look bad-tempered and that's not you, is it?'

Lucy shook her head. Although I am quite pissed off a lot of the time, actually.

'We just want to look a bit fresher.'

'Yes, fresh. That sounds good.' No use-by date stamped across her forehead as though she were one of half a dozen eggs in a box. If she wasn't pre her best-before date, then she must be in her worst-after phase, and that was not a good thing.

'I suggest an especially tailored combination of Botox and Restylane, which is a filler made from an entirely natural non-animal hyaluronic acid. As I say, it's completely natural.'

Deadly nightshade is entirely natural. So's dog shit and snot. None of which I'd want semi-permanently injected into my face. But Lucy banished these thoughts when she saw the before and after photos. The effects were so subtle as to be almost imperceptible. Which was a good thing, wasn't it?

Amanda came alarmingly close and pointed at Lucy's face in the nearby mirror. 'See these furrows? We'll stop those. You'll immediately look so much nicer, more approachable, more relaxed. Then we'll fill in these bits here and then plump your cheeks out a bit. You're quite thin, aren't you?'

'Yes, I suppose. Could always do with losing a few kilos, you know how it is.'

'If you do, you might want to be thinking about having some more fillers. There's nothing more ageing than being gaunt, is there? On the other hand, it's pretty ageing to be overweight, too. Have you had children?'

'Yes, two.'

'It's so hard, isn't it? You can get all the weight off, but your body never quite recovers.'

'No, my tummy . . .'

'The mummy tummy, we call it.' Amanda smiled

as if this was just so cute and cuddly and adorable of them. To use the word that only two people in the world were allowed to use to her, although she had noticed that Jamie used it quite a lot. It was because he never spoke to her directly any more, only to the children and in the third person. 'Well, if you find that you're uncomfortable with that, we can always refer you to our sister clinic. We don't do surgery here.'

Amanda began to draw blue lines across Lucy's face, just like in those TV makeover programmes that she was secretly addicted to. There was a sort of beauty to their symmetry and abundance; she looked like a pale Maori warrior.

'I could fit you in today,' said Amanda.

'No, I mean, yes. No.' Lucy looked at herself in the mirror. She no longer looked like a warrior, but some sort of Kabuki horror mask, the felt-tipped lines only emphasising the confusion in her face. 'I wasn't expecting to do it right away. This was just a consultation. To think about it.'

'No time like the present.'

It was an obvious expression, one that Lucy had probably used herself on many occasions. But she began to examine it. Of course, there is never any time like the present, it's always changing, what a stupid thing to say. She continued to gaze at the mirror; this was her face at the present moment, but if she did as Amanda recommended, then her face would no longer be in the present but in the past. No, not the past, because it wouldn't look exactly as it had done five years ago, it would be a different version. A new you, it said on the brochure. It's not the old you at all. She wasn't about to revive a past incarnation, but create a totally modern one.

One that would not only look different, but be different, too. The old her, the one whose face she was chasing, would never have done this. She could hear her chastising her from the past.

'Why wait for the new you?' said Amanda, as if she could read the thoughts that flashed behind Lucy's lined book of a face.

'Because . . .' Because she still hadn't quite managed to convince herself of the feminist arguments for conceding to society's strictures that women should stay puffy cheeked and smooth, because she had no guarantees that Jamie would sleep with her again anyway, because it was expensive, vain and possibly even dangerous.

'There's no hurry,' said Amanda.

But there is, thought Lucy. She felt as if she was hurtling towards her year's anniversary of nothingness between her and Jamie. It had already been nine months, enough time to gestate a whole baby.

She had got so close to having stuff done to her that she thought she would leave with disappointment if not with a new face. She felt as surely paralysed as if she had already been injected with botulism.

'Can I?' she said. Can I what? Think about it? Or pay by credit card?

*   *   *

The fridge at Sierra's flat was crammed with expensive deli produce, protein-laden stuff like Serrano ham, hard cheese and marinated anchovies, along with a jar of artichokes and some rocket salad. Sierra had been feeling guilty all day about snapping at her mother and had escaped the intimidating solitude of the gallery to stock up on Susie's favourite foods, which she could ill afford.

The flat may have been full of things for Susie to eat but it was empty of Susie herself. The bedroom had been left exactly as Sierra had seen it that morning, but the bony bundle in the bed had gone, taking with her only a few clothes and a holdall. Her mother's suitcase still lay spewing the clothes that she hadn't bothered to unpack on arrival, though Sierra noticed that the Azzedine Alaïa black tube dress that she had long coveted had disappeared. Not for the first time, she wondered what money her mother lived off.

She helped herself to an artichoke heart, and then another, and opened one of the three bottles of wine she'd bought. She sat at the kitchen table, on an old rush-seated chair that her mother had painted purple when Sierra was ten. She felt lonely. Trade had been far from brisk in the gallery and without Tess there to chat to she felt that her voice had become hoarse through lack of use. She worried about her future at the gallery, about the gallery's future, she supposed. She had wanted to come home to her mother, to apologise, to get maybe a bit drunk together, even share a joint, which she didn't really like but she thought it would please Susie.

She couldn't ring Josh since they'd split up. Split up? When had they ever been joined, except in some crappy pseudo porny copulation? They had quite literally never been out. She missed it, though—not the sex, but having something to do.

She got online but couldn't bring herself to message any friends, real or otherwise. She flicked through the texts on her phone for inspiration on who to talk to, or a clue as to where her mother might be. There was a message from Chloe, but she was still too involved in that skanky gig scene that might get her embroiled with a Josh v2. Chloe called the bloke she was sleeping with her 'friend with benefits'. Sierra had thought about using this phrase, or maybe 'fuck buddy', to describe her relationship with Josh, but since he wasn't her friend and there were no longer any benefits, if there ever had been, it didn't really apply.

She could go round to Chloe's, she supposed, to the house that she shared with all her fellow graduates, where they'd complain about how, like, hard it was working every single day of the week and having to get up at the same time every single morning and how big their student debts were while still getting their Brazilians and blowing money on cheap designer knock-offs in Topshop every Saturday morning. Sierra wasn't sure she could face them. Her status as non-graduate who lived at her mum's made her both older and younger than all of them.

She'd just have to wait for her mother to return. If she was coming back. She went to turn on the television and found a note written in her mother's loopy-circles-over-the-i handwriting. It was on the back of an envelope, a gas bill it was her responsibility to pay.

'Back to Spain. Don't wait up. Be back soon.'

Just like that. As if she'd popped out to the corner shop. How could a woman who'd said she hadn't got enough money to pay for the bus afford a ticket all the way to Andalusia?

151

*   *   *

Michael felt that his life was spent busying around a prone Tess. She had been felled by the latter stages of pregnancy and took to the sofa as if born to it. He was round at her flat, again.

'I really deserve a break,' said Tess. 'It's ridiculous that it should have to take getting pregnant to allow me to have some time off, but I'm going to enjoy it.'

'Yeah, right, you need a holiday, Miss-four-foreign-holidays-a-year. Anyway, Sierra says that you've not exactly been rushed off your feet at the gallery,' said Michael as he ticked off items on Tess's hospital bag list.

'Silly girl's in a panic about coping without me,' said Tess. 'She'll be fine. It's not like I'm planning to become a stay-at-home mum.' She giggled at the prospect. 'I'll be back in a couple of months.'

'Really?'

'Yes, the recovery time's much quicker after a water birth.'

'Here's hoping.' Michael and Tess looked at one another. It was a recurrent worry that all three birthing pools at the hospital would be in use when she went into labour. It was, in fact, their biggest worry, since both looked upon labour as a physical challenge that would be surmounted with the ease with which Tess had gone through the rest of her life. Over the last couple of weeks they'd had sporadic texts announcing the fantastic brilliant wonderful news that the most beautiful baby in the world called Finn or Eva or Noah had been born to one of those nice couples from the hypnobirthing class. These were soon followed by an email with

152

a photo of a baby indistinguishable from the last. With each announcement, Michael's nerves increased. The birth, he knew, was inevitable. His presence there, he reassured himself, was not.

'Are you happy to have that casserole again tonight?' Michael asked.

'I'm not hungry.'

'Really?'

'Yes, I feel a bit funny.'

'In what way?'

'Strange. I've got some quite strong fakey contractions.'

'Definitely fake?'

'Definitely. Michael, it's not going to be like the films, I'll have hours of waiting before I even go to hospital and Lucy will be with me by then. And even there, they'll tell me I've not yet started to dilate. Remember what the teacher told us—first labours are long, wait before going to hospital. Besides, I'm so not ready to give birth and I'm not due for another two weeks.'

'If you even think there's the slightest possibility that you're going to go into labour, I think we should ring Lucy,' he said, tightly gripping the strap of Tess's capacious overnight bag, which was filled with outsized sanitary pads, glucose tablets and a water spray. 'I'm not going to be there, I'm not.' Hadn't he read somewhere that a woman's handbag was a metaphor for her vagina? A lovely little clutch with a phone, lippy and keys in it when young, a gaping black hole like the giant changing bag they would eventually carry later on.

'I know, Michael, you've told me often enough.' Tess's voice was sharp. 'You don't think that makes me feel any better, do you? Don't you think I might

153

like the option not to be there?'

'Where's the lip salve?'

'You're changing the subject. I never use lip salve, anyway,' said Tess.

'Says on the net that it's an essential piece of kit. Your lips get very dry in labour.'

'Right, I'm going to be applying lip balm in between contractions.'

'Apparently. The Balenciaga is your birth bag, the Birkin's your hospital bag. See—flannel, sponge, slippers, apple juice, warm socks. Damn, where are your pyjamas?'

'Pyjamas? I've got a gown, thank you—bottom drawer over there.'

Michael retrieved an old-fashioned negligee of the softest silk he'd ever touched, which shimmered through his fingers when he held it. 'Wow.'

'I know.'

'This is like something Elizabeth Taylor would wear in *Cat on a Hot Tin Roof*.'

'Labour sounds so grim that I thought I needed something to make me feel cosseted afterwards. Won't I be the most glamorous mother on the ward? Not that I'm going to be on the ward—you have remembered about booking the private room, haven't you? Make sure you tell Lucy.'

'Is ivory the ideal colour, though? Aren't you going to be bleeding and stuff?' He waved a packet of the outsized sanitary towels that were apparently essential after giving birth.

'Oh, you with your gore, I'll be fine.'

'It's funny to think that your baby's dad might be there.'

Tess frowned. 'What do you mean?'

'Well, he's a doctor, isn't he? Didn't you say that

the sperm donor was a doctor? Hospitals do tend to be full of them, dashing around being handsome and riding on the trolleys and saving lives.'

'Of course. Yes. No, he's not from London. I think he's from the West Country. That's what they told me.'

'I see. Funny accent. Do you think she'll look like him?'

'How should I know? I don't even know what he looks like.' Tess flipped herself and her bump over to the other side.

'Of course not. I forgot. You never met him.'

'No, I didn't. I really can't be doing with talking about this now, honey, not with these cramps. Do you mind staying tonight? Just in case I don't feel well.'

'You don't think you're—'

'No!'

CHAPTER TEN

Baby-soft Skin

'Michael,' came a groan. 'Michael, I need you.'

How many times had Michael dreamed of such a night-time request? He turned over and enjoyed the hardening of his cock. The spare bedroom at Tess's flat was still a gloriously adult enclave. A scented candle sat on the bedside table, along with a pile of magazines and a packet of Nurofen. A huge canvas portraying a man's genitalia in close up, so that the veins looked like silvery purple rivers across a deserted landscape, dominated one of the walls. Michael seemed to remember that it had been Sierra's responsibility to turn the room into a nursery.

The groans continued at intervals of around two minutes. 'Yes,' thought Michael, as he continued to enjoy the replaying of his default dream. It had been a while since he'd used Tess as a tool for pleasure; lately Sierra had been in the ascendant.

Tess's voice became sharp. 'For fuck's sake, Michael.' Tess almost never swore, except with the old-fashioned 'hell and damnation'. 'I need to get to the hospital.'

'Shit, shit.' He jumped up, as panicked about dampening down his hard-on as by what Tess was telling him. He grabbed his pants and a T-shirt. 'You're not really—I thought it was fake labour, false labour, whatever they call it?'

'I thought so too.' She breathed in deeply.

'Out through the mouth,' intoned Michael as he too tried to use breathing techniques to calm himself. 'It still could be, but we'd better get to the hospital anyway.'

'That's what I said.' Each short sentence was punctuated with a moan. Michael looked at her. She was possessed by something so animal that it made his stomach churn. She had thrown open her silk dressing gown and she didn't seem to care. He could see her body. She had evidently had an antenatal wax.

It's not supposed to be like this, he thought, it's supposed to take ages. We're supposed to go for walks and watch videos and I make her food and then Lucy comes and takes her away from me and then later I visit my gorgeous and clean god-daughter.

'Why don't I ring Lucy and wait for her to get here first?'

'Now!'

'Right,' he said, trying not to stare. He had dealt with enough rowdy kids at school, he could deal with this. 'The hospital notes are in the hospital bag. No, the birth bag. That's the black one. Yes, not here. I'll try the other bag. I'm looking through it now.' He shouted through from her room to the spare room where she was still concentrating hard on the thing inside her that was swelling up every minute and pushing out in every direction from within. 'It must be in the living room.' Michael hadn't seen the notes for days. He went out to ring directory enquiries. Why hadn't he memorised the hospital's number? Why had he spent eight two-hour sessions talking about 'why pain is good' and pretending to be the father of Tess's unborn child, but hadn't managed to remember a simple telephone number?

'Hello, yes, can I have someone on delivery? Patient's name is Tess Franklin. She's in labour.'

'First-time mother?'

'Yes.' He swung the telephone out so that the midwife might be able to hear the throaty bellows from the spare room. 'Please, I'm not supposed to be at the birth.'

'The chances are it's the early stages. How often are the contractions coming?'

'All the time.'

'Have you timed them?'

'No, but they're every minute, at least. She's in pain.'

'Mishe, come here!' Tess screamed.

'Listen,' he told the midwife as he thrust the

157

phone out for her to hear. 'She's in agony. This must be labour. Or she's dying.'

Tess was briefly released from her possession to give Michael a look of pure hatred. 'I need to shit.' Michael really didn't like the swearing. Or the nudity. Or—he glanced at her again—the sweat. 'I need to shit.' And he really wasn't going to like *that*.

'She says she needs to go to the toilet,' he said to the midwife. 'I mean the loo,' he added for Tess's benefit, knowing that she had always thought his use of the words pardon and toilet oh so very common.

'Can she speak to me?'

He put the phone towards Tess, who was on all fours, just like she had practised in the sweaty bean-bag-filled room at their antenatal classes. She shook her head and shouted again, 'I need to shit.'

'Oh dear. It doesn't sound like you've got time to get to hospital,' said the midwife.

'What? She needs to go to the loo, she's not going to give birth.' Michael's voice had become squeaky.

'It sounds like she's ready to push. You stay on the line and I'll get an ambulance sent over. Try to get her not to push yet. We don't want her tearing. Just tell her to keep calm and not to push. Have you got that?'

Tess began panting. He covered her raised bottom with her dressing gown and massaged the bottom of her spine, only for her to knock his hand away, hard. She ripped off her dressing gown. Michael looked away.

'Get behind me!' she screamed. Michael felt like he did around horses, remembering that you're never supposed to stand there in case they kick you in the teeth. He grabbed the phone and moved, gibbering into it, calling for the woman who, by appearing at the end of the line, might be able to teletransport herself into the spare room at Tess's art-filled flat.

'Hang on, Tess. You're doing brilliantly.' He was an actor, he told himself, an actor in a medical drama. This was the only way to get through it. 'Don't push, don't push. The ambulance is on its way. Don't push.'

'I'm going to die. It's killing me. She's killing me.' Another groan. 'I never wanted a baby, I don't want this baby. Get it out of me. Get it out of me. Take it away.'

Michael looked again. Two large turds oozed out at his eye level. He grabbed two of the oversized international art magazines from the pile by the bed and scraped up the mess on the floor, and was amazed at just how much it was like picking up the dog poo left by his nephew's puppy. He gagged. Tess seemed unaware of what she had just done. Michael wondered whether he'd ever be able to tell her.

'Oh god,' he said and then shouted it down the phone.

Tess had been stolen and replaced by one of the hippies from the active birth DVDs. Her hair had become dank and floppy, her body shameless. She was transported into a trance, she was a member of the congregation at a born-again Christian service. She moaned and keened.

Just when he thought it couldn't get any worse, Michael was faced with something so horrific that try as he might, he'd never be able to forget it. It was an image that would sit at Tess's shoulder for the rest of their lives, it was like one of those faded spectres of gargoyles that they find when they clean up old paintings, which then forever co-exist with the beautiful public face of the canvas.

Tess was still on all fours, with Michael behind her, when, accompanied by a straining sound, something emerged from her. Although he knew which hole it was coming out of, from where he was sitting it looked like it was emerging from the same place as the shit had two minutes earlier. There, for a second, was a head poking out in the middle of two buttocks. He could have sworn that two eyes opened within that gunk-encrusted ball and looked at him. For a second, Michael found himself staring at the face of this boil on his beloved cousin's bottom. He was sure that the baby was viewing him with an expression of superiority, Tess's genes passed on to the next generation, the family dynamic continuing.

Just as Tess's body was being possessed, so some other force took over Michael. He could do it; he *would* do it.

'Tess, you're doing brilliantly. The ambulance is on its way, but so is your baby. Try not to push. Or maybe another big push. I think we're going to have to do this on our own.' How was he supposed to stop her tearing? 'Don't push, blow on your arm, don't you remember? Blow on your arm. The slower it comes out the better.' Was that right? Or would that mean that the baby would be starved of oxygen?

Another bellow and the head emerged again.

'It's going to kill me,' she shouted. To Michael it did seem like a battle between the baby and Tess, and only one of them was going to survive. Another push. 'I'm going to die.' She's going to die, oh god, she's going to die.

This time the head emerged and stayed out. She was now squatting. The flesh of her thighs was splayed and she had become solid, earthy, not the willowy woman he had loved for so long. He had never been any good at ball games but some sporting instinct kicked in and he held out his hands to catch the bloody sludge that slithered out from within. He felt bad about the carpet, but it would have to go now that it would be a nursery. Perhaps Sierra would be able to incorporate it into her decorating scheme—she had some quite outré ideas.

He held the sprite in his hands and once again they exchanged glances of mutual suspicion. 'Is she OK?' shouted Tess.

'No. I mean, yes, all seems fine, there's toes and fingers and everything. But it's not a she. It's a he. It's a boy.' He laughed at the surprise of it, the fact that it was a baby more shocking than its gender, somehow.

'That's its umbilical cord, idiot. It's a girl.'

'No, it's not. It's a boy—look.' A tiny shrivelled button of a thing, covered in blood, proved his point. 'You've got a baby boy.' Michael had expected to find himself aware of the cliché, the seen-it-a-thousand-times miracle of birth, but he wasn't. He was unique, this baby was unique, and so were they. He didn't fall in love with it at first sight, like they say that parents will, he fell into a relationship that was already complex. He started weeping. The weight of responsibility hung so heavy that he cried with relief that he was not the father and he cried with sadness that he was not.

161

And then the baby began to cry. It was a sound that would soon punctuate Michael's nights, a sound that he would hear in a dog's bark, he would hear when he was away from the boy, but at that moment it was a wonderful noise, the best he'd ever heard.

He manoeuvred the baby round, a task made difficult by the umbilical cord. He handed the baby to an equally naked and bloody Tess. He was distracted by her stomach being almost exactly the same shape as it had been ten minutes before, except no longer hard and fecund, but slightly paunchy. She'd lost at least a stone, though, he knew that from the pregnancy books—the quickest way to lose weight that there was.

'Skin-to-skin contact?' he asked, dredging what memories he could from all those classes. She shook her head and waved the baby away. She seemed to be dripping from every pore, sweat sheened across her body, tears pouring, blood gushing.

He knew he was supposed to think that she had never looked more lovely.

What a lie. Michael was startled, repulsed. She looked a mess, she looked revolting. Tess, who never did; Tess, who had always been a picture of perfection and elegance. He wondered whether he'd ever be able to see anything other than the baby coming out from her bottom and her present bloody nakedness.

'Come on,' he said again, keen to pass the baby over and to separate himself from the umbilical cord that bound him to Tess.

She acquiesced. Leaning against the bed, she held the baby to her breast. Michael smiled at the

162

sight, beginning as it was to resemble the Madonna-and-child image that he had envisaged. He found her dressing gown and wrapped it around her shoulders.

'I'll take a photo,' he said.

'Thank you.' She looked down at the infant. There was no suspicion or fear in her expression. It was almost blank. 'A boy. Me, who never really liked them. Except for you, my darling, of course.' She gave a little laugh, a small step back towards herself.

'Sorry about your carpet.'

'Don't worry, Sierra will probably want to frame the placenta.'

They looked at each other. 'Shit,' said Michael. 'The placenta. It's supposed to come out.'

'I never really got that part.' She continued looking down at the boy with a detached curiosity.

'Third stage, it's called. I think we wanted a managed one. Managed by someone who's not me.'

'What happens? Look, he's on my breast. He knows. How completely weird.'

The doorbell went.

'Thank god,' said Michael, who wondered whether his faith was undergoing a revival.

'I'm the midwife,' said a portly Irish woman, who was accompanied by a second midwife who looked barely old enough to give birth, let alone help other women to do so. Fantastic, thought Michael, looking at the first one—she's the very matronly marvel I was hoping for. 'My word, seems we're late. May I?' She set about cutting the cord and gently took the boy away to weigh him using rudimentary scales and flannels, while the second midwife began examining the carnage around

163

Tess's legs. 'My, my, we are a good-sized boy—four kilos. That's more than eight and a half pounds, a bonny weight for a baby.'

'Eight and a half pounds,' echoed Michael. 'No wonder it hurt. What about the placenta thing?'

'We wait for it to come out from mum,' said the Irish midwife. 'Sure it won't be long now. And because you've had a home birth, however accidental, there may well be no reason for you to go into hospital at all.'

Tess's face was less blurry now; some of those feline features of hers had sharpened once more. 'I don't suppose it will be a problem with the placenta. I've managed to do everything so far, haven't I?' The midwives would hear bravado, but Michael heard a vulnerability that had been born with the boy.

Michael saw both the midwives' eyes go towards her bloodied vagina. He wasn't sure Tess was going to be left as intact from the experience as she'd hoped.

'Your baby certainly seems a happy chap. Ten out of ten on his Apgar,' said the first midwife.

'His first exam,' said Michael, 'and he's passed with flying colours.'

'And now he's at mum's breast like a real pro,' the midwife added.

'Guzzling away,' said Tess. 'Guzzler. Gussy guzzler. Gus. I think I might call him Gus, what do you think? Augustus, maybe, on account of his being born in August. No, Augustine. Augustine Franklin.'

Michael thought that it sounded like the name of an octogenarian American patriarch whose name is always followed by the suffix 'the third',

164

but he nodded in agreement. His teacher's instinct for playground taunts kicked in. 'Augustin', he's disgustin'.' It seemed sort of appropriate, as he watched the boy child squirm at his mother's breast.

*   *   *

Even a day later, Lucy couldn't stop feeling the lines that ran from her nose to her lips. Or not the lines, exactly, because they were now gone, but the small thread of foreign matter that had taken their place. She would wiggle her fingers over it compulsively, in the same way that you would stick your tongue into the gap left by a wisdom tooth removal or stroke a newly manicured nail. It felt funny, the little tube of otherness where what Amanda had referred to as her 'nasolabial lines' had once been. Not unpleasant, just different.

It seemed impulsive of her to have got even the Botox there and then, but it was not as if she hadn't been thinking of it for months. She'd done her research into prices and best practitioners, possible side effects, and exact dosage to achieve a natural, unvarnished look. She had used her professional skills to do a cost-benefit analysis in which she took into consideration the importance of staying reasonably young looking in the workplace, especially when you were as client- and media-facing as she was.

So it wasn't rash of her to have said, 'Yes, you're right, there is no time like the present.'

'You'll feel a small prick,' Amanda had said and Lucy giggled, a juvenile reaction that she put down to nerves.

She had watched the needle hover above her

and known that she could still say stop, no, it's wrong, I'm not anti-ageing, how can anybody be anti-ageing when the alternative is dying? But she didn't. She said, her speech becoming as juvenile as she hoped her skin would be, 'Bring it on.'

And so it was. The Botox hadn't hurt, anyway. There was an argument that it was no different, in political terms, to dyeing your hair, and certainly it was considerably less painful than eyebrow threading (a procedure that made Lucy feel so nauseous that she'd have taken an anaesthetic if it were on offer). There was just an almost pleasant cold numbness.

'That's your elevens done,' Amanda had said.

Lucy had looked quizzical. Well, at least she supposed she had looked quizzical, but she wasn't sure at this point whether anything was moving. She remembered having an epidural when Rosa was born and being told to push and having no idea whether she was or not, so instead she concentrated on screwing up her face into a pushing expression to make up for what she guessed was a lack of movement down there. Now, she spoke to compensate for the lack of puzzlement on her face. 'What do you mean?'

'Your frown lines. Some people have ones, others elevens. You have a very defined eleven. Well, you did have.' Amanda gave a tinkly laugh. All these cute little euphemisms for the enemies about to be annihilated by the practitioners—they spoke of tear troughs, apple cheeks and horizontals, instead of lines and wrinkles like a normal person.

'Now for your forehead.'

Elevens were one thing, her brow another. 'I don't want it to look like a skating rink. I don't want my eyebrows to look raised. Or one higher than the other. Or like I'm wearing a wax mask on top of my face. You know, like that photo I showed you.'

What would Lucy tell people? By people, she meant Jamie. Or would she be like those glassy-faced actresses who always admit that they 'tried it once, but it wasn't for me', despite all appearances to the contrary, as if telling a little bit of truth made up for the subsequent lie.

'Here goes,' said Amanda.

Again, nothing. Lucy wished it had hurt more, that there had been some reflection of the enormity of what she was doing. The teeny tiny dot of pain wasn't enough. She wanted to self-flagellate in some way.

Amanda stood back to admire her work and then said, 'Are you sure you just want fillers in your nasolabials?' God, it sounded so rude, so gynaecological. Which of course made Lucy wonder if really she shouldn't be doing something down there next. 'If I pop something into your cheeks, it will lift your sagging jawline.'

It hadn't even occurred to Lucy before that her jawline might be sagging. Eyebrows, jaws, bottoms, stomachs, they all needed lifting. They weren't just anti-ageing, they were anti-gravity. Next she'd be told that breathing wasn't good for you, that the earth going round the sun must be stopped, that the double helix must be reshaped into something more aesthetically pleasing.

'I think that's fine,' said Lucy. 'For the moment. Do the nose–lip lines.'

Oh my god, the pain. The shock of it. Like a thousand eyebrow hairs being threaded all at once. The thought of it, too, as she felt the needle scrape along the insides of her flesh—like when the dentist's anaesthetic injection scratches across your gum, but so much worse. It had looked so small, but it felt as though someone had inserted an Allen key deep within her cheeks and was wrenching it. She felt sick as she felt Amanda massage the foreign matter into the desired crevices. *If this is non-invasive, what would be considered an invasion?* She felt as though a worm was burrowing through her lines and spawning. She couldn't believe that she would look anything less than misshapen and lumpen; it felt as if Ned's foam football was being pushed into a pocket beneath her skin. She almost passed out. She tried to screw up her face with the pain of it, but realised that she couldn't do that, she couldn't express that emotion any more.

'Now,' said Amanda, looking pleased with the results, not horrified as Lucy felt. 'The fillers will take effect immediately, though many of my clients say that they look even better after a day or two. The full effects of the Botox will take up to a couple of weeks to show. I've been cautious, so it might be that you'll need a top-up. Which is of course complimentary.'

Cautious? How could she have been, when the results felt so reckless? Lucy felt her whole face puffing up, but her brain contracting into a thumping headache.

'Here, take a look.'

Lucy stared at the mirror in shock. *Oh my god,* she thought, rounding out each word in her head. *I don't look that different.*

She looked at Amanda, who was smiling. 'See, the filler around your mouth. Stunning, isn't it? But as I say, you won't really see the full difference for a couple of weeks. That's the joy of it.'

'But,' said Lucy, 'I feel so different.' How can I feel so strange, yet look so like I always have?

'Great, great.'

Lucy's fingers went to her forehead. It felt the way it always had to her touch; perhaps a little more tender at the site of the injections, but on the outside, normal. From the inside it felt as though someone had replaced her tissue with epoxy resin.

She had floated home in a taxi, having not yet formulated what she was going to say to her family. The kids had been playing at a friends' house while Jamie was off, as ever, busy with aliens. She'd made sure she'd kept her face behind an ajar door and didn't think that anything had been noticed until Rosa asked her what the 'hurty' pinpricks on her forehead were and Lucy had fobbed her off with an excuse about a red biro. Rosa, with her obsession with looking at photos of herself and discussing which teachers at school were the prettiest, must never, ever know.

She waited for Jamie. And waited. He came back long after she had gone to bed.

The next day she wondered what he would say. Her face had puffed up so much that her eyes had shrunk. She did look younger, yes, but younger with an anaphylactic reaction to peanuts.

Jamie said nothing.

Either he hadn't spotted it, or he didn't care enough to say anything. She didn't know which was worse. She wondered if she put a Post-it with a big 'check this out' scrawled across it upon her forehead whether he'd notice. Probably not. She realised that if you live with someone, you never really look at each other as you swap timetables and instructions.

Someone at work had asked her if she was wearing tinted moisturiser. To the rest of the world, then, she looked no different. She knew that Amanda would tell her that this was exactly the subtle effect they had been looking for. But it still seemed strange to her that she should look the same, but feel so different. The first time she tried to yawn she found that she couldn't, which only made her want to yawn all the time. She had to wear sunglasses outside at all times because she could no longer squint. She felt permanently detached from the world, as if she were viewing it from a coma. She cancelled all meetings for fear of giving herself away. She needed the time to escape and finger her face with the worms of foam within it. She was supposed to feel confident and sexy, to be able to seduce Jamie with her newfound youth and vigour. He hadn't even noticed. She sat on a bench in the park at lunchtime wondering if she'd ever feel anything again.

Her phone bleeped to tell her she had a message. The sunlight was bright on her screen and now she couldn't squint to see it better. It was from Tess.

'We did it! Augustine George Franklin born 5 a.m., a whopping four kilos. Inadvertent home birth, love Michael.'

Michael had assumed the mantle of modern fatherhood and its first task: the sending of the text announcement. Lucy stared at the phone in confusion, at first thinking it must be from a different Michael. She stripped the message down to its constituent parts but it made even less sense. Augustine, was that a boy's name? Tess was supposed to be having a girl. Born? She was only 38 weeks pregnant and first babies were always late. And early babies were always small; this one wasn't. At home? With Michael? Lucy was supposed to be the birth partner. And what sort of person uses the word 'inadvertent', spelt correctly, in a text?

She was momentarily distracted by the odd sensation of not being able to frown at her phone in disbelief.

*   *   *

Owen got the text too, but was distracted by news of his own. His father, like Tess, didn't make it to the hospital on time. Tess had a home birth and Gareth had a home death.

They weren't even sure what time he'd died. Mari had passed by Gareth's office and glanced in but, only seeing a figure hunched over the computer who didn't bother to respond to her twittering queries, thought it was business as usual. 'He's on the Internet again,' she said to Owen, when he'd made his customary phone call to check on his father's health. 'He must be all right.'

It was only when Gareth didn't come down to make himself the usual Spartan lunch of a slice of corned beef on chewy rye bread that she dared enter his fortress. He wasn't hunched but slumped. She turned his body, and his face was white and indented with the keyboard. She screamed so hard that the neighbours had come round and called the doctor but everyone knew that it was too late.

'It's your father,' said that nice Mr Jenkins when he called Owen. It was a call that he had been dreading for so long that he felt relieved to receive

171

it, finally. He'd always pictured it, with some ghoulish relish, as his father lying on a hospital bed, his breathing constructed by a machine, until the rasp turned into a rattle. Before that, though, but nearly at the end, his father would manage to splutter out the truth about Owen's birth parents. To which Owen was supposed to say, 'You're all the father I've ever needed, Dad.'

As his father had said, nobody got good death scenes any longer.

The emphysema hadn't got him, anyway. As far as anybody could tell, his dying breaths had been the same as his daily breaths. They reckoned he'd had a heart attack, just like any other octogenarian. They'd got so used to thinking of him as an ill man, that they'd forgotten he was also an old one.

Owen had continued working at his office computer for half an hour before he'd rung Ruby.

'Owen, ohmigod,' she had screeched. 'I'm so sorry. I'm really sorry. I feel awful. I'm so upset, oh god, I can't breathe.' This continued for a few minutes. 'I should be with you. I really should, you shouldn't be without me at this moment. Still, at least he got to meet his new daughter-in-law before he went. That must have been a comfort to him. At the end of the day, he had that.'

He got into his car and drove straight to his parents', not stopping at the flat, knowing that he had a toothbrush and spare pair of pants there and could always wear an old pair of cords belonging to his father. Had belonged to his father. Who wasn't his father, anyway.

Mari already seemed a lesser woman. She had been elevated by her marriage. Owen had always thought she couldn't be quite so silly as she appeared to have made a man like Gareth fall in love with her. Now she just seemed like a woman who wore her dyed blonde hair far too long and her skirts far too short.

'Don't leave me,' she cried. 'I can't sleep here alone.'

'I'll stay the night,' he said. 'Of course I will.'

'In my bedroom. I can't sleep in this room alone.' Owen glanced towards the bed. It was an old-fashioned double, half the size of Owen's, which was the biggest available. Bed size inflation had so worked its effect that the one in front of him held the appearance of a single. That generation seemed to be able to sleep in beds far narrower than his own, their men wore shorts that were far shorter.

'Couldn't Caron come?' he asked.

'I don't want Caron. I need a man.' She was a drag queen mid-rendition.

'I'll sleep on the zed-bed.' The one with the springs that coiled their way into your back in the night.

'In my room. Please, in my room.'

When Owen got Michael's text birth announcement the next day, he was so exhausted with grief, the discomfort of a 1960s camp bed and the squeamishness of listening to his mother's sleeping-pill-filled slumber that he felt no response to the news that he'd become a godfather. Clearly a response was deemed necessary as Michael phoned him that afternoon.

'Tess is wondering whether you got the text.' Michael sounded chirpy, high on something.

'Sorry, yes. Very exciting. I'm thrilled, couldn't be more so. How is she?'

'Exhausted. Lost lots of blood. The birth was fine, but I thought she was going to die when they were pulling out the placenta. She's not supposed to use a mobile on the ward, hence me calling on her behalf.'

'Isn't she in a private room?'

'They won't let her. She needs to be under observation because of bits of the placenta being left inside her—too disgusting, can you imagine?—so they've kept her on a ward. Can you picture it? Tess on a ward? She's surrounded by little Bangladeshi women and their very large families. If it weren't for the fact that she's so mad with hormones I think she'd be getting very truculent about it all. How funny, motherhood's mellowed her already. When do you want to visit? I'm the slot-monitor. Could probably fit you in tomorrow.'

'I'm at my parents' house.'

'Nothing wrong, I hope.'

Owen paused. 'It's fine.'

'But when are you back?' If Michael hadn't been so high on sleep deprivation and drama he might have been able to interpret Owen's tone.

'I'll be driving back tomorrow to pick up some stuff . . .'

'Perfect, you can come then. I'll try to get all the godparents to visit in one day.'

*   *   *

Sierra wasn't particularly surprised by the text. She hadn't even been sure when exactly the baby was due, so it didn't seem early to her. Was a home birth actually at home, or was it like those posh invitations that her father's mother had on her mantelpiece that said 'At Home' when they meant a drinks party held in a gentlemen's club?

After much telephone tennis, she finally got to speak to Michael the following day. 'Tell me the gruesome details.'

'It's too gruesome,' said Michael. 'It still is gruesome. She looks like something from a Victorian novel.'

'I bet it wasn't. I bet she just coughed it out and now wonders why others don't find it as easy as she did.'

'True-ish. It was really quick. I think I found it more painful than she did and he was a big bugger too. Just when we were feeling smug and high about how well we'd managed on our own, the placenta got stuck. Then I realised why women die in childbirth.'

'Stuck where?' said Sierra. She didn't really understand the mechanics.

'Up her. Wherever placentas live.'

'Aren't you supposed to fry it and eat it?'

'Well, we might have done if it had come out, but instead we had to rush off into hospital where they drugged her and tugged it out, literally pulled the umbilical cord and she haemorrhaged and it was disgusting and in comparison childbirth was as easy as, I don't know . . .'

'Shitting?' suggested Sierra.

Michael shivered as he thought of how closely the two acts seemed connected. 'I suppose. Oh god, Sierra, it was terrible. There was blood everywhere and this head came out and he looked at me. It was like something out of *Total Recall*.'

'Where are you now?'

'Standing outside the hospital, where the

175

smokers go. And I don't even smoke.'

'Can I come and see her?'

'She'd love that. Lucy's coming in her lunch break. Why don't you shut the gallery up early this afternoon and come then?'

Sierra was interrupted by the nagging child of her phone telling her there was another call waiting. She glanced at it and saw the word 'Susie' flashing up. 'I've got to go.' She cut him off and pressed the answer button.

'Mum?' Please let it be her.

'Sierra, babe, you've got to help me.'

'Mum, are you all right? Where are you?'

'I think I've fucked up again.'

CHAPTER ELEVEN

PHARMACEUTICALS

'She's gone off to wait for the paediatrician,' said Michael to Lucy as they sat in moulded plastic chairs by the side of Tess's hospital bed. Lucy noticed there were bloodstains on the sheets and felt embarrassed by the intimacy. 'There are these endless appointments that happen at random times and apparently it was bedlam last night.'

'I remember that from Rosa and Ned. The babies all have an agreement with each other to cry in shifts so that nobody gets any sleep.'

'It just seems so rude, somehow, that she should be getting no sleep having just given birth. It's like you have to run a marathon and then you don't even get a bit of kip afterwards.'

'How is Augustine?' She said the name self-consciously, as so far she'd only ever seen it written down and, let's face it, it wasn't as if Tess had opted for the name John.

'Gus, we're calling him. Ridiculously gorgeous. I might be biased but when I look at the other babies on the ward, I want to weep for them, they're so hideous in comparison.'

'Why are they being kept in?'

'They want to keep an eye on Tess, because of the haemorrhaging. And Augustine's got a spot of jaundice. Can't let them go home until he looks a little bit less like one of the Simpsons. Bright yellow, he is. It's all just so annoying that after we managed to do it, the birth—'

'We?'

'Oh you know, I was there.'

'I'm sorry about that; you know how I wanted to be the birth partner.'

'You and me both.' Michael gave a theatrical little shudder. 'Oh god, Lucy, it was hell.' She patted him on the arm and he glanced at her. 'You look different.'

'What do you mean?'

'Nothing.' She blushed, or at least she felt as though she blushed. Perhaps this was another cauterised function. He so knows, she thought—despite all the concealer I've trowelled over the bruising, he was just the type to be able to spot work at 100 paces. There was no right way—she was either offended by people not noticing or mortified when they did. 'You were saying, about the birth.'

'Yes, that she did all the birth bit so well and then the stupid placenta wouldn't come out, and now the jaundice. We could have avoided the whole

177

hospital bit altogether and here we are. We'd have been quicker out of here if she'd had a caesarean.'

'How is she?' Lucy didn't know whether she wanted to see her or not. The blood on the sheets had been enough to forewarn her of the incongruity of glorious Tess made mortal by childbirth. She was certainly desperate to see the yellow-hued Gus. When she had first had Rosa she'd felt repulsed by older women grabbing at the baby and wanting to hold her, strangers in cafés asking her questions and pulling back Rosa's blanket. Now that she had left those wondrous hallucinogenic early years behind, she found herself acting just as those women had—crowding newborns, feeling inside the bubble of broodiness that unhappily co-existed with the equally strong belief that she should have no more children. It was Tess's turn now. She would bounce her baby over cappuccinos with other mothers, she'd feel both bored and fascinated by talk of breastfeeding and purees.

Michael frowned. Lucy envied him that ability. 'I don't know. Dazed. I thought she'd be all, you know, Tess-like, about how easy it was, but she oscillates between looking bored and looking terrified.'

'No self-satisfaction whatsoever?'

He laughed. 'There are occasional glimmers of smuggery.'

'Thank god for that.'

'I'm bored of looking at this bed. Let's go for a wander, see if we can find her. I think she said she was having to go down to the first floor to see the paediatrician.'

As they walked, Lucy felt sure he was examining her face. Stop it, she thought, why did you get it done if you didn't want people to look at you? Tonight—no, he's out tonight—this week, definitely this week, she was going to use her newfound youth to seduce Jamie. That had been the point of it, after all. Perhaps she should have been tightened up down there too. That wasn't youthful. She wondered whether Tess would be unable to bounce carelessly on a trampoline ever again. It was one of the ironies of motherhood that before you have children, you never have any need to bounce on a trampoline, yet afterwards, when you're always being dragged onto them, you're unable to do so without fear of embarrassment.

'There she is,' said Michael. 'In my dressing gown. Silly thing had packed the most inappropriate clothing.'

Lucy saw Tess in the corridor carrying a baby wrapped in a waffle blanket. She was surprised and, shamefully, gratified that she had that post-partum-yet-still-six-months-pregnant look that normal women sported.

They hugged and Lucy felt a burst of love that surprised her. She had always worshipped Tess, but this was something different.

'Don't squash him,' Michael warned.

'Oh yes,' said Tess. 'The baby.'

'Gus,' said Michael. 'Isn't he absolutely gorgeous?'

'Oh, Tess! He's perfect.' Lucy's eyes welled up. The Botox, it seemed, had not jammed up her tear ducts. 'I know it's clichéd, but just look at his tiny hands. And his eyes, that extraordinary slate-blue colour they go. And his feet, they're minute.'

'Quite big, actually,' said Tess, as if she were describing a sofa she was thinking about buying for

179

her living room.

'I know. But still, just so miniature. Can I?' Tess shrugged her assent. 'And the smell.'

As they passed the lift, the doors opened and a wheelchair was pushed out. 'Ouch, watch out,' said Tess as it careered into her leg.

'Sorry,' said the porter manoeuvring it. Tess looked shocked, though it could hardly have hurt her at all.

'You've got to be careful,' said Michael. 'You don't want anyone to end up in hospital.' On seeing the porter's stricken face, he added, 'Joke.'

Tess walked quickly ahead and started jabbing the entry buttons to the ward.

The porter frowned at her back and then looked towards Lucy and Gus. 'Cute baby,' he said, in a pronounced Eastern European accent.

Michael put his arm around Lucy. 'Yes, we're very proud.'

Lucy wondered whether he enjoyed the charade as much as she did. She found herself leaning into his arms as she did her best Madonna-and-child smile down at Gus.

*   *   *

Sierra locked up the gallery and got home as fast as London Transport allowed. Which was not very fast at all. The inefficiencies of the Underground allowed her to think over what Susie had said to her, the many layers of which she tried to process.

'I think I've fucked up again.' Again. Like the time she forgot to pick Sierra up from primary school and didn't turn up for three days. Or when she decided that it would do Sierra good to live

180

with her dad for a while, necessitating a change of schools in the year she was supposed to be doing some of her GSCEs. Or when she thought it would be funny to put some hash into the brownies for the PTA cake sale. There was the time when she took it upon herself to tell Sierra and her nice friend Jessica the facts of life in the middle of a fantastical fairy story, despite Jessica's parents not being party to this decision.

'I had some stuff,' Susie continued, 'that I brought over from Spain, for a friend. That I was supposed to give to another friend. And I forgot. Well, I didn't forget. I gave him half and then I was supposed to get the other half to him, which I'd left in the flat, you know as a guarantee, but then I went to a party and overslept and was going to miss my plane back to Spain—I got these cheap flights that gave me only one night in London, sorry love I'd have loved to have seen you but I didn't have time and you weren't at home when I went there—and then, I don't know, silly me, you know what I'm like. It's complicated, but there was a good reason why I forgot. So now he's going to pick it up, no hassle for you, but you have to go and find it for him at home and let him in. I'm trying to make it as easy as poss for you. You don't have to go out of your way at all.'

'Stuff?'

'Bits and pieces. Look, sweetheart, my phone's low on juice. I just need you to get home and give it to a bloke called Jason. He'll be round at one or something.'

Sierra suddenly understood how Susie was funding her life in Spain. She was an idiot not to have suspected it earlier. 'Basically, you're asking

181

me to do a drug deal for you?'

'No, not drugs. Just a bit of hash. Don't get all priggy on me, darling, it's the last favour I'll ask of you, I promise. You'd better get going—it's in a duty-free bag in the jewellery box that's inside an old washing-powder box in the locked cupboard under the sink. Chop chop and all that.'

Chop chop? What was this, a trip to the races? Sierra decided that she had no choice but to dash home, trying to make sense of what should happen as she travelled. By the time she got out of the station, she was no nearer to knowing what the correct thing to do was, either ethically or as a daughter. The two, she was sure, were incompatible. Maybe when she saw the bag and its contents it would become clear. A teeny-weeny bit of weed was going to do no one any harm. Perhaps this Jason bloke would be quite nice and it would all be fine.

In the flat she soon found the box and the bag within. Her knowledge of drugs was limited to the usual occasional spliff and pills. As she began to open the bag, she made a decision: if it's just weed, I'll do it. Please let it just be weed or hash or whatever. Inside the duty-free bag (oh, the banality), there were some freezer bags, the expensive type that have their own ziplock. Not the sort that Susie would ever have invested in for Sierra's sandwiches, or for putting leftover herbs in the freezer. Some of these contained stuff that looked reassuring, like the insides of a herbal tea bag. Others, though, held little cellophane knots of white stuff. And then there were some, bizarrely, that had powder the lurid pink colour of candy floss. It wasn't exactly a factory's load of gear. It

182

didn't look like those sacks of drugs that you see on the news when they get a drug haul. Maybe it isn't even what I think it is, anyway, she considered. I mean, Morocco, southern Spain—that's got to be just weed, hasn't it?

She sat on the bed feeling panicked that she could no longer stick to her decision with ease. Her resolution evolved: if Jason comes in the next five minutes, I'll just do it. The hands on the clock moved slowly round.

After four minutes there was nothing.

Five, six, seven. Sierra felt as though she was in a trance. Or a television programme about the drug squad. She wasn't quite the prude her mother thought her, she wasn't totally naïve about narcotics, obviously—there wasn't anybody her age who was. But what she knew about drug dealing was confined to the kids from school who she always avoided in the classroom because they were all in the lower sets and who mostly left her alone outside. There were a couple who were now in jail and another one was dead. Oh shit, shit, shit. Sierra hadn't hated her mother as much as this since she'd pretended to be her sister to the first boy Sierra had ever really liked.

Eight minutes. Sierra willed the doorbell to go, but instead she heard another sound. A police siren, and it was coming nearer. She ran to the windows at the back of the flat, but couldn't see anything. She opened the door that led out to the walkways and the entrance of the buildings and she could see at the front of the estate, three police cars congregated and officers and dogs emerging from them fast.

Shit, shit, shit. What do people in television

183

shows do now? They flush it down the loo. She ran into the bathroom and looked down into the toilet bowl. Susie had once thrown a Tampax down there and all of the flats in block C had been backed up for weeks. They never show that in the TV shows. She'd have to open up all the bags and throw away the plastic wrappers. But she'd have to clean them out first. And then if the police caught her, she'd be done for concealing the evidence or dispensing with illegal substances or something. She could leave it here for the dogs to find and then blame her mother. Or go out there and confess all—well, confess all on behalf of Susie. I don't want my mum in jail. But she needn't be. She could stay in Spain forever. Do they have extradition with Spain now? She looked out again and saw that the police and their sniffers were running towards block B, known as 'the Bollocks', as it was the worst bit of the estate.

Sierra bundled a few clothes and Susie's very much duty-free goods into a bigger bag and then walked out as calmly as she could. She must have a few minutes before they came out of the flat of those dodgy blokes whose doorbell rang at strange times of the day and night. She walked down the stairs, keeping to the side as far from block B as she could, then out to the front of the estate. She tried to go slowly, to look nonchalant, in that way you find yourself doing when you go through the 'nothing to declare' channel at customs—the difference being that usually you find yourself faking that innocent look even though you really haven't got anything to hide.

She kept walking and didn't look back.

Owen was steeling himself to celebrate a new life when he saw Sierra standing outside the hospital, pacing as though she were the expectant father.

'Hello, darling, what's a gorgeous girl like you doing in a place like this?'

She didn't look particularly thrilled to be there, or to see him. 'Same as you, going to visit her ladyship.'

'I know, I was just . . . anyway, lovely to see you. Shall we?' He offered her his arm, glad of the distraction. You can do this. Owen was not a man usually given to introspection or symbolism, but even he couldn't fail to see the poignancy of the cycle of life and death that was being thrust upon him. Oh blah blah blah, he said to himself, dismissing any hint of sentimentality. 'May I carry your bag?'

She looked at him with the expression of one of those awful women who were offended when you offered them a seat on the tube. Not that he travelled by tube any more these days, thank god.

'I'm fine, thanks,' she said, clutching it nearer to her chest.

Funny, he hadn't had her down as a feminist type. Pity.

As they approached the security at the front desk, she stopped. 'Actually, I'm not sure I can face it. Not today.'

'Me neither.' He hadn't told Tess yet, but as he looked at Sierra's miserable face he felt the urge to outdo whatever was causing her mood. 'My dad's dead.'

'Owen, I'm so sorry. When?'

185

'Two days ago. He was old.'

'Still, that doesn't stop you feeling like an orphan. Though you can feel like that when your parents are still alive.' He liked the way the words always came rushing out with her, beyond the point when it was wise to stop. 'My dad said to me when his mother died that you're never too old to feel like an orphan. I felt awful when he said it because I was thinking that it felt like the first time I'd had a father, you know, because we were talking and stuff. You definitely can't go in there,' she gestured towards the hospital. 'So I guess that makes two of us.' She smiled for the first time and he was reminded of just how glorious it was. The uncharacteristic melancholy that had preceded it only added to her appeal.

He felt a kinship with her that he had so far failed to find with Ruby since his father's death. 'Do you fancy a drink, then?'

'Yes,' she said. 'A drink to parents. Wherever they may be.'

CHAPTER TWELVE

RESTORATION

Lucy couldn't remember ever actually having seduced Jamie. When they had met at the blood donor centre all those years ago, that they would sleep with each other had been as unstoppable as the blood flowing into the plastic bags and then on into the veins of some deserving patient.

They'd gone for coffee and held hands on the

way there as if that was a natural thing to do with someone whom you'd met while lying on an NHS bed. Lucy could have just gone straight home with him then and there, but they waited a couple of hours and a few drinks for respectability's sake. They had spoken of superficial things, but it seemed to Lucy as if they had already made a profound bond. There was something about the blood that did that, just as when she and her school friends had scratched their arms with compasses to let their fluids mingle. They'd called themselves blood sisters. Lucy's feelings for Jamie were definitely not sisterly.

They had hailed a taxi to her house, the one that she had bought with Mark, the one with the bathroom he had grouted, the Edwardian hall tiles restored so lovingly and the cornices that he had cleaned out with a toothbrush.

On the way in, Jamie hardly glanced at these reminders of Lucy's previous life, instead he stared at Lucy without self-consciousness. She looked back at him and the jeans hanging off his skinny frame and the T-shirt with the name of a band she'd never heard of. She filed this under second most erotic moment of her life (the first would always be the blood-pumping moment at the donor centre. She knew even then that it would never be beaten). Then he crossed the hall and they kissed and he lifted up her dress, while scrabbling for a handily placed condom in his pocket. She smiled that he should have been so sure. She pulled down her tights and knickers inelegantly and pulled him into her. He was hard, she was wet, it was perfect. He came quickly, just as she had wanted him to. She was lying diagonally halfway up the stairs. It should have been awkward and uncomfortable, but it wasn't; it was ideal for him to put his head between her thighs and finish her off in less than a minute. He was only the second man she'd slept with since Mark and she found herself even loving the whole condom thing, given that it meant he could lick her out without the yukky thought that he was effectively eating his own sperm, which was instead neatly sealed off in its own rubber bag and left lying somewhere on the floor, only to be found days later.

She shouted as she came and then laughed. She sat up and put her legs around his waist. She liked this wanton woman that she had become with him, most unlike the sensible Lucy of yore. He was so strong that he managed to manoeuvre them both up the stairs and into, what he wasn't to know then, the spare room.

'Can we do it again?' he asked, with the enthusiasm of a boy taking penalties.

She nodded, delighted at his energy.

* * *

But that was then. Lucy did one of the calculations of which she was so fond. They'd had sex more times that first day they'd met than they had all this year and most of last. She had read on the Internet that anything longer than six months counts as a sexless relationship.

That day they had met, he had entered both her and the house, filling them with himself, owning them.

'Wow, do you live here?' he'd asked when they finally lay still across the duvet of the spare room.

'Yes, of course.'

'Really?'

'It's not like I'd be doing this in a stranger's house.' That would be good, though, she had thought, I'd like to do it with him on the street, and in museums and in the sea. The words of the Dr Seuss books she had read as a child came unbidden to her: would you could you in a boat? Yes. It is so good, so good, you see. Now Lucy read those books with Rosa and Ned and would stifle a sad nostalgia about the words.

'It's not your parents' house?'

'No.'

'Wow. How many housemates have you got?'

'None. I had a boyfriend. Not any more. I bought him out.'

'You bought him?'

'His share of the house—we'd bought it together, you see.' Mortgages were clearly a foreign country to Jamie. It was one of the many differences between them that Lucy had found so charming back then.

'You're like an heiress,' he'd said with awe.

Lucy had often wondered since whether he fell in love with her or the house, which was, she later found out, disturbingly similar to the one where he'd grown up in Edgbaston. He went back to the flat where he was sharing the living-room floor with one of his film-maker mates to get his two stripy gypsy bags of stuff and never left. The spare room where they'd fucked was now their daughter's bedroom. The stairs where he'd first screwed her were littered with toys. The bath surrounded by Mark's grouting was now replaced with a power shower installed by Jamie, who'd taught himself

189

plumbing from the Internet. 'I might as well be constructive if I can't be creative,' he'd said, which at the time Lucy had taken as a good thing, but now she realised had been tinged with bitterness.

Meeting Gus, who'd gone from not existing to being a solid baby in the time since she'd last had sex, had made her more determined to carry through her intended seduction. Rosa had been dispatched to a friend's for a sleepover and Ned, bless him, would sleep through in his loft conversion eyrie. While Jamie cooked up a delicious meal, Lucy tried to do the same with a plan of action.

Seduction: the word conjured up a vision of her leaning against the bedroom doorway while wearing sexy lingerie. Everything about the concept was comic and/or dated. Her ideas of it seemed rooted in some sort of seventies sex comedy, a movie made before Jamie had even been born, before his parents had met. Hadn't things moved on at all from then? There was probably some cool, modern way, using a phrase like 'hook-up' and some obscure recreational drugs. She wondered whether to consult some Internet message boards in an attempt to be more modern, but even in their anonymity Lucy knew she would feel naked. She wanted to reserve that for the deed itself.

While she rejected this vision of Elizabeth Taylor in a Tennessee Williams play version of seduction, she was too unimaginative to think of an alternative. What would a magazine tell her to do? You perform a striptease. She could update that into a pole dance to show how down with the kids she was—the girls who Jamie hung out with probably did that in lieu of Lucy's staid old Pilates.

But the nearest thing they had to a pole was a standard lamp which would never bear her weight. You stroke each other all over, but don't actually do the penetration bit. This works you up into a frenzy of frustrated desire, apparently. Enough already, she had to have full-on sex. She looked in the larder for food that could be smeared on and licked off. Honey was too sticky, Nutella too messy. She turned to the fridge—sun-dried tomato paste, hummus, low-fat bio yoghurt? Too middle-class, especially if Jamie were lying across the pine kitchen table, on top of letters from the PTA and a copy of one of those free magazines that estate agents advertise in.

If food was out of the question, then she would just have to be tonight's meal.

Jamie was sitting at the table, watching the latest clips of his interminable film. Lucy had changed into the undies that she had bought for the occasion and deliberately avoided checking out her back view in the bathroom mirror.

She popped a dressing gown on, towelling, bulky, and stood behind him as he typed, massaging his shoulders.

'You're tense,' she said. She had on the rallying voice she used when trying to get everyone out of the house. All jolly and la-di-da, what a lovely day, isn't life such fun?

'Yeah, sort of stuck on this bit.'

'Can I help?'

'No.' Just as she had used her parental voice, he used the 'Well, der, of course not' voice of a small child. When she had chosen a younger man, she hadn't realised just how much younger than her he would feel.

She leaned forward and put her breasts into his hair. It was one of the most unerotic of moves. Every one of her orifices was desiccating with mortification.

He wriggled beneath her. She moved her hands down into his shirt. 'Sorry, Luce, but I really want to get this done.' He brushed her hand away.

She was just about to slink off, to say, 'Yes, of course, sorry. Well, good night then,' as she usually would, but the thought of the pain where the needle of fillers had entered her cheeks made her snap. She had done that for him. The effects of the Botox would wear off after a few months and she was determined to make the most of them while she supposedly looked young and lovely. She spun the swivel chair round. Standing while he sat made her feel bigger than him for the first time, but also mildly deranged, like she might be a psychotic carer with a wheelchair-bound patient she was about to push into a river.

'Look at me.' She dropped her robe and then immediately wished there was some way of picking it up and putting it on again, as it was quite chilly for August.

'Great, Luce, but really . . .'

'I mean look at me properly.' Actually, she thought, don't look at my body in these stupidly uncomfortable and unpractical contraptions that I decided it would be a good idea to wear. 'Look at me.' She squatted so that their faces were level. Amanda had told her that it would take a few days for the swelling to go down and up to two weeks for the full effects of the Botox to magic themselves into view. Maybe she should have waited. 'What do I need to do? We haven't had sex in . . . In a long time, and it's not good, it really isn't.'

'It's fine, Lucy, it's not important.'

'But it is.'

'I'm here, aren't I? I look after the kids. What more do you need?'

He walked out and into the night before she had time to answer.

When she had been doing her research into anti-ageing treatments, Lucy had read that having your frown lines frozen can not only make you look less sad, it can actually blunt your ability to feel that emotion. As she looked at the door that Jamie had slammed in his hurry to escape her, she wished that were true.

*   *   *

Owen and Sierra had gone out for cocktails. Many, many cocktails. Sierra had not spoken much and Owen, to his surprise, had talked a lot.

'Are you going to find out, then?' she asked when he'd told her the story of his birth and his father's death. 'Who your real parents are? I mean, your birth parents. Sorry, Owen, you know what I mean.'

'I do know, exactly.' He was touched at her apology. 'Yes I am.' There—he'd said it out loud for the first time, he was finally going to do it.

'It won't mean you love Gareth any less, you know. He sounds like he's a better parent than either of mine have ever been.'

He was pleased by her use of the present tense. 'You're right. But I couldn't have done it while he was still alive.'

'But you don't feel the same about your mum's

193

feelings. Adopted mum. You know.'

Owen snorted to try to convey how little he cared about Mari's well-being, but revoltingly, he just ended up spurting some of his martini out of his nose. Sierra laughed. 'Don't,' he said. 'Really not good for my image.'

'But it is. Makes you a bit less scary.'

'Which is a good thing?'

She nodded and looked away. Owen felt a sudden need both to parent her and be parented by her. She was so much bigger than Ruby, with generous tits that he'd be able to put his tired head upon. She'd make him feel better. Ruby was away at her nan's, the one who was younger and healthier than Owen's dad, as she had never failed to point out.

'What's in that bag of yours?' he asked.

'Nothing. Why?'

'I wondered if it might contain some overnight clothes.' He checked for her reaction. She looked relieved, as if she'd been waiting for this invitation for a lot longer than this evening. 'Shall we go, then?'

Owen was surprised by Sierra that night. Beneath all those outré outfits and inner-city attitude, she was all enthusiastic and gung ho in bed, as if she were actually one of those girls who'd been to boarding school and dotted their 'i's with hearts and had a taste for lacrosse. In addition, she was rather laissez-faire about contraception, it seemed, something he took care over since a series of unpleasant STDs in the late nineties and that business with the recurrent chlamydia and that weird anonymous letter. She rode him with eagerness and an endearing lack of cool, whooping

194

and at one point even slapping her thighs with the excitement of it all. Bits of her wobbled, which made a change from the aerobicised tautness of Ruby. Yet despite her size she seemed to take up less space in the flat than his fiancée. He had kicked one of the wedding magazines beneath the sofa in shame.

He fell straight to sleep for the first time since Gareth had died. From the unpromising start of a hospital visit, the evening had worked rather well, especially since there was little chance that Ruby would find out. In fact, he didn't see why this couldn't happen more often. He had no intention of leaving Ruby, he was engaged after all and this time he had to go through with it, but Sierra was a welcome distraction and one, if she was as relaxed as she seemed to be, he wouldn't mind occupying himself with again.

*   *   *

Michael sat by Tess's bed, watching and trying not to watch her stick her already chapped nipple into his godson's mouth. Her breasts were pumped up and hard, exactly as though she'd had unnecessary implants except unlike those that he had seen perched on the bony figures of actresses at red-carpet events, these were threaded with almost fluorescent veins and finished off with a nipple the size of a saucer. Like childbirth, he knew that it was something he should find beautiful.

'Can I get you a glass of water or anything?' He might not believe all that he'd read in those antenatal books, but he had at least read them.

She sighed. Tess had always liked to portray

herself as the girl with the crazy, wild life, but it was only now that something so unpredictable had entered the mix that Michael realised how in control she had always been. Now that she was no longer commanding events, Tess appeared to him like a superhero who'd lost their special power. She didn't even seem happy that at last she was being allowed to go home with Gus.

'Don't leave me,' she said.

'I'm not, silly. I'll get you a taxi and everything.'

'I mean, stay with me, at home, in the flat. I can't do this on my own, Michael. I never wanted to do it on my own.'

'Yes you did. Why, you orchestrated the whole thing, like you do everything. And sweetie, you do everything on your own. And very well, too. You'll be fine. Goodness, what a lot of stuff you've got. Are hospital porters like ones in hotels, do you think? Can I summon one and press a pound coin into his hand. What about that nice blond who crashed into you with his wheelchair? Bit of eye candy like that will cheer you up in no time.'

Tess frowned. 'I don't know what you're talking about.'

'OK, maybe not, guess I'll have to take all this stuff.' As he heaved the designer bag that they had so carefully yet inappropriately packed only a week before, he felt as though he were hauling it from a past life. Did all parents feel like this? He meant real ones, the real fathers—that going to hospital to have a baby meant leaving one sort of childhood behind overnight? The gratuitous and heavy buckles of Tess's overnight bag seemed symbolic of some sort of frivolity and uselessness. Part of him wanted to be divested of such fripperies, but most of him was screaming, I never wanted to do all this, not yet—I'm a boy, I'm still a boy. Tess had seemed to suggest that this had all happened against her will, when she had not only asked for it, she had presumably paid money for the privilege of getting knocked up.

He looked longingly towards the security door of the hospital and pictured himself running towards it and going into the street with nothing but his mobile, wallet and keys. He looked back at Tess, who was dressed in maternity clothes. When she had been pregnant they had been tight and glamorous, now they bagged and sagged. Like her body, he speculated.

'Of course I'll come with you, darling. I'll stay as long as you like.'

* * *

Sierra sat in Owen's bathroom. As the morning light poured in, she could examine her smudged make-up and blotchy skin. The cupboards were full of expensive female unguents. Ruby's, she assumed. She had been able to forget about Owen's fiancée last night, but her presence dominated this room, despite the Italian black marble and power shower that only a man would have bought. There was a pink flannel hanging off the sink, a cupboard full of make-up and Tampax, bottles of perfume and bowls full of hair accessories. Sierra felt squeamish about using another woman's products, which was ironic since she had felt no such shame in using her man.

That made it all sound so sordid, when it really hadn't been. They'd had sex, that was true, but afterwards he had held her and stroked her head.

'Darling girl,' he had said, smoothing back her hair. 'That was just what the doctor ordered. Not any doctor I've ever met, mind you, but a doctor I'd happily see privately.'

She had stood up, putting on one of his T-shirts to cover herself.

'Don't,' he said. 'You're gorgeous.'

It might have been a line, she wasn't stupid, but she loved it. They'd talked more in one night than she had in all her time with Josh. She liked him, she really liked him. He was good looking and older and had somewhere to live. Stupid Ruby, stupid cow. Did she know how lucky she was?

Things had been different in the morning. After all that warmth, she had been expecting more of the same with a good helping of croissants, but when she had woken up at dawn, Owen was marooned on the other side of the bed. She knew she shouldn't ask questions, but she couldn't help herself.

'So,' she said. 'Did you always fancy me, then?' She was not unaware that this urge to construct their history smacked of desperation.

'What a horrible word. "Fancy". Next you'll be telling me I'm "well hot".' He turned away.

God, she thought, he sounds like someone's dad trying to get down with the kids.

She realised as she sat on the toilet in his bathroom that with one short night she'd invested her whole future in him. But he wasn't the future, he wasn't even the present. She still had a bag of drugs to hand to a dealer who she had no way of contacting except through Susie, probably nowhere to live once her mum found out how she'd messed it up, the gallery was going down the tubes and, for once in her dating life, she didn't even have a

198

boyfriend. For all her youth and the fact that she lived in an estate not a castle, she wasn't above a princess fantasy and one in which Owen would have fitted the bill of both prince and provider.

She got out the duty-free bag and rifled through its contents. If she got hold of Susie she'd be able to find Jason and give him the stuff. She could try to sell it herself, she supposed, to one of those boys from school who she knew still made a bit of money from it, or Chloe could probably put her in touch with one of her music friends. Or she could get rid of it, chuck it down Owen's pretentious toilet with its chrome bowl. Which seemed kind of wasteful, and her mother had at least taught her not to throw away something that others might have a use for.

She sat on that loo, staring at it, knowing that Owen was outside desperately trying to think of ways to get rid of her, just like a bag of dodgy weed and powder.

The door rattled and Sierra quickly wrapped up the stash and stuffed it back into her overnight bag. 'Sierra, sorry love, but you've really got to get out of here. I've got to double lock, I need to get back to my parents'. My mum's, I mean. No, my parents' house. Chop chop.' Fuck, what was it with that expression that Owen and Susie both used, so tragi-comically appropriate given the coke or whatever in her bag. It must be something to do with their age; Owen belonged far more to Susie's generation than to hers. He pushed the door again, but, as Sierra had triple-checked, it was locked. 'Are you all right, Sierra? Come on, we've got to get going.'

'I'm fine. Just getting myself sorted.' But I'm really not, she thought. I'm a long way from sorted.

CHAPTER THIRTEEN

CHEMICAL COMPOUNDS

'We need to talk,' Lucy said to Jamie. It had been two days since her failed seduction, but this was the first time she had managed to catch him in the revolving doors of her rushing in from work and him rushing out to the film. Their conversations consisted of barked instructions about school bags and playdates in the tiny overlap of their six-o'clock lives.

'Cliché,' Jamie replied.

'I know.' The words are stereotypical, but we aren't, thought Lucy. I am older, richer and keener on sex. I'm the bloke in this relationship. Jamie is younger, prettier and looks after the home and the children.

They sat down opposite each other as if for a job interview. Which it sort of was. Jamie looked down at his feet, shod in fashion trainers. Lucy only ever wore trainers if she was going out for a run. Sometimes she felt as though she were nearer his parents' generation than his. This whole social networking and filming every breath thing, for example. Lucy was using a beginner's phrase book, but Jamie was a native speaker of its language.

'You look different,' he said, looking up at her for the first time that she could remember.

'How?'

He shrugged.

'Better? Worse?'

'Different.' He stared at her. 'You're not

frowning as much.' His own forehead furrowed with this revelation. 'It looks like you've had Botox.' He laughed, as if the idea was ridiculous.

Lucy toyed with the idea of attributing her unlined forehead and filled-in nose-to-lip creases to a new moisturiser. She opened her mouth to say as much, but found herself instead saying, 'I have.'

He laughed again. She couldn't remember the last time she'd made him laugh, but at the beginning they'd spent days in bed doing just that, right until the moment she'd told him that she was pregnant.

'No, really. I've had Botox. And fillers.'

He frowned and oh, how she envied him. 'Like what I've just done to the cracks on the bathroom ceiling?'

'Yes, pretty much.' She could see that he still didn't believe her. Amanda had been right, no one need know. 'Botox freezes your face; fillers, well, they fill it out. Right here.' She traced the lines where small cavities of foreign matter trespassed upon her face.

'Jesus, Lucy, how much did that cost?'

'What it cost is irrelevant.'

'I don't think it is. I thought we couldn't afford extra childcare so that I could get my film finished and then I find out that you've been spending— what is it, thousands of pounds?—on getting your face frozen.'

'We agreed not to pay out for childcare until you actually started making some money from your films.'

'It's all about money with you, isn't it? My creativity has no merit unless it makes some money.'

'We calculated—'

'Your fucking sums. Sometimes life should add up to more than your calculations, do you know that, Lucy? If you'll excuse me, I've got to go and do some work—you know, on my stupid non-money-making film that I can't take any real time off from sorting out your family to work on.'

'But Jamie, we need to talk about, you know, other things. Us.'

'I've talked quite enough, thanks.'

As Lucy watched him go, she thought about the calculations she had used when deciding to make the investment in her face. Knowing what she did about finances and the workplace, she had used that money to keep herself relevant in the workplace for longer. Therefore it was like creating a personal website or wearing expensive clothes to work, something that you should be able to write off against tax. But the real investment, she conceded, had been as a way of keeping herself relevant to Jamie. And in that she had received no dividends.

*   *   *

Sierra got bored of trying out her signature with the surname Williams, especially since it was too much like the name of a tennis player. She moved on to fantasising that Owen would send her a huge bouquet of flowers with a loving message tucked inside. That would make their night together seem like the romantic beginning of something rather than a sordid end in itself. But a whole day and night had already passed (a night which she'd had to spend on the chaise longue in the gallery's office)

202

and she knew that she should start being realistic. But she couldn't stop herself from becoming impatient for the next phase, the one where she and Owen would be properly close and they'd be invited to grown-up houses as a couple and explain, 'It's quite funny, really—we're co-godparents, so we owe it all to Gus'. Sierra even wondered whether she'd go to Owen's dad's funeral and whether she could wear Susie's early Galliano, the one that made her look a bit Mafiosa widow.

But she knew she had two more pressing matters than funeral attire to deal with. First there was the huge hole in the gallery's schedules for November, one that Tess had promised she'd be sorting out on her maternity leave. She had not, of course, heard anything from her boss about returning to work any time soon.

The other, weightier still, was sitting inside a duty-free plastic bag hidden beneath the chaise longue. She felt so skanky. She *was* skanky, washing her clothes in the sink at work where she'd previously only washed coffee cups. She wished she'd also been prescient enough to have brought a clean top with her as she looked down at her favourite vintage blouse, the one with the bow that she could get away with because she was young, but on anyone over 30 would lose its ironic librarian charm. Owen had made some snarky comment about it being 'a bit Aunt Mildred'. Wearing it three days in a row, Sierra noticed, had resulted in the activation of decades' old smells which had been trapped beneath its arms by its original 1940s owner, a woman who like most of those of her era had had narrow shoulders and upper arms.

Sierra had visions of herself as an old woman,

wearing the polka-dotted, pussy-bowed blouse, still worried about having to get her mother's stash past the security at the retirement home. It felt like an enormous boil upon her face that she could always feel, yet nobody else could see. As she had walked through the streets and even taken the Underground to work, it had throbbed undetected within her overnight bag. And the longer she carried it, the less unnerved she was by it.

Her mobile rang, Susie's name flashing up on the screen, again. She'd managed to ignore it all of yesterday, not wanting to let her mother intrude on her fantasy life as the girlfriend of a wealthy and handsome banker. Susie had now rung 27 times. She knew she couldn't deny her mother any more.

'Yes.'

'You're there, at last!' Susie's voice was hysterical. 'Where the fuck have you been? I've been so worried.' Even after everything, Sierra still got a little lift from hearing that her mother might have been concerned about her. 'What did you do with my stuff?'

'I've got it. Here. I'm at work.'

'Jesus, Sierra, I ask one thing from you, one tiny thing and you go and fuck it up.'

'It wasn't my fault.' The same words and tone that she'd used years ago when her failure to turn up to school in the correct uniform had caused the head to contact her mother, which had in turn led to some minor league intervention from social services.

'Christ, my phone's about to die. Listen to me, Sierra. You must go to Jason's and give it to him as soon as possible. He lives in Dalston. Or Haggerston. You know, one of those places out east. I'll text you the address and his number and a time. He's a nice man, really, but I owe him. And you owe me, for everything I've done. If you don't, I'm toast, you get that?'

'Yes.' Sierra was trapped in a bad TV drama. This could not be happening, even with her mother.

'If you love me, you'll do this.'

'But, Mum . . .'

'If you ever want to see me again, you'll sort this out. Just take the fucking stash.'

'It's not that simple . . .'

'It is, Sierra.' Her tone changed. 'Please, my lovely. I've never asked anything of you, babes, just do this one thing for me.' Sierra heard a sigh. 'I love you.'

* * *

It felt to Sierra as if she'd been clutching this bag to her chest forever; it was a cyst upon her stomach. She walked along the canal towards the address that Susie had texted to her, along with an ominous, 'He knows where we live.' It was no big deal, she was just delivering something that her mum had forgotten, like a borrowed designer dress or a cup of sugar.

No big deal? This made her a drugs mule, just like some poor Gambian woman who'd swallowed ten condoms filled with heroin and got on a plane to Gatwick.

Don't overdramatise. It's just some hash and some sort of white powder. It could just be a bit of E, pre-pill stage—you don't know that it's crack or coke.

But it probably is, isn't it? Let's be realistic. She'd

205

Googled drug routes from southern Spain and apparently quite a lot of coke came into Europe via the African coast, like those sad boats of migrants you see when there's a shipwreck.

She sat on a bench, watching a woman and a child throwing breadcrumbs to the ducks. They were inner-city ducks, which meant that far from being deprived they were plump on all the snacks that came their way. The woman was laughing and pointing out the different ducks to the little boy: 'That one's a mandarin,' she said, 'and those others are moorhens. Do you know,' she went on, 'I don't know if that means they're hens or ducks or what the difference is.' She and the boy laughed. What a nice mum she was. Sierra tried to dredge up some happy mother memories. There were plenty, she conceded. She could remember so many times that the radio was on and Susie sang with loud tunelessness along with it, while spinning Sierra around the purple kitchen they still lived in. Susie had been so young that Sierra hadn't been shunted off to babysitters when her mother had gone to parties, but had slept among the coats and been entertained by lovely people who she'd thought of as grown-ups, but she now realised had been little more than children. Her mother had also been really good at making up stories, something that had once enchanted Sierra, about princesses coming from humble backgrounds armed only with their beauty and cunning.

The woman singing out all the birds' names was stout and dressed in a really horrible coat, but to Sierra she appeared to be the perfect mother. Would Tess ever be like that? She'd never wear that coat, for starters. Nor could she see her caring about the ducks.

As Sierra became more engrossed in the scene, she noticed something that should have been obvious to her from the beginning. The boy was blond and the woman was black. Not mixed race, but properly dark-skinned. Sierra's knowledge of genetics was pretty poor, but even she could recognise that it was unlikely that she had been the one to have given birth to the little flaxen-haired cherub. That woman, she realised, is paid to look after that boy and, if the bits and pieces of babysitting she'd done as a teenager were anything to go by, not paid very much at that. She reappraised the scene to see if this piece of knowledge would make any difference to her understanding of what was going on.

It did not.

The woman was laughing and giving the boy information and trying to make it all as fun and yet educative as possible, not because she was being paid, but because she wanted to. They had moved onto quacking, followed by the whole spectrum of farmyard animal noises, the mooing, bleating and baaing.

'I love you,' her mother had said to her on the phone, but had not repeated in her text.

'I love you too,' Sierra said out loud, at which the nanny and her charge turned to look at her. 'Sorry.' The woman just smiled, as if Sierra were another small child in need of love and information about the animal kingdom.

She picked up herself and the bag and approached the canal. There were ducks and breadcrumbs in the water, that was true, but also plastic bags, empty cans and unidentifiable brown froth floating upon its surface. She found a broken bit of concrete at her feet and put it inside the duty-free bag that she was clutching. She felt a yearning to make the sign of the cross, something to mark what she was about to do. With a deep breath, she knotted the top of the bag and threw it into the canal.

There was a splash, then a squawk from a nearby swan. Though it might look as though she were littering, Sierra felt that she was finally getting round to tidying up.

She needed somewhere to live. She looked at her mobile, scanning through her contact list until she got to the letter M. Not for Mum, not any longer, but for Michael.

* * *

Owen went into the office for the first time since Gareth's death six days before, having studiously avoided checking anything other than his private email inbox, the address of which was only given out to women. The colleagues junior to him said curt hellos and then looked away; those more senior, scarce though they were, made a point of coming to offer their condolences in voices that said, 'We're all grown-up about dying' as loudly as they actually said, 'So sorry to hear of your loss.'

His secretary Jan gave him a coffee.

'I'm here for you, Owen. If there's anything, and I mean anything, that I can do.'

Somehow she managed to give the offer a sexual spin, or at least that's how it sounded to Owen. Attractive as she was in her cougar-ish way, he felt he had enough on that particular plate with Sierra and Ruby.

'Coffee's great for the moment,' he said.

'I've been checking your inbox and replying to anything urgent.' She looked embarrassed. 'There are some personal ones that have come into there rather than your other address. I think you ought to look at them. They're marked as unread.'

If Owen had had the physical or emotional predisposition to blush, he would have done so then. His first thought was that Sierra had been sending him filthy messages. She was such a goer, shagging on a first date; she talked dirty, too. The thought of her shouts and pleas, which only a few minutes earlier had given him an injection of lust, now made him feel very queasy. She wasn't going to be one of those women, was she? He'd assumed that she would be as detached as her boss had always been. He should have made sure that Lucy had used his private email account for all those blessed messages about godparental duties.

He opened up his inbox with trepidation. Jan had expunged any spam offering cheap Viagra and a bigger cock and had replied to the work ones. There was only one personal one. It stood out, in bold unread text, shouting at him through the pale irrelevance of all the other messages.

Subject: Loose ends.

Like that, with a capital letter and a full stop, neat, grammatical. The message construction of somebody over 30. Sierra would never use a capital L. She'd probably write something ghastly like 'endz', wouldn't she, being of that same texting generation as Ruby.

No, the subject wasn't what made Owen feel dizzy. It was its provenance.

Sender: Gareth Williams

He stared at it again. It had only arrived yesterday. His mother didn't even know how to use the Internet, or the Interweb as she called it semi-ironically, so it wasn't her being uncharacteristically efficient and getting onto Dad's computer. He supposed somebody else could have set up an account in his father's name, but what sort of a sick joke would that be?

He opened it and read.

Dear Owen,

it began. He scanned to the end:

your loving father, Dad.

He went back to the top again.

If you're reading this, it means that I'm dead. It's an email message from beyond the grave. I thought it more efficient than a letter, and the post office can't delay the arrival of a letter, at least not on purpose.
**   You're confused, I'm sure. I first wrote a version of this email a while ago now and I update it every week. And then I change the date for it to be sent in a week's time. If it ever reaches a point when I can't change the date, it will be sent and you'll be able to read it. Bet you didn't know you could**

time the departure of your email messages until after death, did you, Owen? It was always a source of great pride to me that I was much better at all things technological than you. Sort of like a boffin's version of being able to still beat his son at football. I just hope your mother hasn't unplugged the broadband while hoovering. Surely even she won't be hoovering already? I like to think that the screensaver is still flickering away even with me gone, like a sort of flag in remembrance of me, or a park bench marking where I liked to sit.

Get on with it, Dad. You always could be long-winded.

So I suppose you reading this means either I'm dead or in a coma. Or maybe I'm in hospital for an extended stay. Worse than death.
     I've not got much to say.

Well get on and say it, then.

Except that I think you know there's no father who could have loved his son more than I did you. Sentimental stuff. That's why I saved it for after I was gone. If I could have wished for anything in this world, it would have been to be your real father. Your 'birth father', horrid expression that, but I can't think of another way of saying it. I used to daydream that I was your real dad. I made up lots of stories to explain

211

how that could possibly be true. I know you think I only do logic, but I can be quite fanciful when I want to. I needed to find any way of being your father—I even looked up in the library whether it would be possible to father a child if the mother used the toilet after you (it's not). Silly schoolgirl stuff, but I loved you so much that I was reduced to it.

Thing is, I'm not your biological father. There, said it. I know that's not news to you, but it never ceases to be a shock to me.

Now I'm gone, you need to know the truth about your parents, your real parents. I'm sorry we never got to talk about it. I meant to, you know that, but I couldn't face it. I didn't want my dying days to be about how I wasn't your father, I wanted them to be about how I was.

All I can say, now that I've gone (how strange it is to type those words, but at the same time a relief too), is: talk to your mother. That's it, I'm not telling you the truth, just how you can find it out. Ask your mother, she's got the time to tell you. Forgive her. It's easy to do. I know I did.

And tell her that I always knew.

CHAPTER FOURTEEN

PRESERVATION

'You look so pretty, Mari, it's lucky that black suits you. It really doesn't suit many people. You wouldn't believe the number of people who come into the store and insist on buying black when it completely washes them out.' Ruby stood behind Owen's mother while they looked in the mirror together, sucking in her cheeks and putting on her special department store voice, the one that said 'I'm honest' when Owen knew it was quite the opposite. It had worked on him, after all.

'You don't think it's a bit short?' said Mari.

'Oh no, Mari, you've so got the legs for it. Anyway, it's only just above the knee.' The two women smiled at their reflection. Ruby was a head taller than Mari and her posture, straight-backed and with her hands on his mother's shoulders, made her look strangely older than her protégée. But despite the difference in their heights, they looked alike and they seemed to be morphing into one another before Owen's very eyes. 'Now then,' continued Ruby, 'have you thought about brightening it up just a little?' She brandished a silk scarf in her signature colour—vibrant red, obviously. 'I always think it's nice to have a little bit of colour. Dear, dear Gareth's dead but his spirit's still with us. And he was such a jolly person.'

Owen escaped to his father's office, that place of refuge from feminine frippery being his undeniable inheritance. The computer's screensaver, a double

213

helix, continued to rotate, as mentioned in Gareth's email. What sort of irony had made his father choose strands of DNA to grace his beloved computer after his death? He clicked on the mouse and his father's desktop was revealed, as ordered as his real-world version. He checked the inbox and read the bulletins from scientific journals and checked the sent items, where the email that had gone to his work address was stored. He re-read it. 'Talk to your mother,' it exhorted. Sure, he could talk to her and she'd certainly talk back—god, she never stopped wittering on—but would she say anything worth hearing?

'What do you think, Owen?' Mari came into the office and did a twirl.

'Mum, that scarf's got a skull and crossbones on it.'

'I suppose it does. Ruby says everybody's wearing them.'

'Not at funerals, though.'

She giggled. 'I suppose not. What about the rest?'

'It's fine.' Owen shrugged and turned back to the computer.

Mari sighed. 'You are so like your father.'

'Am I?' asked Owen. 'Am I really?'

'Of course. He never seemed to care what I wore and sat there all day staring into that stupid machine.'

'But what about my real father?'

Mari's face fell. 'How can you say such a thing, today of all days?'

Owen groaned as his mother rushed out to lock herself in the bathroom. Preening in front of the mirror and arranging a skull and crossbones scarf in a jaunty fashion was evidently appropriate behaviour for the hiatus between death and a funeral, but his remark was not. 'Talk to your mother,' his father had demanded of him, and Owen would honour that demand. Just not quite yet.

*   *   *

Over lunch, Owen's ears hurt with the buzz of continual chatter. His sister Caron had always been taciturn and sulky, dark-browed and frowning, just like her father—her real father—but with Mari's IQ. Gareth had once commented, in an unguarded moment, how sad it had been that the roll of the DNA dice had come up with Mari's brains and his looks for Caron.

But Ruby—Ruby could talk. She complimented Mari on every last detail of her housekeeping: 'Mmm, this butter is delicious, is it local?'; 'Oh, I shouldn't, but it's just so yummy, I'll have another morsel—treat myself'; 'I love this tablecloth, seventies retro is bang on trend. My godmother runs an interior design company and they are just so loving this look at the moment.'

His thoughts were finally interrupted by his mother. 'Owen, has your friend Tess had her baby yet? With you as the godfather?'

'I'm a godfather many times over, actually.'

'But this one's special, isn't it?' Mari insisted. 'What with her being such a close friend, and the little mite not having a dad.'

'It's a boy. Augustine, born the day after Dad died. I've not been to see him.'

'You've not met him? Why not?'

'Because my father died.'

'But still. That poor Tess.'

'I think she's OK, Mari,' said Ruby. 'She's really rich, so I bet she's got so much help it must be like being on holiday. My mum had no help with three of her own and my dad was away working all the time. I love these tea cups, have you had them long?'

'It's not the same, though. You can have all the help in the world, but without the support of the father . . . That's got to be so hard for the poor girl. I feel like crying when I think of it all.'

'You're so generous, Mari. I think you've got enough to be crying about at the moment without having to worry about Tess,' Ruby assured her. 'It is her choice, after all.'

Owen turned to his fiancée. 'I've not read a paper today. Need to check something. You couldn't be a poppet, could you, and nip down to the garage for me?'

'But Owen . . .'

'Please. I'll love you forever.' He kissed her nose, which she promptly wrinkled in a way that he used to find endearing. He took a deep breath.

'I'll come with you, sweetheart,' said Mari. 'I could do with the fresh air.'

'Mum, I want to talk to you.'

'Later, Owen. After the funeral. Please.'

*   *   *

Michael had agreed with Charlie and Debs that they should all travel together to the postnatal reunion of the hypnobirthing group. It was his attempt to make sure that Tess didn't duck out of it. She had

216

barely managed to leave the flat in the two weeks they'd been back, still blurry in her blues, and he felt sure that a bit of showing off about the drama of Gus's birth to people she felt superior to would be the perfect antidote.

'Come on, darling,' he said. 'Put on that nice grey dress, show them all how to be stylish and postnatal.'

'Can't breastfeed in it.' She was moored, as ever, on the creamy-white sofa now flecked with posset. All those hypnobirthing classes and nobody ever said that the baby would be feeding every other hour and that it would take the best part of an hour to do it. All the visions Tess may have had about wafting round cafés and galleries with a sleeping baby in a sling were now banished as they realised that no sooner had she got ready to leave the house than she'd be disrobing to feed him once again.

Gus the guzzler. It was just as well Michael loved him. He just wasn't sure that Tess was as convinced.

'Come on, you need to get used to me not being around. School starts in a week or so.'

'Don't leave me.'

'I won't, not yet.'

'Not ever. I don't want to do this alone. I never wanted to. I never even wanted children.'

Before he could question this, the doorbell went and he buzzed Charlie and Debs into the flat where they swapped compliments on each other's babies, with Michael feeling inwardly smug at how handsome Gus was, with his olive skin and mop of blond hair. Little Tallulah, spawn of Charlie, managed to disprove the theory that all babies are gorgeous. He wondered how her parents could resist the temptation to squeeze the infant acne

217

that bubbled across her cheeks.

Gus greeted their arrival with an explosion and Michael and Charlie repaired to the bedroom to change him.

Charlie looked with disgust as Michael wiped away the mustard-coloured porridge smeared across the cloth nappy with the zebra-print outer shell. He insisted on using cotton wool dipped in boiled cooled water, just as the books had told him to. Tess couldn't have given a damn and he was sure she'd revert to chemical-soaked wet wipes once he left. If he left.

'Don't you hate this bit?' said Charlie.

'I don't know, I quite like the smell of it—it's like bread dough.'

'You're weird. So how was it?' asked Charlie. 'The birth, I mean.'

'Fine. A miracle, you know.' He would never tell anyone about the blood and the mess and the moment that Gus had looked like a monster emerging from his mother's arse.

'Debs had a caesarean.'

'I'm sorry.'

'I'm not. I didn't want her lady bits loosened, if you get my drift. My brother says you won't ever have sex again if you don't stay away from the business end during birth, know what I mean?'

'I guess.'

'And even if you do, it's like waving a flag in the Mersey Tunnel and all that.'

'Right.'

'Mind you, it's not as if she's putting out now as it is. Do you think marital relations will ever be the same again?'

'We're not married.'

'You know what I mean, though.'

'We'd better get going. It's just like school, isn't it, don't want to be late for the teacher.'

'That Tallulah child is wearing some sort of football strip,' Michael hissed at Tess as they got into the car. 'It's some sort of ironic middle-class thing, isn't it? Like making them wear T-shirts which say "mother-sucka" and "mine's a yummy mummy".' He was getting a smile out of Tess, at last, and was now convinced that this excursion was going to work. 'I mean, god forbid we should ever use Gus as a billboard to prove how stylish we are, hey, darling?' he said, turning to Gus. 'You in your hand-knitted stripy cashmere and French babygros.'

The suburban house where the hypnobirthing classes had been held hadn't changed, though the lives of all its visitors had beyond recognition. The hall was crowded with pushchairs and Michael overheard two fathers, Mick and Nick or Ben and Dom, talking over their vehicular purchases.

'Nice folding action,' said one with feeling.

'We opted for the travel system,' said the other.

Upstairs, their classmates seemed frighteningly different and yet so the same. The women were all at least a stone lighter, for a start, though they still carried that blousy padded midriff weight. The more aggressive fathers had managed to prise their progeny away from the mothers and were bouncing them so vigorously that Michael was concerned that social services might be called in. Two of them had theirs strapped to their fronts, ready to detonate.

'Ah, the slings and buggies of outrageous fortune,' whispered Michael to Tess, and was rewarded with a weak smile. She was clutching Gus as her talisman, but her chin was up. He

219

realised just how nervous she was about presenting herself to this audience. There were so many firsts with Tess since Gus's birth, this vulnerability underpinning most of them. She settled herself onto one of the beanbags and lifted her top up. He still couldn't believe she could do that, that she could become so prosaic about such a potent part of her body. He knew all the stuff about it being what breasts were designed for, but when anyone said that he wanted to shout, 'No, they're not, they're designed for me to gawp at and to yearn to touch and stroke!' Well they used to be, anyway.

Tess's weren't the only breasts on display. Megan seemed even less adept at maintaining a modicum of modesty as she latched and re-latched her baby onto her breasts, which hung above great rolls of emptied belly flesh. He looked away only to be confronted with another feeding mother, this one with great tubular nipples, dangling and dripping.

'It's a bloody disaster, mate,' whispered Charlie to Michael. 'The wife's never had such giant pups and I'm not allowed to touch them. It's some sort of sick joke.' Except Michael wasn't laughing. 'It's like she's had surgery—in the mornings, they're all enormous and hard and pointy. Porn star breasts, bloody *Baywatch* boobs. Babywatch more like, more's the pity.' He sank back. 'I'm knackered, I'm bloody knackered.'

'I'm sure Debs is tired, too.'

'Doesn't have to go out to work though, does she? Just sits at home with the baby.'

'I think looking after a baby is hard work.'

'But what does she do all day?'

Michael sighed and Charlie looked at him with disappointment. He wasn't sure where Charlie had ever got the idea that they were kindred spirits. He distracted himself by helping Tess arrange the cushions about her and Gus in a more supportive way.

'We're fine,' she snapped.

'Is he a good baby?' asked one of the mothers, Katie, Izzie, Lizzie, whatever, they all looked the same.

'What, as opposed to a very bad evil baby?' snapped Tess. Oh dear, thought Michael, maybe not such a good idea after all.

'Lila's a very good baby,' said the mother. 'Practically sleeping through the night.'

'Yes, so's Gus,' Tess replied, which was true if your night consisted only of the hours from, say, eleven until two.

'Now then,' announced their teacher, who'd lost none of her bossiness. 'I think the men should tell the birth stories.' Or was it Birth Stories, capital B capital S, so mythologised had they become, such a crucial component of having a child, when the birth already seemed like such an irrelevance. 'After all,' she continued, 'they were there too.' Giggles all round. He'd forgotten the forced hilarity of these occasions.

They weren't birth anecdotes, that was for sure. There was no detail too small to be gone into and he realised as he listened to everybody else's birth stories that they were like dreams, or one of his colleagues' tales of public transport hassle—only interesting to those that had been there.

'So we got to the hospital and she was already five centimetres dilated—'

'Six centimetres, I was six centimetres.'

'So we filled the birthing pool—'

221

'No, first we tried gas and air but it made me go a bit funny. I was seven centimetres when we got in the pool.'

Come on, come on. Surely his and Tess's was the only really interesting story.

Two natural births, a forceps, one ventouse and an emergency caesarean later and it was almost Michael's turn. He had gauged the format. You expressed awe at how your wife coped—'She was amazing'—followed by a soupy look, you talked about how nervous you were about driving to the hospital, you made some joke about how useless you were (while simultaneously implying that you showed amazing fortitude).

'Oh well, mate,' said Charlie, on hearing from a fellow father about the traumatic journey from the birthing centre giant inflatable ball to flat out in the operating theatre for the caesarean, 'at least she'll be honeymoon fresh like Debs.'

Michael wondered whether any of them were ever going to have sex again. God, was he ever going to have sex again? What would Tess be like? He'd never know what she'd have been like before giving birth, when she was still 'honeymoon fresh'— to use Charlie's delightful phrase. An unbidden thought: Sierra was still honeymoon fresh.

'Michael, would you like to tell us your story? A little birdie tells me that it was quite exciting.'

'Yes, well. Terrifying, actually. At about four in the morning, Tess came into my room.' Michael looked around and began to explain: 'We were sleeping in separate rooms because she was having trouble getting to sleep, being so large and all.' Tess frowned. 'We normally share a room, obviously.' He giggled and looked around at his audience,

222

most of whom seemed more intent on looking at their bundles. 'So she comes into the room where I'm sleeping, temporarily, and she's in labour and I rush to ring the hospital.' Tess snorted. 'OK, I panic a bit and flap around and then I ring the hospital.'

Then Michael made the mistake of pausing. The room was close, too many people, too many hormones, milk dripping everywhere, babies crying, a veal cart of a room. He couldn't see, the air was too thick with the emotions, of celebration and of mourning; his vision wobbled like a horizon on a hot day. All he could see was the excrement coming out of Tess when she knelt on all fours. 'Shit,' he said. Everyone giggled. He couldn't think of anything else to say so he said it again, 'Shit.' It loomed in front of him. He could almost smell it.

'Birth's a very scary thing,' said the bossy teacher.

Michael looked around. He couldn't breathe.

'Especially for the father,' the teacher continued to improvise. 'I always say it's a bit like the way that you don't get car sick if you're in the driving seat. In a funny way, I think it's almost more painful for the father, having to watch someone he loves go through so much pain.'

Everyone looked to Michael with great sympathy.

'It just came out,' he managed.

'He just came out,' corrected the teacher.

'No, it, they, just came out.' There it was again, he could see them plopping down and landing on the carpet.

Everyone nodded with incomprehension.

'Like I say,' said their instructor turned enabler, 'fathers can often find the whole process really quite traumatic. Beautiful, of course, but traumatic too.'

'He's not the father.' Michael heard the voice but didn't, couldn't, recognise it. 'You see, he's not the father.' He knew it then, those clipped tones, the unapologetic poshness in a world where most had made their accents democratic. He swung round to look at Tess, his turn at bewilderment. Everyone else was doing the same. He glanced around at their audience. They looked on with embarrassed fascination, alternating between looking at the floor and at the couple centre stage.

'Know what you mean, mate—I sometimes wonder where Tallulah gets those lungs from. And those spots, I never had spots like that,' said Charlie.

'But Michael really isn't the father,' Tess repeated.

Michael looked around and as everyone averted their gaze he realised that they all thought this might be news to him too, which was an assumption even more humiliating than the truth.

'No, I'm not. That's right. I know I'm not—this isn't some soap opera revelation.' He forced a laugh. 'Did you think I was?' Nobody answered. 'Whatever gave you that impression? How extraordinary. No, I'm Tess's cousin. Of course. Just Tess's cousin.'

Everyone nodded again, still with that air of incomprehension.

'But hang on there, Mike . . .' said Charlie.

'Michael, my name's not Mike.'

'You said that you were the father, I'm sure. But I always thought you were a gaylord, anyway. What are you doing here, then?'

'Being supportive. It's classes for mothers and

partners. I'm Tess's birthing partner.' Damn, why had he frozen mid-birth story. Now he'd never get to tell them how he'd delivered a baby on his own. Sort of. 'And I'm not gay, actually—not that there's anything wrong with being gay.'

'Right-oh. So who is the little rugrat's father?'

'Tess?' asked Michael.

'The truth is . . .' said Tess and she looked at Michael. 'The truth is, he works in a hospital.' The doctor donor story again, the one that stopped making sense the moment Tess started saying that she'd never wanted any of this, that she'd never wanted to be a mother. Michael stared at her. 'And that really is the truth.' She said it firmly, forestalling further questions. The exhaustion of the last weeks, the thanklessness and the hurt all came gurgling up inside Michael and he felt that it would explode from him in a projectile posset of anger.

'Really, Tess, the doctor?'

'Yes.' He was still poised to strike, so she turned to those assembled. 'But I decided to have a baby on my own. Never quite found . . .' She paused. '. . . a man worthy of having a baby with, you see.'

'Really? Bollocks, Tess.'

'Michael, since when is this any of your business?'

'Since I spent the last two months supporting you through pregnancy and birth and the hell that is the first three weeks with a baby and you've never even said thank you, not once, not even for a glass of water.'

'I never asked you to help.'

'And I never asked you who the father is.'

Their fellow classmates were all staring at their

225

own babies, doing a mime show of checking nappies or lying them face down across their knees, but all the while listening intently, shushing their babies' cries, not wanting to miss the next instalment. Their lives, not particularly exciting before the birth of their babies, had become even more insular since. They'd all had the customary early visit to the local gastropub to prove that having a baby hadn't completely extinguished fun and freedom, but other than that, they were starved of gossip to share, other than that which they read about in the tabloids that they treated themselves to on Sundays. Tess and Michael's performance would at last give them something to talk about and bond the group even more than the near-simultaneous birth of their loved ones.

Tess stood up. 'Gus is unsettled, I think we should go.'

'He's fine, he always is. You're unsettled. You're lying, and since I've been like a father to him, I deserve to know the truth.'

'This is all rather embarrassing.' Tess's legendary composure had returned at last. He'd been worried that it had been thrown out with the placenta. She looked around at the assembled audience, who all coughed at once and shielded themselves from public awkwardness with their newfound baby props. 'I think we had better go.'

Michael looked around. He was stranded among people with whom he now had nothing in common. For a while, he had done, but it was an illusion. They were all in relationships with people they loved, they all had children, they were happily buried in the cement of stability. They knew him to be a liar and his faux family would have to be excommunicated from the group.

'Sorry about all that. I'd better go catch up with Tess.' It seemed to take him an age to rake up the paraphernalia that littered their encampment—the nappy bag, the muslins, the little sheepskin rug for Gus to lie on. The teacher, who had so droned on and bored them for all those months leading up to the birth was finally at a loss for words. 'Bye then, see you soon. Well, probably not. Good luck with it all.' He looked around at the small objects of love that had brought them all together. He felt a pang of curiosity that would never be sated: what would become of them all? Would they know each other forever? Would they fall in love with each other? Drug addicts or prime ministers? Would little Tallulah learn to despise or admire her father? He'd never know now. He wasn't sure he'd even get to watch Gus grow up.

*   *   *

Jamie was at the computer. Again. Lucy wondered whether that was the cause of his lack of interest in her. She remembered there being a friend of a friend of a mum at school who'd got a divorce over her husband's porn addiction.

'Fuck me,' he exclaimed.

I wish, thought Lucy. 'What?'

'Look at this.' He passed the laptop to her.

She stared at some footage of a girl in her underwear who had her hand down her knickers and was saying something about how wet she was. Lucy felt her whole body heat up with embarrassment, anger and a small flickering of desire caused by watching this stranger with the

227

father of her children sitting beside her. 'Why are you showing me this? I don't want to watch this.'

'But don't you see?' said Jamie. 'I think it's that girl, you know the one who works with Tess who came to our party. Sienna.'

'Sierra.' She looked closer. It was difficult to tell from the grainy footage which, she guessed, had been taken on a mobile, especially since it was focusing on the crotch. Or in the parlance of the girl, 'my wet pussy, my dripping cunt'.

'Oh, Jamie, I think you're right.' That brief dart of the erotic disintegrated and she felt utter mortification on behalf of that sweet silly girl. Or maybe she was wrong to, maybe it was yet another generational gap. Sierra was not far off Jamie's age and since he believed life did not exist unless he had shared it on the Internet, perhaps she was the same. Lucy glanced nervously at him and then at his crotch, which to her relief looked as it always did. 'Where did you find this stuff?' Was it some online equivalent of *Readers' Wives*? Users' Girlfriends, perhaps? 'Does Sierra . . . has she put this up on purpose? Does she want you, us, people to see it?' She felt like someone's befuddled mother. She *was* someone's befuddled mother.

'I don't know. Probably not. There's this bloke, Josh, friend of a friend, who's a bit of an IT guy, can do all sorts of special effects on the cheap. You know, for the film.'

'And this is what, an example of his work?'

'No, I don't think so. I was just checking him out before we get in touch with him and he'd posted this on his page. The link said something like "My girl loves to talk dirty".'

So, thought Lucy, the medium is different from

old-school porn but the words are all the same. Men making it, women pretending to love it. 'Do you think she knows?'

Jamie shrugged.

'Don't you think she should?'

'Why should she?'

'Because I'd want to, I suppose.'

'She let him film her, so she can't mind.'

'What, that counts as giving her permission? To have her . . .' Lucy looked at the screen, where Sierra had taken off her pants to reveal a near hairless crotch to the soundtrack of a reedy male voice asking how hot she was feeling and to describe his cock. 'To have her vagina broadcast to the world.'

'She's talking to camera, isn't she? And to be honest, Luce, she doesn't look like she's complaining.'

Lucy shook her head in disgust. 'You've got a daughter. I can't believe I'm hearing this. Can you really not see how compromised her dignity is by this?'

'Lots of women find it sexy, empowering.'

'Oh for god's sake, don't give me that empowerment shit, that "pole dancing is a fun form of exercise" crap.' Empowering—wasn't that the very word she'd used to justify her session with Amanda? But it was different, surely? There really were good feminist arguments for a bit of enhancement. But why, then, did men not feel the same imperative? Oh, Rosa, how I fear for you.

'It's not crap. Jessie goes to these pole dancing classes and says it's full of lawyers and professors and people.'

'Lawyers can be idiots too.'

'I think it might be an age thing,' he said, which shut Lucy up.

*   *   *

They drove home in silence. Tess barked a few instructions to Michael about getting Gus out of his car seat, but nothing more. When they got inside, she poured herself a large glass of wine and he resisted telling her that she shouldn't drink it until after she'd done a feed.

'Shall I go, then?' he asked, finally. 'Home, I mean. My flat.' It didn't sound so bad, especially since he'd been letting Sierra stay in the flat for the last week or so, due to some unexplained issue at her mother's place.

'Why?'

'Because of, you know, all that. The accusing me of being a sad sap pretending to be Gus's father. The lies, the humiliation.'

She downed her glass and filled another before sitting down on the sofa. 'Do you wish you were his father?'

'Yes.' It came out in a high squeak, just when he wanted to sound paternal and mature. He sounded like a gawky boy whose voice was on the cusp of breaking.

'It's what you've always wanted, isn't it, to be with me?'

He nodded.

She stood up and started to undo the buttons on her shirt dress, which went all the way down to the hem. The first three buttons were those that she opened when she needed to feed Gus, but she carried on going. Michael was frozen. Down she went, past her waist, until she reached all the way to the bottom and could shrug off the dress. She stood before him in knickers and a maternity bra. She popped open the cups of the bra, which were designed for easy access—but for a baby, not for a man. Her breasts spilled out and there was something more naked about them encircled by the supporting structure than if she'd taken it off all together. The only thing left covering her was her knickers. He couldn't help but think of the stitches beneath them.

Michael wanted to look away but couldn't, so he tried to focus on her eyes. It was as if she had peeled away her very skin.

'Go on, then. Here's your chance. You can have what you've always wanted.'

He felt he owed it to her and Gus, in the same way that he had to bring her cups of water and calcium-rich food and to burp the baby when he had wind. He put his hand out and touched one of those unfettered breasts, but could not stop thinking about how tender it would feel to Tess, and how he had to be careful around her nipples, where she'd had some cracking.

'You're lovely, Tess, you know that.'

'Go on. Have me.' She looked defiant yet passive. It was the most unarousing combination.

He looked down, hoping that would inspire him, but all he could think about was the shit and Gus's head and all those stitches. Would he be able to feel them with his fingers, with his cock?

'The book said you have to wait until after the six-week check.'

'I promise you, this will be your only chance.'

He sifted through his wank bank, so filled with

images of Tess. On Christmas Day, putting a decoration back onto the tree, her dress lifting up as she did so. Throwing her head back to laugh at a joke that only she and he got, exposing her throat as she did so. Putting her hair into a ponytail and revealing her then unshaven armpits, with their hair a suggestion of what lay further down her body.

Nothing.

He thought of the best time he'd slept with Rachel, in the detention room at the top of the school with the cleaners hoovering on the level below. He pictured Sierra in that playsuit garment that she wore with high heels, which he'd wondered how you disentangled her from.

A flicker, subsiding to nothing.

'Well,' said Tess, 'am I disgusting now, is that it?'

'No, you're lovely, truly lovely.'

'Can't cope with the reality? I only work as a fantasy?'

'No, I want to, I just . . .'

She picked up her dress and put it back on. 'Perhaps you are gay after all?'

Michael felt a chill that reminded him of being in church. He sunk to his knees, terrified that just as Tess as a goddess had replaced god all those years ago, the reverse would happen now. He really didn't want to start believing in god, representing as it would him being sucked back into the bosom of his family, away from the breasts of all the women he'd ever loved and wanted to love in the future.

CHAPTER FIFTEEN

LANOLIN CREAM

Ruby had to go back to work. She would argue this as a sign of her indispensability to the Italian designer label concession on which she worked, though Owen felt that being allowed as much time off as he wanted after the funeral, as he was, could be considered a better indicator of importance.

'I wish I were going with you,' said Mari as they dropped her off at the station.

'So do I, Mari. It's been ever so lovely to get to know you,' said Ruby. They hugged, their spun hair melding to make a blonde blur.

'Mum,' he said in the car on the way back. 'Mum,' he repeated as she seemed not to hear. 'We need to talk.'

She sighed. 'I know.' It was the first time Owen had ever heard his mother concede to any form of knowledge, let alone something as profound as this.

They spent the rest of the journey in silence, an equally rare occurrence. It was a familiar route to him, taking him as it did past his secondary school, which practically had a plaque engraved to him, such was its pride at his achievements. He knew at what points he could overtake and where all the shortcuts took him. What he didn't know was the truth that might be contained in the conversation that would be held at the end of it.

Mari busied herself with making tea when they arrived, but she was less fluttery than usual, more purposeful. She was already morphing into a stranger and they hadn't even had the conversation. He was reminded of those toys, Power Rangers, 'robots in disguise'. She had become an automaton when before she'd always been a little national doll, albeit a kind of inappropriately dressed one in a too-tight miniskirt.

She sat down and Owen got out a cigarette.

'I do wish you wouldn't, what with your dad's emphysema and all.'

'He's not my father and it didn't kill him.' She looked hurt. 'He's not my father, is he, not my birth father?'

'No . . . yes. You know that, we've always been open about how we chose you. And the fact that we love you just as much as if you were born to us.'

'We chose you so that makes you special,' he mocked.

'It's true.'

'Is it? I don't know anything about truth any more.' He got out a scrappy printout of his father's email. 'Dad thinks I should know it. Listen to what he says: "Now I'm gone, you need to know the truth about your parents".'

Mari recoiled as if Gareth's ghost had appeared in the room. 'Stop it, stop it. Don't be horrible, Owen. It's not funny.'

'It's an email from Dad.'

'Stop it, stop it. He's dead. He can't use the computer any more. I always said it would be the death of him.'

'He wrote it before he died but delayed sending it. It's a message from beyond the grave.'

Mari shrank further from him, until she slouched against the Formica kitchen counter. Then she bounced back as she flinched from the still hot kettle, and for a moment seemed to be wondering whether it was less scalding than her son. Owen walked towards her, his gym-honed bulk and dark skin casting a shadow over her tiny blondeness.

She began to cry. He should have felt sorry for her, but he became more irritated. His need to know the truth outweighed a widow's grief.

'I need to know. Dad wants me to know.' He pointed at the email. 'Read it and tell me, for Dad's sake.' She crumpled like the piece of paper he waved in her face and slithered to the floor. He heard her knee crack as she did so. She took the email printout and read it, her lips moving slightly, tears still rolling down her cheeks.

He helped her up off the lino and she sat at the table, calmer now. They looked at one another.

'I'm your mother,' she said at last.

He felt a delayed kindness towards her, mixed with irritation. 'I know you and Dad loved me, and in most ways you are my mother, but I want to know who my real parents are. Don't give me all that "We loved you as if we were your real parents" stuff, Mum—who gave birth to me?'

'I did.'

'Stop it. Who's my real mother.'

'I am. I'm your mother.' Her voice was even squeakier than usual. He sighed and was about to launch into another round of interrogation when he looked at her face, with its full lips and slightly slanting eyes, just like his, and he stopped. 'Go on,' he whispered.

She drew in her breath. 'It was horrible. It hurt so much, much more than Caron. You're so tall and I was so small and I thought it must be punishment for what I did.'

'What did you do?'

'I wasn't married.'

'To Dad?'

'To anybody. Not to your other dad, the one who I fell pregnant by.'

Fell pregnant—what did she mean by that, that she tripped up and found herself impaled on some stranger's cock and nine months later he was born? 'Who was he?'

'He came from far away.'

'Foreign?' Of course—he was always being asked where he was from, where he was *really* from, and had been nicknamed 'Paki' at school.

'From Liverpool, originally. I think his father may have been Italian, though. Dark, like you, he was. Lived in London, a photographer.'

'Drove an MG and said he'd make you a model?'

'How did you know?'

'Oh, Mum.' Looking at Mari, it wasn't hard to picture the naïve 21-year-old that she had been, living with parents whose idea of sex education would not have even stretched to telling her not to do it. 'What happened?'

'I don't really know. It's been so long and I haven't talked about it since we got you. Things that I didn't talk to your father about don't seem to be real, especially not now.'

'Try.'

'I was living at Nan and Granddad's. It was so boring, Owen, you can't understand how bored I was.' Owen thought about the small village with its even smaller mindset and nodded to indicate that he understood all too well. There were mountains there, big enough to shut out the light, but too small to attract climbers and tourists from outside. 'Every day, I used to wake up and pray that something different would happen. I'd think about setting the town hall on fire just to make that day different from the day before and the one before that. I never did. I was always such a nice girl.'

'Go on,' said Owen, but gently now.

'One day, something finally happened,' she said. 'This bloke turned up.'

'He came.' She said it simply but with significance, as though his father's arrival had been the long-prophesied sighting of Halley's Comet or of the new messiah. Owen supposed that's probably how he had seemed to his mother. 'Oh, Owen, he was lovely. He had the car, shiny green, and he was shiny too. You probably think the sixties and seventies was all sex parties and marijuana, but it wasn't, not at your nan's. When I see that time portrayed on the television, it's got nothing to do with me, except for the week that he was there.'

'A week?' His mother put out to some velvet-suit-wearing ponce from London in a week?

'Just a week, yes. He was a journalist-photographer or something and he wanted photos of real people for a magazine. Said it was for the *Sunday Times* colour magazine, though I bought it every week and we were never in it. He'd been to Vietnam already and to Glastonbury, but now he wanted boring people.' She smiled at the memory. 'But he never made me feel boring. He said I was exotic to him.'

Owen sighed inwardly. He felt sure that he had inherited much from this man, not least his corny chat-up lines. He nodded at her to continue. He felt fine now, not faint as he might have expected. He just felt like he wanted to hear the story in as few words as possible and to do that he had to stop himself from interrupting.

'It was only the once,' she said by way of mitigation. 'I wasn't even sure it had happened. I know it must seem silly to you with all your girlfriends and all the sex on the computers and everything, but I wasn't even sure it had happened.'

This, Owen felt sure, suggested something that he hadn't inherited from the man.

'By the time I'd even realised, it was too late to do anything about it. Not that I would have. Girls like me didn't—couldn't, really. Well, they weren't supposed to get into trouble either, but it was a bit late for that.'

'Did you try to contact him? What's his name, anyway?'

'Keith—like Richards, only much better looking. Your granddad tried, said he was going to get him to do the decent thing. I gave him a false telephone number, but he even went up to London, his first time ever, to try to find him.'

'Why did you give Granddad a false number? Did you not want him, my father, to do . . . I don't know, the decent thing?'

'I didn't have his telephone number. He didn't leave it me. And anyway, I didn't want your granddad talking to him, I couldn't bear the idea of Keith thinking of me as some silly girl from a village causing him problems.'

'But he'd caused you problems.'

'But he'd given me so much more. He'd made just one week of my life exciting. It was worth it, and even being pregnant with you was better than just nothing happening at all.' She giggled; all this talk of sex—worse, sex in which she'd taken part.

238

'And you were always such a lovely baby, so big and with your dark mop of hair. You look so like him. You are so like him. A bit of a charmer.'

Owen chose not to dwell on this. He knew he could be described with a lot of old-fashioned words: cad, bounder, chancer, rake. He knew that there were fathers out there, just like Granddad, who'd have liked to take him out and force him to do right by their daughters, especially the one who didn't get back his deposit on the marquee. 'I still don't understand. When did Dad, Gareth, come along? Why did you lie to me about adopting me?'

'We didn't lie, not exactly. Your dad didn't. We did adopt you, sort of, when you were a year old, just like we always told you.'

'Hang on, Mum—it seems like, in every sense of the word, you're losing me here.'

'Nan and Granddad sent me away to have you.'

'Don't tell me, to a convent for fallen women.'

'Don't be silly, poppet, it was the seventies not the 1870s. I went to your aunts' in Pembrokeshire. I had you in hospital and it hurt so much and I was begging them to get you out of me so they did, with a great big pair of forceps.' She shuddered. 'I never did like those salad implements your dad got me for Christmas. I thought no man would ever want me after that.'

'Because you were, what, fallen?'

'No, because of those forceps. We were going to give you up for adoption, proper like, but then me and your aunts, we fell in love with you. There's no woman that can resist you, is there?'

'So what happened?'

'Maureen and Jeanie said that they could look after you until I found a way of getting you back.

239

I stayed with them for three months, I fed you during that time and then I went away to find a way of coming back to you. I came here—don't know why, halfway between your aunts and home or something—got a job as a secretary. I cried every night and I dripped milk for you.'

'Which is when you met Dad? At the labs.'

'He reminded me of you a bit.'

'And him. Keith.' Owen tried to put the man's name into inverted commas, like it was an embarrassing brand name for children's cereal, or a euphemism for menstruation.

'No, not him, I never missed him. Just you.'

Owen realised at that moment that he'd got it wrong all along. He'd always wondered why on earth Gareth had married Mari, why he married down in IQ levels, when it was the other way round. Of course he'd fallen for this comely blonde twenty years his junior, him a fusty lab technician, her an exotic girl with a past. What he should have been asking himself is what on earth Mari would have seen in Gareth.

'And you thought, here's a man desperate enough to take on me and my baby.'

Mari shifted. Owen looked at her. She was no longer the girl-woman he'd grown up with and his father must have fallen in love with. Owen could see the ruthlessness and detachment that must have allowed her to do what she had to do. They stared at one another for a few seconds, a game of chicken which he won.

'Not exactly,' she said.

'What exactly?'

'He never knew about you.'

'Sorry?'

'He married me, quickly, said he was scared I'd change my mind. I almost did a few times, when I thought of Keith, but then I'd only have to think of you to change it back. I told him that a distant cousin had died in childbirth and had wanted me to adopt her little one and could we and of course he said yes. He'd have said yes to anything I asked for then. My aunts and Nan and Granddad promised never to tell and we went to get you, your dad and I. You were almost a year old and walking and had proper hair, cut at a barber's, so beautiful. He fell in love with you right off and you with him. You couldn't hardly speak, but you said "Daddy" to him, or at least that's what he thought. Jeanie told me later that it was the only thing you could say then anyway, "da da da" all day long, but I never told your dad.'

'Did you ever tell him the truth about anything? For fuck's sake, Mum?' He imbued the word with the same disdain as 'Keith'.

She shook her head.

'But he knew, didn't he?'

'I didn't think, I never wanted to. I thought he didn't. He didn't know.'

'But he did. Read his email. He knew.' She began to weep, proper snotty, face-disfiguring tears, punctuated by great gulps of air to feed them. He looked at the woman who was his mother, the one he knew to be his mother in every sense of the word for the first time. She looked so like him, but even more like Ruby.

'He knew, Mum. But he forgave you.' And, he supposed, he would forgive her too. If not now, then in a few months' time, though like his father he'd never say it out loud.

When Lucy phoned her, Sierra had just been wondering what the opposite of derailing was. Railing? Whatever the word, it was happening to her life. Far from feeling sad about having effectively estranged herself from her mother, she felt liberated, like one of those child stars who divorce their parents. And Jason the drug dealer wouldn't be able to find her. Her mother was wrong, he didn't know where she lived, because she didn't live there any more. Ha. Her exile had also proved to be a good thing since she found sanctuary at Michael's cocoon of a flat, while he had been playing Dad of the Year round at Tess's.

She was pleased to have his flat to herself for almost two weeks, but she surprised herself by feeling just as pleased when, a couple of nights ago, he'd turned up and slept on the sofa so as not to wake Sierra, giving her the most almighty shock in the morning. She hadn't dared go back home, or the place she now only referred to as 'Mum's flat', but had borrowed clothes from Chloe and some unwanted ones from Tess, and spent money she didn't have on new underwear. It was quite a relief after years of hoarding and overstuffed cupboards to have what would be described as a 'capsule wardrobe'—even if the mix had proved a little eccentric.

Yes, for a homeless person with few clothes, life was really quite good, but then Lucy had only gone and ruined it all. She knew she shouldn't shoot the messenger and all that, but fuck she was angry at her and that was before daring to even look at what

Lucy had told her about.

She got it up on her screen and initially found herself staring at it dispassionately. The girl seemed so far away from her image of herself that she couldn't process that it could actually be her. For one thing, the girl on the screen was much prettier and thinner than she'd have thought. It's funny, video image was actually more flattering for big-featured girls like her than a still photo. The girl on the computer screen was also a much better actress. If she hadn't known how bored she had felt and how contrived all this 'I'm wet, I'm wet, oh yeah baby' stuff had been, then she'd have believed the girl in the video was having the time of her life. She'd watched a bit of porn, stuff that had got sent around on emails, never anything hardcore, and now she wondered how dead inside the participants had been. And why had she never noticed before how irritating Josh's voice was, the way it veered between Home Counties and hood, the squeakiness of it?

And then it began to sink in. Her whole body mottled with shame. She glanced outside the gallery windows, convinced that every passing person had seen her with her hands down her pants, moaning. The more she looked at it, the worse it became. It was the act of it, the filming of it, the broadcasting of it, it was the fact that she would look like she had colluded in it, given her permission for it.

Just how much shit could be thrown at one girl? Her mother was going to disown her for not carrying out a drug deal on her behalf, she was homeless, and judging by the gallery's accounts and Tess's absence she was pretty sure she'd soon be jobless. And now she was an inadvertent porn star.

What if it went viral? Got posted on YouTube? People would email the clip around to each other with perky little exhortations to 'check this out!' and 'hot stuff from a big girl!'. Comment boards would be filled with people debating whether she should have got all her pubic hair off or just the Brazilian (thank god, thought Sierra, that the video had been taken before she'd let herself get hairy). 'Derek from Derby' would say she was well lardy, fat cow, another message board user would defend her, saying that she was 'curvy' or 'healthy', before someone else would point at her stomach and say it's 'like gross, she should so go on a diet!!!!'.

She felt the shame of a fallen woman. No man would want her now.

Owen would not want her now.

*   *   *

Lucy was worried about Tess. She was acting as if she had been abandoned by Michael, as if she was a poor nineteenth-century virgin misused by the village squire rather than a grown-up who had chosen to get pregnant by an anonymous donor.

It was not as if Lucy had lots of time to give, what with her job, the children, letting Jamie go off to hang out with his friends—sorry, make their important film. Never had so many hours of work gone into so few minutes of celluloid. Short was not a description of the process of making it.

She sat amid the rubble of Tess's flat. Her friend had always tended towards unabashed untidiness, but it had usually been confined to the bedroom while this was verging on some sort of clinical diagnosis. Flowers sat in mouldy dank water; discarded, yellow-stained breast pads and dirty nappies filled the paper bins; wet clothes squatted unwashed in the washing machine. The stench of baby excrement mixed with the rusty tin stink of those blessed sanitary pads that Tess was still using to catch the unceasing tide of blood that poured postnatally was overlaid with the smell of six or seven nappies a day, then finished with a top note of the putrid artificiality of scented nappy sacks. While Tess fed, Lucy ripped around, finding satisfaction in how much easier a flat with one adult and one child living in it was to sort out than a house with four.

'Can we not sort out some sort of maternity nurse?' she asked.

'Mummy did offer me one, but I said I'd rather have the money. Plus I wasn't sure that I wanted some bossy woman living with me.'

'She'd help you.'

'That's what Michael was supposed to be doing.'

'Yes. Well, he's not. Why did he go?'

Tess shrugged. All women were changed by motherhood, but Lucy had never known anyone as changed as she was. All those years, she had wanted Tess to show a bit of humility but now she yearned for that cocksure arrogance.

'Tess, it's completely normal to feel a bit overwhelmed by a baby at the beginning. I know I did.'

Tess snorted.

'I did, I really did. You feel so discombobulated. Especially if you're a control freak like me.'

'Yes, but being a control freak you made sure you were hooked up to a handsome, malleable man-servant like Jamie to do all the domestic work.'

'Is that what you think? That I deliberately set myself up with someone who would be a stay-at-home father.'

'Of course. Come on, Lucy, you never do anything without first considering all the pros and cons. You wanted a baby, you wanted a career. Jamie: the perfect solution. And he's nice looking, too.'

'You're so wrong, really. You're right that I always think everything through, but getting pregnant with Rosa was the one spontaneous thing I've ever done in my life.' And look where it's got me.

Lucy the love actuary knew it all. Once she had split up with Mark she had a few years to find a man to settle down with before her fertility started dropping precipitously. She ought, she calculated, to be in a position to start trying for her first child by 33. Her careful perusal of the statistics showed that she should find someone a few (but not too many) years older than her, who earned a little (but not too much) more than she did and whose parents were still together. Chances of infidelity were increased by him being too successful and wealthy, as well as by being preposterously handsome or working in an industry dominated by those of the opposite sex.

Jamie was younger, hotter, low-to-nil earning and his parents had split up acrimoniously three years before he'd met Lucy. She had long harboured a suspicion that a large part of her appeal was the fact that her house offered him somewhere to store all his stuff, now that the place he had grown up in had been sold.

In Lucy's plans, any decision to have a baby would of course be something that she would discuss with the potential father, this mythical higher-earning two-years-older man, and then would make careful financial provision for time taken off for maternity leave. In fact, to be truly confident of the right outcome, he should be her husband, because married parents were so much less likely to split up than unmarried ones.

So that's the way parenthood was going to happen. And this was the way it did. One evening, she'd wiped herself after peeing and noticed the slimy egg-white discharge that reminded her that she was ovulating. Even if she hadn't had the physical signs of ovulation, she would have known anyway, since it was day thirteen of her punctual cycle.

That night, Jamie had fumbled for a condom.

'No, I'm safe.' She heard the words but they surprised her. She didn't know that she'd ever told such an outright lie in her life. Afterwards, she could have got up and washed herself out. The next day she could have got the morning-after pill. But she didn't. Instead, she lay there and even very slightly tilted her pelvis up so that Jamie's sperm pooled inside her. She tried to rationalise it. It wasn't that she wanted to get pregnant, not exactly, she was just momentarily curious as to whether she could or whether she was one of these women that the papers were filled with, these 'career women fuelling an infertility epidemic'.

She shouldn't have been surprised, in the circumstances, when she discovered that, yes, if you have sex in the most fertile time of your cycle, then, yes, there's a possibility that you'll get pregnant.

You could even say that she'd trapped Jamie, but it hadn't been deliberate; well, not exactly, that's not the way she liked to see it.

Tess was now staring at Gus whose nappy was visibly overflowing.

'I'll do it,' Lucy said.

'Would you? Such a darling, thank you.'

'It's not true, you know. I didn't plan to have a family with Jamie. It's all turned out very differently to what I expected.'

'That makes two of us.'

'But you did plan this, you did plan Gus. I know how difficult it is to get pregnant at our age, especially if you're doing it an assisted way; the odds against it, every month, the grinding rounds of it, the horrible drugs. I didn't have to go through it myself, but I've done enough financial planning for those who have to know how difficult it is.'

'Indeed. It seems some people really want babies, don't they?'

Some people? You really wanted a baby, you must have done. Lucy again wondered what had made Tess, who had so blithely rejected motherhood, change her mind. When she had been worrying, after breaking up with Mark, about whether she'd ever meet anyone else, she had shared with Tess the statistic that was most alarming her: that 40 per cent of graduate women their age were going to be childless. Tess had laughed and said that was the best news she'd had all day.

*　　　*　　　*

However much he knew that it could happen to

anyone, Michael was very unnerved by the fact that he had been unable to feel his old desire towards Tess. But the situation had not been ideal, what with Gus being asleep in his Moses basket in the corner of the room, them having just had a huge argument, and Tess's long idealised body showing vivid reminders of the birth.

The honeymoon was over. The holidays were almost over and he was back at school, preparing for the parents' meetings that heralded the beginning of term. The head had moved him down the school, telling him that they needed their best teachers concentrated in early years, and in some ways Reception was a gift because he got a chance to get in there early, inspire the children. In other ways, he was already sick of flipping phonics, of jellybeans jumping, je je je and ants on the apple, a, a, a.

If phonics was bad, the parents were even worse. He couldn't decide which ones he hated more, oscillating between those that didn't care or those that cared too much. As his was what was always referred to as an 'inner-city' school, his pupils came from what was, also euphemistically, known as 'a diverse range of backgrounds'. This meant there were professionals living in million-pound houses, dipping nervous feet into the waters of state education before yanking their kids out at seven, ten or eleven. And there were those who had lived in the area for four generations, whining about how it wasn't how it used to be. The third group comprised the ones that were making it how it didn't used to be, the various immigrants and refugees.

One day, Tess would be sitting on one of the tiny

plastic children's chairs that teachers make parents sit on (it was, they agreed when they had drinks in the pub, to make sure they knew their place). Michael wondered who she would be sitting with, or whether she'd be here alone. Would there ever be a man that Gus called 'Dad'? He had really believed that it would be him. Fool.

He bumped into Rachel as he made his way out. She smiled eagerly at him and he felt a great shame mixed with a burst of optimism.

'I don't suppose I could buy you a drink, could I?' he asked. A drink that could act as a balm and as holy water, to exorcise the memories of both the night of Gus's birth and that of his failure with Tess.

CHAPTER SIXTEEN

CRITICAL ORGAN SHRINKAGE

'Glad you finally made it.' Tess answered the door accessorised by cashmere, expensive scent and an infant clamped to her breast. Lucy had led Owen to expect that he'd find her weeping in sackcloth, but she looked much as she had always done, straight-backed and composed.

'Sorry,' Owen said with a shrug.

'So, what's your excuse?' She sat down to continue feeding. 'Can you get me a glass of water.' Not a question, but an order.

'I got this for the little one.' He brandished a neat cardboard box. 'What did rubbish godfathers do before Baby Gap?'

She opened it. 'It's for a newborn. And since Gus is a month old tomorrow, he's far too big to wear it.'

'I bought you these.' He threw a small jewellery box in her direction. She opened it to find a pair of emerald earrings. According to Owen's man at the jewellers, it's customary for the father to buy the mother a little gemstone token on giving birth, or at least it was a custom the industry was doing its best to encourage. He and Michael, he felt, were divvying up the father's jobs—Michael had done dirty work of nappy changing and sponging up Tess's discontent, while Owen was doing the old-fashioned showy stuff. He'd have a cigar and a bottle of champagne later.

She smiled. 'Don't think I'm so easily mollified. I'm really rather cross at you, Owen, and wondering if I shouldn't have chosen another benefactor in your particular godfather slot.'

'Try them on.'

She slotted them into waiting ears and wandered to the bedroom. He followed and saw her do her Tess mirror face, head tilting backwards, eyes looking down her nose at her reflection, a pursed pout playing at her mouth.

'They're lovely.' She punched him in the arm. He supposed it was meant to be playful, but it rather hurt.

'It's what fathers do, apparently—they buy their wives some jewel in appreciation at them producing an heir. It's called a push present.'

'You do know you're not the father,' she said with faux seriousness.

'I do sometimes wonder.' He looked at Gus for the first time and saw his dark skin and a certain

251

enthusiasm for breasts that did remind him of someone close to home. And, after all, if he had learned anything over the last few weeks it was that being a father was more than a matter of biology. And more too, he conceded, than buying expensive but tasteful gifts.

'What?' said Tess. 'I stole your sperm, froze it and then implanted it a few years later? Don't flatter yourself.'

'To be honest, darling, that doesn't sound any more implausible than the yarn you've told us.'

'Not you too. What is everyone's problem with what I've done? I've had a baby without a father. Not the first. Not the last. End of.'

Owen felt a rush of grief sizzling inside his head that felt very close to anger. 'I miss my father.'

Tess looked at him and the wetness on his cheeks. With Owen, even his tears were man-size. 'Oh, Owen, why didn't you tell me? Why didn't anybody tell me? I'm so sorry.' She touched his arm but no more, not being one for hugging.

Not as sorry as he felt for himself. 'Are you?'

'Yes, of course. I do know about losing a father, you know. I still think of it as something that defines me, though you're not allowed to. You're allowed to never get over the loss of a child,' she glanced at Gus as she said this, 'but not of a parent. It's part of the life cycle, isn't it, parents die so babies can get born? It's horrible, and I miss him every day.'

'I'm sorry, I probably wasn't very good when your dad died.'

'No one was. Everyone thought I was just being pathetic; Daddy's girl, they all said. Yes, you too, I heard you. I know I like to be the first in everything, first to do yoga, first to go to Laos, first to try eyelash extensions, but I really wish I hadn't been the first to lose a parent. I felt like nobody understood.'

They sat in silence for a couple of minutes, which Owen was the first to break.

'At least you haven't said anything about him not being my real father.'

'As if I would. And he was, anyway, wasn't he? In the ways that matter.'

'My mum was. Is.'

'What?'

'My real mum.'

'I'm so glad you think so. You've always been so rude about her.'

'No, she really is—my mother, I mean. It turns out that she didn't adopt me but actually had me and persuaded Dad to adopt me. Sort of. It's a long story.'

Tess frowned. 'I'm confused.'

'Only Gareth adopted me. Mum—you know, Mari—she gave birth to me.'

'Crikey. It's like one of those films when someone finds their birth certificate and discovers to their horror that they're adopted. Except the other way round.'

'Exactly. I've always thought my parents weren't my real parents and to my horror I discover one day that my mother is.'

'What some women will do to avoid being a single mother, hey?' Tess moved away. 'Tea?' He nodded. 'It's in the kitchen.'

He laughed, relieved that Gus hadn't entirely obliterated the old Tess. 'How's Sierra?' he shouted from the kettle.

'She's fine, you know, a bit shaken up about this naked Internet thing.'

Owen stopped what he was doing and came out to face Tess. 'What thing?'

'Didn't I tell you? We haven't seen each other for so long, I suppose. That nasty ex of hers has put some porny video of her on the Internet—Google Josh Lawson and you can find it. It's a real-life sex tape, isn't that low rent? The younger generation, I don't know. Lucy's Jamie is the same. It's like it doesn't exist until they've made a video of it, called it a documentary and entered it for a film festival.'

Owen looked stricken. 'Is it horrible?'

Tess stared at him. 'Oh, Owen. You didn't . . . you haven't . . .'

'What?'

'You know.'

'No.'

'You have, you've gone and slept with her.' She shook her head. 'Being a godparent isn't like being the best man, you know. You're not obliged to sleep with the bridesmaid.'

'It's no big deal.'

'I wonder if Ruby would think so. And I'm sure it's a big deal to Sierra.'

'She's cool about it.'

Tess shook her head. 'You really are a selfish tosser, aren't you, Owen? The poor girl's got enough on her plate without you wading in.'

'You're calling me selfish?'

'Yes, I am. You can't keep going on sleeping with women and not thinking about the consequences.'

How dare she speak to me this way? he thought. I'm grieving. 'I don't hear any complaints.'

'That's because you never listen.'

'I never got any from you.'

'True, but I'm different from other girls.'

'I think what you've done is far more selfish.' Tess, sitting there, all Madonna-like on the sofa, suddenly seemed to embody a world where men were forever being duped and deceived by women. In the one way that really counted, women were able to know a truth that men could never guarantee—that a baby was really theirs. All the anger and confusion he felt towards Mari welled up inside. 'Deliberately having a baby who won't know his father. My mother at least had the excuse of youth and idiocy. What's yours? It's the not knowing that killed me. That's made me what I am. That's the thing you're denying Gus, knowledge. He'll go to expensive schools, he'll pass all his exams, he'll probably end up at Cambridge and be cracking on pub quiz teams, and everyone will say, doesn't little Gus Franklin know a lot about everything? But he'll never know the only thing that he really needs to know. Who his father is. You selfish cow, Tess.' He felt strong for the first time in a month. He was engulfed by his anger: at Gareth's death and his own birth; about the gilded week all those years ago that his silly mother spent being conned by some small-time Lothario; that Gareth knew but had never said anything; about the decades of wondering who had spawned him; about years of countless women and three, or was it four, fiancées. At that moment, it all seemed to be Tess's fault. 'You really are a selfish monster, Tess,' he repeated. 'You only think of yourself and you make everybody else only think of you and when they've finished thinking about you they've only got energy enough to think about themselves, so they spread your selfishness like a computer virus, you're the email that infects everybody's hard drive and because of you the world is a small bit, just a little bit, more selfish than it would be without you.' The words were out but the blackness remained. He couldn't take them back now, anyway.

'Have you quite finished?'

'Yes?' The certainty had evaporated. That had been the longest speech he'd ever made in his life and he wasn't sure he remembered anything that he had said.

She calmly put Gus down in the Moses basket that perched on wooden sticks in the corner of the room, an oddly primitive ensemble. 'It's funny,' she said, though it was clearly anything but, 'that you should talk about infections.'

'Why?'

'Because it's you, Owen, who is spreading disease through the world, ruining lives, changing them. You did it to me and now I gather you've done it to Sierra. If she's got any sense she'll take my advice and get a test done immediately.'

'She's pregnant?' Owen said with horror.

Tess laughed. 'Quite the opposite.'

Owen grabbed her. The last woman he'd touched like this had been his mother. Her tiny form had been so soft and pliant in his arms that he had felt like he was admonishing a small child not to walk out into the road without looking both left and right. Tess was different. She felt as strong as a man he might tackle on a rugby pitch. He felt no protectiveness, only the old combative urge kick in. He would wrestle the truth out of her, he felt, quite literally. 'Tess, I'm sick of this. What are you talking about?'

'She should go to the clinic and get herself tested for every filthy STD that you've picked up from your eternal quest for an identity through casual sex. I love that girl, I don't want her to have her fallopian tubes ruined.'

He let go of her, but stayed standing, his eyes level with hers. 'What are you talking about? Tess, you have to tell me.'

'Chlamydia, Owen, chlamydia.' He reeled. 'It's not the name of some posh girl you've slept with.'

'I know what chlamydia is. I had it years ago, got tested, took the antibiotics. Sexually transmitted disease, can cause infertility . . .' He stopped and looked at Tess and his brain fumbled towards a truth that he had always known, deep down. 'You?'

She nodded and then pulled her face up to stick her chin out. 'Yes, Owen, me. I really haven't slept with very many men. That's the advantage of being taken out to supper by all these geriatrics—they never actually want to follow through. Mummy made me go for a check-up with her gynae when I got to thirty and he discovered that my fallopian tubes were, to use an inappropriate word, completely fucked as a result of an untreated bout of chlamydia. And I knew who to blame.'

'But why didn't you tell me?' She raised an eyebrow and more unacknowledged truths came into focus. 'But you did.' Owen thought back to the anonymous letter he'd got years ago that told him he needed to get to a doctor. He'd ignored it for a few months before finally getting himself off to a sexual health clinic, whereupon he discovered that he had chlamydia, which had seemed like a good thing at the time, seeing as how they were all terrified of AIDS. He'd taken some antibiotics,

257

sorted it out, done. Might have mentioned it to some of the girls he'd slept with. Might not have. His mate had suggested he have a chlamydia party where he invited them all over to let them know. Instead, he'd gone to the pub and raised a glass to the silent STD and sung a song about it rhyming with Lydia with some blokes from work.

'That letter was from me,' said Tess. 'Obviously. I didn't even bother to disguise the writing.'

Of course, thought Owen, that enormous looping extravagant hand that comes from expensive girls' schools, the one that shouts of confidence even when writing of silent bacteria. He knew it had looked familiar, but recognising handwriting was a bit like recognising makes of shoe—something for girls, not men. 'But I still don't understand what you're accusing me of.'

'Think about it, Owen—your aversion to condoms and my infertility would explain a lot about the way I've chosen to live my life over the last ten years.'

'But you had a baby.'

'Much to my doctor's surprise.'

'And that's great. It's all worked out in the long run, hasn't it?'

'You've got no idea, Owen. No idea at all.'

*   *   *

Michael felt sure that he was never going to have sex again. It was fine, he told himself. Sir Isaac Newton was a celibate. He probably never would have discovered gravity if he'd been distracted by things going up instead of down.

Rachel had been much nicer about it than Tess,

258

but that had only made it worse. He couldn't even say, 'But this has never happened to me before,' though at least it meant he could promise that 'It's not you, it's me,' with a truthful ring. She had said, 'No it's fine, really, it's fine,' but had then started crying, which suggested that it wasn't, it really wasn't. He felt like shit. But then he would have felt like shit if he'd managed to shag her, given that he had no intention of going out with her and he knew that was what she wanted of him. You see, even nice girlish men like Michael can be utter shits when they want to be. He was like Owen. No, he was worse than Owen, because he knew how to be a better person.

And he missed Gus. When a baby first comes into your life, you wonder how you'll ever find time for it. And then, so soon, you wonder how you ever filled your time before.

Sierra was the only bright spot in the gloaming. And she would, he was sure, eventually go back to her mother's flat, drug stash or no drug stash. And she didn't fancy him. And even if she did, he wouldn't be able to get it up for her anyway.

For the first time since he had stopped believing in god and started believing in sex, he found himself making pacts with a higher being. God, if you sort out my impotence (would that make it my potence?), I'll start going to church again. No, I won't, but I'll take Gus to church, occasionally. He's the one you want, anyway, they always want the little ones. Well, I'll take him if Tess lets me. I am his godfather after all.

He looked over at Sierra, who was watching TV as he made them both some supper. His flat was great, courtesy of a shared ownership scheme for key workers, but the sitting room and kitchen were one room and he missed being able to listen to Radio 4 as he cooked.

'Are you sure you don't mind me being here?' asked Sierra for the twentieth time.

'No, I'm sure.' Which was true, despite the problem with Radio 4.

'Do you think you'll ever go back to kipping at Tess's?'

Kipping, what a casual word for those few weeks. It suggested that he'd been squatting as Gus's father, subletting the role. 'It was never a formal arrangement, just a habit that became entrenched. She made it very clear that I was not to mistake it for anything else.'

'I expect you're wondering when I'll find somewhere else to live.'

'No, really, Sierra. To be honest, I quite liked the company at Tess's, so I think I'd be quite lonely if you weren't here.'

'I don't believe you, but thanks anyway. What time's our programme on?'

It had only been a couple of weeks but already Michael and Sierra had developed the customs and rituals that create families. She did the supermarket run, he bought the newspaper, he did the cooking, she washed up. He had the bathroom first, she called out, 'I'm your homey, hon,' when she came back in the evenings and they made up the sofa bed each night. They looked through the week's TV listings together and decided what they would watch; Michael would point out all the important films that she should be adding to her canon and then would forget to save them. They had become a couple in all but one, very important respect.

This seemed to be the story of his life over the last year: he got the domestic bit, Owen the sex. Worse, the casual way she had told him about her and Owen made it clear that she wouldn't have ever entertained the idea that he could possibly be jealous.

'Sierra?'

'Yes.'

'Are you upset about Owen?'

She shrugged. 'Sort of, a bit. And then again, no, not at all. Upset because my life's so shit and confused and I thought he might clear a few things up. Silly, I know. I've heard all the songs from girl bands about buying your own shoes and being your own boss, but . . . I don't know, he seemed like a grown-up man.' She hugged her legs and then stretched one out straight while still holding onto the heel. She was very bendy, Michael noticed, not for the first time.

She continued, 'So, yeah, a bit upset, but then again he wouldn't have solved anything. He's got problems of his own—his dad's just died, he's adopted and he doesn't know who his real mum and dad are, and you know, anyway, he's well fucked up.'

Fucked. He shuddered as he remembered both Tess and Rachel's bodies offered to him as gifts, one gracelessly, one generously, both taken back to the shop.

'You're over him, then?'

'Never really under him—well, not for very long.' Michael tried to banish that image, but then he gave into it and found it strangely alluring. He closed his eyes and imagined that it was he who was on top. When you're in that position, who cares

261

how tall you are? 'To be honest, I'm not sure I should be doing anyone at the moment, after what happened with Josh.'

'What did happen?' She looked at him quizzically and then smiled. 'Nothing, nothing. You don't speak to Lucy much, then?'

'No, should I?' he asked, resolving to speak to her as soon as he discreetly could.

'No. Are you over Tess?'

'To use your phrase, I was never under her.' And that image no longer aroused him. 'What makes you think I want to be?'

'Tess, I suppose—she's basically said as much. And you've got something sexual and not sexual about you, which makes me think she's probably right.'

'What do you mean?'

'Non-sexual in the way that I can be talking to you like this. That it doesn't feel weird to be here alone with you, to be living in your house, to be alone with a single bloke and to be talking about your sexual and non-sexual sides.'

'I'd prefer to hear about the sexual bit.' He heard his voice sound squeaky.

'OK. Sexual in that you have that look in your eye.'

'What look?'

'You've got it now—the you're thinking about sex look.' He shifted and crossed his legs. 'Which makes me think that you're gay.'

'Not that again.'

'Sexual but not threatening. I can't understand how you can be so sexual, and quite sexy in fact, and yet not make me feel uncomfortable or awkward. So either you're gay or you're hopelessly

262

in love with Tess. Or both. I think Tess reckons her allure transcends sexual orientation.'

'Can I be as honest with you as you clearly feel that you can be with me?' She nodded. 'I'm not gay, really I'm not. I wouldn't mind if I were and I do have three very domineering sisters, but I'm not. What can you do about it? I have to come out of the closet and announce to the world, that yes, I love Joan Crawford films and I watch the swimming events at the Olympics, but no, I'm not gay.'

Sierra giggled and pushed her foot towards him in readiness of its evening massage. 'All right, I believe you. Tell me about you and Tess.'

'Not much to tell.' Though there was, or there had been, but only in his head. 'She's always been impossibly glamorous to me. I think she would have been, anyway, as she's so gorgeous and older—she's always been seven years older than me. Always will be.'

'Makes sense.'

'Ha ha. But on top of the obvious attraction of the older beautiful woman to a weedy adolescent boy, her family were just so rich and confident and exotic. It's funny, because looking back it was my family that were properly foreign, with our Polish church and club and narrow circle of fellow Poles, while Tess's dad was English, sort of. But they just used to breeze in and out of our lives like people who lived abroad, in somewhere like Buenos Aires, and were just visiting London for expensive shopping weekends. They'd arrive at our overcrowded house and make it seem even smaller because of their largeness. And their largesse. They always brought presents and stories and he chugged on a cigar and the house would smell of his smoke

263

and her perfume for days, until my mother's aggressive fight-back with the air freshener finally won out.'

'But when,' asked Sierra, 'did you start fancying her?'

He scowled. 'I never fancied her. That's too prosaic a word. I worshipped her. I don't think I ever didn't. Even before I became aware of sex I was aware of her as sexy. It just mutated from me wanting to be her to me wanting to be with her. You know those men who say they always knew they were gay, before they even knew what being gay was? I always knew I wanted Tess. I remember one Christmas Eve we all trooped round to their palace for drinks. Tess stood on a stepladder to put the glass star on the top of the tree. She must have been almost grown-up by then, but it was her job and she always got to do it, even though by this time there must have been nephews and nieces from Lord Franklin's first haul of children. She leaned up and her top rose and I could see her stomach and the top became clingy. I think I was about nine, but that was when I began to think about her naked as much as clothed. She always wore such marvellous clothes. Her mother used to take her to the collections so when everyone else was wearing second-hand black from Kensington Market, she was in couture.'

He sighed and went back to the story. 'You know what it's like as a teenager. You've got so many acres of thoughts to be filled and I just got into the habit of filling them with Tess. Tess turns to me and tells me she's always wanted me. Tess decides that it's time she taught me the ways of love. Tess invites me to stay with her at university and introduces me to everyone as her boyfriend. Boy would have been the operative word since I hadn't even done my GCSEs by then. And it wasn't just that I was younger than her, I looked young enough to be her son.'

Sierra hugged her knees. 'But nothing ever happened?'

Despite his shame, a part of him was proud that she had once offered herself to him, albeit in such a petty and ungenerous way. He considered boasting of this to Sierra, but then realised that ultimately there had been nothing to boast of. 'No, of course not. I was just some geeky second cousin who she liked to favour as a way of pissing off the "ugly sisters", as she charmingly referred to my siblings. And, as I've since discovered, Tess doesn't even particularly like sex, anyway. In the meantime, I've wasted the last two decades mooning over a non-starter.'

'You're not a . . . it's not as if, you've not, well, not done . . .'

He laughed. 'I'm not a virgin, if that's what you're asking. I've had a succession of long-legged lovelies. Of some length. The relationship time, I mean, rather than their legs—though actually that too.'

'Longest, shortest, when, how, when did you lose it?'

They were talking relationship histories— strange, thought Michael. Very strange. 'Lost it aged seventeen to a girl in my English A-level group. My usual MO, wheedled my way in by being such a sensitive girly boy and offered her a shoulder to cry on when she found out that Joe Potts was a hard man in all but one respect.' He felt bad on

Joe's behalf only now. 'Thought it was her fault, couldn't understand why he wasn't gagging for it and only after one thing, just like her magazines told her the boys were. I ended up proving the magazines right and we went out with each other for all of sixth form.'

'Doesn't sound that dysfunctional. Weren't you supposed to be pining for your cousin?'

'I was, really I was—I always used to think of Tess to make sure I didn't go the way of Joe Potts. Who I saw recently and is a fabulous muscle Mary who runs a bar in Tenerife.'

Sierra sniggered. 'Then?'

'University, usual smorgasbord of opportunities.'

'Smorgas-what?'

'An as-much-as-you-can-eat buffet which I barely grazed upon. A couple of relationships that lasted a term, a few that lasted a week, snogged a boy, but only because all the girls were doing that thong-flicking lesbo action stuff. Doesn't really work that way round.' He wrinkled his nose. 'Does the thought of my man-on-man action turn you on?'

'Yeah, baby. What about after uni?'

'Eliza: two years, most serious since my schoolgirl love. Finished because we rather earnestly realised that it wouldn't be forever and so what was the point. Rather premature at twenty-five, don't you think?'

'No, not at all. What's the point, otherwise?'

'That pretty much brings me up to date. What about you? You say you've never been single.'

'You mean what I said that time at Lucy's? I might have been exaggerating for Owen's benefit.'

'Do you miss sex when you're not having it?'

266

If she was going to treat him like some gay best friend, he could do the same back.

'I do. Fuck, that's sad to admit. It's always struck me as crap, this idea of men being much more into sex than women. At least in my experience. It's so embarrassing when you're the one who's more into it as it seems to go against the natural order of things and they make out you're weird. I miss it like food when I'm not getting it. And I have a fiddle myself, but you know, it's so mechanical.'

'Not necessarily,' said Michael. 'I get myself in the mood, get the cine film of fantasy going in my head, a bit of back story . . .'

'Involving Tess, no doubt.'

Not any more. He nodded his assent for fear that the words in his head might articulate themselves by accident.

Sierra continued to torture him. 'It's funny how all that porn for women is about putting sex into some sort of romance,' she said the word with contempt. 'But I find actually, when I do it—you know, myself—it's more about just putting it in, or putting your finger on it or something. Know what I mean? Just doing it. I've got a vibrator,' she continued cheerfully, as if telling him she'd got them a treat of some sticky toffee pudding with crème fraîche for afters. 'I'll show you if you like.'

'It's fine, thanks. I'm off to bed, really tired. The first half of term always kills me.'

'All right, night then.' She looked hurt. It hurt Michael to walk. He had to get into the privacy of his bedroom to play back in his head the very latest fuel for his emissions. He leaped under the duvet and took his cock in his hands.

It works, thank you, it works.

Lucy had emailed all the godparents a photo of Gus with a suggestion that they meet up soon to plan a christening or 'naming ceremony'. He was wearing horizontal green and blue stripes. Evidently with babies you didn't worry about stripes making them look fatter or the camera adding pounds. Quite the contrary: Lucy had included a special mention of his chubby thighs and dimpled bottom, as if these were good things.

Lucy was such an adult. I wish I were her, Sierra thought. Or she was my mother. She would never ask her daughter to do a drug deal for her. If she were my mother, I'd never have let myself be filmed by a porn-loving boyfriend while pretending that I enjoyed it.

Sierra resolved that she too would become grown-up about her very un-grown-up life. In pursuit of adulthood, Sierra wrote a list, dividing the page into two columns, Problems and Solutions. Into the first she detailed: hole in gallery schedules → poss. unemployment; homeless; loveless; motherless. Next bullet point: am online porn star.

She looked at the second column, a great white tower of blankness. She tried to think about the problems one at a time, picking on the first as the only one with some potential resolution. She rung Tess about it.

'You said you'd be in straight after the baby was born to sort it out.'

'Don't be silly, darling, I never said that.'

'You did. You said that nothing would change.'

'And you believed me. It was the hormones

talking. I'm sure you'll work something out. Got to go.'

So that was that. She could leave that month empty, which would screw up the already screwed finances even further, which would almost certainly lead to the gallery going under. Sierra knew that there were graduates with top qualifications struggling to get jobs at the moment. She really couldn't face simpering through another set of interviews and explaining away her lack of degree to get a starting salary that bordered on the minimum wage.

So the alternative was to work something out for herself.

She doodled and she Googled. No inspiration.

She looked at her emails and the photo of Gus again. Her mother had worn horizontal stripes and hooped tights in lots of the photos Sierra had of her. For people above the age of one, they're the preserve of the very skinny, like wellington boots and fur gilets, something that either makes you look very dumpy or very lithe. Sierra thought of that photo her mother had shown her, the one in which she was very pregnant, and all the conflicting feelings of pride and prudishness fermented again. The photographer's name had been Dez. Her mother had always said he was a little bit in love with her, hence her getting so many shoots for the sort of fashion bibles that pioneered heroin and porn chic long before the average Sunday supplement had model spreads that looked like stills taken from a cheap skin flick. Dez what? She wondered whether Susie was still in touch. He must have some great photos, seeing as how he had trailed Susie with such persistence and she in turn had trailed some of the biggest bands of the day. She was pretty sure her mother even had a box of his original prints stored somewhere, though knowing her mother, she'd probably ripped them up and used them as roaches or something. No, she hadn't, she'd seen them there recently, in a shoe box at the top of the wardrobe. For a flat so small it was big on hiding places. Which is when she remembered why she hadn't been there since the day after Gus was born. The flat—did she dare to go back there? What if Jason had got it, she didn't know the word, staked? She looked in her bag for the keys and threw them in the air in a self-consciously devil-may-care gesture to convince herself.

*   *   *

Lucy practised saying the words, 'We've got to talk' every day, but never got a chance to say them. There was a Lucy-evasion programme being enacted by Jamie. Whereas once, he had merely watched television in a different room, after the 'always going to bed exactly half an hour after her' phase, he'd graduated to kipping on the inflatable mattress in the box room because he suffered from insomnia—due to all the creativity, he'd imply.

Now, he just wasn't there. She'd rush in from work, he'd be waiting at the door, ready to go and meet up with the friends he was doing the film with, leaving her to have what she liked to think of as 'quality time' with Rosa and Ned, but in reality was a bath, two fractious kids and bedtime delaying tactics.

'We've got to talk,' she said to Jamie, this time

out loud.

'Sorry, got to go.'

'No, we really have to talk.' She closed the door to the sitting room, where Rosa and Ned were watching their prescribed 30 minutes of DVD, in this case a bit of a Japanese cartoon that had been recommended to her as gender neutral. God forbid that Rosa should get the idea that there were different rules for boys and girls.

Jamie used this distraction as an opportunity to manoeuvre himself to the front door. She ran and grabbed him, surprising herself with this act of near violence.

'Let go of me.' He tried to put his courier bag between them. Is this what it's come to? That I'm having to physically restrain him in order to have a conversation and he's using a shiny messenger bag to put a barrier between us?

'No. Not until you talk to me.'

He pulled away. 'I've got to work. Do you think my work doesn't count? Because I don't earn lots of money and don't have a pension?'

Not this again. 'Of course not, Jamie.' When of course she did, in a way, think exactly that.

He'd got as far as the pavement now, just as the nearby station was disgorging the returning commuters and the street was as busy as it ever got.

He was going to get away, again. She could not let this happen.

'We've got to talk about why we haven't had sex in the best part of a year.' Had she actually shouted? She probably had.

He froze and looked to his left and right, to check if anyone had heard them and to plan which way he was going to escape. 'Lucy! Not now.'

271

He looked stupidly sexy, in well-cut shorts and a T-shirt that showed how those broad shoulders tapered to a slim torso. How brown his arms were and how muscular his calves were, both a product of the energetic football he played with Rosa and Ned in the park, the happy times that she was funding. He had a physicality about him that translated into being good at sport and, in the early days, fantastic in bed. And in the kitchen, on the stairs, in a field one time . . .

'Yes, now.'

'I've got to go.'

'Now.' She bundled him inside.

'The children?'

'They can watch all of that film. It's foreign.'

'So that's all right then.'

They looked at each other and at least smiled.

'Come on,' said Lucy and went into the kitchen to pour herself a large glass of wine. 'So.'

'So?' he shrugged.

He's going to make me say it again. 'Why haven't we had sex? Jamie, are you having an affair?'

He laughed. He actually laughed. Again Lucy felt an urge to touch him, to check he was real, to inflict pain or pleasure or something, just something to get a reaction. She raised her hand to slap him, but stopped so that it hovered an inch away. She felt embarrassed, like when you go to kiss someone on the cheek and end up kissing their lips by mistake. The hand hung in the air for a second, until she pushed it down with the other one, as if it had no functionality of its own.

'What's so funny? It's not a stupid question. Why won't you have sex with me?'

At that moment the answer seemed blindingly

272

obvious: that she was too old, too haggard, too unattractive that she didn't want to hear the truth. Even with her new plasticised sheen of Botox and fillers, she was too ugly for him.

'It's not you . . .'

'Don't give me that bollocks.' He was forcing her to say it herself, the bastard. 'It's because you find me repulsive.'

'What? No.' He moved closer to her. She couldn't remember the last time he had done so. A recurrent image of him was his departing back.

'Well, you certainly don't find me irresistible.' It hurt her to say these words. The one person who should find her attractive didn't. The vaguely flirty dad at school and that TV news director who'd said she didn't need flattering lighting meant nothing to her. 'Is it someone else?'

He shook his head. 'It really isn't. The problem is I find everyone resistible.'

The door swung open. 'The DVD's finished,' said Rosa. 'It was rubbish.'

Jamie leaped up. 'I'll help with bathtime. The guys can do without me on the script tonight.'

*   *   *

The most different thing about Susie's flat was that it was exactly the same. That pool of water on the walkway outside was always there whatever the weather, the purple paint on the door had that ancient scrape on it that looked like a wonky butterfly, the graffiti on the downstairs lock-ups was still unscrubbed.

But to Sierra it all looked new.

Firstly she'd felt scared. She'd always been afraid

273

when coming onto the estate at nights—for good reason, there were some dodgy types. Not so much her neighbours, but people that they consorted with. But it was only just after six and still light. She should have been fine, but this was a different, specific fear—of Jason the dealer, of the police, of retribution of some sort. She wore dark glasses and a hat. She knew they didn't disguise her—quite the contrary, they drew attention to her—but it made her laugh in a hysterical, anxious way when she tried them on, which gave her a small distraction.

She'd first tried walking with a straight, proud back and then had swapped to skulking. This made her feel more self-conscious, so then she tried to walk normally before realising that this was something that was impossible to do when trying, like when a drunk attempts to totter along a straight line.

Sierra glanced up at the security cameras that pockmarked the estate. She had no idea whether they worked. They didn't make her feel any better either way, for even if they were fully functioning, they wouldn't stop her being attacked, just provide some grainy black and white footage for an episode of *Crimewatch*.

Keys in bag, in lock, they worked. She pushed the door and quickly went inside before she could change her mind.

At first she couldn't decide who had visited. It had been ransacked, she supposed, but quite neatly.

'Mum?' It could easily all just be a sign that Susie had returned.

No answer. The cupboards had been emptied and their contents thrown onto the floor, but with little violence as far as Sierra could tell, in her not extensive knowledge of flats being turned over. Whoever had done it had managed to break into the flat without damaging the door and for this she was grateful.

'Is anyone there?'

She went into the kitchen, which smelled of sour milk. All the cleaning products from below the sink had been pulled out and some of the tins and packets from the cupboards. She stood still, like a cat, forcing her ears into a state of alertness. Nothing. The tension would not leave her. She knew that it would not until she had left the estate and been sucked back down into the claustrophobic depths of the Underground.

She went into Susie's room, the one that had become hers and then her mother's once again. She pulled down a large suitcase and threw her clothes into it, piling them up in that dramatic, haphazard way that people in films do when they want to show that they're leaving, they're really leaving. She then picked up as many as she could from where they had been scattered by whoever had been here, this Jason man probably, went into the bathroom and picked out some toiletries.

There was just one more thing she needed. She looked at the top of the cupboard but someone had swept the jumble that had teetered upon it down to the ground. There she found the plastic bag she'd been looking for, the one that bore no resemblance to the one that Jason or one of his associates had so keenly sought and that now lay at the bottom of the Regent's Canal.

She dragged the suitcase to the door and turned round for one brief moment to survey the place where she had grown up. And she had, she had grown up, she really had.

'Goodbye,' she said quietly and then a little louder, 'goodbye.'

She didn't know whether she'd ever see her mother again, but she knew then that she'd never live here.

*　　　*　　　*

At last the children had gone to sleep. Lucy sighed. They must have inherited their extraordinary bed avoidance repertoire from their father.

Jamie emerged from the bathroom, his hand balled up into a fist. Lucy stared at it without fear. She knew he'd never hit her. She almost, she admitted to herself with a dart of shame mixed with desire, wished he would.

'You wanted a reason for the lack of sex. Here it is.' He slowly unfurled his hand and showed her what was within it. His film-making instincts made him do so with a theatricality that irritated Lucy, especially since all that she could see was a small cardboard box with an unfamiliar word across it and a label with Jamie's name and that of their local doctor's surgery, the one where the children had been vaccinated and where she had had her wasted coil inserted. She opened it up to find a blister-pack of bullet-shaped pills. She looked back to Jamie.

'Sorry, Jamie, but what are they?'

'Antidepressants.'

There was too much to take in. Jamie, the beautiful vital boy whom she'd met while he was literally giving life and blood. 'You're depressed?'

'Was, yes. It was terrible. Not any more, thanks

276

to these.'

'But when were you depressed?'

'Last September, October. When Ned started at school full-time.'

Like one of those empty nest mothers that the school mums in the pub had talked about. 'But you were so looking forward to it, you said it would give you a chance to make films again.'

'That's what I thought. I'd looked forward to it for so long and blamed my lack of career on the children, and then I couldn't blame them any more, but I still wasn't making or doing anything. I felt so tired. Tireder even than when they were babies. I used to drop them off at school and then come home and sleep until lunchtime. And you'd come back from your hard day of earning money and ask me what I'd done and I'd lie. I felt so ashamed. Every evening, I'd say tomorrow will be different, tomorrow I'll start writing or get in touch with my mates, but then by the end of breakfast I'd want to go to bed. I hated myself.'

It seemed to Lucy that this was the first time they'd had a conversation since Ned had started school. How had it been that the moment in which they had thought they would be liberated, they had become so shackled. 'I'm so sorry, Jamie.'

'It's not your fault. I know it's not. You've been amazing, supporting me, housing me. That just made it worse. I just felt like I wasn't ready for all this, that my life had accelerated and I'd missed an important stage.'

'The stage where you live in a cool warehouse apartment with other film-makers and have bicycles hanging from the ceiling and random women wearing boy-shorts and tight T-shirts

277

lounging on the sofa. And lots of DVDs stacked up on bookshelves made out of old packing crates.' Lucy had once seen a photo in a magazine of such an apartment, somewhere in Brooklyn or Santa Monica, and had noticed Jamie mooning over it like a teenager looking at pictures of a blonde in a bikini. 'I know, Jamie. I felt that.'

'You did?'

'You kept on telling me how old you were, like a four-year-old, except that you felt you were too young to be doing all these things. "I'm only twenty-nine and a quarter" sort of thing. And every time you did, I felt guilty.'

'Why? It's not like you trapped me into this life.'

Lucy looked at him. Was he being sarcastic? 'No, but I could have had an abortion, I suppose.' Having got pregnant accidentally on purpose.

'No, no. I love Rosa and Ned.' Not me, thought Lucy, you're not including me. 'I didn't want to have children then, not before establishing myself, but they're the best thing ever to happen to me. And resenting the life that they made me lead only made me feel worse about it all. So I'd go back to bed for another few hours. I was like a fifties housewife in need of some mother's little helpers.'

Lucy looked again at the pills, which came in such an anonymous packet that they might well have been for hay fever. 'Which you did get, you got some mother's little helpers.'

'Stay-at-home dad's little helpers,' said Jamie.

'How come?'

'After a couple of months, I finally went to the doctor and she gave me these.' He stroked the box lovingly.

'Did you not think about talking to me? Or

getting some therapy before you necked them?'

He shrugged. 'I thought I'd give them a try. And they're amazing. They made everything better almost at once. It was like a light being switched on. I thought they'd dull me, but they didn't, quite the opposite. I had this energy and optimism, I got in touch with Joe and we started writing and the words came flying out of me. It was like I had the keys to the kingdom.'

'But you, us, the sex?'

'The doctor told me about the potential side effects. I didn't want the pills that can cause weight gain.'

'Evidently,' said Lucy, eyeing up his intimidatingly smooth stomach.

'These ones have fewer side effects—just nasty indigestion, which I've sorted out, and, you know . . .'

'Loss of libido?'

'Yes. Total wipeout. It's not like I can't, I *can* get it up, I just can't be bothered. It's funny because I always thought of sex and wanting sex as so core to my being, but it isn't. In fact, it's great not wanting sex as you've got all this energy to expend elsewhere.'

'It's great?'

'Yes. Honestly, Lucy, I feel better than I have in years. I really think I'm going to make it, me and Joe, get some reward for all our hard work.'

Great, he feels great. When he was offered his Faustian pact between creativity and sex with her, he didn't hesitate. 'But what about us?'

'You want me to be happy, don't you?'

'Yes, of course.' She thought about all those conversations with the mothers at school, about the

279

way their husbands nagged them for sex. The men were humiliated and belittled by their actions, but how much more dignified they were than she was. Women weren't allowed to be the ones doing the prodding. 'I love you, Jamie, I really do.'

'Me too. Love you, I mean.'

'But I need to . . .' God, how to phrase this? Not 'I need you to make love to me', but what? She cleared her throat. 'I need you to talk to the doctor about coming off the pills. I would like us to have sex again.'

CHAPTER SEVENTEEN

SCARRING

'I am so tired,' said Tess.

'I know what you mean,' Lucy replied. She looked at her watch. She felt guilty for stopping off at Tess's before going home to Rosa and Ned. But then, she felt guiltier if she didn't fit in at least one visit a week to check on Tess, who still refused to embrace motherhood.

'You cannot be as tired as I am. Did you ever use a night nanny?'

'No.'

'Well, you had Jamie instead. A night manny?'

'Yes, I suppose.' She also felt guilty about not getting back to Jamie. Today was his first day without the pills. She didn't know whether she should be expecting a transformation—a plunge back into the torpor that he'd described to her combined with a welcome priapism—or none at all.

She needed some change, obviously. She needed the old Jamie back—not the one before he took the pills, but the one before he needed them. 'I was still pretty tired. Still am. I shouldn't be telling you this, but even when they sleep through, you're still exhausted. It's as if you never catch up on those missing nights and even if they don't wake me by crying any more, I get woken by thoughts and worries about them. I think you lose the habit of sleep.'

'I'm sorry,' said Tess, 'but everybody knows there's nothing so bad as the first six weeks with a newborn.'

'Well, it's just as well that you've almost reached that milestone.' Lucy tried to stop herself from entering into the who's-more-tired competition. 'I think you're coping brilliantly. And he's gorgeous.'

'Is he? He's getting bigger.'

'That's a good thing.' His thighs were like a child's stacking rings and Lucy couldn't look at them without giving them a squeeze. She couldn't stop herself glancing at Tess's midriff. She was amazed that it hadn't just snapped back into place without any effort, but still wobbled with post-partum richness.

People talk about how women forget the pain of childbirth, but really they forget every stage just as soon as they've gone through it. As Lucy stared at Gus's sleepy face, she realised she could no longer truly remember the confusion that comes with a new baby, the anxious staring into their nappies as if the contents were oracles, the little tiny milk blister that forms in the centre of their lips, the baby acne that pocks their cheeks and the cornflakes of skin on their scalps. She felt assailed by the perpetual nostalgia of parenthood, the continual mourning of passing phases.

'I am so tired,' said Tess again.

'You said.' Lucy looked over and realised that Tess was crying. She had never, ever, in two decades of friendship seen her cry. She put out an arm and then retracted it. It finally came to rest on Tess's back. 'Sweetheart, don't cry. It's the tiredness and the hormones. Baby blues, they call it, everybody gets them.'

Tess straightened up, not even wiping away the tears, for that would be to acknowledge their existence. 'But I'm not everybody.'

'No, of course you're not. You're doing this on your own, so you're bound to feel even more tired . . .'

'But I'm not everybody,' she repeated. 'I don't behave in the way that they all behave. Everybody else has babies. I don't. I was never supposed to.'

Lucy thought back to Tess's words in the ambulance when they thought she might be losing the baby, when she'd said she had never wanted one anyway.

'What do you mean? You're supposed to have Gus. You're glad you have him, aren't you?'

'After I went to so much trouble to get him, you mean.'

'Did you?'

'That's the story.'

'But is it just that, a story? I don't know, Tess, it's never added up to me. I never thought you'd have children.'

Tess gave a strained laugh. 'Neither did I.'

'So what made you change your mind?' Tess just shook her head so Lucy went on: 'Was it your age, the forty thing coming up? I know you said that there's no role models for childless women our age, but I always thought that you of all people didn't need a compass. I don't know, I just can't picture you having some random man's sperm put into you in hospital. It all seems, how would you put it, just too, too much effort.'

Tess sighed. 'Do you want to know the truth? I suppose you might as well.'

Lucy felt the way she had the first time they'd stayed up all night talking at university: a giddy unworthiness of confidences from this beautiful creature.

* * *

He's clearly done all right for himself, thought Sierra, as she approached the willowy north London house. The veterans of her mother's eighties crowd tended to fall into two very extreme camps. More memorable were the casualties, those that had died of AIDS and heroin addiction. They would sometimes make a quirky little obituary for newspaper readers to tut over at breakfast. There but for the grace of god, her mother would always say, though she believed in neither grace nor god.

Then there were those who had survived and prospered. By the look of things, thought Sierra as she passed the columned houses hemmed by expensive cars, Dez fell into this category. These were the ones who turned out to be boring, according to Susie, who'd invested their royalties and profits into property rather than drugs. Instead of it going up their nose, their money went into a home here, a rental investment there. Accidentally or on purpose these bricks had made them piles.

Sierra looked at the photo that she held in her hands. The one she and her mother had reminisced over the day she'd returned from Spain, the picture that captured the hours in which Susie danced herself into labour. Inside that neat pregnant belly was the girl who now stood on the street, staring at the house of the man whose lens had both lingered on Susie and fluttered around the club in which she had reigned. It gave Sierra courage to climb the steep steps to the front door and to knock. She had found the street name and number in Susie's stained address book and the Internet directory enquiries site had seemed to confirm that it was the right one, but even if it were, he might not be there.

The door was answered by a fat man whose head had been clippered to a number one cut, not in an avant-garde way, but in an 'I'm bald' way. She thought she possibly recognised him from an old Polaroid that her mother had taken, which was in the plastic bag filled with pictures and memories; for once the photographer had been photographed. He had a shyness that separated him from the flashbulb-seeking missiles of the rest of them.

'Mr Dickerson?' The man looked amused. She struggled on, holding the photograph in her pocket to get strength from it and sticking out her other hand to be shaken. 'Derek?' One last shot. 'Dez?' How could she have thought the fat man was shy—he was confident to the point of arrogance. Standing a step above her gave him an additional six inches of height, not that he needed it, and she felt a rare moment of diminution.

This man was so tall. It made her think of Michael, who was not. Lots of things made her think of Michael, she wasn't sure why. And when she thought of him, thoughts of sex were not far behind. Again, she couldn't be sure why. She didn't fancy him, not in the way she did Owen, and, anyway, after that business with Josh she wasn't going to be sticking her hand down her pants for anyone. She felt a moment of shame, as she always did when she thought of it, and swore once again that she would talk to Josh to sort it out.

She looked up at the big man on the other side of the doorway. Something about being temporarily small made her give him a pleading little-girl look to which he responded by shouting up the stairs, 'Dez, my sweet, there's a young lady to see you.'

A thin version of the fat man came down, like an after shot in a Weight Watchers ad. She half expected him to pull out the waistband of his trousers to demonstrate how he'd become half the man he had been without ever feeling hungry! Same shaved head and wry look, but a kindness and, yes, a shyness, that told her she'd found her man.

'Mr Dickerson, my name's Sierra and I believe you knew my mother, Susie Smith.' His face became a deliberate blank. 'I think you used to call her Suze? Here's a photo that you took . . . you took lots of them. See, this is from the night I was born.' She thrust it into his hands. He staggered a couple of steps backwards so she stepped into the hall. 'Mr Dickerson, Dez, are you all right?' He and the fat man looked at one another.

'Yes, Susie's daughter, why of course I knew your mother.' Another exchange of glances. 'You must be, how old?'

'Twenty-three. Nearly twenty-four.'

285

'Twenty-three.' His face became that of a man dividing up a particularly complicated, 'Well, I only had a starter and two glasses of wine' bill at a restaurant. 'My, how you've grown.'

'Not as tall as you,' she said to both of them. 'Makes a change.'

'But your mother's very tall,' Dez said.

'Quite. Not that tall.' Sierra wanted to burst out laughing. Of course Susie had slept with Dez. She'd once told her in a spliffed-out moment that she'd slept with every photographer she'd ever worked with, and another time that she could turn a gay man straight.

'I suppose you'd better come in.' Fat and thin looked at one another with something approaching panic.

Sierra was just about to say, 'Don't worry, you're not my dad,' when she stopped herself. She might as well get something out of her mum being such a slapper for a change. Fortunately for Sierra, her real dad had chosen to do a DNA test on a strand of hair he'd plucked from her shoulder one particularly awful Christmas, so she was unconfused as to her paternity.

'Thank you.' She felt tall again.

They walked upstairs to a first-floor sitting room with floor-to-ceiling windows and wrought-iron balconies. Dez's companion sat on a Louis XV chair reupholstered in shocking pink candy stripes, while Dez stood with his hand resting on its curved back. They could have been parents presenting a united front against a truculent teen expelled from boarding school.

She looked around. 'Beautiful things,' she said. 'I think the times were kinder to you than they were to my mum.'

'Your mother wasn't sensible enough to marry a lawyer,' said the fat man. 'I'm John, by the way. You don't think that Dez's work keeps us in a Georgian townhouse, do you?'

'I see.'

'How is your mother?' asked Dez.

'She's fine. Living in Spain.'

'How nice.'

'Yes.'

'On the coast?'

'Mountains.' They were like parents talking to their son's new girlfriend, all sweet and polite, but having nothing to say. Sierra wanted to put them out of their misery. 'You're not my dad, don't worry.'

Both sets of shoulders dropped with relief. John gave a forced laugh. 'My dear, we never for a moment—'

'You so did.'

'Well, I . . .' Dez stammered. 'It was a possibility. Everything was possible then. I thought you might be coming to tell me and looking for—'

'Financial support,' said John, clearly the lawyer.

'It's something else I'd like from you,' Sierra told them. 'Please.'

'What?' asked Dez.

'Your photos.'

'He doesn't do them any more,' said John. 'He's a book dealer now.'

'But they were brilliant,' she protested. Dez shrugged. 'They were fierce. They captured everything, the people, the stars, those that weren't stars but wanted to be, those that were stars, but who fell, the glamour . . .'

287

'And the squalor.'

'The dance floor . . .'

'And the toilet floor.'

They laughed, tension dissolving. And that's my exhibition title, thought Sierra, The glamour & the squalor: from the dance floor to the toilet floor. 'Exactly, and that's what's so brilliant about them—and everyone's into that time again, especially that whole club scene thing, all that stuff in the decade before I was born. It's mad that you've never exhibited. You have never exhibited, have you?'

Dez shook his head. John clasped his hands together. 'And you should.'

But Dez continued shaking his head. 'I've been asked so often. To sell my work, to exhibit it, but no. So many dead ones, not happy times really.'

'But they were at the time. Do it for the dead ones, then. Do it for those that lived, too, the sort-of survivors. Like my mum. Like Susie.'

'Why are you so interested, anyway?' asked John.

'I run a gallery.' A metaphorical crossing of fingers. 'It's super hot right now, really full-on, but I just want to take us in a bit of a new direction, away from showing a few expensive items to showing something with broader appeal. I want to move into photography and your work is the thing to take me there. Please.' She put her head on one side again; some part of the vulnerable little girly from the doorstep had remained.

John squeezed Dez's shoulder. 'Maybe the time has come.'

'And if there's anything we can do to help Suze's daughter . . .'

Sierra walked out of the gorgeous Georgian house with the feeling that everything was going to be all right after all.

*   *   *

Lucy left Tess's flat with a glow. She reeled with the dizziness of shared female confidences, a feeling that's almost like falling in love, talking, talking, talking, looking at the clock and not believing the time. She had spent time with mothers from school and with people in the office, but they were all not so much friends as work colleagues. She'd forgotten how heady friendship could be, especially the one she had with Tess. It all came back to her now.

Feeling like an errant husband, she had forgotten all about Jamie and the pills, about the children and their bedtime, but instead had drunk a bottle of wine and sat with her feet up on the stained white sofa at Tess's.

The dizziness of a friendship revived subsided enough for her to feel some sadness at the secrets she had learned. Poor Tess. She had never felt pity or even sympathy for her friend before, it hadn't been that sort of dynamic, but now she did and she surprised herself by feeling no joyful superiority in it.

Tess had made her announcement brutally. 'I always thought I couldn't have children. Chlamydia, pelvic inflammatory disease, scarred fallopian tubes, blah blah blah.'

Of course, thought Lucy as she said it, of course. The blurred behaviour of Tess's thirties was now viewed through brand-new contact lenses. The aggressive singleness, the dismissing of domesticity, the unusual freedom from the pressure to settle down, the lack of interest in children—her own or anybody else's—the seeming absence of the backwards-from-40 clock that plagued other women.

All the while, Tess knew that the clock ticked differently for her. That the choice of children had appeared to have been taken from her a dozen years earlier than it was for most women. Lucy thought, almost shamefully, of how much of her own desire to find a man had been about finding someone to father her children. It was more than a coincidence, she thought, that most people happened to find their soulmate at just the right time to procreate.

'How? I don't understand,' Lucy had said.

'Chlamydia, you see—frightfully common, but then I'm not, so it came as a bit of a shock. Mild in most cases, nothing to worry about, but it wasn't in my case.'

'Yes, I know all about it. I read women's magazines.'

'You are an idiot, they're full of nonsense.'

'Tess.' Lucy moved to touch her and did, on her shoulder. 'Don't change the subject. Where did you get it?'

Tess shrugged. 'Owen. Maybe.'

'Owen? I suppose, yes, with his reputation, but then why would he be your friend still? Not just your friend, Gus's godparent. Oh my god, he's the father, isn't he?'

'No, no. Why must everyone speculate so?'

'All right, but then why choose him as the godfather? Why even give him the time of day after what he gave you?'

'He may not have done. Though I think it highly likely, don't you? He's such a terrible slapper. I don't know, it's too strange, I suppose, but I feel like Owen and I are entwined somehow, by what's happened. The strange thing is that when I found out that I couldn't have children, I actually felt relieved. I felt pleased. It was just at that time when everyone was beginning to spawn or fret about it and I felt utterly liberated that I wouldn't have to worry about it. I didn't want children. I never did. I worried, mildly, that I might be abnormal and that I should want to want them, but I really didn't. I actually thanked Owen.'

'What, really?'

'No, not literally. I just sent him an anonymous note telling him to get himself checked out. No, in my head I thanked him. By giving me chlamydia and scratching up my fallopian tubes, the decision had been made for me and I could live my life how I'd always wanted to. I've never thought that every woman should have a child. I love my mother very much and vice versa, but she and my father could have been just as happy without me. I looked around and it wasn't childless women who seemed unhappy, but those women whose children had let them down in some way or who had left them or just didn't appreciate them. Being a mother never really looked much fun.'

'But what made you change your mind?'

'I didn't. I just got pregnant.'

'By IVF? Donor?'

'Sort of. Not by IVF, but the donor bit is sort of true. Gus is a miracle.' She laughed, wryly.

'All babies are.'

'But Gus really properly is. I wasn't able to get pregnant and then I go and do and I wasn't even trying. I'm old, infertile and I have unprotected sex for the first time since I'd made the mistake of doing so with Owen. Even though I always thought I couldn't get pregnant I was very scrupulous about protecting myself from more damn STDs.'

Lucy pulled a face. 'Even with all those old men you used to hang out with?'

Tess laughed. 'Older men. Most of them were in their forties, maybe fifties, which doesn't seem so old now, does it? Yes, even with them, they're probably the worst for those types of diseases. I don't know why I didn't use a condom that one time I got pregnant. I keep asking myself the same question. I didn't have any on me and nor did he, but still, I wonder if somehow I knew what might happen. I got pregnant by accident, and I didn't even realise until I was a couple of months gone. I still could have had an abortion, I suppose, but there seems to be a gulf of difference between not wanting to have a baby and then getting rid of the one you get given. My doctor kept telling me what a miracle it was and, I don't know, it felt sort of churlish not to celebrate the fact.'

'But you're happy now?'

'Sort of. Not really. I think I might have had it right all along. I don't think I'm cut out to be a mother. I mean,' she looked over to Gus who was sound asleep in Lucy's arms, 'I think I love him. And I don't want him to come to any harm. But I'm no more maternal than I ever was. But you know, you're not exactly allowed to reject miracles, are you?'

'So who is his father?'

'He's a doctor. Some doctor, really. I wasn't lying to you about that.'

'Really, someone you actually know? Do you see

292

Gus in him?'

'I don't know. Do you?'

'What do you mean?'

'You've seen him. You've met him. He's the doctor who almost ran us over with a wheelchair, that one time you came to visit me in hospital, he was coming out of the lift. I'm not sure he even recognised me.'

Lucy could remember her feeling of pride as she and Michael, both of them pretending to be something they weren't, had posed as Gus's parents to the Slav-accented man who'd been pushing a woman in a wheelchair.'

'Tall blond man, kind face, good looking?' Tess nodded. 'But darling, he wasn't a doctor, I don't think. He was a porter.'

It was Tess's turn now to look shocked.

*　　　*　　　*

Sierra took Michael out to celebrate.

'Celebrate what?' he'd asked—slightly morosely, she thought.

'I've saved the gallery, my career, my sense of self, my relationship with my mother. Maybe. What else do you need? Anyway, I owe you for putting up with me and putting me up.'

'I've got some marking to do.'

'Yeah, marking this happy occasion. Come on.'

'One drink then.'

'Everything's going to be all right,' she said early on in the evening.

'Really? Your mother still owes some dealer a wodge of drugs.'

'Don't spoil things. Maybe I'll make enough

293

money to pay him off. It will sort itself out.'

Later on she said, 'Actually, everything's going to be brilliant.'

This time, a few cocktails and the best part of a bottle of wine inside him, he replied, 'It is. It really is.'

'Yes, it is,' she repeated. They smiled at one another. Sierra wondered whether her instincts were wrong. The other night, on his sofa, they had been so close, but he'd just left her abruptly. It would have been a mistake, surely, but still she had quietly touched herself in the night and thought of him, worried that she'd wake him and yet half hoping that she would.

There was a pause. He had the face of a naughty boy, chocolate-button eyes and a mouth that always looked like it was hiding a smile. Her head was muddled by drink. At that moment, she wanted to touch him more than anything. She wanted to touch him and then to hold him and then to envelop him. She didn't fancy him, of course not—he was too little, too nice. But she wanted him. No, he wasn't her usual type. She normally went for big men like Owen. Although, maybe it wasn't so much that she went for big men as much as feeling like they were the only ones who'd go for her.

Anyway, she wasn't going to ruin things with Michael. He was like the sort of male friend she always felt she'd have made loads of if she'd gone to university. A nice, just gay enough best friend. Tonight and the other night, it was just drink and loneliness that had tricked her into thinking that she wanted him.

She willed herself to think of Josh and the footage to stop her making a fool of herself again.

She shuddered as the image of her awful moaning and groaning flashed up. It was still there on his page. It hadn't gone global yet, at least, but it was still there and one day Michael might see it and she didn't think she could bear it.

Anyway, he didn't want her, did he? Though there was no way of knowing for sure, if she didn't try something. Should she just touch his leg with hers? She'd try that. That was a good ploy, she thought in her wined-up way—she could always pretend it was an accident.

'What are your hopes for the next six months?' he asked.

Six months? What about the next six minutes? No, she couldn't touch his leg, she'd made her attraction to him pretty obvious the other night. He must know, but he's still in love with Tess. Or not in love with anyone, just not wanting to get off with her. She was so much, well, bigger than him, after all. In fact, it didn't bother her, not at all, but it was amazing how many men had a problem with that. She'd read once that women liked men taller than average, but men liked women smaller than the norm. She could believe it. It wasn't like she minded that these petite, exquisite things stole all the tall men, they could have them, it was just that the small men they left behind often didn't want a girl who made them feel even tinier.

But, she thought, the small men who did go for girls like her were the best of all. Men who were confident enough not to care.

He waited for her response. 'I want the exhibition to be a fantastic success,' she said. 'I want Tess to recognise that and give me a new job title and a pay rise. What else? Somewhere to live that's not my mum's whether she's there or not. Her or me not being pursued by a dodgy man called Jason. I want . . .' She paused. I want you. I want to sleep at your flat but not on the sofa bed, I want to find out whether you're as into sex as Tess says you are, I want to have sex where you look at me and not your computer, I want to go for Sunday lunch at your parents' and meet your three sisters, but most of all I want you to lean over and hold my hand now, just to let me know that I'm not wrong to want you, that if not now, I will have you one day.

Her phone went. She slipped it out of her bag and looked at it to discover the name of their interloper. Owen. She paused. Now he calls. The thing she had longed for and now he calls. What had Owen ever given her? It continued to ring and she looked at Michael. He grinned and raised an eyebrow. She grinned back.

'Who is it?'

'Nobody,' she said as she switched it off. She put her phone back into her bag and took the opportunity to look under the table to see how far her leg was from his. It was just a couple of inches. She sat up, her face red both from hanging down and the thoughts that were racing through her mind. 'What do you want, Michael?' She pushed her leg forward and it met his. She let it stay there. It was like she was playing grandmother's footsteps and if she managed to inch forward without him noticing then she'd win the game and him.

She looked at him. She thought he seemed pained so she moved her leg away.

'For starters, I want your leg pressed against mine again,' he whispered.

She exhaled. 'And then?'

'I want to put one hand beneath the table to stroke your calves. You have beautiful calves.'

'Really?'

'Yes. But I can't reach.'

She giggled and then regretted it, fearing that it might kill the mood. 'No bad thing, my legs are a bit hairy.' Oh god, why did I say that? Now I'll have not only murdered the mood, but buried it six feet under.

Michael laughed. 'As if I care.'

'It's been a while since a wax, you know, everywhere.'

'Everywhere?' He raised his eyebrows.

'You know.' She blushed. She, who had found herself plastered all over the Internet, was reddening like a virgin.

'Sierra, you're killing me. You make me want to do something very embarrassing right here in this restaurant. To prevent it, can you take my hand.'

She followed his instructions. They held hands and smiled at one another. She wondered what to say. She didn't want to scare him off again.

'Michael.'

'Yes.'

'Do you know what I really want?'

He shook his head.

'I'd like to get the bill and go home. Go to your home.'

'So would I.'

'But,' she thought of Owen once again, 'is it all right if we don't, if we do but don't, you know, everything but? Something happened, recently, and I don't want to rush things.'

He seemed relieved. 'That's fine by me. Let's go home.'

'Let's.'

The journey home was excruciating. Sierra babbled to try to quell her need to be kissed by him, a need she only wanted satisfied when they got inside. At last they climbed the steps into his neat flat. There was the sofa in front of the television and the little kitchen where they'd prepared meals and the bedroom off in the corner and her clothes neatly folded beneath the bedding that she tidied up each morning. She wouldn't need to make up the sofa bed tonight.

Don't offer me a cup of coffee or delay the moment any more. Don't let us be awkward even for a second, she silently implored, just kiss me.

He must have heard her. He stepped towards her and at last they kissed. She had to bend her head slightly, but their lips matched. She certainly didn't think he was gay any more.

CHAPTER EIGHTEEN

FLU-LIKE SYMPTOMS

'Owen.' The word, elongated, almost made a sentence. 'What's this?' Ruby brandished the envelope in his face.

'It's a bill, electricity I think,' he said, ignoring his fortunately illegible scrawl across the back of it. 'Not that you need worry your pretty little head about them.'

'You know how awful I am with money. Anyway, silly, I don't mean what's inside the envelope, but what's on the envelope. What's this list thingy?'

He looked at the writing, the fruit of half an hour spent in the pub on the way home. It was a list with 71 entries, though he'd thought of a few more since then. Swedish Anna, how could he forget her? And the Australian female rugby player he'd scrummed with? It was a tally of all the women he'd slept with, or remembered he'd slept with before he'd got that anonymous note from Tess almost ten years ago.

'Your writing's terrible.'

'It is.'

'This one, Cleo, at the end here? And there's a Katie, Sandy—does that say Sandy? Why's it ticked?' He knew that some of them he had told about the chlamydia and they were safe, or at least in his conscience they were. Others he had not told, hadn't thought it very important at the time. Now he was staring at their names and wondering whether their lives were going to be as affected as Tess's had been.

'I'm really embarrassed,' he said, briskly. She looked inquisitive. 'You're going to think I'm awful.'

'Go on.'

'Awfully soppy, I mean. It's a list of girls' names.'

'I can see that.'

'For our daughter. You know, when we have a daughter.'

She snuggled up to him. 'Might be a boy.'

'No, it won't be, because I want a girl,' he said. 'I want a girl every bit as beautiful as you.' God, he was good. He was a born liar. Bit like his real dad, as it now turned out.

'I want a boy just as handsome and clever as you,' she said.

He'd got away with it.

'But I think St Tropez is a bit of a funny name for a baby,' she said. 'And what's this one? Looks like "toilet girl". And what's *this* one?' she asked, pointing to Owen's note to self that read 'CHECK: ds oral count?'.

'I think we ought to start right now,' he said by way of diversionary tactic.

After they'd done it he zipped himself up quickly and stood up to order a cab to take him to Lucy's for their postnatal godparental summit meeting.

'I don't understand why I can't go,' said Ruby.

'Because you're not a godparent.'

'I'm married to one, aren't I?'

Owen felt momentarily dizzy, which he attributed to standing up too quickly after sex. 'Not quite yet.'

'Sweetheart,' said Ruby. 'It's ever so good that you're mourning properly, really it is.'

'Thanks.'

'Your dad, Gareth I mean, was a wonderful, wonderful man.'

'Yes, my father was.'

'And I'm so impressed that you're getting in touch with yourself at last and working through some of the issues you had around your parents.'

'Thanks. I can sense a "but" coming here,' said Owen.

'No, of course not,' she protested. 'It's just that it's been a month and a half now.'

'And?'

'I think your dad would have wanted you to have named the day, don't you?'

'What day?'

'You're such a tease. Our wedding day, silly.'

'Oh, that.'

'I've done all I can without having a specific date in mind, but we've really got to book a venue or all the best ones will be gone. All my magazines say you need to have decided on a date at least a year before the big day and I don't want to wait that long. Anyway, it would make your mum so happy.'

'My mother, yes, my mother,' he said abstractedly. It still shocked him to say that word and know that it was true in every sense.

'She told me at the funeral that nothing, nothing in the world, not even your lovely dad coming back, would make her happier than seeing us get married. It's karma, isn't it, the great cycle of life, that he should die so that our new life together can begin.'

Owen thought about the funeral. Ruby had looked beautiful, if a little overdramatic, wearing a full mantilla over her face matched by a figure-hugging black dress. His mother's dress had been even tighter, though that was not by design but due to the fact that Mari's nostalgia for life with Gareth had taken the form of comfort-eating forgotten foods. She had spent the days after his death munching her way through plastic tubs of chocolate mousse topped with UHT foam, crackers with Primula cheese spread and endless bowls of Angel Delight. 'Your father always loved me in this dress,' she said mournfully as she put it on, while at the same time chewing on a Peperami stick.

Ruby had accompanied Mari down the aisle, slowly and musically, as if in preparation for the next time they'd all be in church together, while Caron trailed dumpily behind, pulling her high-waisted black trousers away from where they had got stuck up her bum.

'Owen,' said Ruby, jolting him back to the

301

present. 'Forget about your father.'

'Sorry?'

'I don't mean forget about him, obviously we'll remember him forever and ever, god rest his soul, amen. I mean, move on. It's what your father would have wanted.'

'My father?'

'Gareth, I mean,' she said. 'Not the other one.'

Owen felt he finally understood that there was no other one. That Gareth had been his father and always had been, from the moment they'd set eyes on each other and Owen had said, 'Dada'. All that stuff that parents tell adopted children about how they're special because they're chosen was true. Gareth had chosen to take Owen on, because he loved Mari, but also because he loved him. And just because he was a good man, the best of men.

'I do need to do something for my father,' said Owen, distractedly. 'You're right. We can talk about it later.' He promised himself that from now on everything would be done for his father, his father Gareth.

*   *   *

Michael sat in the living room waiting for Sierra to finish in the bathroom. They'd shared a bed each of the three nights since their kiss. They were decorously keeping on their underwear, the way actors do in films and which Michael had always thought very unnatural. Sierra was even wearing a bra each night, which was filled with the glorious breasts that he'd admired the very first time he'd met her. She had made it very clear that she wanted to take things slowly; she'd muttered something about having been burned by something to do with this Josh bloke and a video, and by what had happened with Owen. At first he had been very relieved by this suggestion. He knew that there was a risk he'd have the same problem he'd had with Tess and Rachel. Two times was just an unfortunate coincidence, but with three women? Then there would be every chance that it was a permanent affliction. Which seemed a very strange turn of events, since he'd spent his life up until this point worrying about just the opposite problem.

The more he tried to force himself not to conjure up the image of Gus's head emerging from Tess in birth, the more it came unbidden.

But after lying next to Sierra, he began to feel confident that he had exorcised the infant that had been suckling on his libido. Sharing a bed with her was like one of those trust exercises that couples experiencing sexual dysfunction are prescribed, the ones where there is no pressure to do anything, but instead they're supposed to stroke each other with feathers until desire overwhelms them. Of course, he couldn't be sure that it would work with Sierra, but the painful releases he'd silently organise for himself in the bathroom indicated that it would.

Maybe it was better not to try. It was enjoyable, in its way, this making out like teenagers and a bit of dry humping finished off alone. It had to be preferable to more failure. I'm overthinking it, he realised, the one thing I never had to think about and now I am. His body hadn't served him well in sport and he lacked good hand-to-eye coordination, but in the sex Olympics he'd always been told he was gold medal standard. Now he was choking it, like some no-hoper British tennis player at

303

Wimbledon.

He had to stop thinking about it. No, no, not the Gus-head-coming-out thing again. He waved his arms as if he could actually bat the image away.

'What are you doing?' Sierra had emerged from the bathroom with a towel wrapped around her, tucked in at the front in that way that girls must get taught at school, because he'd never managed to do it so that it gathered in such an appealing way.

'Nothing. I suppose I'd better get ready too.'

'Yes. You should.' She clamped her lips together as if to stop herself from saying anything else, then looked down at her towel. She was a picture of dejection that skewered Michael.

'Come here,' he said. I'm not going to do anything. We are allowed to kiss and hug, that's part of the programme, this weird couples sexual rehabilitation that I never signed up to. It's fine. He had got the impression from her before that she was all liberated and perma-up-for-it, but maybe that was just for Owen.

She came and sat next to him on the sofa. She's naked beneath that towel, he thought. It seemed an even flimsier barrier than the underwear she slept in. He could pull at it like the trick magicians do with the plates on the table, I could just whip it off in one move. Or I could just touch her, under there—I could do that coughing thing where your hand just lands there, just like I used to do fifteen years ago. Ahem, cough into hand, lay it back to rest on her tit, under the towel. Not quite sure how that's going to work. And isn't it rather disgusting to cough on your hand and then put the germy thing on them? Michael, you're overthinking it again.

He tentatively touched the towel. Even with his gentleness, the girl-knot that she had created fell apart and the towel slid off. His breath quickened as he saw breasts finally freed from the prison of those vintage-style bras. Before he had time to think, he leaned forward and licked her nipple. She shivered, he hoped with pleasure. He moved over to the other one and then glanced down to see if she was wearing pants. She wasn't. Oh my god, there's a naked Sierra sat atop a towel on my sofa. As he continued licking the nipples that tasted of the shower gel that he had bought, the one that offered zingy minty freshness, he moved his hand down. She was wet. He slipped his finger inside and it became moist with her, all the better to remove it and lightly circle and stroke her clitoris.

'For fuck's sake, Michael, fuck me,' she cried out.

He grabbed a condom from the drawer on the table by the sofa and pulled down his trousers quick before either she or his subconscious could change their minds. He plunged in and his cock felt harder than he had ever known it and she yielded yet clenched it, he could feel her muscles tightening around it.

She rolled him round so that she was now astride him, grinding herself round and round his cock. Oh god, he thought, not yet, not yet. This time he forced himself to think of Gus to stave it off. He pressed his thumb lightly on her so that as she made those circular movements it moved her closer towards it. Think of Gus's blood-covered head, he told himself, but the image wouldn't come any more, he could think of nothing but how good this was and how glorious her breasts were and how well his thumb fitted against her and how safe his cock felt within her, how both hard and soft she was inside.

'Not yet, not yet,' she cried. OK, not yet, oh please soon. 'Now, now.' She pushed herself against him and he felt her twitch around his cock as permission. He thought the condom must be overflowing like a burst dam, since all the weeks with Tess and all the years of loving her, the sadness and the happiness, the frustration he had felt with Sierra, it all came out.

He was surprised as he wiggled out and removed the condom that its contents were quite normal. He'd expected it to sparkle like glitter glue or be rainbow coloured, something to denote the magic and the otherworldliness he felt.

They lay back, concertinaed on his Ikea sofa. 'Fuck,' said Sierra, her word of choice of the last few minutes.

He nodded, unable even to utter that.

'I thought you were never going to do that.'

'I thought you didn't want me to.'

Her eyes welled up and she began to cry. When Rachel cried, Michael had wanted to stab rusty forks into his eyes to distract himself, but Sierra's tears were contagious.

'I'm sorry,' she said. 'I'm just so relieved.'

'Me too.' They looked at each other and began to laugh.

*   *   *

Lucy had told Jamie that he was welcome to join her in the reunion of Gus's godparents that she'd organised for that night, but he said he needed to get on with the editing. Since dropping the pills,

306

he'd had the 'flu-like symptoms' that had been mooted by their Internet research but did not yet seem to have had a drop in the creative energy that he was expending on the film. Nor had she had proof that the other side effect of the selective serotonin re-uptake inhibitors that he'd been taking had been resolved, since the old go-to-bed-half-an-hour-later regime was being maintained.

As she'd changed out of her work clothes and into what she hoped conveyed casual elegance, she had examined herself in the mirror. Her face, she was sure, had improved, but she wasn't convinced that it looked as different as it felt. Even apart from the fact that Jamie still avoided her, she wasn't sure it had been worth the pain and the cost. Would he even be looking at her face if they ever had sex again? Surely it was her body that would look most different to the pre-maternal ones of his contemporaries? Perhaps she'd got it all wrong when she had plumped and smoothed her face as if it were pillows and a duvet. She felt the trace of hardened foam that burrowed through the folds between her nose and the side of her mouth and with her other hand the loose skin around her belly. Maybe she should invest her savings elsewhere.

'More, anyone?' she asked Owen, Sierra and Michael. She'd gone for one of those all-in-one pomegranate seed, avocado and bulgar-wheat loaded salads that all women love and men seem to think of as bird food (in all senses). Owen had even asked where the meat was, though Michael had been lavish in his praise, only further promoting the idea that he wasn't a hundred per cent hetero.

'Yes, please,' said Sierra. As she leaned over to grab the serving spoon, Lucy noticed her hand brush over Michael's. She left it there for a second and they glanced at one another. It's like that, is it? thought Lucy, surprising herself with a little ache of envy, unsure as to whether it was due to the comfortable fondness she felt towards Michael, or his and Sierra's togetherness, at the wonderful newness of it, the way they'd be having sex all night and then again in the morning. She guessed that Michael would be good in bed. And Sierra too. They would be a cosy little twosome of goodness in bed and on the stairs and on the beach. Just as she and Jamie had once been.

*   *   *

As Sierra had dressed to get ready for Lucy's dinner party, she'd been promptly undressed by Michael. She hadn't washed since. The condom had contained it anyway, which saddened her. She wanted to feel the slow dribble of sperm down her inner thighs and to be able to take in its doughy yeasty smell to remind herself of the utter loveliness of sex with Michael. She thought she'd never be unselfconscious again, that sex would always be in split screen, with fuzzy footage of her from Josh's camera phone forever playing beside the actuality of it. But she'd forgotten all about that humiliation as she concentrated hard on coming. She'd surprised herself with that, too. Usually when she started sleeping with someone new, she'd be thinking too hard about giving a good impression and making sure that the bloke enjoyed it. And it wasn't as if she didn't care whether Michael had a good time or not, just that she assumed he would be and that anyway the best way to ensure that he did was to have one herself. She knew him well enough to know that her pleasure was his.

When she came she felt a release and moments later, when he did, a relief. Who knew that little old, unshowy relief could be the most glorious and euphoric of all emotions?

When her hand had glanced over his at Lucy's table, she had felt the hairs of it tingle against her like an eyelash kiss. In combination with the crisp wine, she felt a bit dizzy.

She escaped to the loo. When she wiped herself she pressed and left her hand there against the aching memory of what had happened earlier that evening and in anticipation of what would happen that night. She saw a shadow through the Edwardian frosted glass of the bathroom door and quickly stood up and composed herself. In the mirror she saw a girl with the look that all make-up aspires to create: reddened lips, flushed cheeks, huge pupils.

She opened the door to find Owen, who had been hitting the prosecco and moderately priced wine provided by Lucy. He fell against her, pushing her back inside the bathroom.

'God, Sierra, you're so sexy.'

'Thanks, but—'

'And so kind. You understand me, you know what it's like not to have a father.'

'But I do have a father.'

'Ruby doesn't understand me.'

'Oh, really.'

'Please look after me.' He grabbed her, quite roughly. Sierra felt a jolt of fear, of his roughness but more of Michael coming in at this moment and drawing the wrong conclusion. He would be hurt and confused, she knew. She felt sick at the thought. Shit, she realised, I love him. She was surprised, both at the way the words formed so clearly in her head and at the emotion that they expressed. I actually love him. She had been in love before, or at least that's what she had told her friends, but she wasn't sure she'd ever loved anyone. It wasn't what she'd been expecting; it felt closer to what she had always wished her mother would show towards her but never did, a sense that she could never be happy unless he was. She shook Owen off so hard that he collapsed onto the floor. He grabbed at her and put his head between her legs, muttering something into her thighs.

'Owen, get off me. Now!'

'Come on, Sierra, we had fun, didn't we?'

'Get your hands off me or I'll start screaming.'

Owen looked stricken. 'Oh god, I'm so sorry, I didn't mean anything. I thought you wanted to. I feel awful.'

'Owen, I'm sorry, really I am, but I'm not the answer. You're engaged.'

'Not any more.'

'Since when?'

'It's not actually official yet. But honestly, I'm not going to marry Ruby. You're too lovely for me to marry Ruby.'

Sierra couldn't help smiling at the utter ridiculousness of him. 'Bollocks. You just don't love Ruby enough. It was obvious you weren't going to marry her.'

He slithered down to the floor again. 'You're right, of course you're right. I was never going to marry her.' His face was contorted with concentration and then he smiled and sat up.

Sierra could almost see the light bulb above his head. 'That's not what I'm supposed to do, it isn't. I know.'

'What?'

'What I am going to do. It's all clear.' He started singing, 'I can see clearly now the rain has gone,' in his gloriously deep voice. Sierra wondered whether she'd be able to sing if she'd been born in Wales.

'Good, I'm happy for you, Owen. I've got to go, Michael will be wondering where I've got to.'

'Michael?' He managed to sneer and look amused simultaneously.

'And Lucy. The others. We four musketeers.'

'So I suppose a grope's out of the question?' said Owen.

Sierra smiled. She knew that he didn't really want her and that he knew she didn't want him, but he still had the courtesy to pretend to try. It was a form of politeness and she was grateful for it, while even more grateful for the fact that for all his faults he hadn't pushed her any further than he had.

*   *   *

Owen remembered what he'd come into the bathroom for and stood up and did one of those long drawn-out pees that would intimidate other men in urinals. He looked in the mirror and tried to pick some of those goddamn seeds out of his teeth. On the whole, this ageing thing didn't bother him, not having ovaries and all, but recently he had found himself surprised by little signs that he had never been told about: the long single white straight chest hair that dangled near his nipple; the way that food either got caught between his teeth more, or always

311

had done but only now bothered him; that a bruise would form and stake a semi-permanent tenancy on his shin. This was in addition to all the things he'd been told about: the holding of newspapers at arm's length; the salt-and-peppering of his stubble; the dodgy knees.

He stared at his reflection. He looked like a father. He should be a father. He had a clock, not a biological one, but it was ticking nonetheless towards 40 and he felt like a taxi that had just put its light on and would end up with the next girl who happened to stick her hand out. He really had believed that he'd marry Ruby, although if anything she was even more unsuitable than his previous fiancées. He had only come nearer to doing it because he was nearer to the age at which he felt he should settle down.

'I've got something to tell you,' he announced as he returned to the godparental table. He laughed at the thought that they had been chosen to provide moral guidance to Gus. 'I'm Gus's father.'

He enjoyed the look of shock upon their faces, especially Lucy's. 'No, you're not,' she said.

'Not technically, no. But he sort of wouldn't exist if it weren't for me.'

'What do you mean?' asked Michael.

Lucy stared at Owen and he realised that she knew already. 'I gave Tess chlamydia, which gave her . . . can you explain it, Lucy, since I'm guessing you know all about it?'

'Untreated chlamydia,' she recited, 'can cause pelvic inflammatory disease, which in turn can scar a woman's fallopian tubes which can be a cause of infertility. But making Tess infertile does not mean you're responsible for Gus's conception.'

Sierra had gone pale. 'You don't still have it, do you?'

Michael had by now grabbed her hand. Owen felt a sense of injustice to this. She was mine first, he whined inside like a child; I bagsied her, you little upstart. He shook his head. 'I cleared it up years ago. You're fine.'

Michael glared at Owen.

'I do sort of understand what you mean, Owen.' Lucy had a trace of sympathy in her voice. 'There's a sort of logic to it. If she hadn't thought she was infertile . . .'

'What?' said Michael. 'She wouldn't have gone for donor insemination and had Gus? It's a bit tangential, don't you think?'

'No, I don't,' said Owen. 'It's my fault that she had to do this, that she couldn't conceive naturally, but something good has come out of it, so if I was a part of the cause then I should be a part of the result.' He was formulating this argument as he went along. It seemed to be a good one, sort of or at least not entirely without reason. 'I'm going to be like a father. I'm going to take financial responsibility.'

'That's not a bad idea,' said Sierra. 'Have you seen the gallery's accounts?'

'And moral responsibility.' Michael snorted with laughter at this. 'I am. What's so funny? If my dad, by which I mean Gareth, who I think of as my real father, if he's taught me anything it's that being a father has nothing to do with biology. Women just use men as sperm donors, don't they, Lucy, especially in this case? Quite literally with Mr Tall-doctor-come-in-a-bottle man.'

'You weren't there at the birth,' said Michael.

313

'I was. And with the nappies and the stuff and the waking. You don't even know what a nipple shield is, do you?'

Owen had an inappropriate picture in his mind of a warrior princess complete with conical armour, but resisted the temptation to say this. 'They're for the breastfeeding. I don't think that's very important, do you? OK, so I wasn't there at the birth, what with my father dying and all, but I'll be there now.'

'You can't just swoop in with your money, your horrible, overpaid, City-boy wages, and buy yourself a role as a father. Wanker.'

'What did you call me? You tossy, camp primary school teacher.'

'Ooh, like being a primary school teacher is an insult, is it? Is that what you think? You might have to change your mind about teachers when your so-called son Gus goes to school. Pretty much sums up how crazy you are to think that you're enough of an adult, enough of a man, to be a father to him.'

Owen lifted up his arm to shove Michael, not hard or anything, but just to remind him what would happen if they did have a fight.

'Stop it,' said Sierra.

'What, you'd rather we were having a fight over you?' said Owen. Bloody Michael, the self-righteous little git, he's got Sierra, why can't he just let me have Gus? And Tess, he thought with sudden clarity. She's the only woman he'd ever managed to be friends with, certainly the only woman he'd slept with who had remained his friend afterwards, who hadn't got all clingy and wedding-wanting like the others.

'I don't want you to have a fight over

anything,' said Lucy. She shifted uncomfortably in her reclaimed 1950s Scandinavian kitchen chair. Probably partly because it was bloody uncomfortable, thought Owen, and made for teeny tiny Danish girls. 'Michael, calm down, he's not going to take Gus from you. Owen, I think it might be more complicated than you realise.'

'It's not.'

'It is. You're right about the fallopian tube thing, but not about there being no father. There is a father.'

'Yes, the sperm donor. The doctor man.'

'What I'm going to tell you is confidential. Promise me, all of you.'

'Cross my heart,' said Michael.

'The father isn't just a label on the back of a sample. Tess slept with a man and got pregnant.'

'I don't understand,' said Owen. Actually, what I most don't understand is how for once in my life I'm trying to do the decent thing, I'm trying to do what Gareth would do, and everybody's trying to stop me.

Lucy sighed.

'Explain,' said Michael.

'I feel disloyal, but we are the godparents, after all.'

'Just get on with it,' said Owen.

'You're right, in a way, the infertility did lead to Gus. Tess genuinely never wanted children, she really didn't. You know how she's never been ordinary, mortal, like the rest of us. Having children would have been what the little people did. When she discovered she was infertile, or they thought she probably was, then it confirmed that idea of herself. Like some sort of Greek god, she wouldn't spawn

315

in the usual messy way.' Lucy turned to Owen. 'She was grateful to you.'

'That's good,' he said. 'I think.'

'Bollocks,' said Michael. 'She didn't need to be infertile not to have children. She could have just chosen not to have children.'

'Yes, of course,' said Lucy. 'But it was a great relief not to have to make that choice, to feel that instead it was preordained. That way she didn't have to fear regret at not having them, as it wasn't her decision. She didn't have to count down the years and approach gay friends and think about doing it on her own. She could just live her life in the oddly day-to-day way that she always has done. You know, that sort of permanent impermanence of hers.'

'No, not really,' said Owen.

'I know, exactly,' said Michael.

Ooh, I'm so sensitive, look at me, I'm Michael. Sanctimonious twat, thought Owen. 'But where does this doctor come in? Who is Gus's father?'

'He's not a doctor. You've met him.'

Michael looked befuddled.

'Sort of. He's not a doctor, he's actually a hospital porter. Tess did genuinely think he was a doctor. In fact, she was horrified when I pointed out that she'd got confused by the scrubs. I've never seen her look so shocked. She really wanted him to be a doctor, she says because she liked the irony of doctors not being able to sort out her infertility, then a random doctor doing exactly that. But, though she'd never admit it, I think it was more that she liked the idea of her child having such well-educated and clever genes. You know, if you were going to choose a sperm donor, it probably

316

would be a tall blond-haired doctor, wouldn't it?'

'And I know this paragon of manhood?' asked Michael.

'Not know, exactly. We bumped into him, do you remember, at the hospital—the one who ran a wheelchair into Tess's feet? She went off really quickly because she didn't want him to recognise her and do the maths.'

'Yes, I think I do remember, vaguely. As you say, tall blond good-looking type.'

Owen looked at him and did an old-fashioned limp-wristed gesture.

'Fuck off,' said Lucy, Sierra and Michael in unison.

'He said something to us about Gus,' Michael remembered.

'He thought Gus was ours. And that's what Tess wanted him to think. He was a one-night, or -day, stand that had unforeseen consequences.'

Owen felt all his grief for Gareth bubbling up again. It was like this. He had always thought that you grieved and it got better, but it was jagged and would pierce him at unexpected moments. He could plot it like a stock price graph during a crisis. His eyes welled up, much to his annoyance.

Lucy noticed the wetness and cocked her head to one side in that annoying way that people who pride themselves on being empathetic do. 'She never would have risked getting pregnant if it hadn't been for the fallopian thing, nor kept Gus.'

'And this is supposed to make me feel better how?' he said.

'That you're still right, you are sort of the cause of Gus.' She turned to the others. 'Tess was in hospital that day having her annual obstetric

317

check-up results. Vondra paid for her to see her consultant privately and Tess has always been a good daughter. They told her the usual, that her tubes were rotting, a bit like an old rubber garden hose—those were the very words they used, apparently. Nice. But this time, they also added that it looked like she was perimenopausal.' She looked at their blank faces. 'It means that she wasn't ovulating much either, so the chances of getting pregnant were even more miniscule. She left and went to a bar across the road to toast herself and her childless state. There she met Teodor. It's Croatian. It means "god's gift".'

Michael made a face. 'Well, he is very tall and godlike, isn't he?'

'Wanker,' said Owen. 'Teodor, I mean, not you. She shagged a hospital porter called Teodor?'

'You could put it like that. She was celebrating a certain sort of life, I guess, and meeting a handsome younger man in a bar and taking him to a hotel fitted in with all that. The consultant had given her odds of something like a million to one to get pregnant naturally—a combination of her age, the eggs she had left and the scarred tubes. Then there were the risks that even if she did get pregnant, it would be an ectopic pregnancy. There was something about beating the odds that made Tess not have an abortion, even though she genuinely hadn't wanted to get pregnant in the first place. You know what she's like. To get pregnant would have been a normal thing to do. To get pregnant when it's a near impossible medical miracle would be different enough from all the rest of us to go through with.'

'Don't believe you,' said Owen, grumpily. 'Why

make up all this story about the donor?'

'She was embarrassed. I mean, it is a bit embarrassing to get pregnant at our age by a one-afternoon stand. If it had been a donor then she'd have been in control, wouldn't she? It would have been deliberate—what's that phrase people always use? "A much-wanted baby". She was trying to persuade herself of this as much as anyone else.'

'What's his surname?' said Sierra. She'd been staying out of the conversation until then. 'Teodor's.'

'I don't know. Something Slavic, I suppose. She doesn't want him to know about Gus.'

'But he should do.'

'No, he shouldn't,' said Owen. He surprised himself with his vehemence. 'Just because he shagged her doesn't make him the father.'

'But it does. My father was like that, it was never that serious between Mum and him, and he's not been around much, but it's been really important for me to know him. I'd be even more fucked up if I hadn't. I don't think I've got a mum any more so at least I've got someone. Teodor should know about Gus. What he chooses to do is up to him, but he should know.'

'But I'm going to be his father. I'm going to be all the father that he needs,' said Owen. He knew it sounded silly and overdramatic, but he also knew that he'd do all he could to make it true.

CHAPTER NINETEEN

Turn Back Time

'You're not gay,' said Sierra. 'You are so not gay.'
My life, she thought, at this one moment feels
perfect. That's how good Michael had been, her life
felt perfect despite being homeless, motherless and
quite possibly jobless, with her only prospect being
a career as an amateur porn star. 'Again. You are
so not gay.'

'I'm not gay. I am so not gay,' echoed Michael.

'No, you're really not.'

'I know.' He shrugged. 'What did I tell you?'

'It's awful,' she lay back on his bed, 'that there's
no way to describe someone being totally hot and
fabulous in bed without it sounding really corny.'

'Or porny,' added Michael. 'But you can try.'

She flinched as she remembered number two on
her list of problems, the removal of her own little
homegrown porn on Josh's page. She hadn't dared
to look at the page for weeks now. 'You are totally
hot and fabulous in bed. I am so glad I didn't sleep
with you earlier. Do you know why?' He shook his
head. 'Because if I'd slept with you earlier, I'd have
always worried that I loved you because you were
so fan-fucking-tastic, quite literally, rather than just
loving you for being you.'

He leaned backwards. Away from her, it seemed.
She had been too keen, hadn't she? He was going
to go off her. Owen had gone off her because she'd
been too enthusiastic, that's why he'd never called
her, when in reality she had only been pretending

320

to be that up for it anyway. What on earth made her say that she loved him? She didn't; well, she did, as a friend, and now she'd found out that she loved sex with him, but that didn't mean she *love* loved him. She glanced across at him. He was so incredibly pretty, like a boy singer or the sort of actor that adolescent girls go to see in the same film eleven times over. That in combination with the fact that he seemed to know Sierra's body better than she herself did made him lethal. Who'd have thought it? Owen was supposed to be the hot one, but it turned out that Michael was the one who had pierced Sierra.

But she'd ruined it. How could she have been so uncool? Hadn't she learned anything?

'Sweetheart, what's wrong?' he asked as he stroked her hair. He had stroked her all over the night before, so very slowly and lightly that she could bear it no more and she had come immediately just by grabbing his thigh in between hers. Then he'd started stroking her again and he had entered her and she demanded that he come immediately, which he did, so that they could start again at one all. Pretty soon they had upped their scores to two all.

She toyed with being enigmatic and aloof, but kind of thought that she'd blown that role already. 'I don't love you. I mean, I do, I mean before we kissed I could have said, "You know that Michael, I love him, he's great." I probably did say that, I don't know. But now I can't say things like that any more without it being too, well, you know, mad girl, and I just forgot temporarily that there were new rules and it came out, but I don't want you thinking anything of it and going all man on me and suddenly not being my friend.'

He sighed and pulled her towards him. There was no height difference between them when they were lying down. 'Sierra, from the first moment I met you properly, at Tess's house that night, I thought, now there's a girl who doesn't know when she's said enough.'

'I've ruined . . .'

He gave her a look. 'We've got so much to look forward to, you and I. I know that. And one of those things will be working out whether we love each other.'

'Love love, I mean, you know I love you as a—'

'I know that, and I know that I probably will, at some point, not very far away in the future, know that I love love you. But let's not have all our pleasures in one go. Personally I'm rather enjoying the fact that I've discovered that the girl who I like best in the world is, by very fortunate coincidence, also the one with whom I am deliciously and outrageously sexually compatible. So, what do you think—a little less conversation?'

'And a little more action?' She pressed into him and he scooped her perfectly; they were like one of those ballroom dancing partnerships where they were always in step and would have to be awarded ten out of ten for technical merit and artistic interpretation. As they kissed, she felt herself become wet, and thought of that phrase the girls at school used to use: 'He's so fit, he gives me a wide-on.' She was just about to share this with Michael, when she thought to herself that maybe it wasn't too late to introduce a note of mystery into the proceedings.

Later, they sat in companionable silence as they read the Saturday papers in a nearby café. Sierra had never noticed before just how much newsprint was devoted to the subject of when women should give birth, but now that Tess had made her choices, it made Sierra think about her own.

'When do you think the best age to have a baby is?' she asked Michael.

He looked mock-stricken. 'First she tells me that she loves me, then she's asking me to father her children. This is like the worst fling ever.' Her face fell. 'Joke, Sierra, joke.'

'Seriously, it says here that more and more women are leaving it too late and they can't have IVF and they're not with anyone and it's their fault for having a career and stuff.'

'What about men?'

'It doesn't say anything about them.'

'Well, perhaps the problem lies with them rather than women. I always thought I wouldn't want to be a father for at least ten years, it's always ten years away, which would make me the age of all these women that are being blamed for leaving it too late.'

'I wouldn't want to have a baby on my own, I know it's old-fashioned, but I've been a child brought up in a not very old-fashioned way and it gives me a different point of view. I really think Teodor needs to know and I think Gus needs to know back.'

'Sierra,' he said, and she could imagine what it would be like to be in his classroom. 'You stay well out of this.'

'Yeah, of course.' She nodded, while at the same time wondering what would happen if you Googled the hospital and the name Teodor.

*　　　*　　　*

Owen couldn't remember a time when he'd felt more nervous. His interview at university? Losing his virginity? Confessing to his first boss that he'd misdirected some investments? Telling fiancées mark one, two and three that he wasn't going to marry them? Or was Ruby fiancée number four? Either way, she hadn't reacted well when he'd told her. He had looked at the photo of Gareth throughout to give him strength and had remained unmoved by her hysteria and claims that he'd stolen the best years of her life. 'Best years?' was all he had managed. 'Best months, surely.'

He kicked the fallen leaves of the tree-lined streets near Tess's flat for half an hour before finally ringing the doorbell. She probably wasn't even in. Please be in. Oh please, let her not be in.

A foreign accent answered the intercom.

'Is that Lady Franklin? It's Owen.'

'Darling boy, my darling Owen. My favourite man, come in.' As he arrived at the door, he was swept into an embrace that smelled of beauty halls in expensive department stores. Vondra's jet-black hair became buried midway up his chest, like Gus's would do in a baby carrier. He felt a sudden urge to be one of those men accessorised with a baby in a carrier. 'My Tess is crying, she is so tired, so very tired, because she has only one man in her life, not two. If only you were the father of her baby. You're not the father of her baby, are you?' He thought

324

she was joking, but her eyes pleaded.

'I'm not. But I'll try to be.' He liked the way it sounded.

Vondra looked at him with confused gratitude.

'Owen,' said Tess. 'Fancy seeing you here. A second visit, we are honoured.' Her voice was cool, but Owen could see that her eyes and nose were red, while her black cashmere top was decorated with a snail trail of snot and posset.

He went to hug her, but she skirted away from him.

'Can we talk?'

'Mummy, darling, would you mind taking Gus out for a little spin?'

'I take him to the shops where everybody says he's the most beautiful baby, the most beautiful in all the world, they all agree.'

'Can I hold him first?' Owen surprised himself by asking. The baby felt both too hard and too soft for him to manage, requiring him to be simultaneously firm and gentle in a way he only normally managed when having sex.

'He's not going to go off,' said Tess.

'Be careful of his head,' said Vondra.

Gus was warm, like a hot water bottle, and felt stronger than Owen had imagined he would do. Owen looked into his eyes with the expectation that some flash of recognition would pass between them, but they looked unfocused and still that otherworldly slate-blue colour which rendered the pupils almost indistinguishable from the iris. It made Gus look as though he'd been taking Class A drugs. Owen looked to him for a sign, like the 'Dada' that he himself had given Gareth almost four decades earlier.

Vondra moved to take Gus away but Owen beat her off with a 'You're right, he is beautiful' and continued staring at him. He tried to do his psychic command thing again: give me a sign, he thought, and then scoffed at himself inwardly for believing that you could transmit thoughts to a baby who wouldn't be able to understand them anyway.

And then it happened.

'He smiled at me.'

'He's so smiley,' said Tess, herself smiling as if for the first time. 'He's the smiliest of all the babies we know. He smiles at everybody. Some of the other babies aren't even smiling yet, even at eight weeks, while he's been doing it for ages. It's not wind, don't let anyone tell you it's just wind.'

'The idea that my grandson would be windy, the idea.'

Owen looked at Tess and then at Gus. 'He's still doing it. Hello, little man, what are you smiling at? His smile is just like yours, Tess, but with fewer teeth.' The smile transformed Gus from strange alien to something recognisably human.

Vondra joined in as all four of them caught smiling from each other.

It was the sign. Living his life along the precepts of 'What Would Gareth Do?' had made everything so simple.

Owen was bursting with his desire to do something good for a change and to do it now, but Vondra seemed to take an age to bundle Gus up in a complicated sequence of under and outer garments, finished off with a foot muff and an ear-covering hat. Tess intervened to give the hat a tweak and to check that the buggy was fully unfolded. Gus gave another gummy smile as if to encourage Owen and then he was off. They were alone.

'He's adorable.'

'I know.'

There was a pause between them. There often was. Owen had noticed that Michael and Tess talked to each other continually and quickly in imitation of their beloved wisecracking movies of the thirties, but when he was with Tess it had often been in silence. He looked at her. She was going to help him out. He repeated the mantra to himself: What would Gareth do?

'I'm sorry,' he began.

'What for? I don't mean that I don't think you've got anything to apologise for, I'm just intrigued as to which of your misdemeanours you're feeling contrite about exactly.'

'I'm sorry that I gave you chlamydia. Obviously. And I think I know what it means that I did.'

'Enlighten me.'

'I know I'm not Gus's father.'

'You don't say.'

'But he needs a father.'

'Not this again.'

'Please, listen to me, Tess. He does need a father. Not whoever supplied the sperm.' He emphasised the word supplied. Whatever Sierra said, it didn't make any difference whether he'd supplied it in person or via a phial. 'My, what do they call it these days, birth father was a seventies sort of sperm donor and I know I've no desire to ever meet him. He's nothing to me. But my dad, my real dad, Gareth, was no blood relative of mine, but he was everything a father should be and more. My mother's a silly bint who got herself knocked

327

up and I owe her nothing for that, but I owe her everything for choosing the right man to be my real father.' He didn't know that he'd ever talked about his feelings at such length, certainly never when suggesting an engagement or breaking one off. 'What makes her my mother is not that she bore me but that she found Gareth for me.'

Tess shook her head.

'Well, and the other stuff too, the looking after me and cooking her horrible custard and telling me how handsome I was getting as I grew up to be a man.' Tess smiled and he saw in her the baby he had just been holding. 'And not that I would ever compare her to you, but you're on your own and I want . . .' He gulped.

'Spit it out.' Tess arched a recently plucked eyebrow. Owen was momentarily distracted by the awareness that she hadn't let herself go despite this talk of tears and tiredness.

'I would like to be more than a godfather to Gus. I'm not saying you have to marry me.'

'Indeed. I'm not sure I want to be the fourth Mrs not-Williams. Or is it the fifth? And anyway, what would Ruby say?'

'She's no longer an issue.'

'Part of the ex-fiancées club?' He nodded. 'Oh, Owen, you are such a cad.' He liked that she called him that. Ruby had screamed at him, called him a cunt and then said, 'Excuse my French.'

He shrugged. 'You and me, Tess, you and me. Neither of us are very good on feelings, are we?'

'No, I suppose not. Not until Gus came along, anyway. Now I've got too bloody many of them.'

'Exactly. That's why I want to be his sort-of father rather than just his godfather. I'll support

328

him financially, we can buy a house together. Like I say, we don't have to be a couple, but we can be parents. Gus wouldn't be here if we hadn't slept together. Doesn't that make me his father? Or near enough? He wouldn't be here without me.'

Owen didn't know what was supposed to happen here; he didn't watch that genre of films unless forced to by a girlfriend. Did he and Tess embrace one another, and kiss, and tell each other that they had always loved each other? Would they fall into bed with one another to seal this love? Had he always loved her? If he squeezed her tits, would milk come out?

Tess shook her head again, but smiled. 'We can't tell each other that we love one another and that we always have.' Christ, how did she know? 'Because it's not really true, is it? Though it would be nice if it were, sorting out as it would my financial and parental worries . . .'

'And any sexual ones,' added Owen, suddenly feeling a protrusion of desire. Maybe this could be your reward for doing the right thing, he thought.

Tess laughed her knowing laugh and Owen felt that feeling ebb away. 'I suppose. Look, we can't have that happy ending, much as I'd like it. But we can have another. One that we'll just have to work out while we go along.'

*   *   *

Sierra proofread the invitation yet again, convinced that surely there must be a mistake that would proclaim to the world that she was an imposter, the mini-me to giant-Tess. 'Franklin Art,' it announced, 'invites you to a unique preview of the photographs

of Derek Dickerson on 14 November from 6 p.m.'
Address, correct, postcode, telephone, email.
It should read 'Sierra Barton-Smith invites you
to', really, but oh well. Franklin Art still sent out
card invitations, the old-fashioned way, to their
long-standing customers—sorry, *clients*—with the
B-list invitees merely emailed.

The very last of the card invitations sat on
her desk, daring to be sent. She addressed it and
put the stamp on. And then, for good measure,
she emailed one to the same person from her
computer, using the surname and address that the
unprofessionally helpful receptionist had given her.
As she pressed send, she almost tried to grab the
message from the ether that it had now entered, but
it was too late. The deed was done. It didn't matter,
she told herself. It was unlikely to get to the right
person and even if it did, what were the chances
that he'd show up?

Sorting out the photo negatives and the display
with Dez had been like doing the most marvellous
school project with a proper father. 'My dear girl,'
he'd say on greeting her at the door of the house
that was as tall and thin as he was, while John
scurried off to make them both tea, 'let us journey
to the eighties.'

He had pushed the scroll bed to one side in the
spare room for them to work through the boxes
of photos. At first the work had been uncreative,
merely sifting through piles and trying to match
them to the divorced negatives. She'd cursed him
silently for having been so careless with his art, but
once they'd done this donkey-work, she had found
herself beginning to throb with energy. Nothing,
not even sex with Michael, had matched the high

of finally feeling useful, of seeing her potential and knowing that one day, if not now, she'd reach it.

Today was their final chance to whittle down the exhibition photos and to work out a theme for them. 'If you don't mind,' said Sierra, 'I want it to be called The Glamour and the Squalor, brackets The Dance Floor and the Toilet Floor. Close brackets.'

Dez frowned. 'I was thinking more Putting on the Blitz? You know, like the club.'

'That is so camp,' said Sierra.

'It's not like I'm suggesting Fade to Gay.'

'No, but I bet you thought about it. No, it works to have the high and the low thing. People get off on it, they like to see people punished for being beautiful and fashionable, and it makes the exhibition much easier to organise.'

'So like your mother,' he said. 'She always got her own way.'

'And never ever say I'm like Susie again.' She continued leafing through their shortlist of images. 'So many brilliant pictures . . . ' They were, all of them—she couldn't decide which of the babies to kill. There were photos of men in shiny blue eye make-up; girls in clingy dresses and lace-up DMs; stars, has-beens and never-weres; faces crowding into mirrors like multiple Narcissuses. 'I like this one,' she said, holding up a picture of a woman's perfect naked body accessorised only with a pair of huge black hands. 'Very Mapplethorpe. Except rather heterosexually erotic. Very sexy girl.'

'I'm glad you think so. It's your mother.'

'Urgh, I feel sick,' said Sierra, but she continued to examine the image.

'So did she, at the time. Turned out she was

already pregnant with you, darling.'

Sierra stared hard to see some glint of herself in that flat stomach, but there was none. What did she expect? It wasn't as if Susie looked very maternal even now.

'I feel excited and a little alarmed at the prospect of seeing your dear mother again.'

'What do you mean?'

'At the exhibition, of course. She is coming?'

'No, I don't think so. I don't know.'

'My dear girl, why ever not? She must be so proud.'

'She asked me to do something for her and I didn't. I failed her.' Or she failed me, for years and years. With that, Sierra burst into tears and cried upon Dez's shoulder, and he held her like the father she'd only known on arbitrary weekends.

*   *   *

Owen was feeling pretty good about himself. It was true that he missed Ruby, but any girl-shaped hole was filled with the satisfaction of helping Tess and Gus. It made him feel a little bit closer to Gareth, which was all he wanted.

Actually, it wasn't true that he missed Ruby. He missed sex with Ruby. He was usually so good at getting it, but he felt so exhausted by his visits and support of Tess that he didn't have the energy to prowl. And, in a rare moment of self-awareness, he wasn't sure that prowling was seemly for a man of his age any longer.

He thought about Sierra and how he'd come close to forcing himself on her in the bathroom. She was hot. Ruby had all the sexual passivity of

332

a beautiful girl: yes, I know I'm lovely, that is my gift to you, now get on with it. Sierra was so much more fun. Damn it, he should have got some more in when he could. What he would give for another good gawp at those tits of hers.

Hang on, he thought, Tess had mentioned something about a sex tape on the Internet. Google Josh Lawton, was it? Or Lawson? Josh, it was definitely Josh, that had been her boyfriend's name.

Eventually he found what he was looking for and did the usual random befriending that happens on such sites. This, he hoped, would provide a useful stopgap. It was a temporary drought, of that he was sure, and a little homemade Sierra love would be just the ticket until he gained enough freedom from Tess to get out there again.

His cock stiffened before he'd even opened the link. As he made out the grainy still of Sierra, before pressing the triangular play button, he thought, this was going to be good. Oh yes.

This was exactly the sort of 'sexy stuff' his mother had feared the Internet was full of for his father. Damn it, why was he thinking about his mother? He turned the sound up. Sierra, you dirty thing, you gorgeous thing.

His father would never have looked at anything like this, he was sure. Come on, get back, don't think about Dad. Come on, Sierra, pull them off, that's it. Let's see what you've got.

Mari had said that Gareth was her knight in shining armour. All that time, he'd saved her from a miserable life and Owen from living with his ageing aunts, and he'd never even told her that he'd known all along.

Oh, Sierra, do you like it? Is it really wet? Come

333

on. Come on. Damn it.

Gareth saved a fallen woman. Like Gladstone or something. He didn't drag them down further by lording it over the fall.

Stop it, think about the screen. That's it, show me what you've got. The sound of Josh's voice asking Sierra how she felt merged with Owen's own pleas. Both were repellent.

Owen pressed the triangle on the clip again and it turned into the double quote mark of a pause. But it wasn't a pause, it was a full stop.

He opened up his email system and began to type, slotting in the address of a friend at one of the City's top legal firms. Put this in legalese, he said, really threatening stuff about unauthorised dissemination of unauthorised material, whatever fuck off is in legal terms, cease and desist or something. He went back to the page where Sierra was frozen with her hands still down her pants and found Josh's contact button. Send it to Josh person, would you? he typed. Send.

He leaned back, his hands still cradling his cock. He felt a sort of release.

*   *   *

When Lucy's friends were younger, if they ever wanted to make a move on someone, they'd just get very, very drunk. Lucy was not a big drinker herself and sometimes wondered whether she had stayed with Mark for the whole of her twenties because she wasn't sure how she'd ever get it on with someone else without the lubrication of alcohol. As she remembered from her pre-Mark days, there was always that moment when although you knew it was going to happen, that it had to happen, there seemed to be an invisible force field preventing your lips from meeting.

It was hard to get together with someone for the first time. It was even harder, oh so much harder, to get together with someone you were already together with. She had never sought strength in alcohol before, but she couldn't see any other way.

She analysed, as was her wont, the barriers between her and Jamie's re-consummation. There was the time elapsed, now eleven months. There were the pills, but they were no longer being taken. Lucy had shamed herself by rifling through the bathroom cupboard and Jamie's drawers to make sure that this was the case. It was, she felt, as though Jamie was making a choice between the pills with their attendant creativity and her, like an eighteenth-century opium eater or a drug-addled beat poet. There were the children and the fear that they might burst in on them, and the therapy they'd need in 20 years' time to get over the horror.

She planned, of course, the whole thing. A neighbour's much-loved nanny was staying overnight, bought off with £10 an hour and talk of a business trip. She booked a hotel in an urban part of town with a restaurant that was praised by reviewers for its sharing plates and fine wine. Jamie was told to meet her for a meal there. She didn't mention the bedroom bit. She wasn't entirely sure that she would do so at all and the sensible economist in her felt aggrieved at the potential waste of money.

She went up to the bedroom first. Not to lay out rose petals on the bed or anything, Jamie might be being a bit of a wife about not putting out, but he wasn't a girl. She had a shower, moisturised every part of her and used a pair of nail scissors on her bush. She was on the cusp of the generations when it came to pubic waxing—she couldn't do that landing strip or all-off thing that those younger than her took for granted, nor could she leave it untended. Instead she got it done at the beauticians so that there were no stray hairs peeking out of her pants, a country lane of hair rather than a motorway. She put on newly bought underwear. Again, she wasn't sure if this was just part of the cliché she was shoehorning her evening into or whether it would make any difference to his desire for her. It's all about the confidence, she told herself. She couldn't resist having a bit of a hoick of the skin around her stomach and then again around her face, before trying to remind herself that it wasn't about her age.

'You look nice,' he said, as he ambled into the hotel bar where they had arranged to meet.

Round one. 'Thanks.'

'What's this about? Dinner and stuff?'

Don't scare him off, there must be nothing less conducive to sex than talking about it. Not in the beginning, though. He used to ring her when she was at work and she'd lock herself in the toilets to listen to him. 'I just thought we never get out.'

'We do, with Rosa and Ned, all the time.'

'I thought it might be nice to eat somewhere together that doesn't involve asking them whether they'd prefer the chicken goujons or battered fish pieces with chips or salad.'

Jamie laughed. 'Why do we bother asking them if they want chips or salad?'

'Because it makes us Good Parents. Anyway,

let's have a ban on talking about the kids.'

'All right.'

There was a minute's silence. It could have been embarrassing, but Jamie hammed it up and they both laughed. So far it was going better than expected.

'How's the edit?'

'It's good. Better than good, it's amazing. Honestly, Luce, I'm getting somewhere at last.'

There seemed to be something so youthful and male about the way he could say this. Lucy would never say this of her own work, for which she was generously remunerated. 'I'd love to see it. Would you show it to me?'

'Really?' She was surprised that he should seem so touched.

'Yes, of course.' You never offered and I never asked. 'And it's been going fine recently?'

'Yeah, great.'

'I mean, since you . . . the pills . . . you know.'

'Yes.' He looked at her, properly, in the face. She knew that he never looked at her full on any more when he had failed to notice the bruising after the Botox and fillers. Did he know what she was asking, what she really meant when she asked whether his creativity was undimmed by coming off the pills?

'Good. I fancy a cocktail, don't you? Something strong.'

*　　　*　　　*

The small tapas-style dishes were the closest that Lucy and Jamie had got to sharing bodily fluids in almost a year. She even ventured so far as to drop one of the pork and fennel polpette with a spicy dipping sauce into his mouth at one stage, and licked her fingers afterwards with as much lasciviousness as she could muster without feeling completely idiotic.

'Another bottle of wine?' she asked.

Jamie frowned. She looked at him and tried to frown too. She was glad to discover that there was now a smidgen of movement in her brow. Not proper movement, but at least a hint that there might be. 'What time have we got babysitting until?'

'School pick-up time. Tomorrow.' He looked confused. 'We've got a room.' She beckoned to the waiter. 'Can I put the bill on room nine?' She stood up. She realised she was very drunk. I shouldn't be being too organised, too forceful, that's exactly what got to Jamie in the first place. But if I'm not then we'll never get anywhere. Oh, for god's sake. She handed him the door card, partly in an attempt to give him some power, partly because she remembered that it had been quite tricky to work out when she'd done it earlier, and she'd been sober then. Gosh, she thought, I haven't been drunk in years. It's actually quite nice.

He looked for the signs pointing the way to the bedrooms and she stopped herself from telling him exactly where to go. Her head started one of her interminable analyses of modern-day feminism. Was it bad that she'd got to sit in the comfortable banquette seat in the restaurant? Was it worse that she was pretending to be more incompetent than she was? She slipped a little on the stairs. Was it worse that she was in fact being genuinely incompetent on account of having drunk too much?

He managed the complicated lock-light arrangement of the room with aplomb. Ooh, masterful, she said to herself. See, I can do this. I am woman, he is man. Now I throw all my clothes off and drape myself across the bed. No, oh god, I just can't do it.

Jamie looked at her as she stood awkwardly at the door. He put his hand to her face. I hope he can't feel the fillers, she thought, and then, it's nice, I haven't felt this hand for so long, only the rough, greedy hands of my children. Even in her drunkenness, she knew better than to dive down and feel the disappointment in his trousers, so she put her hand around the back of his neck and began stroking. He moaned lightly, which could be taken either way but she decided to give it an optimistic interpretation. She wanted to push him to the bed and get on with things, but she thought back to the ballroom dancing lessons she'd done with Mark, one of those things that was supposed to revive their dying relationship, and knew that she had to let Jamie lead, even if he would do so as incompetently as Mark's box step.

He smiled at her. She loved his smile, though it seemed so intimate that she blushed. It was madness that contemplating sex with someone you knew so well, who'd seen you give birth, should be so much more exposing than it had been that first time she and Jamie had fucked on the stairs. He took her hand away from his neck and moved it down to his crotch. She almost gave a yelp of astonishment as she felt its hardness, but stopped herself. It was like a rare woodland creature that she couldn't risk scaring away with any loud noises or sudden movement.

They moved gently towards the bed. She couldn't speak. Even breathing might be too much. He pulled down his trousers and pants to halfway down his thighs. She put her hand back where it had been, but now she could feel his flesh directly. She didn't dare look at it or move but just carefully wrapped her hands around it. Please don't go, don't leave me now, she implored it. She had made sure not to wear trousers or tights, nothing to come between them, only underwear, which she removed with the other hand. She lay back, still holding his cock but not doing anything more assertive. She worried that she might be too dry, but as he entered her she was relieved that the lubricant of alcohol had worked in all ways. It was like some very complicated NASA operation where each stage carried with it another set of odds to indicate failure. Step one, entry, success. Step two, maintain. She left her legs apart but squeezed her pelvic muscles just like she'd been taught to while pregnant, to avoid later urinary incontinence. Is it pronounced Kegel as in key-gel or kay-gel? Just do them. Being Lucy, she'd taken these diktats very seriously while pregnant with both Rosa and Ned, and was probably one of the few women in history who'd done the requisite daily number, including the ones where you had to try to graduate your squeezing as if your muscles were a staircase. She did this now with Jamie and thanked all the practice for the fact that she could do it without making an odd tightening face of concentration.

He moved very gently in and out. She lay inert, but for the muscles within her which squeezed in time to his motion. It was all so understated that they could have practically done it beneath the duvet with the kids in the room. Please don't leave, she implored his erection, stay with it. She wanted him to come quickly so that they would have done it and she could tell herself that it had only been a minute, an hour, a day since they last had. Would making orgasmic sounds encourage this or scare him off? She breathed more heavily as a compromise. Even this seemed an effort that might destroy the silent sense of achievement. She counted in her head. If he gets to 20 thrusts and still nothing has happened, then I'll do a bit of gripping, shouting, upward thrusting, something.

Sixteen, seventeen, eighteen . . .

'Yes,' he said and she was glad that he too, for all his creativity, was driven to cliché. He rolled off her and she put her hand between her thighs to verify. His sperm oozed out as forensic evidence.

'Yes,' she said too. She couldn't stop grinning. She glowed like she had after they'd had sex for the first time in that house where their children now lay sleeping (were they sleeping? She hoped they weren't playing up). This two-minute anorgasmic, unathletic congress felt to her to be the best sex ever. She wanted to high-five him or something unerotic like that because it didn't seem sexual, more the completion of a marathon after an intensive training programme, or Rosa's first length of the local swimming pool.

She swung herself round to lie on top of him, at last giving herself permission to do something mildly assertive. She didn't know what to say that wouldn't be cheesy or break the mood. So she kissed him instead. She kissed him without the fear that he'd get the wrong idea or roll away in case it was a prelude to more, with his flaccid cock curled away from him.

He kissed her back.

CHAPTER TWENTY

FRESHER FACED

'You seem very calm,' said Michael.

'I am,' Sierra told him. 'Everything's done. I am a wonder of efficiency.'

'You're just a wonder to me.'

'Really, am I? Do you think so? Why? I'm not really, you know, I'm not. I'm a bit of a mess, what with my mum and stuff, and you know I think you're great and I'm sorry about being a bit of a flake and talking too much—'

'Shhhh.'

'Thanks for everything. I couldn't have done any of this without you, really I couldn't.' She surveyed the 40 framed prints that hung around the gallery. They were keenly awaiting the red 'sold' stickers to cluster about their frames. She'd organised dozens of exhibitions for Tess: she knew the caterers; she had all the addresses on a computer programme that worked with the sticky labels; she knew how to hang pictures in a way that sucked in customers as ruthlessly as any supermarket that puts sweets by the checkout and milk at the back of the store. In some ways, she told anyone who'd listen, it had been easier to organise this exhibition than any of the others because she only had to satisfy herself. What she hadn't known and didn't tell anyone was that it turned out she was even harder to satisfy than Tess had been. Those many days she'd sat fuming with resentment at Tess's imperiousness and glory-taking, longing to be her own boss, but she hadn't realised just what a bitch of a boss she herself would make. A boss that made her one employee work twenty-hour days, that screamed at the framers when one of the pictures was bordered with wood that had a grain running in a different direction to all the others, that fretted about the punctuation in the picture list. Sierra the boss made Sierra the employee such a wreck that every night she'd sweat through anxiety dreams of nakedness, surprise A-level examinations and lost plane tickets. And in the morning Sierra the boss would berate her employee for having such prosaic and clichéd dreams in the knowledge that Tess would have never been troubled with such tedious imagery.

She had expected Tess to involve herself, just a little bit, and she was both relieved and disappointed when she didn't. Whatever happened to all that 'I won't let a baby change my life, I'll be back in the gallery before you know it' stuff? Tess had acted as if it was more than she could stand just to hear Sierra's voice on the telephone, let alone help her make decisions about who to invite.

She locked the door of the loos. 'You are Sierra Barton-Smith,' she said and then whispered it for fear of someone hearing. 'And you are the hottest young gallerista, gallerina, gallista, whatever in London and this exhibition will be the making of you.'

Tess owed her this chance, her mother owed her Dez and his photographs and most of all, thought, Sierra, she owed this to herself. By the end of the evening, Tess would either be thanking her for saving the gallery or cursing her for daring to interfere in her oh-so-private of private lives.

She does seem calm, thought Michael, a hell of a lot calmer than I am. He felt nervous on so many levels that he couldn't work out what it was that was making him quite so shaky.

He was swathed in anxiety about his girlfriend's first exhibition. It didn't matter to him how successful Sierra was, he wasn't in a high-octane career himself, but he knew how much it mattered to her despite her apparent cool.

He was always nervous of seeing Owen, big-cocked, Mr Macho, fast-car-driving, strapping six-footer, slept with Sierra and Tess—that Owen. STD-spreading Owen, he could now add to the list. How was it possible for them to have both slept with Sierra? Owen was everything that he wasn't. He didn't know whether it was Owen as his girlfriend's ex-lover or Owen as his godson's ersatz father that he most feared. Hadn't Owen announced to them the other night that this was the role he was making for himself?

To be worried about your girlfriend's previous lover was a vaguely legitimate cause for concern. Stranger was his fear of seeing his cousin Tess again. Somehow he'd managed to avoid her since the awful showdown at the antenatal group reunion and the embarrassment of her offering herself to him. He knew he should have got in touch with her. Wouldn't that show he was a man, a great big brave man? He'd had a hundred imaginary conversations in his head, as he always had done, but these days none of them ended up with Tess and him having sex. Her sexual allure had been destroyed along with her pelvic floor muscles. And anyway, Sierra had then come along and had been the first woman to vanquish completely the untasted, untested rival that was Tess.

When it became clear that Tess wasn't going to apologise, he'd had to replace his conversations with new ones where they'd bump into each other and make everything fine between them again. But why would he ever find himself accidentally walking in Holland Park? And Tess never came to family gatherings any more.

So the window of opportunity for reconciliation became narrower and narrower, until it came to pass that his great rapprochement would have to come at Sierra's great exhibition.

He longed to see Gus again. He was shocked that a person so briefly in his life could leave him so full of yearning. Sierra was a balm to this ache, but he wanted to hold Gus again, to sniff his cradle-capped head, to feel both the solidity and weightlessness of his body. Sierra had told him that Tess was going to bring him along. He wondered whether there would be any recognition in those watery eyes.

If it weren't for Sierra and the happiness she had brought him, he didn't know how he would have coped with Gus's absence. He had sympathy now with those idiot men who dress up as superheroes and climb towers to publicise their campaign to get greater access to their children. And Gus, as Tess had been so firm in telling him, wasn't even his child.

But he and Sierra were happy, they really were. He said that to himself again and again, not to convince himself, because he needed no convincing, but to congratulate himself. He had never been happier with a woman. As he prepared lessons and marked spellings, he would write an essay for himself in his head in answer to the question: 'Sierra and Michael are in love. Discuss this analysis of their relationship and analyse its potential longevity.'

Or was it a multiple-choice question? Sierra and Michael love each other because a) they have the best sex b) they make each other laugh c) they have mutual respect or d) all of the above?

It was all of the above, that was true, but it was more. He had never been with someone who he made so evidently and truly happy. Sierra was the woman to whom so much had been given—good looks, an innate intelligence, that dirty laugh, but at her christening the bad fairy must have said to the gift-bearing good fairies, 'Well, I shall ruin them all by making sure she doesn't recognise them in herself'. Her needing him was sometimes needy, but most of the time it just made him feel like the world's strongest man. He was daily pumped with the sort of recognition and love that doesn't come when you first meet somebody, but a few months into a relationship when you're sitting together on the sofa being boring and you look at them and you think, 'Of course, it's you and it's so easy'.

Michael knew that he would never have had the sofa moment with Tess, and that Sierra would never have found it with Owen. The thought of Sierra being denied such reassurance caused Michael more pain than the prospect of him being alone for the rest of his life.

And there was another worry, too, one that he couldn't access but that skulked just beneath his consciousness, like one of those unspecified dreads that sometimes fill your stomach. He tried to access it, but knew that it was just something Sierra had said, in an offhand way, about an invitation that she had sent out and the way she'd closed her computer down as if viewing porn when he'd come home one night.

Sierra emerged from the bathroom having painted on a face of defiance. He caught her eye and gave her a reassuring nod as she went to work her charm on Dez and his partner. He looked at the door, wondering which of his fears would be realised.

He did not have to wait long. Tess sashayed into the gallery first, her lush post-partum body squeezed into a ripe S-shape of Edwardian proportions. She was closely followed by Owen, who wore Gus in a baby sling as other men might sport a six-pack stomach on the beach. Look at me, his demeanour said, oh this? Really, it's nothing, comes naturally to me.

Fucker, thought Michael. He realised that although he'd got Sierra, Owen had got Gus. He wondered whether Owen had got Tess, too, but realised that he didn't care any more, that the prospect of being replaced as Gus's almost father was far more dispiriting.

*   *   *

Owen hoped that Gus wouldn't posset on his suit, which he'd only just picked up from the tailors and flattered his broad-shouldered slimness. He accessorised its delicate pinstripe with a dark purple tie, handmade shoes and, of course, a particularly cherubic child. He was, he liked to think, like a walking, talking version of that bestselling Athena

347

poster of the bare-chested man holding the baby: all strong masculinity but so visibly in touch with his feminine side. His friends who'd become fathers had always told him that babies were a babe magnet, especially if you were unencumbered by a wedding ring.

Babies also gave one an excuse to sit it out, perfect for the taciturn man about town. He watched with detachment as Sierra and Tess did their dance of compliments, each more extravagant than the last as they worked their way up from shoes to haircuts.

'You look amazing, Sierra, you make me look even more raddled than usual,' said Tess.

'Rubbish, I'm the one who looks like I've been having broken nights for the last two months while you look like you've been on holiday.'

'Those shoes are amazing. Don't tell me—they're vintage Manolos.'

'But that shrug is incredible, it's like something from a costume drama.'

'Handy for breastfeeding, actually.'

They both looked splendid. Post-partum Tess looked more like Sierra than she had before, now bosomy and bounteous. He'd love to trampoline between those two sets of tits. I wonder if there'd be any chance of a threesome? Though the nearest he'd come to three-in-a-bed action of late was the night Tess had allowed him to sleep on the floor in her bedroom in order to wind and change Gus.

He continued to jig up and down and survey the room. That Michael was giving him a look. What was that about? Sierra was ignoring him too, which was a bit rich after the way he'd curtailed her little porn career. 'But you love me, don't you?'

348

he whispered to Gus, kissing him on the top of his sleeping head.

*   *   *

The gallery was filling up quickly and before long, there were too many people to see the photos. Not that it mattered, since everyone was more intent on getting their drinks and made only cursory compliments about the photos on the walls. He'd lost Tess, who was in the corner of the room with Sierra, pitching in with the red stickers.

A rather tired-looking blonde in purple silk sidled up to him.

'Yours?' she said, nodding towards Gus.

Owen paused and then answered, 'No, he's not.'

'Your girlfriend's?'

Again a pause. He was never very good with words, but he wasn't sure one existed for his particular relationship with Gus. Maybe he should just marry Tess and then he could be Gus's stepfather and she his wife. Would they have sex if they got married? he wondered. Or would he be allowed sex with other people? He became lost in the possibility of asking another woman to marry him.

'You don't seem to know,' laughed the blonde.

'No, not my girlfriend's. He's a friend's kid, actually,' he said. The woman moved a few inches closer to him. Although gratified that the baby sling thing worked as a pulling tool, Owen was rather horrified that a bird older than him might think she stood a chance. Even Tess almost seemed a little ancient, given that his most recent conquests— Ruby and Sierra—had been firmly in the twenty-something bracket. The woman glanced at his wedding finger and then came within inches of him, only Gus blocking her way. He was just about to make his excuses when he decided to put into practice his current mantra of What Would Gareth Do?, his manual for living. What would Gareth do? Why, he'd be courteous to the older lady, show her some respect. He wouldn't look at her only slightly crepey bosom and think 'nice tits for her age'. And actually, she was maybe only 45 or so, which, hard to believe, was almost his age.

'Gorgeous baby,' she purred. 'So handsome, look at his face. Couldn't you just cover it in kisses?'

'Yup.'

'So what brings you here?'

'I know Tess and Sierra.'

'Do you?'

'This is Tess's baby, in fact. And you?'

She gestured towards a photo of a woman sandwiched between two famous gender-bending pop stars. 'I'm sort of the star of the show.' Her eyelashes actually fluttered. It made her look epileptic.

'Right. You look amazing.' His interest was pricked by the image of a woman of such startling beauty. 'Were you a model?'

'Am a model,' she said. 'That's me too, though you can't see my head.'

'Just your body,' he said, staring at the nude. It was really quite erotic to be talking to a stranger while staring at a photo of their naked body. He thought about the footage of Sierra again. Wish I'd downloaded it onto my desktop, since it had now been removed from that tosser's page thanks to his mate the lawyer. He glanced at the woman again. Yes, a bit scraggy, but with an appealingly filthy look about her. She was now even licking her lips, my god, she's actually put her finger in her mouth to suck. Those clichés worked like a charm on Owen and he found his groin straining, despite having a sleeping baby strapped to him.

*　　　*　　　*

Sierra was beginning to feel the first stirrings of satisfaction. She had already bagged some sales— more tonight than in the last few months put together. Not to be a bit supermarket about it, but high volume, lower cost was proving to be an effective strategy. She scanned the room, wondering if she would see the invitee she dreaded arriving, though it had been her stupid idea to ask him to come.

In looking for the man she didn't know, she saw a woman she did. She bustled through the crowds, trying to accept their compliments graciously as she did so, and realising that she still had a lot to learn from Tess.

'Mum,' she said when at last she reached her.

Susie grasped her. 'Darling, I'm so proud.'

Owen looked with confusion from Susie to Sierra and then to the photo again. 'You're Sierra's mother?' he spluttered.

'Yes, I am. I'm Susie. Pleased to meet you.' She offered up the hand that only a few seconds ago she'd been sucking erotically.

'But Susie, Mum, what are you doing here? You told me that you'd never be able to come back to the country, that I'd fucked your life forever.'

Susie glanced at the photo of her, resplendent

351

behind them. 'Darling Dez,' she said. 'He always did have a soft spot for me.'

'I don't understand.'

'He rung me, got the number off your phone I suppose.'

'And?'

'I explained the spot of bother I was in and he's sorted it out for me. I think he rather enjoyed it, in a slumming it sort of way—you know how these posh gays are with their lowlife chums. Went into what he called the ghetto and everything, all of two miles away from his rather lovely house, with a bag of used notes. Just like a gangster film, he said.'

'He did that? Why?'

'I guess I must still have it.' She smiled as she looked at the photo of her former peachiness.

He did it for me, thought Sierra. People who aren't your real dad can do paternal things. She looked at Owen, who was rocking on his feet to keep Gus asleep on his chest. Oh shit, what have I done?

'He's very rich, though, so it's no big sacrifice. Have you seen his house? If only I'd married as well as he did.'

That was where it all went wrong, thought Sierra, Susie hadn't married well or worked hard. If you've got a beautiful body and no qualifications that's all that's open to you, and silly Susie had got pregnant with Sierra instead. All the glamour and the adulation was so fleeting. She looked at Owen again and remembered how she'd entertained a brief fantasy of being rescued by him, of all her financial worries being over and having a rich husband and not having to work. If she'd done that she'd never have enjoyed the feeling of triumph that she now had as she surveyed the throng at the exhibition, her exhibition.

'So you're back?' she said to Susie.

'Yes, darling, I'm back at the flat. Isn't that marvellous? You can come home now.'

'Home? I suppose I can.'

'And you must come and visit,' she said to Owen, stroking his arm as she did so. He at least had the decency to look uncomfortable.

Sierra snorted and walked back to the sales desk. As she did so, she saw the arrival of a new guest, the one she had been unsure about inviting, and she diverted her path towards the door to intercept him.

*　　　*　　　*

'So,' said Michael.

'So,' said Tess.

'Here we are.'

'Yes, here we are.'

'Are you just going to repeat what I say? Because if so, then perhaps you could start with, I'm so sorry, Michael, for making such a scene and embarrassing everyone at the antenatal group.'

'I am sorry. I really am.'

Michael reeled. Tess apologised even more rarely than she swore. 'Sorry. I mean, as in what did you say, not as in I'm sorry. I've got nothing to apologise for, have I?'

'Sorry. I was ungrateful. Blame the hormones or something, I was so snappy. I felt furious at everything and you seemed to be the best person to take it out on.'

'Bet you're not taking it out on Owen.'

353

Tess laughed. 'Believe me, Michael, I am. I'm making his life miserable.'

Michael thought about the chlamydia and the sex with the two women he loved most in the world and the money, the height and the access to Gus and he was glad that Owen was being punished. 'Really? Do tell. Are you making him change Gus's pooey nappies? Making him tidy your bedroom—which, by the way, is a disgrace? What else? Make my day and tell me that you're flaunting your newly magnificent embonpoint and yet have no intention of ever putting out?'

'That and so much more. When I use the fancy reusable nappies, I make Owen empty the nappy pail.' They laughed. 'I've missed you, Michael. So has Gus.'

'Have you? Bet Gus thinks of Owen as his fake father these days.'

'There will always be a special place for you in our lives. And in my flat, sleeping on that uncomfortable bed and cleaning the kitchen.'

He thought of Sierra and knew that he'd never return to Tess's as anything other than an occasional visitor. In the ever-changing game of Twister between him, Tess, Owen and Sierra, he felt that the positions were now happily calcified. He sought out Sierra to give her a smile of reassurance and saw with some jealousy that she was talking to a tall, blond man with his back to them who then turned to look their way. Tess followed his gaze and her whole face puckered and she aged before his eyes, like Ursula Andress at the end of *She*.

'I don't understand,' she said as she continued to stare at them.

'About Sierra? Well—'

'Sierra? Not her,' she said, her eyes still fixed. 'Him. What's she talking to him for? What's he doing here?'

'I don't know. Who is he?' At that moment, Michael realised that he, too, recognised him. 'What the . . .'

'Hell,' Tess completed.

'It's the hospital porter.'

'Doctor, I really thought he was a doctor. That's what he told me. I can't believe he lied.'

'So it's true, then, about him—about Teodor and Gus?'

'You know his name?' She shook her head, not in contradiction but in disbelief. 'I'm going to kill Lucy. There she is. Lucy!' she shouted across the heads of the private view. 'Come with me.'

'I'm not sure it's entirely her fault. You'd better kill Sierra. Unless I do it first.'

'What have I done?' said Lucy and then looked in the direction Tess indicated. 'Oh. How on earth . . .'

Sierra did have the good grace to look embarrassed as the three of them approached. 'I was just talking about you. I believe you know Teodor.' She said his name as though it were a complicated foreign dish on a menu. Teodor himself looked most confused and Michael realised that there was a hierarchy of knowledge with Sierra at the top and this man at the bottom.

'Tess,' he said. 'It is Tess, isn't it?'

'Yes, it is,' she said. 'Nice to see you again.'

'And you. You look very well.' He had attractively accented English and doctor or porter, Michael could see why Tess might have decided

355

to celebrate her child-free existence with an inappropriate tussle with the man. 'Your friend, Sierra, told me that I should come, that there was something I need to know. About you. I don't understand.'

'Tess, he's really grizzly, I think he needs a feed,' said Owen, who approached the group carrying a crying Gus.

Teodor looked at the baby and then at Tess. 'It was you I saw at the hospital, that time. With your friends, these people. I thought yes, but no, you look so different.'

'Well, yes, childbirth does do that to you.'

'How old is she?'

'He. He's three months. Three months and one week.'

Michael saw Teodor mouth some words in another language and then begin to finger each of his knuckles in succession. It reminded Michael of what he had been taught to do when you needed to do your Hail Marys but didn't have a rosary to hand, or the way of calculating the nine times table that he showed the Year 3s.

'Twelve months,' said Teodor. 'A year.'

'Tess,' said Owen. 'I really think you need to get on with the feeding. Who's this?'

'This,' said Tess, 'is Teodor.'

Owen froze and for a moment Michael thought that he would drop Gus. He would never have guessed that one day he'd feel sorry for the man.

'Can I?' said Teodor.

'Not unless you can breastfeed,' snapped Owen, but Teodor reached out and gently took Gus into his arms and began to mutter to him in a language no one else could understand. Gus, with a sense of cinematic poignancy inherited from his maternal grandmother, stopped crying and looked up with shocked curiosity.

'You told me,' said Teodor, 'that we didn't need to, you know, that this couldn't happen.'

'We didn't. I thought I couldn't,' said Tess. 'That's what they told me at the hospital, that I couldn't. And I didn't want to, I really didn't. Please don't think that I used you. Good god no, never wanted a baby but I got one anyway.'

'He is a miracle,' said Teodor, the man whose name meant gift from god.

'Yes, he is,' said Tess. The four godparents made an awkward tableau around the parents and child like some latter-day nativity. 'Don't you think,' she said, looking at them all, 'he is somehow divine in its true sense?'

'Like some sort of messiah?' asked Michael. 'Surely your delusions of grandeur don't stretch to that?'

'And you're not exactly a virgin,' added Owen.

'I don't think I'm Mary, but Elizabeth. You know, John the Baptist's mother, the one who gave birth despite being old and infertile. I didn't want him, but now that I've got him I will do all that I can for him.'

Teodor continued to stare in shock. The bewilderment gave his face a saintly look. Either that or it made him seem a bit dim, thought Michael. Time will tell.

EPILOGUE

'You look gorgeous,' said Michael. He'd watched a television programme that fitted men with sensors to discover exactly where their eye line was when faced with a woman. No ultraviolet device was needed to show where his eyes were zooming. 'You really do.' He made a *Carry On* sound of approval, but because of his intrinsic campness it came out more Kenneth Williams than Sid James.

'Thanks. Another borrowed stroke stolen vintage Vivienne Westwood number, courtesy of Susie.' She looked down at her cleavage. 'You don't think it might be a bit slutty for a baptism?'

'No, I like it, though you might want to put that cape thing on. The priest will be rethinking his vows of celibacy when he sees you. I'm wondering if I can stay celibate for the journey there.' They kissed. Sierra was very tolerant of having her make-up mussed.

They picked their way through the shoes and handbags that littered the living room and shouted goodbye to the sleeping bodies beyond bedroom doors.

'I don't know how you stand it,' said Michael. 'It's so sordid in here. Surely they're worse than your mother,' he observed of Sierra's friend Chloe and her two flatmates.

'Really very similar, in fact,' said Sierra. 'The using my facial products as foot softeners, the nicking clothes, the lost phone chargers, the moods. And they all eat such weird things, like nothing but cereal for three days, followed by a meal consisting only of frozen peas. Whenever I offer to cook they all say no, they're not hungry, and then scavenge leftovers from my plate. I can't leave cheese in the fridge for a second.'

'You don't have to live here. You know you can live with me.'

Sierra smiled. 'But I love it here. This is my uni, the one I missed out on. I'm sick of always being older than my age. It's like my mental age and my physical age have finally coincided. But I love you too.'

'There's that rule, you know from Armistead Maupin.' She looked blank. There was so much she needed to know, that he could teach her. When he and Tess made *All About Eve* references, she showed the same ignorance, which was no bad thing since Tess had pretty much accused her of wanting to steal her life like the eponymous heroine. Which was unfair, really it was, because without Sierra, Tess wouldn't have a professional life left. It was only thanks to Sierra's reinvention of the gallery as a purveyor of overpriced photographic nostalgia for a recent pop cultural past that Tess had something to return to from maternity leave now that Gus was almost six months old. 'He wrote that you can have two out of three of the holy trinity of great job, great flat and great lover, but never all three at the same time.'

'Well, it looks like I've proved them wrong then. Come on, we'd better get going.'

'Off to renounce the devil.' Michael looked at Sierra and thought it very unlikely he'd be able to renounce the sin of fornication.

'Are you going to? I thought you said you weren't going to stand up at the whatsit . . .'

'The font.'

'That's the one. I thought you said you wouldn't be able to do that.'

'I don't know. I haven't decided yet.'

*   *   *

I'm free, thought Owen as he escaped from Tess's flat without pram, nappy bag or Gus. His life ricocheted from his office to yet more work, looking after a baby and being shouted at by its mother. The What Would Gareth Do? philosophy of life had succeeded in helping him to act the gallant knight to two women so far, one of whom was imperiously ungrateful and the other didn't even know what he'd done.

His excuse was to buy cigarettes. 'Don't be long, you've got to look after him while I get ready. And I really don't like you smoking,' said Tess.

'But I don't smoke anywhere near him.'

'But it's on your clothes, that's enough. I hope you can live with yourself. Teodor always smells so nice. Do you know, he's never had a cigarette in his life.'

Teodor, oh saintly Teodor, the angel to Owen's devil as they silently fought for paternity rights over Gus. It started off with a couple of visits before Christmas, but in the six weeks since then it had upped to weekly ones, usually on a work-day afternoon thanks to his shift pattern. The very shift pattern that had enabled Gus to be conceived in the first place.

Owen quizzed Tess as to what went on during these visitations.

'You know,' she'd say.

'I don't, actually. What?'

'Parent stuff,' she'd say vaguely. 'He's keen to be involved.'

He wasn't sure what this mysterious parent business was, given that he and Tess talked of little other than Gus and how extraordinary he was, with his precocious ability to pull himself up to standing and marvellous way with a carrot stick. He looked at fathers in the park and he couldn't see any difference between what he and they were doing, but he feared that if Teodor were to arrive at the swings, the other men and he would have some special handshake to mark them out as the real DNA providers.

He'd taken up smoking again with a vengeance. He wasn't getting regular sex (which he gathered did make him like the other dads they'd meet) so he needed some vice, and cigarettes now offered him the guilty pleasure that he'd first got from them 25 years ago.

'Twenty Camels, please.'

He sucked on his cigarette on the street outside the newsagent and thought about when he'd last had sex. Ruby, oh Ruby, who made those funny squeaking noises throughout even when he knew she wasn't really coming. He didn't think he'd ever gone so long without it.

'Goodness, you look like you need that.' He glanced up to find himself looking at a woman of about thirty carrying a thick wad of Saturday newspapers. 'The cigarette, I mean.'

He smiled. 'I do.' He smiled again, this time doing the one marked 'rakish'. She was small with a milkmaidy face. He offered her his pack.

She shook her head. 'I only smoke with coffee or

booze.'

'Coffee, then? We can sit outside.' He gestured towards the café across the road. As the smoke filtered through his body, so did the flirtation. Glorious addictions both.

She shrugged. 'Why not?'

*   *   *

The first person Sierra saw was Owen hiding behind the church as he attempted to blow smoke up and over the head of Gus sleeping in his new baby carrier, one even more expensive and complicated than the last.

'Don't tell Tess.'

'Promise. You all right?'

'Yes, I am. I'm doing really well, thanks. You?'

'Great, yeah, fabulous.' She said it as a reflex response to an enquiry from a man you've slept with and who wasn't interested in repeating the experience, but as she did so she realised that it was true. She breathed in as if to inhale this rare moment, when you're content but not too dizzy with it to recognise the sensation. The gallery seemed to be doing well, she loved sharing a flat, and even Josh's sex tape seemed to have fallen off the Internet, pleasing her on two levels: first that it was gone and second that the man on which she'd wasted her body at least had some decency. 'I'm happy,' she said out loud.

Owen looked as though he were about to say something, but he just smiled.

*   *   *

363

'Baptisms are the new weddings, apparently,' announced Lucy to Michael and Sierra as they huddled outside the imposing Gothic façade of the church. 'I've got lots of friends who don't get married and then have whopping naming ceremonies with shamans and party planners and presents instead.'

'I suppose there has to be some reason for it,' said Sierra. 'Do you know I've never been to a christening before? What is the point of them, exactly?'

'You get to go to better schools if you're Catholic,' said Lucy. 'I'm sure Gus will be off to some fancy pants private number, but Tess is keeping her options open.'

'Only if Owen's paying,' said Michael.

'As I expect he is for the champagne we'll be having afterwards,' said Lucy. 'It is a lovely way of celebrating Tess's new family.'

'I thought friends were the new family?' said Sierra. 'I read that somewhere too, along with something being the new black and something else being the new rock and roll.'

'Or are family the new friends?' Lucy said, distracted by Rosa and Ned jumping the hard stone steps of the church two at a time. 'Don't do that, it's dangerous. Come here.'

'Hello, Mr Wasiak,' Rosa said to Michael. Lucy could have sworn she giggled coquettishly at him. 'I like your tie.' Lucy had a brief vista into a future when Rosa would buy inappropriate clothes and take endless photographs of herself wearing them. Or worse, not wearing them. She wanted to stop Rosa's ageing as much as she'd wanted to prevent her own, to keep them both frozen as they were or

364

even to reverse time to some imagined idyll when they were both at their cutest.

'And that's a lovely dress you've got on,' he said.

Rosa did a twirl. She'd grown out of the pink phase and, in keeping with the whole growing up too quickly thing, had moved onto black. Lucy had stopped complimenting Rosa on her appearance. It was not that she wasn't gorgeous, she was—albeit quite strapping—but Lucy had noticed that almost everything said to girls involved their looks, while Ned was always told how good he was at football or how clever he must be.

She couldn't protect Rosa from the forces of consumerism, she knew that, all she could do was to love her as much as she did and to try to set her a good example of what being a woman was.

'Where's Tess?' asked Michael.

'Owen was with Gus, but I can't see him now.'

'He's always with Gus. I hate to say it,' said Lucy, 'but he's really surprised me.'

'Yes, he's marvellous, isn't he?' Michael retorted.

'Now, now,' said Lucy. 'It's not a competition. I never thought he'd take his responsibilities so seriously, especially after you-know-who turned up. He's even talking about helping to buy a house. But you've done loads too, Michael. Tess knows she wouldn't have got through this without you. A hybrid of you and Owen is pretty much the ideal father.'

'His money, my domestic skills,' said Michael. 'We're like a sitcom married couple, Owen and I.'

'Don't forget Teodor's beauty,' Sierra added.

'Thanks for that,' said Michael, upon which Sierra kissed him in a manner most inappropriate for a religious event.

'Get a room,' said Lucy, but benevolently. She had less to be envious of now. She flashed back to last night, when Jamie had lifted her skirt as she cooked supper and bent her over the kitchen table, just as she had fantasised he would all those months ago. They hadn't actually had sex, of course, that would be too much to hope for, but even a grope was joyful congress of sorts. It wasn't like they were doing it all the time, at most once a week. Who am I kidding? At most two or three times a month, but after an absence of almost a year, it felt like wanton abandon. 'Typical bloody Tess,' said Lucy. 'She gets pregnant by mistake and decides to go ahead, but instead of Gus having no father, he ends up with three times the number of fathers as a normal child. And better ones at that.'

'You're doing all right,' said Michael, pointing at Jamie who was tipping Ned upside down.

'I am, I am.' For the moment that was good enough. She fingered her face where the filler had been, but was slowly shrinking to nothingness. She missed the comforting feel of the foreign body to her touch and it had lasted far better than the Botox. Neither of them, she told herself, had been the cause of Jamie's return inside her. Although, she thought, still feeling between her nose and the end of her mouth, the fillers had definitely made some difference to her life. Yes, she told herself, she'd drop the Botox for sure. The other stuff, well, there was no need to be too hasty about it, was there? Jamie would spot it this time, but she didn't care about him. It was Rosa who must never know.

'Speak of all angels, here she is,' said Michael. 'The mother of the baby.'

'Darlings,' Tess purred. 'Great shoe,' pointing

at Sierra's vertiginous heels. Lucy had missed the email that went out to all women which said that you had to refer to trousers, jeans and shoes in the singular, as well as the one which said that it was empowering to wear hooker heels. She knew she sounded old, but really, how did other women walk in those heels as high as a hand span? 'And happy belated birthday, my love,' she said on kissing Lucy. 'Still think you should have had a party.'

'Maybe I will. It's not so bad after all, this being forty business.'

'Where's our godson?' said Sierra.

'With Owen.'

'And the godson's father?' asked Michael.

'Teodor,' corrected Sierra. 'He's only one of Gus's fathers, really.'

'With my mother,' said Tess. 'She just adores him. Feels some sort of kinship with him. Immigrant sensibility, I think. And he is rather adorable, isn't he? I could have done so much worse. And he's a Catholic, you know, so Michael, if you don't feel you can do the honours at the font . . .'

'I will, I will.'

'Really,' said Sierra. 'Are you a believer all of a sudden?'

He grinned at her. 'God, no. Actually, that's not right. It's not that I believe there is a god, it's just that I can't be so sure that there isn't.' He took her hand. 'And talk of the devil, the one that I promise I will renounce or denounce or whatever, here comes Owen. Is he capable of going anywhere without Gus strapped to his six-pack? Looks gratifyingly tired, though, which is something. Hello, Owen, are you well?'

'Bloody great, thanks. Here we all are again.'

'Here we are,' repeated Lucy. 'Do you know, it's about a year since we all first met, round at Tess's that evening. You know, when she asked us to be godparents.'

They glanced round at one another. Michael and Sierra with a look of lust and love in equal parts, the night before and the night before that flashing up on the screens in their heads, along with their unexpressed hopes for a future that didn't end in silences and avoidance. Lucy felt only happiness for them and for herself. Owen shuffled awkwardly, using, as he seemed so often to do these days, Gus as ballast against the world. He was wondering whether he'd ever go to a church for his own wedding.

'So much has changed since that night,' said Lucy. 'Mostly for you, Tess, of course, but for us too. We didn't even know each other that night. Gus seems to have changed everything. Do you remember how I said that my midwife told me you didn't become a grown-up until you had a baby or lost a parent?'

'Great,' said Owen. 'I must remember that next time I'm sad about my dad. What a bonus.'

'Sorry,' Lucy apologised. 'That was tactless of me.'

'It's fine. I do know what you mean. A bit,' he said. 'I have changed since Dad died.'

'That might be true for you,' said Sierra, 'but I still don't think becoming a mum or dad automatically makes you a grown-up. I don't know, it's more that you become a grown-up when you stop being someone's kid. Like I'm not Susie's kid any more.'

'Lucy is right, in a way,' declared Michael. 'Gus coming along and bringing us together has changed everything and made us sort of grow.' He mimed sticking his fingers down his throat in case this sounded too much like it was taken straight out of a tome from the mind-body-spirit section of a bookshop. 'Or does that give credence to Tess's narcissistic notion that Gus is the new messiah?'

'I never said that. But he is my miracle baby, the one that was never supposed to be and yet very much is. Too much, sometimes.' Tess looked at the four of them. 'He's our miracle baby. Thank you for all you've done.' They shuffled awkwardly at all the sincerity. Tess lifted up an imaginary champagne glass. 'To the four of you. Gus's proper grown-up godparents.'

ACKNOWLEDGEMENTS

Thanks to Arabella Stein for her wisdom, acumen and old-fashioned long lunches and to all at Abner Stein, especially Kate McLennan, Sandy Viollette and Ben Fowler.

I feel very lucky to be published by Hodder. Carolyn Mays and Francesca Best are editorial alchemists, ably assisted by Katy Rouse, while Karen Geary and Lucy Zilberkweit do a phenomenal job in publicity. I'd also like to thank Sarah Christie as the designer responsible for bringing such freshness to the cover, and Jason Bartholomew and Alice Howe in the rights department.

Amber Burlinson brings her eagle eyes, thoughtfulness and grace to the copy-editing process.

Other writers are my work colleagues in this sometimes lonely process. Wendy Jones and Ali Knight have provided support and sounding boards. Elizabeth Buchan said something to me so pertinent about just getting on with it instead of waiting indefinitely for the muse that I persevered with finishing this book. I'm grateful that she shared the benefit of her experience.

Dr Sandy McBride of the Royal Free Hospital shared her dermatological wisdom to help me with this book (and with countless other unrelated paediatric skin conditions). Thank you for your patience.

Debbie Perera and Maria Bañeres have been on hand to help look after the children, while Lorna Hobbs, Selina Macnair, Francis & Charlotte Hopkinson have done a lot unpaid.

Bini Adams has been right with me for the last thirty years of growing up and not growing up. Her parents Brian and Cynthia were always so willing to listen to our gossip, hopes and neuroses.

And, as always, Alex, William, Celia and Lydia have provided love and distraction.